Moonstruck

BOOK TWO OF THE GWEN ST. JAMES AFFAIR

NICOLE MCKEON

TOWER ROOM PUBLISHING

Content Notice

PG-13

This book was written for an adult audience and contains mature themes that may not be suitable for every reader. Content includes but may not be limited to:

- Swearing

- Violence and violence toward minors

- Death

- Alcohol use

- Grief

- Assault

Contents

For Tommy
You were the first person who taught me to love someone else more than I loved myself.

1

A Day at the Zoo

SAM

Sam never wanted to pick a pocket so much in his life. The visitors of the New London Zoo crowded together, staring in oblivious rapture at the sleeping baby unicorn. He could have stuffed his hands into their pockets while blowing a kazoo; they never would have noticed.

To make matters worse, the late spring day was balmy, and half the men unbuttoned their jackets and waistcoats to take advantage of the breeze. The flash of expensive watch chains, rings, cufflinks, and jeweled brooches caught his eye no matter which way he turned. Little coin purses dangled from wrists, and the bulge of wallets screamed at him from vest and trouser pockets.

He could clean this place out before anyone realized what was missing, and now that he owned fancy clothes, he would blend in. No one would look at him twice as he made off with their possessions.

Sam folded his arms and tucked his hands safely under his armpits.

Imagining dipping his fingers into someone's waistcoat and walking away with a shiny timepiece was a bad idea. He wasn't a thief anymore; he was the ward of Lady Gwenevere St. James, and everything he once lusted after, like food and new boots, was part of his daily life.

He and his sister were respectable now, and they could do things only wealthy people did, like buy sweets at a bakery, or stand around with other wealthy people watching a baby unicorn sleep. Neither of them needed to steal. He leaned on the rail and told himself he was glad about that.

Lady Gwen joined him, her umbrella and hat combining to cast as much shade as a small tree. She used a heavy black umbrella instead of the white lacy parasols the other ladies had. Unlike the rest of the crowd, she didn't display her rank and wealth with jewelry. Whatever money she carried was tucked away in places Sam couldn't guess at. The last time she paid for something, the cash had been under her hat. Hard to pickpocket a lady's hair.

"Why the long sigh?" she asked.

He thought over what to say. This was the first time he'd ever visited the zoo without having to hide from security, and he was nearly fourteen years old. Instead of dodging guards and scaling trees, he strolled from exhibit to exhibit as if he didn't have a care in the world.

"I...thought the unicorns would be more exciting," he said, feeling a bit deflated. He couldn't very well tell fine, upstanding Lady Gwen he missed the excitement of being sneaky. "All they do is lie around and sleep. I don't understand why everyone was so keen to see them. They don't look like nothin' but skinny horses."

"Don't look like anything," Lady Gwen corrected with a smile. "Do try to avoid double negatives before mid-day, my dear, they make my teeth ache."

Sally leaned far over the fence to peer at the little white animal and said in a dreamy voice, "I don't know how you can say that, Sammy. They're perfectly magical. Look how small the foal is with its pink nose and bit of horn poking out of its fetlock."

Sam frowned at his sister, then at the beast. It was smaller than a horse, with spindly legs more like a goat, and a little downy tuft of a beard on its chin. Its neck was long, and feathery hair decorated its cloven hooves. Okay, it was a goat-horse. Horse-goat? Hoat?

He blew out a bored breath and said, "Can we go see the lions instead? Or at least something with claws and teeth?"

Lady Gwen considered him. Her dark eyes sparkled with laughter, but her voice was solemn when she asked, "Sally, why are there so few unicorns in captivity?"

"Because they are both clever and elusive," she said, as if reciting a passage from a book. "Their white fur takes on the hue of the light reflected by their surroundings, and they're as nimble as goats, so they can climb trees and sheer cliffs to flee pursuers. And if a unicorn is cornered, it can strike with its hooves and horn."

"And how many men have unicorns killed?" Lady Gwen asked.

"Twice as many as lions for every human encounter."

"Why?"

"Because men expect lions to be dangerous."

Lady Gwen gave him an affectionate pat on the shoulder. "There's a lesson in there somewhere, Samuel."

So, the unicorn was more interesting than he thought, but the beast still just lay in the shade, panting, with its legs curled up to the side.

"Can we at least see a manticore or something?" he asked.

"Manticores are only a myth, I'm afraid. If they are real, we've never spotted one. There are none in this zoo, in any case. However,"–Lady Gwen pulled a watch out of some pocket so well concealed Sam hadn't even seen it–"we can walk to the crocodile exhibit. Inspector Hardwicke will meet us there shortly."

Sally sighed one of those girlish sighs, full of secret wishes. She thought nobody saw, but every time the inspector visited, Sally's cheeks turned pink. But Sam kept that knowledge to himself, and his hands in his pockets, as they walked along the paved path toward the crocodile pit. A welcome breeze lifted the sweaty hair off his forehead and mixed the sticky-sweet scent of caramel apples with the ripe odor of dung and musk.

Lady Gwen raised her parasol as if she had a grand idea. "While we're walking, let's make good use of our time. Sally, what are the medicinal uses of monkshood?"

Sally rattled off an answer filled with words that sounded like a foreign language, so he ignored them. Ever since they moved into the townhouse, his sister had been on a mission to learn everything about everything. She spent hours curled up in a chair in the study, reading obscure books by the steady light of dwarven lamps. Lady Gwen seemed to think it was a good idea, so they talked about useless facts whenever Sally's tutor wasn't teaching her how to be proper.

Girls. Couldn't they just enjoy a few quiet moments to think?

Sam had a tutor, too, but he was learning to read and speak like a gentleman, not memorize rubbish about plants. The speaking part was harder than the reading. He would always sound like he was from the Narrows, but as long as he had money, who cared how he sounded?

"Did you catch any of that, Samuel?"

He hesitated for only a moment before answering. "You can use it for fevers, gout and"—what was the word?—"rheumatism."

Lady Gwen blinked at him. "So you can. Well, you cannot. Don't get it into your head to muck about with any. Just touching the plant could kill you. But those are a few of its traditional uses. Well done."

"If it's so dangerous, why are we learning about it?"

She stopped walking and bent to look him in the eye. "Of all the things to learn in the world, what do you suppose we should know most about: the innocuous things or the things that can do us harm?"

He thought that over as they approached the crocodile pit, wondering if he should learn about crocodiles, too, since they were dangerous. Inspector Hardwicke waited there, almost a head taller than the people around him and twice as wide. His hair was a few shades lighter than Sally's dark blonde, and he had the jaw of a boxer. His hands were also large and capable; hands that needed wide pockets.

Sam smiled and flexed his smaller, more nimble fingers.

The inspector must have heard them coming because he turned, bowed his head, and smiled at Lady Gwen for just a moment too long. That gave Sam the chance to slip away from her side and blend into the crowd around the viewing platform.

"Lady St. James," Tony said, using her formal address the way he only did in public, then bobbed his head at Sally. "Miss Dawes."

Sally blushed. She was such a ninny. The man barely even glanced at her. What did she have to blush for?

"Good morning, Inspector," Lady Gwen said, stepping close enough for a handshake.

Sam edged around a woman and her children to slip up on Tony from the right side. The man was right-handed, so when he reached out to shake Lady Gwen's hand, it pulled the fabric of the coat away from his body. Sam slipped his fingers into the exposed pocket.

Nothing. The inspector was learning.

He backed up, hurried around the edge of the crowd, waited a moment as if he'd lagged behind, then ran in from the opposite direction, waving and shouting, "Tony!" before tripping and plowing into Sally's back.

She squealed and tumbled forward into the inspector and the three of them slammed together with an *oof*, arms flailing as they steadied themselves. Sam brushed his hands over all the usual spots, but no wallet, watch, or money clip bulged from any pocket.

Tony righted himself, straightened the two of them, and asked, "Are you all right?"

Sally blushed again, this time as red as the roses Mrs. Chapman, Lady Gwen's housekeeper, put on the table in the foyer, and mumbled something about being fine.

"Samuel," Lady Gwen sighed. "That was clumsy. A little subtlety goes a long way."

The inspector narrowed his eyes, then widened them as realization set in. He patted a spot on his jacket with his right hand before checking the more obvious places Sam already searched.

Gotcha.

"Not this time, scamp," Tony said, satisfied his possessions were safe.

He shrugged. "You're getting better, I guess."

Tony was a good cop and an honest man. He'd never win this game. Sam hid his amusement behind a mask of disappointment and said with a shrug, "I suppose so."

"Shall we have a look at our reptilian friends?" Lady Gwen asked.

The four of them made their way around the crowd of spectators to an open spot along the fence. A steep embankment lay on the opposite side of the wrought iron, leading down to a pond where the dozing crocodiles sunned themselves or floated lazily through the green scum on top of the water, leaving brownish trails behind them.

A few of the onlookers leaned far out and pointed as one reptile sank beneath the surface. That was a precarious place to balance. What would happen if one of them fell in? After a scream and a great splash, the crocodiles would sink and turn to swim toward the unlucky victim. They would flounder up the muddy bank, yelling for help. Some people would toss jackets down the slope while the braver citizens held hands to form a human bridge.

But those big lizards were faster than they looked, and when one or two climbed the bank and opened their toothy mouths—

"What news?" Lady Gwen asked the inspector.

Sam pulled his attention away from the daydream and focused on listening while his eyes roamed over the scaly predators.

"We've been watching the building and every delivery for months. There is no sign the mysterious Mr. Capstone has been communicating or paying anyone from the orphanages by hiding bribes in the laundry deliveries," the inspector said. He sounded tired as he took off his hat and ran his hand through his hair.

Lady Gwen said, "Then either Mrs. Edwards was lying about the bribes, or Mr. Capstone reneged on their arrangement."

"I doubt whether he had agreements with the other orphanages since no more children have gone missing under suspicious circumstances."

Suspicious was the inspector's code word for magic. Sam shivered despite the heat. He remembered what magic felt like the first time he'd encountered it, so many months ago. It felt like home; a mother's arms reaching out with the promise of love and safety. That lie dragged him down a narrow alley at night where the only person waiting for him was a kidnapper.

No orphan who ever dreamed of being rescued by their long-lost family could resist such a thing.

Luckily for Sam, his sister was with him. Sally fought like an angry badger, but she was no match for a full-grown man. Sam had tried to save her but got a knock on the head for his trouble and spent the rest of the night running back to the townhouse on Grosvenor Square with tears streaming down his face.

Lady Gwen and the inspector tracked the kidnapper, saved Sally, and stopped the witch before she sacrificed the orphan children to save her sick daughter. If there were no more kidnappings, maybe it really was over. Maybe he could sleep without nightmares, or waking to Sally's muffled crying through the wall that separated their rooms.

"I am glad to hear it," Lady Gwen said. "Though it makes catching him much more difficult."

"Assuming he is a real person."

Lady Gwen made a very un-ladylike sound.

"I know you don't want to admit it," the inspector said, keeping his voice low enough to blend with the hum of the crowd. "But we must consider whether Mrs. Edwards lied to cover her involvement. It is possible the witch worked directly with her to arrange the kidnappings. Mr. Capstone may not exist at all."

"Do you believe that?"

He sighed and rubbed the back of his neck with one hand. "No. I don't. But it's been months with no proof. If I don't find something convincing soon, my superiors are going to recall the men I've been using."

"I know how much you've fought for this investigation. Don't lose heart. There is one piece of her testimony strongly in favor of Mr. Capstone being a real person: the particulars Mrs. Edwards provided. If we assume she was lying, she fabricated details strangely unrelated to the truth. Why make Mr. Capstone an elf who wanted to kidnap the orphans to scare humans?"

"Why, indeed?"

"And Lady Monmouth's plan to save Clai—her daughter, did not rely on public fear." Lady Gwen's voice caught on the girl's name, and Sam flinched. He held Claire's hand as she died, her skin slowly growing cold once the spell keeping her alive vanished. She'd only been a year or two older than him. Of course, sacrificing other children to save Claire was wrong, but in a strange way, Sam envied Claire for having such a mother. If their father had loved him and Sally half as much, perhaps he wouldn't have abandoned them.

The wind picked up again, dragging away the stale mud and pond water scent of the crocodile pond and bringing with it... voices? What sounded earlier like the faraway buzzing of bees matured into the ruckus of rhythmic shouting.

The conversation behind him paused.

Lady Gwen tilted her head to listen. "Another demonstration?"

"A big one," the inspector said. "Went several blocks out of my way to avoid them, but it was peaceful."

"That brings us to my point," Lady Gwen said in a voice Sam strained to hear. "I think this Mr. Capstone business is more likely tied to the impending legislation for equality. He is the only piece of the puzzle that doesn't fit into Lady Monmouth's plan to save her daughter through sacrificial magic. She used compulsion to control everyone she worked with, but no spells were inked upon Mrs. Edwards when we questioned her at the orphanage."

"The bit about scaring the humans is suggestive, I'll grant you. But it would only make Parliament less likely to approve the bill."

"I never suggested which side of the affair he was on. If he is working for equality, he may be misguided in believing humans would acquiesce through fear. But if he is trying to suppress the bill because he does not want elves and dwarves to be granted hereditary titles, perhaps he seeks to discredit them."

"True, enough. But we can speak of it another time." The inspector's voice carried a tone that said he meant something other than what he'd said, but Sam wasn't sure what. When he spoke again, it was lower and harder to hear. "You still plan to go through with this?"

Through with what? It didn't sound as if the inspector liked the idea of Lady Gwen doing whatever it was. Sam began weaving through the crowd, casually shifting his weight and leaning as if he were only trying to view the exhibit from a better angle.

"You know what we saw that night," Lady Gwen replied in the same tone she used when teaching Sam something he wasn't interested in learning. "Just because the Fae have done nothing overt since Samhain"—she said something he couldn't make out above the growing noise of the protests outside—"and unless we know how she gained access to that magic, there will be nothing to stop them. And if Mr. Capstone is still active, I will not risk anything happening to Sally. She's already been touched by magic, and that leaves traces."

Sam's stomach tightened into a fist.

"We will learn nothing if you work yourself until you cannot function. Don't think I do not see it on your face."

"That," her voice was crisp and detached, "is not your concern, Inspector."

He ignored her switch to a formal address and stepped closer, raising his hands as if he would hold Lady Gwen's, but stopped. "You are taking too many chances, Gwen. I don't—"

Inspector Hardwicke didn't finish his thought, because the protesters neared and the next shout of, "Polity for equality! Polity for equality!" was loud enough to make everyone turn. Vibrations from hundreds of feet made the ground tremble.

"What's a polity?" Sam asked.

Tony spun, surprised to find Sam standing behind him. He smiled and held up the inspector's badge and wallet. The man's jaw tightened, and Sam dropped the pilfered items onto his palm, still grinning. Tony wouldn't ask how he knew where the items were, and Sam wouldn't offer the information. That was part of the game.

"Better luck next time, guv."

Tony stuffed his valuables back into his pockets with thin lips and a grim expression. "I thought I had you."

"I guess you need more practice, after all."

A loud crash sounded outside the zoo's walls, followed by a single scream. That scream was joined by another, then another, growing like a snowball, picking up shouts of indignation and ending in a sustained howl from the crowd of protestors.

"That doesn't sound promising," Lady Gwen said.

"It does not," the inspector agreed.

Behind them, the crowd of zoogoers shifted and muttered. The atmosphere of the place changed. Like dropping ink in water, the sense of discomfort and fear billowed out in invisible tendrils, infecting everything it reached. Sam's whole body tensed, muscles primed to move, to flee, to hide.

Sally met his eyes, the same knowledge on her face. The lessons taught by life on the streets were carved beneath the skin, down in their very bones.

"We should go," Lady Gwen and the inspector said at the same time.

"This way," the inspector said, and ushered them down the path leading away from the front of the zoo. A gust of wind dragged all the tree limbs toward the fleeing crowd, and Sam's heartbeat sped up at the acrid burn of smoke in his nostrils. Something in the city was on fire. The ground continued to shake.

Zoo visitors who weren't hurrying toward the exit stood frozen, staring wide-eyed at the walls. Even people without the finely honed senses of street urchins felt the sense of impending danger.

"Come on," the inspector ordered in his most officious voice. "Don't just stand there, move along! That's right, ma'am, this way, please."

Their party gathered more frightened visitors, crowding and pushing for space, making it hard to breathe. They bumped into one another and muttered in frightened voices every time a scream rose outside the wall. Several people tried to part from the group, only to be reeled back in by fences and Tony's voice. Sam did not want to be trapped among them. Sally's fingers clamped painfully around his wrist, the only thing stopping him from breaking away at a dead sprint.

"Keep calm," the inspector called to them over the rising shouts, cries, and crashes in the city. "Everything will be fine. We're going to the opposite side of the zoo, where we can exit safely. Sir, stay with the group, please."

A siren wailed nearby, soaring above the racket. Several ladies cried in distress, clutching their hands and their children with equal vigor. The air reeked of sweat and fear. Something, or someone, would break soon.

Lady Gwen turned and said over her shoulder in a low voice, "Stay close to me."

Sam recognized that tone of voice. Sally tightened her grip, and he squeezed back.

The smoke thickened, the coughing started, and they huddled together like frightened sheep being driven before the storm. Inspector Hardwicke was the sheepdog, snapping at their heels.

A horse screamed. They flinched and froze. The shouting and screaming reached a crescendo, followed by a crash that made Sam jump. The wall not ten feet in front of them crumbled inward in a cloud of dust and madness. For a heartbeat, everything moved in slow motion; a fancy new fire engine followed the tumbling brick as it toppled sideways through the broken wall and onto the path, dragging with it a team of flailing horses. A ton of wood and metal crashed to the ground, the siren stopped, and the huge brass reservoir broke. A wave of shin-deep water rushed toward them hard enough to knock everyone off their feet.

He lost grip of Sally's hand and rolled backward with the tide, gasping as water forced its way down his mouth and nose. He hit the iron fence post that separated the path from the smaller exhibits and hung on, coughing as the water finally abated. The shiny brass siren horn, etched with runes to amplify sound, lay in a muddy puddle at his feet.

A mob swarmed through the break in the wall, some holding signs, some wearing the frantic expression of hunted animals, and others with the bright gleam of destruction in their eyes. They ran in every direction, leaping over the sopping bodies of visitors who lay sprawled on the ground.

"Sally!" he yelled, but the crowd caught him up and forced him along in the press of running bodies.

Lady Gwen screamed his name.

Instinct took over.

He turned with the tide and ran as fast as his sturdy legs could carry him, trying to separate himself from the crush, searching for the first opportunity to break away into some place dark and hidden. But they pressed against one another like a living wall, and when one person fell, the rest trampled them in their haste to flee.

Sam squeezed between two men, avoided getting kicked, and scrambled toward the edge near the fence. Someone stepped on his foot. He stumbled, grabbed a sleeve to steady himself, got knocked off his feet, and hit the path hard enough to force the wind from his lungs.

Someone stepped on his leg and he cried out, trying to roll away, but stomping feet hit the ground everywhere. If he didn't move, they would crush him. A hand curled around his wrist and pulled. Sam scrabbled at the stone, trying to break free even as someone kicked him hard in the ribs, trying to leap over his body.

He landed hard on the pavement again, this time on his side, but kept rolling and panting, sobbing with every other breath. If he stayed on the ground, they would crush him. Sam pushed to his feet to find himself on one of the lanes that turned off the main path toward a closed exhibit. He'd rolled beneath the barricade.

He was safe.

At least, he thought he was safe until he looked up into the face of the person who pulled him free.

2

Witches and Riots

GWEN

All current evidence suggested one inescapable fact: I was cursed.

No matter where I dared take the children over the last year and a half, disaster was guaranteed to strike. Our candles set fire to the evergreen tree during the Yule festival, causing quite a distressing fracas. In the rush to quench the blaze, Sally's hair got stuck in her caramel apple, much to the amusement of her younger brother. The young man she had been speaking with found a less sticky companion to impress with his dimples.

Sally hid in her room for two days following the affair.

At the May Day celebration, Samuel stole three watches and a pocketbook full of money, which I was obliged to return discreetly, resulting in several uncomfortable conversations with men who found my proximity—and my unmarried state—intriguing.

And both children insulted Viscount Hennings at the opera, causing a rather exciting shouting match between the viscountess and myself. The three of us were forcefully removed from the building when it was over.

In the children's defense, the viscount *did* have the face of a rat.

So, when a figure in black appeared atop the wall of the zoo as if by magic, experience told me our mildly inconvenient situation was about to get interesting. The figure paused for a few heartbeats, crouched on the top of the wall, then turned to look directly at me. My breath caught.

Before I could blink or call out, the figure fled down the top of the wall with perfect balance, then leaped into the bushes inside the zoo as if the wall were not over ten feet high and disappeared into the manicured undergrowth. No one else seemed to have noticed.

People who cover themselves head-to-toe in discreet clothing tend to be troublemakers, especially ones who scale ten-foot walls like cats and make superhuman leaps into vegetation. Should he choose to cause mischief, I did not want to be trapped by a herd of frightened civilians while trying to protect the children.

Sally and Sam looked at me with wide, worried eyes in pale faces as I told them, "Stay close to me," in the serious voice Mama always used.

They nodded and crowded against me. Even the children were smart enough to know that something was wrong beyond a mere rowdy protest. The air was thick with energy, like the buildup before a storm, and my nostrils burned as caustic smoke grew stronger on the breeze.

If I were a cat, every hair on my body would have been stiff with apprehension. I was prepared for anything... except for a fire engine crashing through the zoo wall, dragging with it a team of screaming horses. There was barely enough time to snap open my umbrella and crouch in front of the children as bricks sailed through the air.

Two hit the open canopy in quick succession, and rings of pale blue energy rippled through the fabric where they struck, like pebbles falling into a still pond. The runes engraved on the shaft of the umbrella pulled the kinetic energy from the canopy panels and stored it for later use.

"Delilah," I muttered, "you are a genius."

Despite how well it protected us from flying debris, the umbrella did have a flaw: it wasn't transparent. So, I didn't see the wave that crashed into my legs and pulled my feet out from under me. Cold rushed up my body as I gasped and floundered, trying to right myself while careening off other floating visitors.

The water plastered me against the trunk of a smallish tree before it subsided, leaving me chilly and bruised. Where were Sam and Sally? Where was Tony?

Sprawling figures littered the ground like windblown leaves after a rainstorm, gasping and groaning as they climbed to their feet. Sally clung to a fence post, but her walking dress hung in heavy, wet folds, and dripping locks of blonde hair were plastered to her face.

Tony held the elbow of an elderly woman as she tried to stand, but a mob of rioters poured through the breach in the wall and knocked everyone standing back to the ground. They split and spread, swarming the shocked visitors in a tidal wave of stinking, frenzied bodies.

Humans, elves, and dwarves rushed down the lane in both directions. I grabbed the bottom branch of the tree and swung my leg up, pulling myself out of the danger just as the throng passed beneath me.

And there was Sam, his light brown hair swallowed up in the churning mass. I screamed his name, but it was too late. He'd been dragged downstream. I waited for the endless tide of fleeing citizens to pass, then slipped out of the tree, retrieved my umbrella, and ran to Sally.

"Are you all right?" I asked, cupping her cold cheek in one hand.

She nodded, though she looked dizzy, and pushed the wet hair out of her face. "Where is Sammy?"

"I'm going to find him. I promise. You stay with Tony and help him get these people out of here. Can you do that, darling?"

She blinked, then resolve settled on her like armor. "Yes, ma'am."

"Good girl. Tony! I'm after Sam."

The inspector's brown eyes snapped up to me, took in the scene, and his mouth flattened into an unhappy line, but he nodded.

"Take care of Sally. I'll be back."

I turned toward the empty lane where I last saw Sam and ran. Well, that wasn't entirely true; one cannot run in wet, heavy layers of skirts and petticoats. Let us say I galloped. With all haste. In truth, my chest was so tight it was difficult to breathe well enough for anything more than a trot.

As I rushed past, people unlucky enough to fall lay bruised, bloody, and groaning—but alive. I could not stop to help them.

The mental image of Sam's sturdy little body on the ground, wet and broken from trampling feet, drove me on.

I hiked up my skirt, baring an immodest amount of leg, and ran. The screaming caught my attention before I realized what was happening. A man, clothing still dry, grappled with a wet woman, pulling her hair with one hand and the coin purse tied around her wrist with the other. She curled in on herself, gripping the strings of the purse to her chest as if she were drowning and it was a lifeline.

I jerked the umbrella up, braced the handle against my shoulder, and pressed the button concealed along the lower end of the shaft. The energy stored from the impact of the bricks burst from the tip of the umbrella in a stream of force and hit the man in the small of his back. The wood warmed beneath my hands.

He shouted, arched his back, and spun to see what hit him. By that time, I reversed my grip on the umbrella and brought the handle—a decorative raven's head Delilah carved of oak and lined with bands of iron—crashing down on his head. He crumpled into a boneless heap.

"Run that way," I called to the woman as I passed. "Follow the inspector. Brown jacket!"

She lifted her skirt and fled.

I splashed through the puddles at breakneck speed, images of an injured Sam spurring me on, until I skidded to a stop to see him standing next to a pale-skinned woman in a dark dress that covered her from ankles and wrists to her neck. She was absolutely still, clean, uninjured, and unafraid. Something in the way she held herself caused every warning bell in my head to ring simultaneously.

With slow deliberation, I turned the handle and the shaft of the umbrella in opposite directions, and with a click, a slender, rune-engraved blade slid free. A translucent shimmering, like the walls of a bubble, rose around her and the boy.

"No, wait!" Sam yelled, holding out both hands, eyes flicking between the pale woman and me. "She saved me from the crowd. Don't attack her."

"Samuel," I said in a voice that belied the heart-pounding fear in my chest. "Are you alright?"

The woman opened both long, elegant hands and held them out to her sides. "The boy is fine, Lady St. James, as you can see. I pulled him from the crowd when they might have trampled him."

"You'll pardon me, but I wasn't speaking to you. Samuel?"

"I'm fine, my lady. Promise." But there was unmistakable fear in his wide eyes and shaking hands.

"Come here to me, then."

The woman didn't bother to stop him, and Sam crossed the bubble as one would cross a pit of snakes, every moment expecting something to go wrong. The field of shimmering energy let him through, much like poking a finger into a jelly.

I stepped between them as soon as he was close to me, held the point of my rapier low, and decided that being polite was the least I could do while threatening her life.

"Thank you for protecting the boy."

"If you would like to thank me properly, you'll put away your sword and accept my invitation to join the Triumphant Sisterhood for supper tonight. I believe you know the address?"

My fingers tightened around the raven's head handle. I had not seen nor spoken to the coven of witches styling themselves The Triumphant Sisterhood since they'd given me the clues I needed to track down Lady Cassandra Monmouth, a rogue member of their coven who resorted to sacrificing orphan children to save her terminally ill daughter.

They sent me a note shortly after I killed their former sister, re-questing a meeting. I ignored them and commissioned protective amulets for everyone I loved. Apparently, they didn't intend to be ignored any longer.

I would have preferred to turn my back on the woman and re-move Sam to some level of safety… but then she did me a good turn by helping Sam. I owed her, and I took karma seriously enough to recognize the debt.

"Who am I speaking to?" I said as I slid the blade back into the umbrella shaft.

"You may call me Deborah."

"After the prophetess?"

She smiled. "You are reading too much into the name, lady."

"Names have meaning, Deborah. One should not take them lightly."

"Wise. Will you join us?"

Sam's clammy hands clamped around my wrist. He hadn't been trampled into the dirt by rioters, or abused by some vulture who took advantage of legitimate protests to prey upon distracted at-tendees… and I had witches to thank for it.

"What are the terms?"

"The terms?"

"I do not know what Madame Matilda told you about me, but if you think I will accept an invitation from your *sisterhood* without agreeing upon binding terms beforehand, you have not been told enough."

Was that surprise or respect flickering in her dark eyes?

"Dinner begins at eight o'clock and ends promptly at nine o'clock. The invitation will be extended to the inspector, should you wish, but to no others. We will guarantee the safety of everyone in your party from the time you enter the carriage on Grosvenor Square to the time you enter your home again."

"And you require nothing from me or my guest?"

One corner of her mouth quirked up. "We will accept nothing you do not offer freely."

"Free of persuasion, extortion, blackmail, threats, magic, or drugs?"

Deborah laughed delightedly. The sound was light and airy, at odds with her severe dress and tightly coiled hair. "One thing Madame Matilda had right: you are suspicious. Yes, of course. The only persuasion we intend to use is mundane."

I gave myself a moment to look for loopholes, then a few extra moments, just to make the woman wait.

"One question, before I agree," I said.

"Ask."

"Did the sisterhood have anything to do with the protest becoming a riot?"

The amusement faded, and she clasped both hands together in front of her. "No."

I looked for the signs Tony mentioned were common in liars: sweating, fidgeting, uncomfortable eye contact... but my gut said the woman told the truth.

"Very well. Tell your mistress I will accept the invitation under the terms we discussed."

She smiled and bowed, wiggled her fingers at Sam, and walked away as zoo security and the metropolitan police charged toward them. They jogged right past the woman but stopped and questioned us thoroughly. She must have used a spell that screened her from sight.

As Sam and I answered questions, I thought of how nice it must be to walk about unseen. Had I that power, I would most likely abuse it.

By the time we were free to find Tony and Sally, Sam and I shivered despite the sun and set off at a brisk walk to warm up.

"Lady Gwen?" he asked.

"Yes?"

His jaw worked for a moment. "Are you sure that woman isn't like the unicorn?"

"Oh, I'm certain. That woman doesn't hide how dangerous she is."

He made a dissatisfied noise in the back of his throat. "No, it's not that. It's just, earlier today when we saw the unicorn, I couldn't stop thinking of how— of how easy it would be to fleece everyone there."

He sounded so ashamed of himself that I nearly laughed.

"They were so distracted," he continued as if trying to justify himself. "They couldn't stop looking at the thing, and they never would have noticed if I slipped a couple of fingers into their pockets."

"But you didn't?"

"No," he sighed.

"I see. I appreciate your honesty, Sam. And your thoughts. She might very well have been a distraction. I promise I will think on it."

He nodded and walked next to me with his head down in thought as we passed the exhibits, groups of gossiping visitors, officers trying to reestablish order, and patrons searching for the missing members of their parties.

When we reached the other side of the zoo, Sally and Tony stood with a huddle of blue-uniformed officers near the monkey exhibit. The constables chatted with Tony, their gold buttons throwing reflections on his face and brown jacket.

Sam took off like a bolt of lightning and threw himself at his sister. Sally had repaired some of the damage to her ensemble and pinned her hair back out of her face, looking more like a young woman than a sixteen-year-old girl. She caught her little brother with an exultant whoop of joy.

A shiver of longing raced down my spine. I remembered what it was like to be held by the person who knew you best in the world, to be worried for, and to feel that when you were together, everything was right with the world. But I lost her a long time ago.

Ophelia, my twin sister, jumped into a faerie circle when we were sixteen. She stood amid the red-capped mushrooms, teasing me for being superstitious. When they stole her, she was looking right at me with wide, terrified eyes; simply disappeared, as if she'd never been there.

No one believed me. They thought she'd run off with a paramour, or been kidnapped. But Lia would never have left me.

I spent the last ten years searching for ways to get her back, learning everything I could about faeries, who had been locked away in the Sunset Lands thousands of years ago after the Great War was over. I studied the occult and witchcraft. I learned how dwarves use artificers to capture and control natural forces. I stuffed my brain with every myth, faerie story, and hint of magic I could find in every library, ancient ruin, and obscure temple I knew of.

Nothing had gotten me closer to finding Lia. Not until last October, when Cassandra Monmouth started kidnapping children. The spell she used hadn't only been a source of power for healing her daughter, it was a key that opened a doorway between the mortal world and the Sunset Lands. And Lia had been standing on the other side.

I wanted my sister so badly that I was tempted to let five children, including Sally, die to open that door. But I hadn't. I'd broken the circle, killed Cassandra, allowed her daughter to die, and let the door close. Sally was alive, as were the rest of the children.

But Lia was still gone.

The great gaping void inside me yawned and stretched, flexing its claws, as Sally held Samuel against her chest. Tony looked at me, understanding in his eyes, and the spell broke. I didn't need or want sympathy. Other things must be done.

"Lady St. James," Tony said. "This is Sergeant Honeycutt. Looks like he'll be heading up the investigation into the riot."

"Pleasure to meet you, Sergeant. Any luck discovering what turned a peaceful demonstration into a riot?"

"One side says it was the demonstrators throwing bricks, the other side says it was the opposition. But we have reports of a man in black from both sides. No one was able to identify him, but I have my men scouring the streets."

"What do they say the man in black did?"

"Agitating, mostly."

"That's rather vague."

"Witness reports of events like this often are, my lady. Now, if you'll excuse me. Tony." He doffed his domed cap and turned to issue instructions to the waiting officers.

I pulled Tony to the side, away from the milling officers and the children. The muscles of his arm shifted beneath my grip as he allowed me to lead him away, a frown drawing his dark blonde brows low over his eyes.

"I saw the figure in black," I told him.

His brows raised. "Really? Where?"

"He leaped the wall before the fire engine crashed, ran down the top of it, then jumped into the bushes and disappeared."

"That sounds rather acrobatic."

I glared at him. "Now is not the time for your skepticism. I am telling you, I saw the figure."

"Was it an elf?"

"I don't think so. The dynamics weren't consistent with Elvin bodies. They are graceful and elegant. This person was as tall as a human or elf, but their movements were powerful and predatory and with a greater range of motion. More... explosive."

"What does that mean? It couldn't be a human or an elf?"

"It could be," I allowed, biting my lower lip in thought. "A human could pull off a stunt like that with the right training. Elves are more capable but less likely to try."

"I'll give you that, but it's thin."

I folded my arms and raised a brow at him.

He pulled on the cuff of his jacket and shook his head. "Alright. Write everything you remember. I'll compare your notes to the reports the Sergeant collects and we'll see what comes of it."

"Thank you."

"You're welcome."

"There... is something else."

Tony folded his arms and pursed his lips. Mama gave me that exact look every time she caught me doing something improper, like trying to hold a seance with my dolls at twelve years old. "What's that?"

I took a deep breath. "Will you go to dinner with me tonight?"

His eyes widened, making it easier to see the gold flecks that speckled the rich brown of his irises, but he hid the expression quickly. One corner of his mouth curled up. "I thought you'd never ask."

He joked so rarely that I smiled back without thinking. When he smiled at me like that, it was hard not to remember the feeling of his mouth when he'd kissed me after our ordeal last October.

I wrote it off as the exuberance of the moment since he'd never tried it again. I didn't want to admit I was disappointed he'd never tried because I would have to refuse him. Tony wasn't the type of man to be comfortable with a casual tryst behind closed doors.

It wouldn't suit his idea of honor. And he deserved the love of a woman who could give him the constancy I would never offer. The man was infuriatingly proper. Which made teasing him even more fun.

"You're rather charming when you smile, inspector. You should try it more often. Your face won't crack, I promise."

The boyish charm disappeared. "What do you want, Gwen?"

I put my hand on my heart, as if wounded. "Whatever do you mean?"

"You only compliment me when you have something up your sleeve. What is it?"

I cleared my throat. "The witches have requested the pleasure of my company, and I'd like to drag you along if you don't mind."

"When?"

"Eight o'clock."

"Shall I meet you there or at home?"

"They've guaranteed our safety from my door to theirs and back."

"And you trust them?"

"Of course not. That's why I have you.

The three of us huddled together on the ride home, quiet and cold as a spring storm rolled across the skyline, beating a steady rhythm on the roof of the coach and bathing the cobblestones in cleansing rain. A little cast-iron dwarven heater sat on the floor at our feet, pumping out heat saved by placing it in the hearth every evening.

"At least our toes are warm," Sally said.

"Take small blessings where you can find them," I agreed.

"You shouldn't go," Sam said.

Sally and I both turned to look at the boy. His cheeks were flushed, but his jaw was set, and he stared determinedly at the heater.

"Go where?" Sally asked.

"To the witches," Sam said.

Sally caught her breath, her face draining of color. She'd been a sacrifice in the stone circle the night I'd abandoned Lia, and she still had nightmares. I hadn't intended to tell her till I was back safe for that exact reason.

I clenched my fists, but said calmly, "I am quite capable of protecting myself, Samuel. And I'm bringing the inspector with me."

"You can't trust those ladies."

"I know that."

"But—"

I turned and took the boy's hands, forcing him to look at me. His brows were so low they hid his eyes and his mouth pursed in a stubborn frown. He was still small for his age, and looked no more than twelve years old, though he was nearly fourteen. It was his eyes that betrayed his maturity.

Sam and Sally lost their mother when Sam was quite young, and their father abandoned them a few years later. For a long time, they had no one to rely on but each other. We spent the last year and a half learning to live together and trust one another, and here I was exposing myself to the kind of people both of them feared.

"Do you remember when you told me you were afraid the woman who saved you was like the unicorn?" I asked.

He nodded.

"I agree with you. She is dangerous. But there is something important you must understand. *I* am the unicorn, Sam."

I waited for him to process my meaning. The boy already knew I was capable, but his fear overpowered his common sense. When he nodded, it was uncertain. Not convinced. I sighed and leaned back, digging into a pocket hidden in the folds of my wet skirt. When I pulled my hand out, a large white canine tooth lay in the center of my palm.

"See this?"

"Is that—a tooth?"

"It is. Do you know what it's from?"

Sally gasped and poked at it with her forefinger. "It's not from a werewolf, is it?"

"Very good," I congratulated her. "How did you guess?"

"Well, according to *Monsters and Myths*, werewolf teeth are twice the size of a common wolf, and I've never seen one that big. And it's not serrated like a shark. No cats get that large, either, except maybe tigers."

"You're right. And do you know how I happened to come by this tooth?"

Sam frowned a moment, then looked at me in astonishment, his mouth hanging open.

"Yes," I said, watching his face fill with awe. "If I can kill a werewolf, do you really think a few witches scare me?"

Worry and respect warred on his brow, but the latter finally won out, if only barely.

"I suppose not," he said, at last. Then, after a moment, he asked hesitantly, "Will you tell us how it happened? How you killed it?"

I laughed. "That, my boy, is a long story for another day. We're almost home."

When we arrived at the townhouse, Mrs. Chapman was waiting on the front step. The garden was in bloom and sparkling from the rain, but my housekeeper stood with a stern expression on her birdlike face and her bony knuckles pressed into her hips.

"Just look at the three of you!" she scolded. "You're not fit to be seen. I wouldn't be surprised if you've caught a cold. Come on, then. Get upstairs and out of those wet things. For shame, my lady, look what you've allowed to happen to the children."

When Sally first came to us, an injured laundress from the east side Narrows, Mrs. Chapman was certain the girl would steal us blind. Now she fussed over the both of them as if they were her own, scolding them as thoroughly as she scolded me.

"Get those shoes off! Don't track mud across my clean floors," she said while waving a dust cloth at the boy's feet. "For shame, Master Samuel."

It hadn't taken the children long to become accustomed to my housekeeper's scoldings and tirades. She ran the house with a crabby iron fist, and I loved her for it. It was much more straightforward than Mama's gentle, manipulative reproaches.

I placed my umbrella in the receptacle just in time for Aristotle to land on my head. The raven cawed happily and dug his talons into the soggy straw of the hat.

"Squishy!" he said while squeezing.

I swatted at him. "Will. You. Get. Off?"

"I'm hungry."

"So am I, you selfish bird. Hasn't anyone fed you?"

Mrs. Chapman flicked her dust cloth at Aristotle, who launched himself off my head to land on the umbrella handle that bore his resemblance. "Of course, I have. That little fiend ate more than he's worth, and that's the truth."

Aristotle shook his tail feathers at Mrs. Chapman. She snapped her cloth at him again, and he sailed away into the study, making a sound that could only be described as avian laughter. The rogue.

We separated at the top of the stairs; the children going one way and I the other, to strip out of our soggy clothes. I stumbled into my room, dropped the hatpin on a tray, and pried the soggy straw out of my curls. The hat was ruined.

Aristotle sailed in as I tossed the hat into the trash bin atop the empty bottle of brandy. He perched on the edge of my chest of drawers, his head tilted to the side as he stared out the window.

I closed the door and peeled myself out of my dress, lying it on a chair for Charlotte to send to the laundry.

"I almost lost the children today," I said, shivering in my damp chemise.

"Lost?"

"Well, not quite, I suppose. But almost."

He considered me, black eyes shining in the steady light of the dwarven lamps on the wall. "Save the girl."

A great, heavy sigh worked its way out of my chest. I plopped down on the bed and lay back, careless of my wet hair. "I've not figured that out, either. For all I know, I never will, and Lia will be stuck in the Sunset Lands forever."

Aristotle landed on the coverlet, then climbed onto my stomach, circled a few times, and got comfortable. I ran my fingers down his soft back, and he made a contented little purring sound while I cried.

3

Gwen Gets Hired

GWEN

Aristotle helped me prepare for dinner by plucking out the curls Charlotte so carefully styled and pinned atop my head. The maid tried to include fresh flowers in the arrangement, which the bird found quite intriguing. We had to chase him out of the room to finish the affair.

I almost gave into my sense of irony and wore something guaranteed to offend the witches, but decided at the last minute to mind my manners. Offending the morals of the Triumphant Sisterhood would likely offend Tony, too, and we'd been getting along too well lately to risk him scowling at me again.

So, Charlotte and I chose a simple, dark blue, off-the-shoulder gown with beadwork on the bodice and elbow-length black gloves. The amber amulet that kept the witches from interfering with my thoughts sat pillowed on an impressive amount of dècolletè, which had nothing at all to do with Tony being my dinner guest.

Lamplight shone through the open door of the study when I reached the bottom stair, and I was unsurprised to find Sally inside, curled in a chair near the fire with a book in her lap. Sam was busy near the window, teasing Aristotle with bits of food.

Unlike the rest of the house, which was more functional than decorative, the study had a distinct air of personality. Wall-to-wall bookshelves on the right hand side held enough books to qualify as a library, complete with trinkets I'd gathered on my adventures on the continent and Africa.

Gadgets, experiments, inventions, and chemistry equipment littered the shelves and the worktable behind my father's desk, which sat across from the large hearth. A bank of floor-to-ceiling windows lined the wall facing Grosvenor Square and let the last orange light of sunset bathe the room in a dreamy glow.

I stood and stared at the homey scene for a long moment, locking it away in my memory as one of those rare moments of perfection.

Sally looked up, and her eyes glowed with appreciation. "You look magnificent."

"Charlotte will be gratified to hear it. She fought *that* beast"—I tilted my head at the bird—"for an hour to make me presentable. Come, don't leave me in suspense. What epic tome of knowledge are you consuming this evening?"

Her cheeks turned pink, and she lowered her eyes. "Arrogance and Assumptions. It's a novel, and not educational, but a *woman* wrote it."

"No need to justify yourself, my darling. Reading is for pleasure, too. And that book is certainly educational. Observe the relationship between Anne Baxter and Mr. Dalton. If that isn't a masterclass education, call me a fool."

Sally's shy smile was like the sun coming up. Lia and I hid our romance novels in every conceivable location and read them by candlelight far into the night. Mama knew, of course, but we never allowed ourselves to believe she did.

"Masterclass education about what?" Sam asked.

"Maybe you'd know if you'd bother learning to read," Sally said.

"I can read."

"Barely."

Sam dropped the treats he was teasing Aristotle with and stuck out his jaw. "What's in books that I can't learn in real life, anyway?"

"You'd know if you applied yourself. It's not that hard, Sammy. Besides, just think of everything there is to know!"

The boy folded his arms and glared at his sister beneath lowered brows. "I know stuff 'cause I done it. Not 'cause some dried-up old prune in glasses told me."

I raised both arms and said, "Children, please. No fighting except on Saturdays when I can sell tickets."

"I *can* read," Sam muttered, still glaring at his sister.

"I know you can," I told him. "And what's more, you're right. Not everyone learns everything the same way. Some people learn certain subjects best by seeing other people perform them or by trying themselves. Other people prefer to learn by reading first. And most subjects require a combination of all techniques."

"See?" he said, widening his eyes at Sally.

"But Sally is right, too. There is a world of information in books you cannot get anywhere else. Did you know you can learn from the old emperors of Rome? Or the great philosophers of China? There is even an entire book called *The Art of War*."

Sam narrowed his eyes at me. "You swear?"

I turned, pulled a little red leather-bound novel from the shelf, and wiggled it enticingly. "It's right here."

Sam hopped off the chaise and took the book, turning it over and then squinting at the first page.

"Appear weak when you are strong, and strong when you are weak," I quoted.

Sam looked up and raised his brows. "Like the unicorn!"

"Exactly like that."

He ran his hand over the cover, seeming to consider, then said, "Okay. I'll read it."

"Brilliant. Sally, you'll help him with any of the hard words, won't you?"

"But—" She looked down at her own book, then her pretty features settled into lines of resignation. "I suppose so."

Mr. Yates's steady footfalls sounded in the hallway.

"That will be James with the coach, Mr. Yates?" I asked.

My butler entered a moment later and bowed. "The inspector has also arrived, ma'am."

"You are courtesy itself, as always, Mr. Yates. And you," I said, turning to the children, "are absolute treasures. Take care of one another while I'm out and don't stay up too late."

Both of them looked at me as if I lost my mind. Darling children. I picked up my umbrella and followed Mr. Yates into the hall. I was nearly at the front door when I heard Sam's running footfalls. He grabbed my wrist a moment later.

"You'll be careful, Lady Gwen. Won't you?"

His eyes, the warm brown of maple syrup, were earnest and concerned. My heart gave a little lurch.

"Of course, I will. And the inspector will be there. Better to tell the witches to beware of me." I winked and messed up his hair, then let Mr. Yates escort me outside before I started crying. It was a long time since anyone but Mama worried over me.

I never wanted children. There was too much to see and do to give up my freedom, and using my body as an incubator for ten months was more than a little off-putting. But the longer the children lived with me, the more they felt like family. And despite the disasters that plagued us whenever we traveled even a short distance, they made me feel less alone.

Perhaps I could see myself as a very dedicated great-aunt. That was a cheerful thought.

Tony stood by the door of the carriage wearing the same suit he'd worn to Mama's ball in October. The jacket fitted his wide shoulders, tapering down to a narrow waist accentuated by a black vest. What the inspector did to stay fit was a mystery, but it was all too easy to imagine what hid beneath the layers of fine wool and linen.

His blonde hair, always just a bit tousled, was combed back, leaving the clean planes of his face on display. The angled light of the street lamp carved the sharp line of his jaw, contrasting the softer line of his mouth.

When he saw me, his hands tightened into fists and he stopped breathing for a moment. It was not in the least gratifying, and I can say with confidence that I did not blush. He opened the carriage door, swallowed noticeably before handing me up, and climbed in behind me.

Once upon a time, Tony had been afraid of riding in a closed vehicle alone with me, certain it would impugn my honor, but his scruples withered under the pressure of familiarity. Still, once the door shut and we jolted into motion, the space felt entirely too small.

His knees brushed mine with every bump, and the air seemed filled with the warmth of him. It had been too long since I'd bedded a man. I needed a distraction.

"That suit fits you rather well," I said, then winced. I didn't mean to say that. What had I meant to say? Something innocuous and polite about his appearance, surely, but not that.

The corners of his mouth curled unwillingly. "I had it tailored."

I looked everywhere but at him. "I can see that."

"And you look..." His eyes strayed to the amber necklace, lingered a bit too long, and flicked back up to mine. My skin flushed with heat. He cleared his throat. "Incredibly elegant."

I squeezed the handle of my umbrella as if I could snap it in half. "Charlotte does work magic."

Tony nodded—one of those jerky, uncomfortable nods—and turned to look out the window. I searched for an inane topic to keep us occupied, but nothing came to mind.

"Are you wearing your amulet?" I asked, at last.

"Ah, yes. It's here." He pressed his hand over his chest.

"Good."

We sat and stared at one another across the aisle. His breathing sped up. I swallowed. He licked his lips. The carriage jolted to a stop hard enough to catapult Tony out of his seat. I squeaked and leaned back as he caught himself, both arms on either side of my head, his face mere inches from mine. His breath smelled of peppermint. I remembered exactly how soft his lips had been as I looked into his eyes. They were the rich warm brown of roasted chestnuts, inviting and absurdly comforting.

His pupils dilated as his gaze drifted to my mouth. A little thrill of excitement went whizzing down my spine, and I held my breath. He was going to kiss me.

Tony blinked, then sat back in a rush.

"I'm sorry," he said.

I released my breath slowly and told myself I was not disappointed. "Think nothing of it. Could have happened to anyone."

James appeared at the door and let down the foldable stairs. Tony stayed cramped in one corner of the coach, leaving plenty of room for the footman to hand me down so I didn't trip over the acres of skirt necessary for formal gowns.

Stupid, inconvenient, impractical things.

Tony dropped to the pavement next to me and we both looked up at the square grey stone building that dominated this part of the block.

"Let us see what the witches want, shall we?"

Tony held out his arm. I took it, and we climbed the stairs.

The two-story marble foyer was empty, as usual, and our steps echoed back to us as we crossed to the grand staircase. Patricia stood at the top in a plain black gown, hands folded neatly, face as serene as the first time I met her.

I'd been searching for kidnapped orphans at the time, and the witches offered help in the form of a crystal necklace. How they knew I would need it when I forced my way through the magic circle to save the children was still a mystery.

"Lady St. James, Inspector Hardwicke. This way, please."

Patricia guided us away from the large sitting room with the fireplace, where I was introduced to Madame Matilda twice before, farther down the door-lined hall and up another set of stairs at the end.

The dining room was a comfortable size, lacking the grandeur of the foyer, with a hearth on one side and a long, dark table in the center. If we were dispensing with the standard pre-dinner chat, the madame must have something pressing on her mind.

The woman in question stood at the head of the table. Madame Matilda was tall and slender, with olive skin that glowed and long, dark curls spilling elegantly down one bare shoulder, accentuating the column of her neck. She wore a ruby-encrusted chandelier necklace that perfectly matched the color of her lips and gown, and inclined her head just enough for welcome.

"Lady St. James. Inspector Hardwicke. Please." She gestured to the open chairs nearest her. "Sit."

As we sat, other witches filed into the room and sat in unison, not saying a word.

"Creepy," I muttered to Tony.

Of course, it was intended to be. The entire situation was a display meant to put us in our places and make us just uncomfortable enough not to be confident.

So I smiled winningly at the silent witches and said in my most cheeky voice, "It is lovely to see you all again. It has been too long. I hope your families are well?"

A few pairs of uncertain eyes flicked between me and the leader of their coven, who didn't let a hint of irritation show on her face. Deborah sat near the end of the table, covering a smile with her hand.

"Shall we begin?" Matilda asked, sliding into her seat.

On no signal that I could see, servants in white entered the room through two concealed doors carrying silver trays of steaming food.

"Madame Matilda, you look ravishing. That necklace is exquisite."

She raised an amused brow at me and snapped open her napkin with a neat flick. "Thank you. I believe I have remarked before on the quality of your amber pendant. I'm pleased to see you wore it again. It is becoming a favorite of mine."

"I do aim to please."

She smiled, gave Tony an appreciative glance, and said, "I'm certain you do. I have not thanked you yet for joining us tonight, but I can assure you, your presence is most appreciated."

I hid my irritation by opening my own napkin. The madame's voice and manner were the picture of the highest breeding; perfectly modulated, unflappable, and magnanimous. And she fully intended to keep me in my place. She also wanted to make it clear, from the beginning, that I owed her thanks for sending an acolyte out to protect Samuel. Though, how she knew he would need protecting was anyone's guess.

My thanks would establish a debt, so I said, "Much like the service you so graciously rendered my ward."

One corner of her elegant mouth curled, but she didn't acknowledge my dodge. We sipped soup in silence long enough to allow the moment to pass and to enjoy the talent of her cook.

Finally, when the silence became uncomfortable, she said, "As I am certain you have guessed, the Triumphant Sisterhood did not invite you here merely for your company, charming as it is."

Tony tensed next to me, only just recognizing the carefully worded insults she'd been gently lobbing in my direction since we entered the room. He hadn't enough experience with the velvet-covered barbs of high society to see them for the carefully crafted manipulation they were.

I put my hand on his leg under the table, and he froze. Better to give him something else to think about.

"I assumed as much, though—to put your mind at ease—I would have joined you for the entertainment if nothing else."

Her smile tightened, but she was too well-bred to give anything away. She waited for the second course to be served before continuing. "Let me dispense with the niceties, then, and get right to the heart of things. We need your help."

I almost choked on my fish.

"Pardon me?"

Madame Matilda dabbed the corners of her mouth with her napkin, folded it, and laid it on the table. The other witches followed suit. Tony shifted uneasily beneath my hand, his thigh muscles flexing in a rather distracting way. He did not remove my hand.

"Lady St. James, this is Frances, Lady Chatsworth," Madame Matilda said, extending her hand toward the young woman across the table from me.

Lady Chatsworth? Matilda just gave me the real name of one of her coven, which was reason enough for surprise, but Lady Chatsworth sat comfortably at the peak of fashionable society. To gain her notice and approval was the goal of every debutant. An invitation from her was never turned down. I, of course, had never received one.

When I first met Madame Matilda, she assured me that the Sisterhood was composed of powerful women who carefully protected their identities so they might continue their philanthropy work—and their witchcraft—without drawing the ire of their families. If Lady Chatsworth was a member of the coven, they had far more social and political power than I suspected.

Something interesting was happening here.

I masked my surprise, fell back on my mother's training, and said, "Lady Chatsworth. It is a pleasure to make your acquaintance."

A pair of round hazel eyes surrounded by dark lashes stared back at me. She was lovely, approachable, and earnest, like a flower waiting to be picked. She bobbed her head and said, "Please, call me Frances. I hope I may presume upon you that far, if you'd be so good as to help us."

"And you must call me Gwen."

She gave me a tight smile and a hesitant nod. Her invitation wasn't from the warmness of her heart, but from the hope of relief. I turned back to Madame Matilda. "Please, go on."

"Inspector, as Lady Gwen's guest, I expect we can rely on your discretion?"

Tony bowed his head, just enough for acceptance, not enough for respect. Matilda's eyes narrowed, but she turned back to me.

"Frances, perhaps you would prefer to explain?"

Frances swallowed. "My unfortunate situation, Lady Gwen, is this: my housekeeper, Ms. Honeycutt, has disappeared. She appears to have vanished from our country estate just over three weeks ago. We searched the countryside. I have tried scrying. We have even performed several more complex spells, yet nothing I can do reveals her to me."

What? A coven of witches manipulated me to a secret dinner to ask if I would help find a runaway *housekeeper*. It was ridiculousness of the highest order. Then again, I imagined what I might feel if Mrs. Chapman disappeared, and my heart gave a little hiccup. Perhaps it wasn't so strange.

"Forgive me, but you cannot be serious. This table represents a gathering of some of the most powerful people on this island and you would like *me* to find the woman instead?"

"We cannot become involved," Madame Matilda said. "I imagine you can understand why."

Of course. To keep their connections and identity a secret, the witches would need to manage their social relationships carefully. If enough people learned who they were and what they practiced, the lot of them would be arrested.

"Her absence distresses me so greatly, I—" Frances put one gloved hand on her chest. "I have not been able to bring my power properly to bear. And the coven suffers without my support."

The rest of the women at the table looked at their sister with a combination of concern and empathy.

"Surely Inspector Hardwicke is a better candidate to assist you in this way," I said.

"No," Madame Matilda said, her voice firm. Frances echoed her, but her voice was an octave higher with fear.

She shook her head and said, "Involving the police would bring far too much attention to my house. That is something I cannot risk."

"And as you have solved such complicated mysteries in the past," Madame Matilda said, "you are the best option we have."

"I am holding a week-long celebration for my husband, the earl's birthday, at our estate in the country next week. It is the perfect opportunity for you to find Ms. Honeycutt, as you'll have access to my estate without restriction or suspicion."

I shook my head, bewildered. "You cannot have thought this through, Lady Frances. You know who I am. If you invite me to your home, I will tarnish your reputation more than if Inspector Hardwicke were to investigate."

"Not if people think this is your attempt to re-enter polite society," Madame Matilda said in a sweet-as-sugar voice.

Frances nodded, eagerly. "I will undertake to be your sponsor. With my support, no one can deny you for long."

I sat unmoving, trying to puzzle out why a well-bred lady—trained from birth to see her staff as tools more than humans—would undertake such trouble to recover a missing housekeeper. And why the offer of re-entering a society that cast me out made a little bubble of hope burst in my chest.

"I am sorry, ladies," I said, pushing my chair back to stand. "This is not an affair in which I can involve myself. I have urgent matters to see to and responsibilities here that I cannot easily walk away from."

Mr. Capstone, among them.

Florence clenched her fist around her napkin, sending Madame Matilda a desperate glance.

The dark-haired woman stood. "Of course, we intend to pay you for your trouble. The last time we spoke, I believe you expressed some interest in the provenance of a spell that opened a door to the Sunset Lands?"

The spell Cassandra Monmouth used. Matilda had assured me they didn't know how she discovered the spell. My blood ran hot, then cold, and my hands started shaking. It was everything I could do not to hyperventilate.

This was the key to finding Lia.

This time it was Tony's calming hand that settled on me, wrapping around my arm in both warning and comfort. But it didn't matter. Matilda may not have known why, but she'd just hooked me as securely as any trout.

It didn't matter why the housekeeper of Lady Chatsworth was so important, or what other machinations the witches were planning. If I had any chance of finding a way to Lia, I would take it.

"How can I be certain you have this knowledge?" I asked. There was no hiding the desperate hope in my voice.

"Deborah," Madame Matilda said, never taking her eyes off my face, "if you please?"

Deborah rose and left the room, only to return with a large, leather-bound tome in her arms. She handed it reverently to the head of her coven, who placed it on the table in front of me.

If the book had been made of solid gold, I could not have desired it more. It was bound by hand in dark leather, worn thin on the edges of the spine. Swirling designs that may have been early magical symbols were embossed on the cover, and two elaborate gold clasps held the pages closed.

I bent to examine the symbols, reached out to touch them, then gasped and jerked upright. "Is—is this the Mordegant Grimoire?"

"It is."

"The spell is here?"

"It is."

"Swear it."

She examined me for a long moment, then traced several symbols on the cover with the tip of her finger—I followed the pattern with hungry eyes—and unlatched the clasps to flip it open carefully. The women around the table let out a collective sigh. Madame Matilda stopped on one yellowed page—vellum?—and leaned back so I could inspect it.

I immediately recognized the symbols Cassandra dug into the ground of Monmouth estates, inked into the calfskin in black ink that weathered to a dull red.

"And you will give me this spell if I can locate Ms. Honeycutt?"

"Gwen," Tony warned, tightening his grip.

I ignored him.

Madame Matilda said in a slow, deliberate voice, "If you can locate and return Ms. Honeycutt, I will give you this book."

My mouth went dry. "This book is priceless."

"So is Ms. Honeycutt."

The tension in the air was so thick it smothered every breath, and so heavy that no one moved. Something much bigger than I understood was happening here. And if the Triumphant Sisterhood was willing to part with a grimoire that I had only heard whispered rumors of, they had bigger plans than simply restoring a coven member to her full magical capabilities. I was being manipulated as surely as if Madame Matilda were inside my head.

But Lia lay on the other side of this spell.

I held out my hand. "We have an agreement."

4

Sam Makes a Visit

SAM

The carriage bumped away down the street, carrying Lady Gwen off toward the witches. Aristotle stood on his shoulder, flexing his feet, and the book sat heavy in his lap. Sam had only vague memories of his mother, but none that included watching her leave to do dangerous things while he sat safe behind stone and glass. He didn't like it.

"Don't worry so much, Sammy. Lady Gwen knows what she's doing. And the inspector is with her. He won't let anything bad happen."

Sam turned and considered his sister, comfortable in her chair with her feet tucked up beneath her dress. She'd adapted to this life faster than he. Sally was older and still remembered their mother and her lessons, which was probably why she'd always sounded more like a lady than a laundress. And why she seemed to fit into this new life so much more easily than he did.

"You didn't see those two like I did on Samhain. There was only one witch, and she had Lady Gwen and Tony *both* tied up in chairs. You would have died if I didn't get them out."

Sally frowned at her book. "Well, I'm sure she's learned a lot since then."

"Yeah, when she falls asleep at her desk? When Mr. Yates has to carry her upstairs?"

"That's not your business, Sam."

"Well, no one else does anything! The duchess is off in her country house, you sit there with your face in books, and not even Mrs. Chapman—"

Sally slammed her book closed and scowled at him. It was her *don't push it* expression. "I am helping, you little idiot. Why do you think I'm trying to learn so much? I can't do anything if I don't *know* anything. If I go blundering into Lady Gwen's affairs, it would be worse than if I did nothing."

"How can you learn about what she's doing if she won't tell you or let you go with her? You won't find Mr. Capstone in those books."

Sally visibly shivered at the name. "If—if Lady Gwen thinks I should know something, she'll tell me."

Sam snorted, dropped the book onto the chaise, and stood. Aristotle launched himself into the air and took up his favorite post on top of the head of the statue near the window, leaving Sam free to stalk around.

Why was his sister being so stupid? Hadn't they been fooled, abandoned, left in the dark enough times for her to know the only people she could really trust were him and herself? Not that he didn't believe Lady Gwen, but he'd seen her sip from that bottle in the locked drawer of her desk when she thought no one was looking. She wasn't like their Papa had been, drunk and mean, she didn't even open the drawer that often... but Papa hadn't always been that way, either.

Sam clenched his fists until they hurt, then said, "I'm going to bed," and stalked up the stairs. He would not sit back in the safety of this house and wait until something happened to Lady Gwen or to Sally.

He could do something.

He waited till Sally's door closed. He waited till the house was quiet, and the only sounds were the stretching and settling of the wood. He waited till he was certain even Mr. Yates was asleep, then crept down the servants' stairs, let himself out through the kitchen door, and disappeared into the shadows.

The night air pried at the collar of his jacket and the cuffs of his sleeves with chilly fingers, but found no way past the fine wool. His shoes made no sound on the cobblestones because Sam knew how to walk without making a ruckus. He'd wrapped a bit of rag around each shoe and tied it off at the ankle so the *X* Mr. Yates carved into the sole couldn't give him away. Now Lady Gwen couldn't track him in the inevitable mud of the New London spring.

It took nearly an hour to leave behind the more fashionable districts of the West End for the east side Narrows. The broad thoroughfares squeezed down to thin, wandering alleys, and the proud homes and shops gave way to looming, crooked buildings cobbled together out of the brick bones of older buildings. Rickety wooden additions had been stuffed into every available opening to give as many people as possible someplace dry to sleep. It was like the city cut off its own foot and added a poorly carved wooden peg in its place.

Lines filled with tattered clothing pinned like mourning flags stretched from one building to another, crossing the streets and flapping disconsolately in the breeze. Sam avoided the garbage, broken wagon parts, puddles, and human waste as if he didn't notice it. He recognized the gaunt faces of the men and women forced to sleep on the street, and stayed clear of them all.

He knew the rules, and he kept his eyes open, seeing everything, especially the symbols carved or scratched or drawn onto the grimy surfaces of bricks and doors and window panes. They were bits of Thieves' Cant, a language made by people like him to communicate without alerting the bobbies. There was a curving symbol that meant one could fence stolen goods inside; a series of lines that said the boarded-up building was safe for orphans; something that looked vaguely like an *A* with a circle attached that meant you could earn money off your back if you needed a meal.

Finally, he caught sight of his target: a symbol carved into the doorframe of an impressive old building. The One Tear gang ran this part of the Narrows, and there was always someone on this corner to control who entered and who left.

"Oi. Stop."

Sam froze. He'd been waiting for that.

A boy Sally's age materialized from the shadows, slapping a club against the palm of his left hand. "Seems you've strayed into the wrong part of town."

Sam took off his hat and lifted his chin so the flickering light of the gas street lamp landed full on his face. The boy stopped.

"Sammy D? Is that you?"

"It's me, Turney."

"Where the 'ell did you steal them togs from?"

"Little bloke on the west side. During the riots."

"Smart, that. Bet the watch was everywhere."

"They was."

"You should know better, wearing all that here. I won't take it from you, but you know who will."

Sam plopped his hat back onto his head and considered the older boy. Smallpox scars marred his cheeks, and heavy-lidded eyes stared at him from above a nose broken more than once. He was one of the oldest members of the One Tears, and while he could be hard, he'd always been fair. If he decided not to be fair, Sam was ready to run.

He put his hands in his pockets—a sign he wasn't worried—and said, "I was hopin' you might lend a hand. Ever hear anything about a Mr. Capstone?"

"Sounds Dwarvish. What'cha want with him?"

"Is that Sammy D?" another voice called from the shadows.

"Aye, I think it is!"

"Welcome home, Sammy."

Two rail-thin boys and a girl taller than Turney walked into the lamplight from the direction Sam had come. They weren't

One Tear, so how did they know who Sam was? He didn't take his hands from his pockets. That would show fear. Instead, he positioned his weight so he could take off at a run in any direction at any moment.

"What do you want with me?"

"It ain't what *we* want, ya tosser. It's what *he* wants."

Turney raised his club and stepped in front of Sam. It was a stupid move. He didn't owe Sam any loyalty, not since he left the One Tear years ago, but it made Sam's heart squeeze a bit. He could run now if he needed to.

"Keep your 'air on," the tall girl said to Turney. "We ain't 'ere 'urt the boy. It's the King what wants him."

Sam's stomach hit his shoes as if it had just jumped out a window. Now that they were closer, he could see it: the black cloth ribbon worn around the upper left arm. To any stranger, it would appear to me a band of mourning. But anyone who lived on the street would recognize it as the marker worn by those in direct service to the King.

He turned and ran smack into the chest of another boy, who grabbed his arms before Sam could twist away, and wrenched them up behind his back.

Sam grunted and jerked, but the boy only pulled harder. White flashes of pain shot from his shoulders to his elbows and he froze, panting. He should have known the first group was a distraction. He should have known!

And he'd carefully concealed his escape so no one would know where to look for him. Lady Gwen wouldn't appear this time.

His stomach churned with fear, and he twisted again, desperate to break free in spite of the pain.

"No use fighting, cully," said his captor. "If the King wants you, he gets you."

As they dragged him away into the night, Sam watched Turney stand as if frozen, his face sick in the lamplight, the club hanging uselessly from one hand. He was too smart to interfere.

No one escaped from the Cutthroat King.

Much like the religion it once served, the old gothic church had been abandoned for more years than Sam had been alive. It was probably full of ghosts. When they pulled him through the hole where a gate once stood and into the small courtyard, he planted his feet on the broken paving stones.

"Wait," he begged. "You can't take me in there! It's haunted."

The boy holding his arms sniggered and lifted, dragging Sam's scrabbling toes across the moss-grown path. Empty windows stared down at them from the face of the crumbling edifice, a holy place that lost its soul.

One at a time, they entered, swallowed up by the dark of the nave. The pews were sacrificed to the cold New London winters years ago, stolen and hacked to stove-sized pieces by anyone brave enough to enter. They reached the transepts and stopped directly across from the sanctuary.

The tall girl pulled something from her pocket and flipped it around Sam's head. He tried to pull away, but the boy tightened his grip on Sam's arms, and she tied the cloth around his eyes with a few practiced motions.

Without his eyes to rely on, his other senses sharpened. The musty stink of rotted books and human waste scratched at the insides of his nostrils and the still air pressed clammy hands against his skin. Every groove in the floor was a chasm as he felt his way forward in the dark.

They turned too many times for Sam to keep track of, and then the air cooled, becoming frigid as they started downward. Whether they walked for minutes or hours or days, Sam couldn't say, but fear rose to choke him with each step.

"Password?" a gruff male voice said, and Sam nearly jumped out of his skin, swallowing a yelp before it could make him look weaker than he already did.

"Twice-baked fish," the boy said.

"That's yesterday's password, twit."

"Oh, ah—bobby long limbs."

"Go on."

Sounds grew louder and echoed strangely. Laughter, bawdy talk, some sounds Sam would rather not have heard, coins, the clatter of plates, and then everything went silent.

They stopped.

Someone pulled the blindfold off Sam's head, and he blinked, squinting into the light. He was in a cavernous hall, like the nave of the church, but different. Rugs of various shapes and sizes covered the floor, which was scattered with tables and long benches filled with humans, and a few elves and dwarves eating, playing cards, flirting, drinking, and more. It reminded Sam of a public house, only bigger and shabbier.

He spotted several street toughs he knew by name and tried not to look them in the eyes.

At the head of this room was a throne-like chair carved of wood with silver spoons inlaid in intricate designs that reflected the fire of the candles and hearth. On the chair sat a man all in black, one leg casually draped over an arm. He dressed more like pictures Sam had seen of Robin Hood than any modern man: tunic, leggings, boots, and things of that sort. A crown of spoons rested on his head but didn't look as ridiculous as it should have.

"My lord," the boy said. "We've brought you Sammy—that is, Samuel Dawes, sir."

He stumbled when they released him, then caught his balance and looked up. The eyes that stared back at him from the King's face were dark and hollow. It would be a mistake to show weakness beneath a gaze like that. That's how orphans ended up dead.

"It took you long enough, Smith. Bring the boy closer." His voice was like his eyes, deep, dark, and hollow.

Sam didn't wait for them to take hold of him again. He threw his chest out, lifted his chin, and strode forward.

"Well done, little rat. Better to bend when the wind blows than snap, eh?"

Sam didn't know how to respond to that, so he said nothing. A few chuckles echoed from the back of the room.

"You've been a hard man to find since you left us for the more opulent side of town. Every time we've tried to contact you, that woman has intercepted our *messages*."

Sam's fingers tightened into fists and said through clenched teeth, "She's a lady."

The Cutthroat King threw his head back and laughed. "No, little rat, not your mistress. The crone who keeps her house. She is as fierce as she looks. But no matter. I thought you would return at some point. And here you are. You must be wondering why I've brought you here."

Sam nodded.

"Since you've changed your... allegiance, shall we say, you are now in a position to be uniquely valuable to me. You have noticed the unrest in the city?"

When Sam didn't answer, the King made a motion with his hand and the boy who had dragged him down here elbowed him in the ribs. Sam grunted and doubled over.

"Manners cost us nothing. Remember that."

"Yes, sir."

"Unrest," the King continued as if the exchange never happened, "is bad for business. When people are afraid, they guard their valuable possessions much more carefully. Doors stay locked and windows get barred. Transports acquire extra guards. Men with money stop making deals. You understand?"

"Yes, sir."

"Smart boy. Now." He lowered his leg, leaned forward, and braced his elbow on his knee. "You have a special gift, my rat. You can appear to be a squirrel. Instead of being chased with a broom or killed, people give you nuts. I need you to use that gift to learn everything you can about a man named Lord Edgar Ashcroft. Repeat the name to me."

"Lord Edgar Ashcroft," Sam said, mind spinning furiously.

"I need leverage against Lord Ashcroft. Something so bad that he will do anything I ask to keep people from finding out about it."

"You mean to blackmail him."

The Cutthroat King smiled. It was a slow, dangerous thing with sharp edges. "Indeed, I do."

Sam swallowed. He'd imagined sneaking back onto the streets a hundred times, but it had always been for the excitement, the freedom. He'd never dreamed of this. And now that he was here, he also imagined Sally's disappointed eyes.

"No," he said before he could stop himself.

A few surprised gasps sounded behind him, but he ignored them. The King's smile grew wider, like the crocodiles at the zoo. He leaned closer, his face a mere foot away, his eyes like caves.

"Is that wise, Samuel Dawes? A boy like you, a boy who belongs nowhere, needs friends. Otherwise, how can he protect himself and the people he cares about?"

Sam's heart turned into a rock and dropped out of his ribcage to sink into the pit in his stomach.

"Of course, it is up to you, after all. I can find another squirrel to help me if you will not. Your sister is a lovely girl. She may be just the type to tempt Lord Ashcroft into divulging sensitive information. Most men are careless with their words after—"

Sam's fist flew before he realized what he had done. It stopped with a smack when the King caught it as neatly as a spider trapping an unwary fly. The King tilted his head, amused, and squeezed until the bones of Sam's knuckles rubbed together.

"Does this mean you will be my pet squirrel, Samuel Dawes?"

"Y-yes, sir," he ground out as dull pain throbbed in his fingers. Before he could stop himself, he blurted, "If you'll tell me about Mr. Capstone."

The King released Sam's fist, raised his brows, and leaned back. "Mr. Capstone, eh? Is that why you strayed back into the nest? Interesting. I believe, little squirrel, that if you do as I ask, you will find out about Mr. Capstone, and more. Hennings?"

A man stepped out of the crowd, rested a heavy hand on Sam's shoulder, and pulled him away from the throne. Just like that, he was dismissed. He was alive... but not free.

"Bring him," the King said.

A commotion rose from the back of the room, and jeering broke out in the crowd. One burly man and an elf, who was nearly as tall and thin as a lamppost, dragged a limp form between them. They dropped the dirty man on the rug in front of the throne. He raised his head on a wobbly neck, unkempt beard waggling as he panted.

"This man," the King intoned, "took by force what can only be freely given, or rightfully paid for. We do not live by the laws of the upper world but keep our own councils. He committed a crime against one of our own. That cannot be forgiven."

The King descended the stairs at a leisurely pace, as if taking a walk on a summer afternoon. The kneeling man began to blubber.

"Peg," the King called, his voice soft.

A woman in mismatched brown clothes stepped forward, her jaw clenched, her eyes hard.

"What will be his punishment?"

She glared down at the sobbing man for a long time, as if she could burn him to ash where he stood. Sam's heart threw itself against his breastbone and nervous sweat beaded above his upper lip.

Finally, she said, "Let him bear the King's smile, my lord."

"So it shall be," he replied and pulled a dagger from his belt. He slid behind the kneeling man as quick as a striking snake, fisted his hand in the man's hair to pull his head backward, exposing his throat, and—Sam turned away, squeezing his eyes shut.

When he opened his eyes again, a pool of blood stained the rug, and the crowd cheered.

5

Party Preparations

GWEN

I was finishing my morning coffee and enjoying the spectacle in the study when the formal invitation arrived. Mrs. Chapman brandished a feather duster in one hand and a bag of treats in the other as she chased Aristotle off every surface that needed dusting. She placed several treats on the opposite side of the room, waited for the raven to investigate, then dusted the shelves, books, and trinkets as if the hounds of hell were nipping at her heels. As soon as he finished the bribes, Aristotle flew back across the room, plopped himself down in front of her, and tried to pull the feathers from her duster.

"This—little—fiend—" she said as she tried to pry the duster from his beak, "will not let me get a thing done. If you do not remove him, my lady, I will use his tail feathers when my duster needs replacing. Just look at the damage!"

She shook the duster at me, not realizing how much she looked like an irritated vulture as she glared at me above her hawk-like nose, covered from pointy chin to knobby wrists in the black dress of her station.

"Do you truly believe he will allow me to trick him out of his favorite game?"

"What I believe is that the two of you conspire to torture me for your own amusement."

"Why Mrs. Chapman, what a thing to say. Aristotle and I are the absolute souls of courtesy and consideration, are we not, Mr. Yates?"

Mr. Yates entered the study a moment later, carrying a white envelope on a silver tray. "I would never dream of contradicting a lady, ma'am," he said as he presented the tray.

"A very diplomatic answer," I congratulated him as I opened the envelope.

"And what is that?" Mrs. Chapman asked peevishly.

"It is an invitation from Lady Chatsworth."

A moment of shocked silence followed that remark. I did not receive invitations. Outside of Mama and the morbidly curious guests who attended her rare parties, I was cut off from good society. It was a constant vexation to my loyal housekeeper, who was more insulted on my behalf than I could ever be.

"An invitation to what?" she asked, breathless.

"A celebration at Chatsworth Manor."

"A country party?" she asked, her voice two octaves higher than usual. "*This* weekend?"

"So it would appear."

"But it is Thursday! How could she send an invitation so late? You are nowhere near ready. Charlotte! Charlotte, come to me at once!"

Mrs. Chapman flew from the study in a confusion of feathers and skirts to call the upstairs maid, Charlotte, and begin organizing and packing whatever suitable dresses I possessed... which was, unfortunately, nowhere near enough for how many clothing changes were expected.

But I wasn't attending to parade myself in front of her guests. I had a mystery to solve and a mythic grimoire to win.

"Mr. Yates, will you call James to bring around the auto, please?"

His normally composed expression shifted just enough to appear pained. "Are you certain, ma'am? The last time you drove that contraption, you came home with a pigeon stuck in your hat."

I stood and patted his hand. "Worry not, my friend. Delilah is contriving a wind-screen for me. And I promise to drive more slowly."

When I opened the door to the Iron Rose Industries workshop, the bell tinkled, and I said, "Delilah Irons, you are a genius. Your umbrella performed in desperate circumstances exactly as it did in the laboratory. There wasn't even any heat leakage."

Delilah yelled, "Wait!" over her shoulder.

She stood in front of the forge with her sturdy legs braced apart, holding a glowing piece of metal suspended between the teeth of foot-long tongs. With deft ease, she placed the metal on her anvil, pulled a hammer from her belt, and beat the red-hot billet into shape.

I knew better than to interrupt, so I turned toward the few scarred wooden chairs only to see Percival Bywater bent over a piece of cloth spread on one of Delilah's worktables. Percy was pure elfin elegance; tall and slender with wide, blue eyes angled up at the corner, sculpted cheekbones, and skin so richly dark it was almost blue.

"Percy! What is my favorite hat-maker doing in the Artificer's District?"

In truth, Percy was far more than a milliner; he was an artist in cloth of the highest degree. Hats were merely his specialty.

He looked up from his work and smiled. "When my best client asks for a magical coat, a magical coat she gets. I needed Delilah's expertise in finishing the engraved wire and testing it." He looked around the room as if someone might overhear and whispered, "I don't know enough about finishing runic sentences, so I could not be certain I wasn't selling you a death trap. I need your money too much."

"Flattering."

"Just wait till you try on the coat," he said and winked.

The hammering stopped and Delilah strode to the front of the shop, wiping sweat from her forehead with a dirty rag. She walked with fists clenched as if she were always on the edge of throwing a punch.

She'd tied her dark curls back in a handkerchief, and a pair of elaborate goggles rested on her forehead. Soot stained her tan cheeks, leaving smudges across the bridge of her button nose.

Delilah might only reach my elbow in height, but the dwarven woman was sturdy as a granite block and one of the more commanding people I'd ever known.

"Come for your gadgets, eh?"

"How charming to see you, too, Delilah. Yes, I'm quite well. Thank you for asking."

One side of her rosebud mouth curled into a smile, but she only said, "I don't have time for polite formalities, Gwen. The annual guild inspection is only a week away, and I've got to pass to maintain my membership."

"You'll pass."

She snorted. "Of course, I will. That's not the point. They've been trying to run me out of the guild since they admitted me. And when those uppity inspectors show their sparking faces in my shop, I want the rating to be so good, they pull out their whiskers in frustration."

That mental image made me laugh till I remembered more serious business. "Where will you be storing our, um... experiments?"

"In my warehouse, but that's all I'll tell you. Fleur is unloading everything. There won't be a scrap of magic left in the Iron Rose when they arrive."

Fleur was Delilah's fiancée and partner. The slight Elvin woman had bullied her way into the Iron Rose and taken over the front desk so Delilah would not scare off so many customers. It had taken me months to finally meet the one person capable of telling Delilah Irons what to do, and now I was desperately fond of her.

"I had hoped she'd be here," I said. "I brought her another sachet of Mrs. Chapman's tea."

"She may return before you go. If not, you can leave it with me."

"You won't forget it?"

Delilah scowled. She had a very good scowl. "I didn't forget it last time."

"That's not what Fleur said."

"You are planning to reveal your discoveries, eventually?" Percy asked around a mouthful of pins, interrupting what was sure to be a lovely argument.

Delilah and I exchanged less hostile, but more uncertain, glances as our minds shifted gears to the question of how to control the dangerous magic we discovered.

"Yes," Delilah said, slowly, "but not until we're sure everything is safe. And not until we know it can be regulated and controlled. It's one thing, controlling natural forces like heat or wind through artificery. And I must make my mark on every piece that leaves my shop. There are laws and rules, both from the government *and* the guilds, to regulate its use. But they cannot regulate magic."

Percy snorted. "They certainly can. Otherwise, witches wouldn't be banned from the city."

"Banning it is one thing," I said. "We are talking about regulation. Magic wasn't meant to be wielded by mortals. The forces are too great. That's why it twists the bodies of the witches"—most witches, anyway—"who use it. But magic that doesn't have to pass through a body, magic that can pass through runes instead? With the right runic sentence, a fishwife could carve a magic spell on her walls and do... god knows what."

"She could blow up the slagging neighborhood, is what," Delilah said.

Percy stopped what he was doing and folded his arms. "Magic is power. Don't we want power evenly distributed? Isn't that what all this is about? Why else would you be funneling so much money into the push for equal representation or the women's suffrage movement?"

"That's different," I said.

"How? How is that different?"

"Because there are no limits, Percy," Delilah answered. "We're not talking about just a few simple spells to make life easier. If a witch tries to channel too much power, it will break her body and kill the spell. But the runes will hold up to a certain power level, even if it kills the witch. D'you even remember how we discovered this?"

His face blanched, and I didn't blame him. Someone used artifice to power spells that lured orphans to be kidnapped.

"No limits," she repeated.

Percy sighed and leaned back against the table, then jumped up to make sure he hadn't wrinkled the jacket. "I suppose that makes sense," he allowed. "I'm just tired of tyrants maintaining power by hoarding knowledge and resources."

"That," I said, putting a hand on his arm, "is exactly why we're testing everything. There is a bigger game, afoot. In fact—" I looked down at my hands, then clasped them together. "That's why I'm here, D."

"Spit it out."

I explained as much of my situation as I could. A year and a half ago, Delilah made me take an iron promise by smearing my blood on the head of a sledgehammer. If I didn't tell her the truth, the metal I betrayed would take my life someday. And it was Percy who told me the magic we discovered was from the faeries, creatures banished from mortal lands for thousands of years.

They deserved to know what I was after.

"You?" Percy said once I finished. "A country house party?"

"I can do very well without the incredulity, thank you. And yes, me. This may be my only hope of getting my hands on that grimoire. Once I know more about the spell, it may give me a better understanding of the wall separating mortals and faeries. Perhaps enough to stop faeries from coming through."

That *was* the truth. Or part of the truth. Nearly two years ago, faeries tried to get through the barrier that divided the mortal world from the Sunset Lands. After thousands of years of separation, most people believed the fae wars to be no more than a mythological justification for the mass death that caused the dark ages. But the war was real, and at the end of it, the faeries were locked away in the Sunset Lands.

And now at least some of them wanted to come back. I was lucky enough to stop the spell before the gate opened, but that didn't mean they wouldn't try again. If I understood how the spell worked, we might learn enough to keep it closed for good... after I rescued Lia, of course.

Percy's delicately arched brows drew together in distress. "Are you certain that is wise, Gwen? If this magic is as dangerous as you say?"

"Don't worry," I told him. "I will research everything with the utmost caution. And, anyway, I have to find and return the house-keeper first."

"You're going to do all this during a country party?" Delilah asked.

"Yes."

The two of them shared a meaningful glance, then burst into laughter.

"Perhaps I should spend my father's money on artists who don't insult me," I said.

"Oh, hush," Delilah snorted between bouts of laughter. When she got herself under control, she continued, "I'll be back with your gadgets. In the meantime, why don't you try on the coat? Percy hasn't shut up about it all morning."

"Genius can never be spoken of too highly," he said, and lifted the wool jacket off the table with a flourish.

Deep grey-green, a color that might disappear into forest shadows, the jacket was long with a row of double buttons up the breast. From the waist down, it opened enough to allow me freedom of movement. Both the cuffs and the lapels were turned out and embroidered with flowing vines that mimicked the spell on my umbrella, though there was no mechanism in the coat for redirecting the energy. Too many impacts and the jacket would simply burst into flame.

Unfortunately, we hadn't figured a way out of that yet.

In addition to the spell, Percy used the rest of the fine engraved wire I'd purchased from an artificer in Egypt, felting it into the inner lining of the jacket. The wire was nearly indestructible. I say nearly because the power gathered in the magic circle I'd disrupted fried my first magical coat. Except for herculean feats of magic, however, the jacket was, for all purposes, a coat of armor.

Percy held it up, then stopped and squinted at my arms. "Have you been training? How am I supposed to maintain proper measurements if you continue putting on muscle? You must warn me of these things, Gwen."

"If you would like me to stay alive long enough to continue patronizing you, do not complain about my choice of exercise."

"But jiu-jitsu? Fencing? Surely you can exercise in less... bulky ways?"

"More ladylike ways, you mean?"

"Ways that won't force me to alter your clothing so often. And before you look at me that way"—he pointed accusingly at me—"it changes the lay of the runic sentences I've embroidered."

I sighed. The last thing I wanted was to expect the protection of a garment only to be injured. "Very well. But I don't see that I *can* put on much more muscle without changing my whole life."

I slid my arms into the sleeves—which were only a tad snug—buttoned the buttons and twirled. One should *always* twirl, if one gets the chance.

"Yards of wool and it's light as linen," I said, running my hands down the sides and reveling in the softness.

"That's because of the spell you and Delilah worked out. There are pockets on the outside and the inside," Percy said as he peeled back the skirt. "I've embroidered them with the spell you found for preserving food. We will have to test it, but I don't think you'll lose anything you put in those pockets."

I stuffed my hands into the pockets—deep pockets lined with satin—and purred. "You, my friend, deserve an award of some kind."

"I don't need awards, darling, just your money."

Delilah returned while I was in the middle of my second twirl. She snorted, gave me an exasperated eye roll, and began plunking things on the table.

"This one," she said, holding up a small funnel that resembled a gramophone, "has been engraved with the runes that amplify sound. I haven't worked out how to specify only the sound of voices, so it amplifies all sound. Be careful."

"I'm going to look like your father using this," I said, inspecting the little trumpet. Delilah's father had emigrated to England from Brazil to join the Artificer's Guild of New London before she was born. Pirates attacked his ship off the coast of Spain and fired cannon barrages for hours. His hearing never recovered from the noise.

Despite that, he opened his own workshop and reached Master Artificer within a handful of years, fabricating a head rig with brass funnels on either side to help him hear his apprentices while working a forge. He looked like a small, red-faced elephant while wearing it.

Delilah laughed. "That's a vision I'll not get sick of. Here is the other."

Inside a little leather case lay two cylindrical devices roughly the length of my forearm. She'd engraved neat runic sentences in concentric circles that looked more like decorative elements than commands to manipulate natural forces.

A lens, something like a telescope, closed the cylinders on one side, but the other was flat metal with nothing but the Iron Rose insignia engraved on its surface.

After reading the sentences, and noting the commands to collect and store, I asked, "Is this a lamp?"

"Not quite. It's a torch. I based it on a recent invention that uses electricity. But this one charges in the sun, just like dwarven lamps, so it's far more efficient. Turn it on, here." Delilah pressed a little switch near the front of the device. A beam of light shot from the lens in a neat line, lighting up the ceiling like a spotlight.

"Ooh," I said, pointing the beam around the workshop.

"Don't blind me with it," she grumbled, pushing the end of the torch back toward the ground. "I used several lenses to concentrate the light, so the beam is powerful. It will even warm you up if you sit in front of it long enough."

"This is lovely, D, but"—I turned the torch off and examined the lens—"what will I use it for?"

Delilah threw her arms in the air. "How do I know? I just make the gadgets. You're the one who has to figure out how to use them."

I narrowed my eyes at her as a suspicion crept into my mind. "You saw someone's invention and knew you could improve upon it, didn't you?"

She rolled her eyes and huffed, but her cheeks turned pink.

I laughed and slid my new gadgets into the protected pockets of my glorious coat, then spun one more time for effect. Delilah stalwartly ignored me, but Percy gave me a smug grin.

"Well," I said, spin over, "you two have properly outfitted me for battle. Don't forget to bill me."

"We won't," Delilah said.

"You'll have to remind me later, Gwen, because I'm coming with you," Percy said.

I froze. "I'm sorry?"

He began packing his tailoring supplies into a satchel and said, "I'll be coming with you."

"Why on earth would you want to come with me? Do you need a vacation? Just bill me extra and take whatever time you need."

"I was going to do that, anyway. No, I'm going with you because you need me."

Delilah and I narrowed our eyes at him.

"Explain," I said.

Percy sighed and shook his head while picking an imaginary piece of lint from his shirt sleeve. A useless gesture because he was always flawless. "Gwen, Gwen, my darling Gwen. Have you ever spent a week in the country?"

"Of course I have."

"At a house party?"

"No."

He nodded to himself as if that explained everything. "Do you have any idea how important your clothing will be during this little getaway? Especially if you want to avoid embarrassing Lady Chatsworth and convince her fashionable friends you are trying to make a comeback into society?"

"Please do not patronize me, Percy. Of course, I know. I simply do not have the time to expand my wardrobe. I will make do."

"That is exactly my point. I want you to patronize *me*."

"Percival Bywater, if you don't say exactly what you mean right this instant, I will not be responsible for my actions."

"I will handle your wardrobe. The job of the gentlemen will be to hunt and gamble and show themselves good sportsmen. But the job of the ladies will be to parade themselves in the highest fashions. And despite your excellent taste, you make little effort to stay abreast of the latest trends."

"I have more important things to do than—"

"It's not an accusation, my dear, merely a statement of fact. I can alter your current dresses on location, and I have several mock-ups for day dresses, tea gowns, evening gowns, and even a gaming ensemble I can bring. It would be nothing to alter them to your measurements."

It wasn't a bad idea. The type of people lucky enough to receive a coveted invitation to a party held by Mrs. Chatsworth were too wealthy and too indolent to value anything other than power, and they displayed it by parading their wealth in the most extravagant ways possible.

The witches made one thing perfectly clear to me during our uncomfortable dinner: they wanted to maintain their secrecy. So, to earn the book without drawing attention, my ruse must be believable.

I took a deep breath and sighed. That was apparently all the blessing Percy needed. "Brilliant. That's settled. You can fetch me on your way out of town. I'll need a room with plenty of space, preferably somewhere close enough that transporting the clothing won't take long."

"And how much are you going to charge me for this magnanimous service?"

Percy smiled a brilliant smile and said, "Enough to launch my fashion line, naturally."

"Naturally."

Delilah positioned herself between us and the front door of her shop. She stood with her feet braced and held a hammer between two hands, her brows low. "If the two of you don't get your soft hands and naked chins out of my shop in the next thirty seconds..."

Percy and I ran for the door, only to plow into Fleur.

The woman was short for an elf, with a shock of fine red hair that floated around her head and eyes so green they almost glowed. Pale lashes and non-existent eyebrows made her extraordinary eyes even more prominent. If Delilah was a dark cave full of secrets, Fleur was an errant sunbeam.

"Gwen! Percy! How lovely," she said over the top of an armful of boxes. "Give me a minute, will you?"

She slid through the open door, dropped her boxes, kissed her disgruntled fiancée quickly, and then threw herself into my arms for a hug. No one hugged more often or with more enthusiasm than Fleur.

"I've brought you more tea," I said once she released Percy, who set about fixing the damage her hug had done to his cravat.

"You are an angel," she said and pocketed the tea as if it were a jewel someone might steal. "I see the jacket is finally ready. You look so elegant. I assume this one will not explode?"

We both eyed Percy as the tips of his ears darkened and turned red. "That was an early model," he said. "And it was your fault for throwing a hammer at it. It will withstand significantly more damage now, without... you know... catastrophic failure."

An amused grin twisted one corner of Fleur's mouth, and she winked at me.

After a few more moments of chatting, Delilah dragged Fleur inside and shut the door with a decided *click*, followed by a chain rattling and a bar clunking into place. We clearly needed to make ourselves scarce. Percy and I strolled down Artificer's Row grinning, arm in arm, toward the turnabout where I parked the auto.

"Can I trouble you for a ride back to my shop?" he asked.

I laughed. "You've already troubled me for a lot more than that."

"It was for your own good."

"So it was."

"You do look splendid in that coat, by the way."

"If you think you can soften my temper with flattery, you are absolutely right. Please, do it again."

The sun was just low enough to peek between the smokestacks of the workshops, now and then filtering through purple or orange smoke and making the drab buildings glow with pastel colors. It was strangely festive, despite the rust stains that made the buildings look as if they were crying.

"You will bring Sally with you?" Percy asked. "You're going to need someone to help you dress."

"I suppose I'll have to unless you have altered the clothing for easy access?" I waggled my brows suggestively, and he laughed.

"No, I made them for women who prefer to let their lovers do all the work."

"Lazy."

"Indeed."

We bantered all the way back to his shop, where I left him off with a promise to collect him early in the morning. James would have quite a time tying all the trunks down for the journey. The idea of changing clothes that many times in a day merely for show made my eyes roll so hard I nearly gave myself a headache—and almost hit another pigeon.

I pulled up to the house, left the keys for James, and climbed the stairs, dreaming of a hot bath. I found Tony, instead. Charlotte had served him tea—was it already so late?—but the cup sat on the table, cool and untouched.

He sat with his elbows on his knees, flipping a silver franc over and over across his knuckles, his brows drawn together in a pensive frown.

"Inspector," I said, "I wasn't expecting you today."

Tony stood and pocketed the coin, then brushed the wrinkles from his jacket with a self-conscious glance in my direction. "I know, I am sorry. But I could not in good conscience wait."

"That sounds rather serious," I said, taking a seat across from him and helping myself to a cucumber sandwich.

"I don't think you should go to the country."

I paused with the sandwich halfway to my mouth. "And why is that?"

"Gwen"—he picked up his teacup, considered the cold tea, and put it back on the saucer—"I wouldn't presume to lecture you, but doesn't it make you in the least suspicious that the witches sought you out for this affair?"

"They have a hold over me with that book, and they know it."

"But do they know *why*?"

"You are the only one who knows why."

His eyes widened. It was a sign of trust I hadn't extended to anyone else. "If they don't know why," he said after a moment, "then they are offering you an invaluable bit of knowledge purely because they know you want it. And that, in itself, is deeply suspicious."

"Will you sit? You're making me nervous hovering that way."

I swallowed the rest of my cucumber sandwich while Tony regained his seat, then asked, "Why does a woman become a witch?"

He blinked at my non sequitur. "Power, I suppose."

"Exactly. Everyone wants the ability to influence the course of their lives, but witches accept a greater risk than most because their power can corrupt and destroy their bodies. Only, the Triumphant Sisterhood has discovered that working through a coven protects them from the destructive power of magic. That makes them both self-willed and clever. And people who are both self-willed and clever have a very particular blind spot."

"They assume every clever person wants power," he said, nodding.

"Precisely. But I do not desire this knowledge for my own gain. At least, not entirely. If they knew why I truly wanted this spell... Well, I suppose it's a good thing they do not."

We sat in silence for a while before Tony said, "I cannot convince you to stay?"

"I made an agreement. I will honor it. And I fully intend to get my hands on that book."

He sighed and stood up, then picked up his hat. "I suppose I have no choice but to go with you, then."

I stared at him. "Am I to be confounded by well-meaning men at every turn?"

"What?"

I stood as well and stepped around the table to place myself squarely between him and the door. "I appreciate your concern. Truly. But you have important matters to see to in town. Mr. Capstone is still a mystery, and I told you about the dark figure I saw during the riot."

"There is a good chance Mr. Capstone is nothing more than obfuscation. And, as for the figure you saw, we know nothing about who they were or why they were there."

"Tony—"

"New London is full of officers who are more than capable of protecting the city while I'm gone. They likely will not even notice my absence."

"There is no need for you to absent yourself. I am going to a country party to do a bit of snooping, nothing more. I would not take Sally and Percy with me if I thought they would be in danger."

His jaw clenched. "I don't like the idea of you out there on your own with no one to help you."

"Do I have to show you my werewolf tooth as well?"

His mouth hung open for a flabbergasted moment. "What?"

"Nothing. Look, I have survived this long on my own in far more dangerous environments than a weekend party in the country. I will be fine. Percy and Sally are going with me."

I said the last as if the two of them would offer some kind of protection, rather than being a constant worry. Tony looked down at his shoes and blew out an exasperated breath. I placed my hands on either side of his face and waited for him to look me in the eye. When our gazes locked, a little shiver ran down my spine.

"Your concern means the world to me, but I need you to know that I am capable."

"I know you are, I—" He pressed his palms against my hands, holding them against his skin, and closed his eyes. "I can't shake the feeling that if I'm not there, you will be hurt and I won't be able to forgive myself."

When he opened his eyes, our bodies were only inches apart. The heat of his skin burned right through my gloves, which I hadn't bothered to remove, and his peppermint breath made my mouth water. His eyes roamed over my face, lingering on my lips.

"Fire! Help! Murder!"

A black bullet whizzed through the door and buzzed within inches of our heads, making Tony duck with a muttered curse. Aristotle flapped around the room screaming warnings, then landed on the table next to the tray of tea things. He glared at us for a few heartbeats, then began stealing sandwiches.

We stood staring at one another, but the spell was broken. Tony put his hat on and I accompanied him to the foyer, where Mr. Yates opened the door.

"I'll see you in the country," Tony said, and touched the brim of his hat before escaping. I didn't even have time to argue.

I swore, jerked off my gloves, and said, "Men are such frustrating, condescending, jackanapes! Except you, of course, Mr. Yates."

"Of course, ma'am."

I stalked up the stairs, muttering curses and wondering how I was going to pull off this deception while searching for a lost woman with an entourage to look after *and* an inspector dogging my heels.

If I could not find a way, any hope I cherished of bringing my sister home would be snuffed out. And Lia's absence ate at me.

I peeled out of my clothes without calling for Charlotte, ripping seams and shedding hairpins as I went, and climbed into bed. It was early, but I could not bring myself to care.

There was a fresh bottle of brandy in the bedside drawer. I took a few long swallows that burned comfortingly down my throat to settle in my chest, a little warmth to hold the emptiness at bay, and snuffed out the light.

6

The Investigation Begins

GWEN

"Yes, your luggage is still safely tied down," I said for what felt like the hundredth time.

Percy pulled his head back into the carriage and pointed out the open window. "I'm sure James is a wonderful driver, but safely tying down luggage is not the same as waterproofing it."

I closed the book I'd been trying to read and pinned Percy to the spot with my eyes. "Delilah etched all of your luggage herself. Would you like to tell her you don't trust her work to keep the rain out?"

"Not precisely."

"And James is one of the most competent and trustworthy people I know. Take it on my authority. Your luggage will be fine."

"If we would have traveled by train—"

"We've been over this," I said, cutting him off, barely able to keep a growl from my voice. "I do not trust my life to people I do not know if I can help it. I want influence over how my journey is carried out."

"Train conductors are highly skilled, Gwen. It's much faster and safer than—"

"Have you ever seen a train accident, Percival? No? I have. I will choose the manner of my travel, thank you. If you would prefer to take the train to Cambridgeshire, I will be happy to drop you and your luggage off at the next station and buy you a ticket."

The idea of traveling on his own must have done it, because Percy leaned back, released a slow breath, and in an overly calm voice. "You're right, of course. There's nothing to worry about."

"Exactly."

"Except bandits," Sally said.

Percy's spine stiffened, and I threw my hands up in the air. "Sarah Elizabeth Dawes, are you trying to torture me?"

She hid a mischievous smile behind her hand.

We had been closeted together for three hours, and it would be several more before we reached Chatsworth Manor. Percy fussed about his luggage when he wasn't explaining to me exactly how he planned to alter his designs to my less graceful, non-elfin frame, and Sally only emerged from her book when she could cause a little mischief; usually by teasing Percy.

It took months for the girl to fully come out of her shell at home, but despite her growing confidence, she was still hesitant and deferential around others. She was intimidated by Delilah—who wasn't really?—and treated her tutor, Mrs. Mosswood, like a stranger even though she had lessons with the Elvin woman several times a week.

So, I wouldn't chastise her too much for teasing Percy, whose eyes now darted from window to window in search of bandits, even if it inconvenienced me. Perhaps he merely needed a distraction. I'd already trotted out the story once this week, so I might as well make good use of it.

"Percy?"

His eyes were wild when he dragged them back to my face.

"Have I ever told you about the time I killed a werewolf?"

Percy and Sally both raised their brows and said, "You what?" at the same time. Sally's book lay forgotten in her lap.

"I was traveling through the continent some years ago when I heard rumors of werewolves plaguing some of the smaller villages in the Jura mountains, in France. That was along my route from Switzerland to Calais, so you can imagine my unease."

They both nodded.

"I prepared myself with silver and several other little inventions, just in case, but hoped I would have no use for them. As it turned out"—I dug the tooth from my pocket and held it up for them to see—"I did."

"Ohhhh," Percy breathed as he leaned forward to get a better look. The tooth was as long as my pinky finger.

"How did it happen?" Sally asked.

"Quite by accident, in fact. A thunderstorm forced us to seek shelter, so we stopped at a village inn for the night. It was one of those country places, small and suspicious, where the innkeeper made us prove we were not fae before she sold us the rooms."

Sally snorted, but Percy looked perplexed. "But... the fae have been gone for thousands of years."

"People in the country have longer memories than those of us who live in the hustle and bustle of the city. Being superstitious keeps them safe. We were strangers dressed in queer clothing and the inn probably only rented occasional rooms to hunters, woodsmen, and farmers from the surrounding villages. We were an oddity, you see?

Just after we paid for our rooms, a woman barged into the lobby carrying a nearly dead man over one shoulder. She and the man were soaking wet, covered in mud and blood, and she looked like a cornered coyote that would snap at anyone who came too close."

That wasn't precisely the truth, but I promised Alix and Cyrus to keep the actual events to myself for the safety of everyone involved. Perhaps Sally would learn the truth, someday, but that was a story for another time, and this version worked well enough to keep these two distracted.

Percy put one hand on his chest. "Was he dead?"

"No, but he was close. She asked for a room, and the innkeeper said they were full. She demanded a room, and the innkeeper said, 'We do not house monsters in this establishment.'"

Sally's mouth drew tight with anger. "What did the woman do?"

"She put the man on the floor and drew a silver dagger."

They gasped.

"I took the woman aside, told her to sneak the man into my room, and helped her care for him. He was badly wounded, and if they had stayed in the storm, he likely would have died. They were werewolf hunters, and he was injured during a desperate fight."

"Werewolf hunters?" Percy asked, narrowing his eyes at me.

"Oh yes. Monster hunters are much more common than you might think."

His mouth pursed in disbelief, but he allowed me to continue. If he had a hard time believing that, the next part would test the limits of his trust.

"A nearby village was being tormented by a pack of werewolves, and they—"

"Wait a moment," Sally interrupted. "Werewolves don't run in packs. They're too violent and territorial for that. At least"—she dropped her eyes—"that's what I read in the bestiary."

"And you are correct. But this time, they were. Which is what drew the hunters in the first place. Only the very best hunters could have saved the village from that pack, and there is no finer werewolf hunter than La Cape Rouge."

"Oh, for the sake of the golden rule," Percy huffed, throwing his hands in the air and leaning back against the bench. "I thought you were telling us a real story, not a fairy tale."

"I was."

"The Tale of Red Riding Hood is nothing but a story meant to scare girls into obeying their mothers and distrusting strange men."

"There is a little truth in every story."

He glared at me, truly offended, and folded his arms over his chest to stare out the window, this time neither checking the knots that tied down his luggage *nor* searching for bandits.

Sally also gave me a dirty look.

"What? You don't believe me, either?"

She lifted her book and went back to reading.

"But I didn't even get to the exciting parts," I said plaintively.
The rest of the ride passed in blissful silence.

Thanks to modern technology and an obscene inheritance, we
didn't have to change horses during our journey. The coach had
a suspension that made pulling infinitely easier for the horses and
more comfortable for the passengers. A Guildmaster Artificer discovered a way to transfer the weight energy of the coach to motion
in the wheels. The coach didn't pull itself, but once the horses got
the bulk moving, it required almost no effort from the animals.

As a result, we reached Chatsworth in only a few more hours.
The village was small and tidy, with thatch-roofed houses and
surrounding farms painting an idyllic country picture. The manor
sat in splendor within walking distance of the village proper, a
three-story high baroque monstrosity with too many windows to
count and sprawling lawns that required several full-time garden-
ers.

"Oh my," Sally breathed. "It's... expensive, isn't it?"

"Yes, my dear, it certainly is. The income required simply to
maintain it is shocking."

"And," Percy said in a dreamy voice, "Lady Chatsworth puts
that income to excellent use in her wardrobe."

I laughed. "You are only here for my benefit, eh? You're here to
make a name for yourself with the current leader of fashionable
society."

He sniffed. "I can do both things at once, thank you."

We were third in a line of coaches arriving a day early for the festivities, and once we disembarked, they ushered us inside behind the other visitors and showed us to our rooms. It would, of course, be the height of bad manners for our noble hostess to see us when we were dirty and fagged from our journeys.

Our townhouse on Grosvenor Square was well fitted up, but this home was the ancestral seat of the Earl of Chatsworth, and it was absolutely lavish in every detail. From the thick carpets and silk wallpaper to the mile-high windows and priceless paintings, the place was worth ogling. Several tapestries hung in places of honor, creations of such magnificent size it beggared the imagination to think of how many thousands of yards of wool, silk, and gold thread were used to make them.

Sally's eyes bugged half out of her head the entire way, and it wasn't until the door to our equally impressive room closed behind us that she let out a huge breath and threw herself on the bed to recover.

Percy's room was in a different wing of the house, not being an invited guest but being a member of my party, and I wouldn't see him unless we called for one another by sending servants with notes. Which would make transporting my costumes easier, but socializing with Percy incredibly difficult.

"Remember," he whispered in my ear as we trooped into the manor, "you are supposed to be making your comeback into society. Obey the rules. And, Gwen, for the love of the golden ratio, please parade yourself like a peacock and tell every interested lady that I am the genius behind your beauty."

"You may depend upon it," I promised.

We changed clothes and cleaned up using the washcloths and basin of steaming water left for us.

"How did they know when to leave the water here?" Sally asked as she stuffed the warm cloth into her armpit—the girl was shy in many ways but remarkably comfortable with nudity—and began scrubbing.

"They didn't. Look at the runic marks beneath the lip of the basin."

The bowl was painted with an angular, interlocking design pattern that nearly hid the engraved runes.

"That one says heat," Sally said, bending to squint at the engravings, "and that one... I can't tell what it is."

"The bowl captures the heat of both the water and the room, and releases it back into the water rather than letting it dissipate into the air. That water should stay warm for a few more hours."

A knock made both of us jump. Sally helped me fasten the damnable buttons, then hid behind the dressing screen while I opened the door. A servant stood in the hall with her eyes respectably downcast and said, "Lady Chatsworth requests the pleasure of your company, ma'am, unless you are too tired from your journey?"

"Of course not," I said and followed her out.

She led me through the long hallways, past other new arrivals, and up to the third floor, where the servants lived. The room was nicely sized, if not large, and comfortable, if not ostentatious. Only the housekeeper, butler, steward (if he lived with the family and not in a private residence of his own) and cook would have rooms this size. The flowers on the table, lace-edged curtains, and delicate watercolor painting in pastel shades confirmed this was the housekeeper's room.

"Lady Gwen, I am so grateful you're here," Frances said. She stood near the window, one hand on the chest of drawers as she watched her guests arrive. The servant girl curtsied and disappeared down the hallway.

"Lady Frances, it's my pleasure. This is your... Ms. Honeycutt's room?"

Her delicate brows raised. "Yes, it is. I wanted you to see where she lived. I thought that might help."

"Let us hope it does," I said, and began examining the room. The bed was neatly made, a pair of dress shoes placed at the end of the bed and a few humble pieces of jewelry on the bedside table, all laid out like a store display. "How long has Ms. Honeycutt worked as your housekeeper?"

"I hired her shortly after I married the earl. His old housekeeper was ready to live with her son to be close to her grandchildren."

"How nice. How many years is that?"

"Five years, nearly."

I opened her desk drawer, pawing through the contents. "Five years and she is so dear to you?"

"Of course she is," she said, insulted. "When I moved to Chatsworth, I had no one. Important men are always busy. I could not count on the earl for company. But Ms. Honeycutt was a constant companion, someone who also had a stake in caring for and running this home. She is my friend."

"I see," I said. "Was this the last place anyone saw Ms. Honeycutt?"

"No. That is what I'd like to show you next. If you'll follow me?"

I left the housekeeper's room and closed the door, certain Lady Frances Chatsworth was lying to me.

She led me again through the maze of hallways and to the china room. While smaller homes might have a mere cabinet for their fine china, the manor house of a powerful family had an entire room that remained locked unless the housekeeper opened it for cleaning or to provide settings for the table. This room was about the size of a large closet full of neatly stacked shelves with plates, saucers, bowls, and cups, all lined with paper to protect the finish. A work table with a box of polishing tools and a stool were the only piece of furniture in the room.

I stopped just outside the door, which opened into the hallway. "This is where she was last seen?"

"Yes. She counts—counted—the china every evening before bed."

"It was night?"

"Yes. Our upstairs maid said goodnight to her at around ten o'clock."

I stood in the open doorway and spun, taking in as much information as possible. "How did you find the room when you first investigated?"

"The door was open," Frances said with her hands clasped in front of her. "And there was a stack of bowls on the table."

I knelt near the table and ran my hand along the floorboards. There it was. I stood, searched for the bowls, and started counting.

"There was a broken bowl on the floor when you found the room open?"

Her brows raised. "Yes. There was. The maid was already cleaning it. I think she wanted to hide the evidence."

"Perhaps," I muttered. "Has Ms. Honeycutt ever done anything unwise, unexpected?"

"No." Her voice was firm, her eyes hard.

"Calm down. I am not accusing your housekeeper of anything, Lady Frances. Not yet. Right now I am simply... looking."

The air from the open door smelled like lilacs from the flower-filled vases the servants kept fresh on every table. The window curtains were pulled back to let in the sun, casting a rectangle of warm light at my feet. Beneath my hands, the table was worn, familiar.

"This is the first night of the full moon, and you said she went missing a few weeks ago?"

"Nearly a month now, yes."

"Has Ms. Honeycutt ever broken a dish before?"

Frances's brows furrowed. "No, I do not believe she has."

I straightened my skirt and rubbed my hands together. "You have not told me whether you have any suspicions about what may have caused your long-time servant and friend to disappear."

Her jaw worked for a moment as she decided how to respond. "I have wondered if she received some kind of bad news or had a dark secret. Nothing I imagine seems to fit what I know of the woman. She has always been honest."

That sounded like the truth, but it did not match my impression of events. "I have an idea of the events that led to her disappearance, but I have one last question. Might I see the ledger where she recorded her count at the end of the day?"

Her eyes widened, round as the eyes of a doe, and she turned to pull the ledger from the shelf, then laid it on the table and opened the book to the last marked page. I examined the book, compared pages, and then positioned myself where the woman must have stood while working.

"Ms. Honeycutt stood here," I said, "judging by the wear in the wood where her skirt would have rubbed the table night after night. She was completing her evening ritual around ten o'clock when she saw something that frightened her."

"How—how can you know that?"

"Both her room and this ledger tell me she was a meticulous woman. You said she has never broken a dish. And yet she misprinted the incomplete final tally of bowls in this column. See?"

Lady Frances leaned in to see the number two with a jerky line extending from the tail.

"People make marks like this when startled. There are no other marks of this kind in her records. She was so shocked that she dropped a bowl, which landed on the wood floor, here," I pointed to the rim-shaped dent in the wood. "Whatever she saw or heard affected her so profoundly that she did not warn anyone, or return to her room to pack. She simply left. I would venture to guess that all the doors were still locked in the morning?"

"Yes," she said faintly.

"And Ms. Honeycutt is one of the few people in your household with keys to every door, is she not?"

"She is. Was."

"No food was missing from your pantry or the kitchen?"

"None."

"Then I have no reason to suspect my current hypothesis is incorrect. Particularly because while standing here"—I turned and pointed through the open door to the window across the hall—"she could see down the hill and into the village. People tend to flinch in the direction of the noise or sight that startles them, and the ink drag on the number points directly at that window."

She stared at the window as if it might melt off the wall and said, "But what could she possibly have seen to cause her such fright that she would flee? Our home is safe."

"Apparently she did not think so. Had the woman any contacts or business in the village?"

"Of course. Many contacts, naturally."

"Then that is my next step. I shall set off tomorrow morning. What time are the festivities to begin?"

"Breakfast begins at ten, of course. Then shooting, lunch, afternoon tea, dinner and cards, and so on. In the way of every party."

"Of course," I echoed, as if all of that were perfectly expected and I had not left the country before properly participating in society because my short-lived engagement ended—well, it was no use thinking of that.

We gave one another polite dips of the head, and I followed her back down to the second floor and knocked on Percy's door. He made some kind of grunt I assumed meant I should enter, so I opened the door, stopped, and stifled a laugh. Fabric lay over every available surface in the room. Measuring tape was draped around his neck, various pieces of cloth and lace stuck to his clothes, and he was bent over a portable sewing machine like a bee with its head in a flower.

"Don't laugh," he said around his mouthful of pins, "or I'll leave a seam open so it rips at an opportune time."

"You would never risk your creations out of spite."

"True, alas. What do you need?"

I checked the hallway, closed the door, and said in a low voice, "Just to warn you to be careful. Lady Chatsworth is lying to me, and I'm not sure why."

The rhythmic clicking of the sewing machine stopped, and he turned. "About what?"

"She knows more about this disappearance than she's telling me, but I cannot fathom what it is. Not yet."

He thought for a moment, then nodded. "Alright. Will you be going down to dinner tonight?"

"I intend to hide until being seen is absolutely necessary."

"Then I will deliver your first ensemble before you dress in the morning."

"Thank you," I said, then turned to go.

"Gwen," he said before I left. "Be careful."

I winked at him and strode back toward my room, wondering what Ms. Honeycutt could have seen that scared her so badly, why my hostess was lying about it, and whether that lie was likely to result in my own disappearance... or worse. Hopefully, the village held the answers.

7

Hitching a Ride

SAM

He stood at the window as the coach rolled away, his stomach tied in painful knots. Lady Gwen and Sally were going to the country for the week, expecting him to be safe at home, and he was about to sneak off and break what he was certain were several laws.

He had little choice, but that was his own fault. Had he truly believed he could walk back into his old life without consequences and be the hero who found out about Mr. Capstone when even the inspector and Lady Gwen could not?

"I was stupid," he told Aristotle.

The bird clicked its beak and croaked, "Stupid."

Sam sighed and pulled the curtain closed. The only thing he had to be grateful for was that there were no lessons today. He wouldn't have to sit in front of his tutor and say stupid phrases like "The quick brown dog chased the clever red fox over the fence" while his tutor corrected his pronunciation.

And Chapman would be closeted with Monsieur all day to plan meals for the next week. All he had to worry about was Yates, who seemed to be everywhere all at once. Sneaking out without his notice was easier to imagine than accomplish.

Sam fed the rest of his breakfast to Aristotle, who swallowed the leftover sausage and biscuit with delicate avian greed and carried his plate to the kitchen.

"What are you doing sneaking around, Master Samuel?" Chapman demanded when he poked his head into the steamy room. She stood by a wide wooden worktable next to Monsieur, who was scribbling something on the menu.

The leftover scent of baking bread mixed with the aroma of roasting poultry to make the room smell like everything Sam dreamed of as a boy. Even though he was full, his stomach cramped with the hollow pang of remembered hunger.

"Just bringing in my dish," he said, standing innocently inside the door.

One of the kitchen maids took it and plunged it into the sink, which was nearly overflowing with soapy water.

He crossed to the table and leaned over to peer at the paper, then poked a finger at the writing. "What's boeuf bourg—burg onion?"

"Never you mind," she said, waving her bony fingers at him.

"Something guaranteed to tickle the hunger of even a sturdy little boy," Monsieur said with a flourish of his pen.

"See that you wash your face, Master Sam," the housekeeper said absently. "You've jam on your cheek."

She turned back to the menu, dismissing him from her notice.

He nodded with a "Yes, ma'am," and closed the kitchen door. With a self-satisfied smile, he patted the pocket where several sweets, which he filched from the counter with one hand while distracting them with the other, now lay hidden, and took the stairs two at a time.

Mr. Yates was safely puttering around in the study doing something or other, which would make it infinitely easier to slip out unnoticed.

When he reached his room, he began pulling out supplies he might need: his knife, a leather satchel, a canteen Sally gave him as a Yule gift, a length of slender rope he kept coiled under his bed, a warm cap, and several other obscure things boys always have tucked away in case of an emergency.

But, most important, was the disguise. He rolled the rug aside, pried up the loose floorboard, and pulled out the messenger cap and jacket the Cutthroat King gave him before his henchmen escorted—or, rather, dragged—Sam back to the surface. The uniform would almost guarantee he went unnoticed, even in the halls of Parliament, where servants and messengers were rumored to constantly scurry about.

The last thing Sam did was pull clothes from his drawers and bundle them up into a vaguely human shape before stuffing them beneath his blanket. It would fool anyone on a quick glance, though not for long. But maybe that would be enough.

He padded to the end of the hall and slipped down the servants' staircase to the basement. Lady Gwen didn't keep many servants, and those who were working were already on the upper floors, so the basement was empty.

Despite the relative privacy, Sam snuck through the long hall, past the wine cellar and larder, and edged toward the servants' hall. His entire body was listening to be certain no one was inside, but it was quiet. Except... Sam covered his mouth before he could scream and ducked just as a rustle of feathers flashed past his face.

Aristotle made an acrobatic turn in midair, then landed happily on his shoulder, squeezing hard with his claws.

"You cannot come with me," Sam whispered, trying to pry the bird off his shoulder.

Aristotle clicked his beak sharply in front of Sam's nose, making him flinch.

"Go on, you're going to get me caught."

The raven tilted his head, then opened up his beak as if to let loose a caw that would bring the house down on his head.

"Shh," Sam said, pinching the beak closed. "Stop it. Look, I know you don't want to stay cooped up in the house, but if I take you with me, I'll get caught. But I left a window open for you."

Aristotle stopped struggling and blinked.

"I did, I promise. But you'll have to figure out which one, okay?"

For a moment, Sam was afraid the raven would give him away, but Aristotle finally stopped squeezing, gave him a chuck under the chin with his beak, and flew off back toward the front of the house.

With a sigh of relief, Sam made his way into the still room, where no one would look for him. That was close.

The stairs there were almost always empty. He peeked out the top of the stairs and into the stables above. There were three ways out of the house: the front door, the servants' entrance (which was in the basement but too close to the front door for his comfort,) and the carriage house, where the horses, coach, and Lady Gwen's auto were kept.

That was the safest way out, as far as Sam was concerned, because he could always pretend to be visiting the horses if anyone caught him. But he was in luck. Within moments he was on the street, making his way toward Parliament and praying he didn't get caught. Even Lady Gwen wouldn't be able to save him from the consequences if they found him spying on a member of the House of Lords.

Carriages, hackneys, horses, autos, pedestrians, trolleys full of tourists, hawkers selling maps, and all manner of other madness made the broad street outside Westminster the best place in the world to disappear... but the worst place to overhear anything important.

Sam slipped between the foot traffic like a fish swimming downstream, taking full advantage of his now respectable appearance to get close to the building without being noticed. He might have even nicked a wallet, a watch, and a ring... just to keep in practice.

Sam figured there were two options: brazen his way inside and find information by asking for it, or wait a bit to see what he could overhear. The first option was likely faster, but may also get him caught. The second would take longer, but had the benefit of anonymity.

He chose option two, and if that didn't work, there was always option number one. Sam followed the crowd toward the visitor entrance to Westminster Palace and loitered on the sidewalk, far enough away from the guards to safely listen to people chat, catching bits of information here and there.

"I heard they tucked her away in a little country cottage before her condition became noticeable."

"There isn't enough support for the bill. It will die on the floor."

"She had an entire basket full of oranges, all the way from—"

"Fifty pounds sterling—"

"Broke his arm in the riots—"

"Delivery for Lord Ashcroft."

Sam looked in the direction of the speaker without turning his head. A boy a couple of years older than himself, perhaps Sally's age, held a parcel under one arm as he spoke to one of the guards.

"Take it round to the delivery entrance," the guard said in a bored tone while waving other visitors through.

The boy nodded and took off at a brisk walk. Sam put his cap on and followed.

"Them guards, eh?" he said, coming up alongside the boy.

He flinched, then looked down at Sam, noticed the cap and satchel, and visibly relaxed. "They're always making life harder," he agreed. "If they'd just let me in the visitors' entrance, I could be in and out in a few minutes. Not like I'm bothering no one. The guests don't even see blokes like us."

Sam nodded, knowingly. "Besides, you'd think they'd want the MPs and all to get their mail fast as can be."

The older boy snorted.

"I got one for Lord Rutledge," Sam said, pushing self-importance into his voice as he threw out the name of a lord he'd overheard Lady Gwen complain about.

"Yeah? Lord Ashcroft for this one."

"You ever seen him?"

"Who, the lord? Sure," the boy said, "loads of times. Tall bloke with a dark beard. He likes his tea delivered direct. Gets special blends and all whenever new shipments come in. Mostly another courier picks it up, but they bring me in sometimes."

This was exactly what Sam needed. If he pushed too hard here, the boy might grow suspicious. Sam needed to use a little tact, a skill he sorely lacked. He had been too little to run cons, but he *was* quick and quiet—perfect for sneaking and pick-pocketing. Mostly that only required the minimum contact between him and his mark, so he never developed the skills the adults used to run cons like the fiddle game or the Spanish prisoner.

He was going to have to brazen it out.

"And I bet that just takes even longer," he said, voice heavy with irritation. "Like they don't know you have other deliveries to make."

The boy sighed. "It is what it is."

"I say," Sam said as if just realizing something, "I've got to go round anyway, and this is my last delivery of the morning"—he patted the bag—"I could drop yours off, too, if you want."

The older boy looked down at him, a hint of suspicion in his eyes. "What would you do that for?"

Hell. Sam shrugged and tried to put every drop of nonchalance in his voice he could muster. "I never seen the inside of Parliament, is all. Lord Rutledge has his own courier, but I always wanted to see it. Heard it's a sight. Maybe they'll bring me in if I'm carrying the tea."

The boy narrowed his eyes. Damn, he'd lost this one. But then he laughed. "It ain't all it's cracked up to be, but I don't see why not. Save me half an hour, anyway. Here." He held out the parcel.

Sam reached to take it, but the boy held tight and said, "See it gets inside, mind you. It will mean a whipping for me if my mistress gets a call the tea wasn't delivered."

Guilt washed over Sam in a sudden wave, but he held his breath and ignored it. The boy was too trusting. For all the effort this took, Sam could rob a dozen couriers and fence their goods before anyone knew a delivery had never been made. But he promised himself the tea would make it inside.

"Cross my heart," he said, and took the package.

The boy started to turn away but Sam stopped him with a, "Wait!" He dug into his satchel and pulled out one of the sweets he'd swiped from Monsieur that morning. It was a truffle of some kind, but it lit up the air with the smoky aroma of chocolate and espresso and some other spices that made his mouth water.

"What's this, then?"

"Just a thank you," Sam said. "Nicked 'em this morning."

The boy laughed again, took the treat, touched the brim of his cap, and disappeared into the crowd.

Sam continued around the side of the building, which was bigger than any building had a right to be, amazed at his luck. That was far easier than he'd anticipated. Maybe he could do this, after all.

He queued up in a line of couriers at Black Rod's Garden entrance, making his way toward the front with agonizing slowness. It had taken him long enough to get here, and the sun was descending in the western sky. No doubt Chapman already noted his absence. There was going to be hell to pay when he got back, but nowhere near how bad it would be if he failed the Cutthroat King.

Once more, he remembered the man whose throat had been cut, lying in a pool of his own blood. The King looked directly at him after that display and smiled in a way that turned Sam's guts to water. It was too easy to imagine Sally or Lady Gwen in his place.

"State your business," the guard repeated for what must have been the hundredth time that day.

"Tea delivery for Lord Ashcroft."

The guard tilted his hat back and peered at Sam with pursed lips. "You ain't the regular boy."

"He come down with the putrid sore throat," Sam said, managing to sound both regretful and fascinated.

The guard nodded, as if that boring explanation was expected, and called through the gate, "Tea delivery for you-know-who."

"Send him in," came the response.

The guard motioned him through the gate.

Another orderly waited inside with a book and a pen, wrote something in the book, and said, "Office two-four-three" without looking up.

Sam had no idea where that was, but he wasn't about to give that away. He hurried into the building, trying not to gape. Lady Gwen's house was the nicest building he'd ever been in, but Westminster Palace was grand on an entirely different scale. His shoes echoed on the marble as he walked, eyeing doors and trying to orient himself.

"You lost, luv?"

A washerwoman watched him from above a pair of circular spectacles, both hands resting on a mop handle.

"No," he said, offended.

"Suit yourself," she said and began pushing the mop.

Sam gritted his teeth and peered at the doors, then gave up. "I need office two-four-three," he said.

She gave him a sly smile and said, "One hall down, and two to the right."

Sam was well on his way when he turned down the hall and froze. A dog sat patiently outside an office door... but it wasn't just *any* dog. It was made of brass, gears, rivets, and belts that whirred under metal skin carved with delicately etched runes.

He'd never seen anything like it. Fascinating gadgets were all over Lady Gwen's study, and artificers could make any number of mechanical wonders, but something like this? It looked to have been patterned off a mastiff but was about half the size. Which meant it was still bigger and heavier than he.

Sam didn't realize he'd taken a few fascinated steps forward until the dog turned its huge head and fastened black eyes on him, its mouth opening up in something approximating a doggy grin. Only, it did not look happy.

Would the thing attack him with those huge metal teeth?

The door to his right banged open, and Sam squeaked in fright. The dog stood in alarm, and a booming voice said, "Oh my! Great stars, what are you doing, lad?"

Sam stumbled a few steps back and fumbled with his parcel. He only managed to utter, "It's—I've got—I just—"

The gentleman who opened the door was a bear of a man with heavy shoulders, thick arms, a round belly and long, drooping mustaches.

His voice was deep but his cheeks seemed not to be interested in forming words, so they flapped around loosely when he said, "By jove, it's not my dog you're afraid of, is it? Courage, lad! Ripper is only a construct, aren't you, boy?"

The dog wagged its tail.

"A con—a construction—" Sam was too shaken to get the words out.

"A construct, boy. He ain't alive, for heaven's sake. Only protects me if something goes wrong. Made by the dwarves, you know. Ain't but one of him. Monstrous expensive. Anyway"—he clapped Sam on the shoulder with a beefy hand—"you can go about your business safely. Where are you headed?"

"Two-four-three."

"Why, that's just across the hall, there. You've already made it. See to it, now. Ripper, come along."

The dog stood up and followed its owner down the hall, making clicking noises on the marble as it walked. He must ask Lady Gwen about constructs. Maybe he and Sally could afford one.

Sam took a few moments to catch his breath, reminded himself of what he needed, and then knocked on the door.

It opened on the third knock to show him the surprised face of a handsome, dark-haired man with a black mustache and beard with a streak of white on either side of his chin. A black overcoat swirled about his shoulders, proof he was preparing to leave. Bloody hell.

In seconds, the man took in the situation, eyes landing on the parcel in Sam's hand. He said, "No time. Come along," and took off down the hall at a surprising pace.

Sam opened his mouth, glanced at the office door—where countless important papers must be hiding—winced, and followed the man who must be Lord Ashcroft. He hoped.

The Lord strode through the building, giving a few respectful nods, and Sam hurried along in his wake, clutching the parcel like a lifeline. They exited the building within seconds of one another, turning toward the street where a line of coaches waited. Outside the door of one coach stood a pretty, plump woman in a fine dress. She had cinnamon-colored curls tucked beneath a broad-brimmed hat, freckles on her dark cheeks, and a smile that made his knees a little weak.

Pretty or not, that was the face of a perfect mark: someone kind who assumed the best of everyone. Were he to be caught stealing from her, she'd be more likely to forgive him than call the bobbies.

"Good afternoon, my darling," she said to the lord as they neared the coach. "Everything is packed, as you can see. I hope your day was pleasant. Who is this?"

"Courier," the lord said, then motioned to Sam with one hand. "Here, hand me that tea. Now scramble up top and secure that luggage, would you? That knot appears loose."

Sam delivered the parcel—glad to be rid of it—climbed to the top of the carriage and tightened the knots that secured the luggage. When he climbed down, the woman was saying, "Would have been so much faster to take the train. Only a couple of hours and—"

"We have been over this, dove. Ah, here you are, boy," he said, noticing Sam, and tossed him a coin that Sam caught without thinking. "Be on your way."

What was he to do now? The lord was leaving, and he had no way of knowing where or how long. Would the Cutthroat King accept that? Likely not.

Nothing for it but to nod and slip away into the crowd. Or, at least, appear to slip away. But a desperate plan took hold of his brain with both hands. He passed between the two coaches, as if to cross the street, then ducked and slithered between the wheels while the man and woman spoke. He could never hang on to the frame of the carriage long enough to get anywhere. What could—he dug the rope out of his bag just as the door opened and the woman stepped up.

He looped the rope and worked it between the left and right braces twice, then through the rear axle, and tied it off before the door closed.

Lord Ashcroft shouted out the window, "Walk on!"

Sam nearly dove into the makeshift sling he'd created, feet on one end, head toward the center of the vehicle. The coach jolted, swinging him forward with nearly enough force to hit his forehead on the floor, then pulled out of line and into traffic.

Sam let out an explosive breath. He'd made it. He could continue his mission. The rough hammock he'd fashioned was even relatively comfortable. A truffle from his bag, which rested now on his stomach, made a perfect celebratory treat. He popped it into his mouth, well pleased. Until he realized that he didn't know where they were going or how he was to get back once they got there.

And the hammock wasn't as comfortable as he thought at first. After an hour or so, the thin rope began rubbing, putting too much pressure on his shoulders and legs. It grew colder. Soon it would be nightfall, and it became harder and harder to keep his weight evenly distributed so he did not slip between the coils.

His muscles grew cold and stiff. His stomach growled. The constant rocking made his stomach climb up into his throat, and the constant creaking and bouncing of the wagon made his head ache. Where were they, and how was he supposed to get back? This had been a stupid, terrible plan.

He was lost somewhere in the countryside with no food, no money, and no idea how to get home. Smarter to give up now, while he still had some hope of walking back to New London. The coach stopped, rocking him forward hard enough to hit his head on the underside of the floorboard.

"Fresh horses," someone called.

Sam's cramped body went limp just long enough to topple out of his ropey prison. He bit back a cry of pain, but the clatter of changing horses and tack was loud enough to cover the sound of him crawling out from under the coach.

He wanted to lie down in the bushes and sleep. Nothing in his life had ever sounded better than the soft, grassy earth. But the smack on his head woke him up enough to clear his thoughts. He'd come this far, and he could still see the expression on the King's face when he said, your sister is a lovely girl.

Shadows from the swaying trees covered him like a cloak as he waited, eyes heavy, muscles burning, throat dry and aching. The driver and the coachman climbed up. It was Sam's turn. With a groan, he hoisted himself into the footman's position, and nearly lost his grip when the horses started pulling.

His fingers didn't want to behave and fumbled with the leather strap of his satchel, but he eventually managed to hook it around the handle. It crossed his body and under one arm, a support he could lean against, strong enough to take his weight when his legs eventually gave out.

And they would. If the coach changed horses, that meant there was still a long way to travel, and he wasn't certain he'd be alive by the end of the trip.

8

Dark Riders

GWEN

Sally double-checked the buttons on the back of my blouse, a frilly white confection with layers of lace, and pronounced me suitably attired to go down to breakfast... but I didn't want to.

"You go on," I told her. "I'll just go down to the village."

She rolled her eyes at me and said, "You told me you needed to convince people that your visit had nothing to do with the missing housekeeper. Everyone will be down for breakfast on the first morning, won't they?"

"Yes," I allowed, grudgingly.

Sally folded her arms, looked me in the eye, and said, "Then stop being a baby and let's go downstairs."

My mouth popped open. I intended to say something clever, but nothing came out. The girl was right. I had to face this and get the experience over with.

"Very well, then," I said with aplomb. "Lead the way, my little dictator."

Sally was getting very good at rolling her eyes. She led me down the hall and we became part of a disjointed migration of well-dressed, over-bred gentlepeople, following one another toward the scent of sausage, eggs, kippers, and other confections.

The women wore something similar to my ensemble, a blouse and skirt suitable to the more informal atmosphere of breakfast, but Sally stood out with her blonde hair down and tied back in shining waves. As my companion, not an invited guest, she could participate in the breakfast buffet but would take the rest of her meals separately, as would the members of the other guests' parties. So this was the only meal we would share over the weekend.

The pang of sadness I felt at that surprised me. Since Sam and Sally came to live with me, we shared most meals together, unless I was out of the house. Daily life had taken on a comfortable rhythm that made me realize how alone I'd been before they found me.

Mrs. Chapman and Mr. Yates were very dear to me, as dear as family, but their own scruples about class and rank meant they would never be as open with me as they could be with one another. But Sam and Sally were too young to have been corrupted by the system. Once they had gotten used to their new places, they'd been more frank and honest than anyone else in my life since losing my twin sister. I regretted the lack of that connection, even for so short a time.

But I didn't have long to regret it, because we entered the breakfast hall and I had to put on my *I deserve to be here expression*. Long tables were arrayed with more food than the average family would see in a week, and people were scattered about with their plates, chatting in groups. There was even a balcony opened for those who enjoyed dining al fresco, with cool morning air blowing the sheer curtains in inviting waves.

"Shall we eat outdoors?" I asked Sally.

She glanced around the room, taking in the guests in their finery, then swallowed and nodded. Everyone was so consumed with their food and conversation, I thought I might make it through the line without being noticed. Perhaps this wouldn't be so bad, after all.

We joined the line, slowly working our way down the table, and I allowed myself to believe that perhaps my past wouldn't catch up to me after all. At least, until I heard the first voice say in incredulous tones, "... St. James?"

A few more voices joined the chorus and soon the conversation in the room hushed as they watched me from the corners of their eyes. Would I throw a fit and destroy the breakfast table? It was a tempting thought. My cheeks grew hot and my stomach twisted itself into knots. I could imagine what they said to one another. *Isn't that Lady St. James? Her sister disappeared under mysterious circumstances—probably an indiscretion the family tried to hide. She was quite the wild young thing, totally undisciplined. She destroyed her fiancé's sitting room in a pique during a party, did you know? They had to bribe the boy to get him to marry her in the first place. Scandalous behavior, her poor mother is a saint. Now she is seen all about town with an inspector from Scotland Yard, most improper. What is Lady Chatsworth about, inviting her here?*

My teeth were grinding hard enough that they should have been nothing but dust in my mouth. Concentrating on filling my plate was nearly impossible with the venomous hum of gossip and speculation ringing in my ears. Nothing I did would convince these people that I was making an attempt to rejoin "polite" society. Polite, indeed.

Sally's hand on my arm stopped me from mindlessly piling more sausages on my plate. Her eyes were soft, but her jaw was tight and her lips pressed into a thin, angry line. She said, "Just dogs barking, my lady. Like you said."

I told Sally the same thing nearly two years ago when we overheard two women gossiping. Of course, that did not feel quite the same as a whole room with their judging eyes locked on my back, but I hauled up a reassuring smile from somewhere deep in my gut, raised my head, and sailed through the rest of the line. Ignoring the whispers that were *just* loud enough to be overheard, but not so loud as to be crass, was a bit more difficult, but I managed.

When we had our drinks in one hand and our plates in the other, I led Sally across the room and onto the balcony. As soon as we were out of doors, conversation returned with a vengeance, everyone chattering like squirrels.

Tables were scattered across the balcony far enough apart for privacy but close enough to allow separate parties to converse if they chose. We sat at the table farthest from everyone else.

"You should say something," Sally said, as soon as she sat.

"It would only give them more ammunition, dearest girl."

"So? Choose the biggest one and take them down a peg. That will teach the others to pick on you."

I smiled at her across the table, a genuine smile filled with all the affection and humor I felt. Heaven help the ton if Sally Dawes was ever unleashed upon them. "The biggest one is our hostess."

"Then the next biggest," she said, undeterred, and began ripping a breakfast roll apart.

I could have argued with her—I probably should have—but I liked her indignation. Besides, what was the point? My ruse would only last long enough to find Ms. Honeycutt. I had no intention of again tying myself or my happiness to this group of insipid, cruel, and useless humans. Besides that, I was suddenly and surprisingly hungry. In fact, I was so intent on eating that I didn't realize a woman stood near our table until Sally cleared her throat.

"Forgive me for intruding on your breakfast," the woman said with a little curtsy.

I forced a bite of sausage down with a painful swallow, dabbed my lips with my napkin, and said, "Not at all."

"I am Edith, Lady Ashcroft. I don't mean to take up any of your time. I just wanted to encourage you to ignore those—those people who speak unkindly of you. They do not merit your notice, and I hope they will not chase you away from the party."

It was difficult not to stare at the woman, not only because she was as soft and pretty as a flower, all lovely round curves and delicate lines, but because her facade of kindness was almost believable.

"Thank you very much for saying so," I told her, "but I never let other people control what I can and cannot do."

Her cheeks pinkened, and she said in a low voice, "I admire that. But please, do not let me keep you from your breakfast. Good morning."

And then she was gone, her pale skirts swishing behind her. Sally beamed, but I didn't have the heart to tell her that the woman probably only meant to ingratiate herself so she could ferret out any gossip worth sharing. And I didn't want to think about it anymore.

A servant approached the table with a small silver tray bearing an envelope with my name written in familiar script. I thanked her, opened the envelope, and read the brief note.

I laid my napkin on the table and stood. "Have you finished?"

"I suppose so. The sun feels nice."

"It does. We can enjoy it while we walk into the village. Come along. We have more important things to do than parade ourselves for the entertainment of Lady Chatsworth's guests."

Such as finding out if anyone in the village held a grudge against Ms. Honeycutt.

***

"They will not hold lunch till this afternoon," I told Sally over my shoulder as we trooped down the path toward the village. "That should give us enough time to check in on To—the inspector, and to get the lay of the land."

"Will we make it back in time to change our clothes?"

I took off my watch and handed it back to her. "Here. You keep track of the time and if it gets close, beat me over the head with my umbrella."

She grinned and fastened the band. "Yes, ma'am."

The village awoke far earlier than the manor, and the citizens were already well about their business. We crossed the stream that divided the village from the grounds of the manor by way of a stone bridge and followed the packed dirt road onto the high street, where the heart of business lay.

"Housekeepers of Ms. Honeycutt's station rarely have the time to form casual acquaintances," I told Sally. "So the logical place to start asking questions is the businesses she would have frequented for herself and the family."

"Would she not send a maid to the village for her?"

"Not for her own business. That would be a misuse of their time. She would walk down herself, on her Sunday afternoon off."

"But Charlotte and Mrs. Chapman have far more free time than that!"

"And if our lovely companions at the manor knew how I run our home, they would be both disgusted and mortified."

Sally snorted as we pushed open the front door of the dry goods store. As in most small villages, the dry goods store carried food staples like flour and sugar, but also bolts of cloth, ribbon, buttons, sewing needles, and pomade. An officious-looking elvin woman stood behind the counter, her straight black hair pulled back into a neat bun, not a wrinkle or stain on her white apron.

She flinched when the wind caught the door and slammed it shut, but recovered quickly and asked, "How can I help you to-day?"

"Good morning," I said in my cheeriest voice. "I would like a bag of caramels, please."

She opened the glass jar and picked out the sweets with a pair of tongs, dropping them one by one into a paper bag.

"I hope you won't mind, but I was just wondering if you re-member the last time Ms. Honeycutt stopped by?"

The tongs paused only a moment, but it was a noticeable pause. "Are you from the manor house? They already came by and asked their questions."

"I'm only visiting. You might call me a detective of sorts."

She nearly dropped the bag. "A detective? Do—then the lord and lady suspect some kind of foul play?"

Sally abandoned me and began peeking through the neatly arranged piles and displays. "They don't know what to believe, and I would like to help. You see, from what I understand, they had a good relationship with Ms. Honeycutt, so it seems strange she would disappear without taking her leave of the family."

"I cannot say I know the situation well enough to determine what the lady would do or not do, but—well, it is none of my business. To answer your question, it has been more than a month since she bought a bag of peppermints. That was the last time I saw her."

"Did she have a sweet tooth, then?"

"She rarely missed a Sunday. That will be a penny unless I can interest you in anything else?"

"Just more answers, if you have them."

She raised her hands and shook her head. "I cannot help you."

When Sally and I left, I handed her the bag of sweets. "Save a few for Sam."

"Not likely," she muttered, then slid the bag into her pocket and frowned. Since that particular expression was her thinking frown, I waited to speak till she came to whatever conclusion was brewing in her clever mind. After a moment, she leaned toward me and whispered, "She was afraid."

I took Sally's arm in mine and urged her off the stairs and onto the road. "You have a good eye. You're right. And if I would have pushed her, she'd have found an excuse to disappear into the back. But that's only one store. There are more. Onward."

We visited the apothecary, the cooper, the blacksmith—a dwarven man with a singed beard—and the tinker. Each proprietor was nervous and eager for us to be on our way. And they all said the same thing: Ms. Honeycutt was not a woman of easy intimacy, and she'd been gone at least a month.

Our last hope was the tailor, who worked out of her own parlor, according to the blacksmith. Her cottage was near the end of the row, squat and neat, like most of the homes, with a little trail of smoke dancing up from her chimney despite the warm morning.

A thin girl in a maid's uniform opened the door when we knocked and showed us into a parlor that smelled like menthol, mint, and lemon. A frail old woman sat in her chair by the fire, a white lawn shirt on her lap, needle flashing in the firelight.

"Skirts are ten cents," she began in a voice as thin as wet paper, but I cut her off and said, "Mrs. Haverly, we are not here to have our clothing tailored. I was hoping I might ask you a few questions."

The needle stilled, and the woman looked up at me over the rims of her spectacles, her watery blue eyes calculating. "Do you, now? Then you'll need to pay me, for this is my only income since poor Mr. Haverly died and I cannot answer questions *and* sew at the same time. Ten cents will do it. Martha?" she called to the maid, "Bring in some tea. Have a seat."

Sally and I exchanged a glance, then sat on the doily-covered couch. The maid appeared with a tray and set the tea things down on the small table. Mrs. Haverly gave me a pointed look, so I began pouring the tea. I liked the old woman already.

"Sugar?" I asked her.

"Two, please. And cream."

"I'll be honest with you, ma'am," I said, handing her the cup.

"I should hope so."

"I am trying to discover what happened to Ms. Honeycutt, the housekeeper at the manor. But everyone I've spoken to has been hesitant to answer questions."

"And no wonder, what with the dark riders and all."

"Dark riders?" Sally asked.

"There's many as say they've seen them about on a full moon, on their dark horses."

"Have you seen the dark riders?" I asked.

"No, but those as have seen them say they're all in black and riding black horses, though no one can tell exactly what they're wearing."

A bit theatrical, that. There were several mythologies and folk tales that included ghostly riders in some form or other, whether it was a spectre of death, an ill omen, or some way to explain the missing young men and women who decided country life was not for them.

"Are you willing to talk about Ms. Honeycutt?"

"I'm too old to have anything to risk, young lady. And that's what you're paying for, isn't it?"

"Indeed it is." I set my cup down and folded my hands in my lap. "When was the last time you saw Ms. Honeycutt?"

"Oh, sometime three, four weeks ago. Maybe a bit longer, but not much."

"And what did you speak about?"

"I've never spoken to her. Only saw her walking to and fro on the far side of the lawn near the forest, there." She pointed out the narrow side window to a view of the edge of the Chatsworth lawn that ran into the forest where the earl and his guests would be shooting.

"Did she do that often? Walk by the edge of the wood, I mean," I asked.

"A few times a month, I might see her in the evenings."

"Yet you've never spoken to her?"

"Not once since she's been here. They do all of their own tailoring and mending at the manor."

"I see. Do you have any reason to believe Ms. Honeycutt might have any enemies?"

"Enemies? No, nothing I've ever heard tell. And I would know it." She placed one finger alongside her nose. "Tailors do hear everything."

Apparently, they did. By the time Mrs. Haverly finished telling us every secret she knew about everyone in the village—including a rather scandalous affair between the blacksmith and the owner of the dry goods store—Sally was pointing at the watch and widening her eyes at me.

I thanked Mrs. Haverly for her time and the tea, left her significantly more than ten cents, and followed Sally back through town. The few people who saw us on the street quickly found very distracting and engrossing things to do that did not involve answering questions.

"What is your assessment?" I asked Sally as we passed the house of a woman who stared at us through her drapes.

Her brows drew together, her mouth pursed in a pout of concentration. "I think there is more happening here than Lady Chatsworth is telling you."

"I think you're right."

"But she wants you to find the housekeeper, and she knew you would ask questions in the village, so she wouldn't be able to hide anything."

"That is a dangerous assumption, but I won't fault your logic. There is something you may not have seen. Look." I stopped near the last house on the street before turning toward the manor and pointed to the stairs beneath the side entrance.

"Is that... a saucer of milk?"

"It is. And bread soaked in honey."

She blinked. "They're making offerings to fairies?"

"These people are superstitious, and Lady Chatsworth knows it. When people blame childhood illness on changelings and leave offerings of peace to the fairies, their information will always be colored by their own fears."

"So, you must sort through that to the truth beneath it."

I smiled and touched her cheek. "Just so."

She beamed at me.

We stopped at the small but neat public house, ironically called *The Crooked Nag*, and asked for Tony. Purple smudges lined his eyes, but his suit was clean and his hair and cheeks were damp.

After we stepped outside, I asked, "Did you just arrive?"

"On the evening train," he said, squinting against the sunlight. "I traveled the rest of the way by post. The experience left quite a lot to be desired. Be grateful you took that smart coach of yours. I sat next to a rather bilious old woman for more than an hour, and I hate to speak ill of the elderly, but I can still smell whatever she ate for breakfast the day before."

Sally grimaced, and I laughed at his put-out expression.

"What have you learned?" he asked.

I explained our discoveries while he made his thinking face, which looked less like contemplation and more like he was sizing one up for a good beating.

"Something isn't right," he said.

Sally folded her arms, pleased with herself for coming to the same conclusion, and I nodded. "I cannot tell what it is, yet," I said, "but I agree."

"Perhaps I should see if an inspector can intimidate them a bit."

I scowled at him. It was my best scowl, one that said, *you promised, remember?*

He blew a deep, irritated breath through his nose and ran a hand through his hair. He hated not being involved. After a moment, his expression cleared, and he said, "The Sisterhood can have nothing to say about very observant tourists, can they?"

"Tony—"

He raised his hands. "I'm simply a tourist, taking in the pleasures of the country."

I snorted, and he grinned in triumph. It was his charming, boy-ish grin that I could not resist. It softened the lines of his face and made me want to ruffle his hair.

"Time," Sally said, her voice soft but insistent.

"Here," I said, pulling one of Delilah's clever torches out of my pocket. "Delilah made these. I don't know if we shall need them, but I cannot use two."

"What is it?"

I pressed the switch, and he flinched, nearly dropping it. He turned it over and examined the engraved brass, squinting at the marks. "I'll be—that is a clever little device, isn't it?"

"Indeed. You'll never lose your keys in the dark. If you can find the torch, that is. Charge it in the sunlight, just like a dwarven lamp."

He nodded but didn't seem to be paying me much attention as he flicked the switch on and off and on again.

We said goodbye to Tony, who was still puzzling over his new torch, and walked back across the bridge toward the manor. Sally and I replayed the morning conversations to see if anything meaningful coalesced from the nonsense when I noticed a bit of smoke filtering into the sky through the trees of the earl's forest. It appeared just where Mrs. Haverly claimed to see the erstwhile housekeeper going for her walks.

The forest belonged to the Chatsworth estate and was set aside purely for the use of the earl and tenants with express permission. He was the only one who could allow hunting or harvesting, and this was not the season for burning.

"You hurry back to the manor," I told Sally and hiked up my skirt for a walk in the grass. "I'm going to see where that smoke is coming from."

"But you don't have much time," she said, a note of panic in her voice as she eyed my unsuitable-for-luncheon blouse and skirt and calculated how long it would take me to change and fix my hair. She was getting rather good with those calculations.

"I have time for this," I assured her. "Will you make certain to lay everything out?"

She scowled at me but nodded, and we set off in different directions: Sally toward the culture and refinement of an exclusive country party, and I to find out why smoke was rising from a place no one lived. Did it have anything to do with the mysterious disappearance of a woman no one claimed to know well?

I was going to find out.

9

Hagstone

GWEN

The sun had burned the dew off the grass, keeping my boots dry as I trudged across the lawn. But dew drops still hung from branches and leaves in the wood, and stray beams of sunlight broke through the canopy to turn them into glowing jewels. It was also several degrees cooler, which made me grateful for Percy's magical jacket. I hung the umbrella from my left forearm by its curved handle and took full advantage of the wool-lined pockets.

A much-used footpath began where the lawn met the forest. Unseen from a distance, it threaded through the trees, presumably connecting the village to the estate. Was this where Mrs. Haverly, the garrulous tailor, had seen Ms. Honeycutt so often? Was the housekeeper secretly meeting a beau? An angry wife or an accidental pregnancy could certainly explain her disappearance, given that domestics would be immediately dismissed for fraternization.

I followed the path, pushing further into the woods in the direction from which I'd seen the smoke, ears pricked for the faint report of rifles. Straying too close to the hunt was a bad idea, even though I wore a veritable suit of armor. Wood smoke cut through the scent of wet vegetation. Who would burn wood now when the forest was set aside for the use of guests during the celebration? I increased my pace. I didn't have as much time as I convinced Sally I had.

The path wandered through a small thicket to open on a clearing right out of a fairytale. Sunlight shone golden on the thatched roof of a small wattle and daub cottage that stood a stone's throw from the path. Herbs and flowers grew around the foundation, and wattle fencing kept the small garden separated from the encroaching forest.

It was such a charming sight that I began walking toward it without consciously changing direction. At least, until I stepped on a pebble that sent an arrow of pain up to my ankle.

Cursing, I stumbled to the side and plucked the stone from the mossy undergrowth. It hadn't been a pebble at all. The stone was roughly oval in shape, half the size of my palm, and a perfect circle had been worn through the center. By rain, or by design? Sally would like to see it. I put the stone into my pocket and hurried toward the cottage. Ms. Honeycutt wouldn't have taken refuge so close to the manor, or she would certainly have been discovered, but intuition told me something in this cottage would help me find her.

The rich aroma of herb gardens bathed in the sun washed over me as I neared, basil, thyme, and rosemary making my mouth water. A string of bells, shells, and sticks hung from the door latch, so rather than knocking on the door, I rattled the bells with one finger. The musical chiming hung in the air long after the trinkets stilled.

A small, sturdy woman with a cloud of untamed white hair opened the door. She was no taller than Sam and didn't seem to notice the twigs caught in her hair or the beetle industriously munching a leaf still attached to one. Bright brown eyes assessed me through a maze of wrinkles. She said nothing, only nodded and stepped aside to offer me entrance. It was not a formal invitation, which meant only non-magical beings could accept it.

I stepped carefully across the threshold and into the fragrant hut. Drying herbs hung from the ceiling, and battered wooden tables hosted piles of rough clay bowls, pitchers, and pots. Sunlight streamed through the open shutters, and several small birds flew in to rest in the rafters, steal a few herbs, and fly out again.

The old woman closed the door and began dropping dried herbs and berries into a large stone mortar, grabbing them from separate piles without looking and stopping now and then to tilt her head, as if listening. Satisfied, she picked up the pestle with her stained fingers and began grinding in a smooth, familiar motion that added the homely sound to the already enchanting atmosphere of the place.

I sat down on the small quilt-covered cot next to the hearth and waited, feeling instinctively that she did not desire a response. When she finished grinding, the woman tilted the mortar into a little leather sack, tied it off with a piece of twine, and turned to me with an expectant expression.

I stood and held out my hand. When she placed the sack onto my palm, it felt heavier than it should have. She patted the sack, nodded, and turned back to her table.

"Did the housekeeper from the manor ever come to you for magic?" I asked.

She paused. "Not spells. Herbs. Not a witch."

"I know these are not spells," I said. "But they have a magic of their own, do they not?"

"Who knows what the sky sees? Why it cries, and why its tears bring life? Only the plants know. Who knows what the earth feels, why it opens itself to touch and defilement? Only the plants know. Who knows what the trees remember? What the log hears as it rots?"

"Only the plants," I said as if it were the answer to a riddle.

She nodded.

"So, Ms. Honeycutt needed to know things only the plants know?"

"All creatures need the knowledge of the plants. Need it in their guts, and in their bones."

"What knowledge did Ms. Honeycutt need?"

"The knowledge of passing things, and things that were."

I stared down at my own little bundle of plant knowledge and asked, "And what knowledge do I need?"

She put her bony hand on my forearm and squeezed. It was absurdly comforting. "Drought causes deep roots. And the dandelion does not ask the rose where it may grow. You will see the truth through the eyes of stone."

Something deep inside me unlocked, and a rush of heat spread out from my chest, but the door was still closed, and I couldn't tell where to find it. I swallowed and nodded because that was all I could do.

"The earth never breaks a promise. And it gives to those whom it will." She patted my pocket and the stone inside bumped against my thigh.

"A gift?"

She smiled a gentle smile that brought tears to my eyes. They filled up and ran over my cheeks like snowmelt over the banks of a river, and I was powerless to stop them. She reached up and wiped the tears away with her thumbs, nodded, then turned back to her work. My time in the cottage was at an end.

I didn't want to leave without paying her somehow, though I suspected she would have no use for coin and she'd said the stone in my pocket was a gift from the earth. What else could I—reaching beneath the hem of the jacket, I dug into my skirt pocket and removed the werewolf tooth. I placed the tooth on the table next to a stack of clay jars. Sunlight turned the tooth white, and it glowed against the stained wood.

The only thing I could do was leave. I closed the door reluctantly, feeling as if I'd just experienced something profound but not able to discover what it was. That unlocked door stood somewhere inside me, waiting to be opened, vibrating with promise, but I had no map with which to find it.

My feet carried me slowly away from the cottage, but only because there was nowhere else to go. I turned back, wanting one last sight of it, but the place was gone. Gone, or hidden, or hiding.

With some effort, I dispelled the enchanted haze that hung about me and forced the gears in my brain to begin turning. Wise women lived on the outskirts of many villages, selling their remedies or trading them for goods or favors. It wasn't uncommon. People spoke about such women in low voices not meant to be overheard, and they visited them in secret. They were the last resort when medicine or hope failed.

So why had Ms. Honeycutt visited? She'd said that the woman needed to know about passing things and things that were. That encompassed too many subjects for my comfort and helped me find her not at all. I needed something more concrete, or I would never get my hands on the book... or Lia.

A dark form darted across the path several yards in front of me and I froze in the shadow of a great oak. Dark riders? The gears in my mind ground into place and started spinning fast enough to make me dizzy. That was the dark figure I saw at the zoo. I was running before I consciously decided to follow them.

They ran with inhuman speed and grace, gliding over the earth and slipping between trees as if made of shadow. At my fastest, I only barely kept them in my sight, and I was far less graceful.

Tree roots reached up to grab at the toes of my boots, slowing me further, as the figure disappeared in the shadows only to flash through sunbeams many yards later. Before long, they'd lose me in the tangle of the woods, and we were drawing dangerously close to the hunt.

The report of gunfire grew louder. We hadn't tested my jacket against gunfire while a person wore it, and I wasn't keen to be the first.

"Stop!" I called. "Wait!"

The figure darted to one side and disappeared into a thick stand of saplings. I skidded to a halt, umbrella in one hand, bag of herbs in the other. What did I think I was going to do with the herbs? I dropped the bag into the opposite pocket and held the umbrella in both hands, listening. Silence reigned, punctuated only by the distant report of rifles.

Birds stopped singing, and even the chipmunks took cover. Animals knew when predators were about. A few leaves shifted in the breeze, but nothing else moved. I held my breath and balanced my weight on the balls of my feet.

The figure broke from cover and stood poised to move. The lean, wide-shouldered figure felt instinctively masculine though only the hint of a face was visible beneath the hood. Intelligent malice polluted the air around him like poison gas.

He sniffed, then cocked his head to the side and stared at me for what felt like an eternity. Did he expect me to speak? I had no intention of giving myself away so easily. Seeming to sense this, he straightened, drew a pistol from somewhere in the folds of his ragged clothing, and leveled it at me. I snapped open the umbrella. He fired.

Bullets hit the canopy, three in quick succession, sending pale blue ripples out from each impact and heating the shaft as the runes diverted and stored the kinetic force.

I didn't dare lower the umbrella to see where the hooded figure was, or I'd be dead before I could blink. My ears rang from the crack of the gunfire, but my instincts told me a man this dangerous would not turn and run while I was vulnerable. He would follow one attack with another.

Beneath the edge of the umbrella, a black-booted foot struck the ground. I released the stored energy in a single rush. It burst from the tip hard enough to take me off my feet. I landed on my arse with an *oof* as the figure sailed backward into a stand of saplings, breaking branches as it crashed through.

My umbrella had no more power to throw, so I clicked the handle and unsheathed the blade. It glowed dully from transferring so much energy. I was a fair hand with a rapier, but if that failed and he came at me directly, I would have only the skill I earned at hand fighting.

But I was nowhere near as fast, and if he had even a modicum of skill, he would kill me.

Waiting for him to ambush me from cover was stupid, and if I did not follow, I'd lose him for sure.

"The only difference between bravery and stupidity is success," I muttered and pushed to my feet.

I waited, listening, my heart thundering. But nothing happened. Birds began singing, and dull metal glinted at me from the leaf mold where he'd been standing. I picked up the revolver, likely knocked from his grip by the force of the blow, and examined it.

A stock weapon, no artifice or distinguishing marks of any kind. I tucked it in next to the leather sack in my pocket. Sally was right. Something was happening at Chatsworth that extended far beyond a missing housekeeper. And I was about to be very late for lunch.

By the time I opened the door, Sally was fully dressed and glaring daggers at me. A pale ivory dress, absolutely frothing with layers of lace and ruffles, lay on the bed. Bows, ribbons, and embroidery adorned the elbows, hem, and neckline. In general style, it was very much the common fashion, feminine and delicate but structured enough to show off the corseted waist.

But Percy had created a design with an elegant simplicity of line, a confidence that didn't require excess. Unlike other afternoon dresses in pastel shades, Percy used a black silk belt and bows at the elbows—and around the absolutely enormous straw hat—to turn the dress into something understated, yet unafraid.

I could not even deny that I wanted to wear it.

"Stop staring at it and turn around!" Sally ordered, already fumbling with the buttons on the back of my blouse. "What did you do to your skirt?"

"I fell on my arse while fighting with a dark stranger in the woods."

"You... of course you did."

"Save the scolding for Mama, my dear. You'll never do it justice."

We removed my garments and cinched me into the afternoon dress in record time, then piled my hair atop my head in a loose bundle of curls. Sally slid the hat pin through the mass of straw and hair as if she'd been doing it all her life and examined me to be sure I fit the current fashion—a nod of approval. I must've passed inspection.

She batted my hand away when I reached for my umbrella, shoved a dainty parasol at me, and said, "Go!"

I rushed down the stairs, hoping I was only fashionably late, and stumbled into the garden. Women in white lace dresses festooned the grass, their enormous hats like lily pads on the surface of a pond. They gathered round folding tables in loose groups or sat on blankets that the servants laid out in artful arrangements, complete with wicker baskets and pillows for comfort.

It was the picture of well-bred elegance, and I fit in not at all. Oh, I was born to it, certainly, but these women and I were not the same sort of creatures. Lia and I had been too wild to tame easily, and while Mama trained us well, she had been far more liberal with our education and manners than New London Aristocrats would accept. And I spent the last decade outside society, where rules and social norms changed quickly.

To pull off this ruse, I had to convince them I was meant to be there. Several heads turned my way (one cannot hide where one looks when a hat the size of a wagon wheel turns with one's head) and the whispering began.

There were two distinct options: to continue into the garden as if I did not hear the gossip, or to do something absolutely flagrant and ridiculous. Lady Ashcroft appeared and saved me from being forced to decide. Her cheeks were flushed with the warmth of the afternoon and she smiled winsomely beneath her enormous hat. She could not stand too close, of course, but she somehow managed to take my arm and lead me into the fray.

"Lady St. James, I am so glad you've come. You made quite an entrance. Everyone is green with jealousy. I would not be surprised if black sashes appear on every dress tomorrow."

I could not pry my arm from hers without being rude, and she at least maintained the fiction of goodwill, so I had no choice but to play along. "If they do, Lady Ashcroft, I will eat my hat. Listen." I stopped and turned to face her. "I feel compelled to warn you that showing me kindness will do you no favors, and I dislike the thought of you suffering the ill will of your peers on my account."

She made a little noise, something like a *pfft*, and waved her gloved hand to dismiss the idea. "Since when do we treat people kindly in the hope favors? And, to be honest, I am selfish. I admire people who do not let the whims of society lead them around by the nose. So perhaps I am hoping your strength will rub off on me."

We sat on one of the blankets and dug into the wicker basket, pulling out cheese, grapes, small sandwiches, cold chicken, pastries, and other assorted delicacies. She chattered on while I nodded obediently and made noises of confirmation where expected. The only question was how long it would take for the woman to inadvertently admit her real desire in speaking with me.

"Are you intimate with Lady Chatsworth?" I asked while she sipped lemonade.

"Enough for polite society, certainly. She is a charming woman, after all."

"Had you ever the pleasure of meeting her housekeeper, Ms. Honeycutt?"

Lady Ashcroft stopped sipping, confused. "No, I don't believe I have. Though I have seen her on occasion. Tall and rather elegant woman, for a housekeeper. Why?"

"Oh," I said, waving the question away, "I always find a lady's relationship with her housekeeper says a great deal about her. This is my first time visiting, so I thought I might ask someone who would know."

"I see. I wish I could be more helpful in that regard, but, to tell the truth, I have only seen Lady Chatsworth interact with her house—Ms. Honeycutt, one time. But their intercourse seemed civil."

And that was it. Servants were expected to be invisible, and no one ever took the trouble to pay attention to them. Unfortunately, if a guest took an interest in any servant, even only so far as conversing with them, the servant was likely to be reprimanded at best and fired for putting themselves forward, at worst. Lady Ashcroft might be civil, but she was no different from the rest of them.

The hunting party returned to share in the afternoon delicacies, stopping every conversation as they strode into our midst like conquering heroes. Men in buff trousers and smart hats joined their wives or sisters or fiancées, plopping down onto chairs or blankets and bragging about the day's exploits over their icy drinks.

Lady Ashcroft stood, so I was obliged to stand as well when a man strode toward us. He was clearly a sportsman, with sun-tanned skin, an upright figure, and a dark beard with streaks of grey on either side of his chin. He had intelligent eyes and capable hands, and he smiled when he saw his wife.

"How was the shooting, my lord?" she asked when he reached us.

"Most successful. I think we will enjoy the fruits come suppertime." He leaned toward her, either to take her hand or something else, then batted at the copious feathers that didn't allow him near. "Blast these bothersome hats. I will rejoice the day they fall out of fashion. Not that you ladies don't do them justice, of course," he amended, seeming to remember he was not alone with his wife.

"Not at all, Lord Ashcroft," I said. "I, too, look forward to the day we will not be obliged to put our necks through such strenuous exercise on behalf of fashion."

He barked a short laugh and Lady Ashcroft said, "My darling, may I present Lady St. James?"

The smile fell off his face, but he rallied and wrestled it back into place. More for his wife's sake than for mine, I thought. Still, it was commendable.

"Lord and Lady Ashcroft," a dulcet voice said in tones of rapture, "I hoped I would see you here!"

A woman approached, wearing the absolute height of fashion—which made it look like she was being devoured by aggressive sea foam—and reached out for Lady Ashcroft's hand. "You were not at dinner last night," she continued, looking between the two of them as if their late arrival was a personal affront they should apologize for.

"You know how busy politics is before the close of Parliament," Lady Ashcroft said.

"Oh politics, pish," the other woman said. "I am only glad you're here now. And who is this?"—she meant me—"I do not believe we have been introduced."

I steeled myself. The woman had a pinched but clever face, and while her voice was sweet, it was the saccharine over-sweetness of rotting fruit.

"This is Gwenevere, Lady St. James," Lady Ashcroft said. "Lady St. James, this is Arabella, Lady Covington."

"A pleasure," she said.

"Charmed."

"Lady St. James, I simply must commend you on your gown. Such a brave choice. The black is really very striking. I could not take my eyes off it."

Ahhh, now we were back in territory I understood. The backhanded compliments were a slap in the face with a silk glove, clearly understood by everyone and never to be exposed for the fear of pulling off the glove and discovering a rotting hand inside.

I fought the heat rising in my cheeks.

"Indeed," Lady Ashcroft said. "It is an extraordinary dress, so elegant. Lady St. James, you must tell Lady Covington who your designer is. I'm sure she will want to purchase one."

The smile Lady Covington offered was a thin veneer to cover her insulted surprise as she said, "Of course."

Lady Ashcroft feigned not to notice the hostility, smiling as if all were right with the world. Lord Ashcroft observed the entire affair with a combination of amused indulgence and speculation. Who did he think was winning this gentle duel?

"Lady St. James clearly has impeccable taste," Lady Ashcroft continued. "I will be surprised if she does not challenge you as the fashion plate of society."

Lady Covington's affected enthusiasm was venomous. "I am most excited to see your gown tonight, Lady St. James, If we are all to be following your lead, soon."

"Then you simply *must* stop by our table after dinner so you might examine it more closely. Lady St. James will be joining us for partners' poker, and I am certain she would be so good as to let you see firsthand what the new fashion is to be."

"You may depend upon it," Lady Covington said, before giving me a tight smile and exiting while her tail still had a few feathers left in it.

Lady Ashcroft incinerated the woman, and I wasn't even obliged to speak a word. I blurted, "I think I am in love with you, madame." And then could have immediately bitten off my tongue.

But both the Ashcrofts laughed, Lady Ashcroft behind her hand, and Lord Ashcroft with a belly laugh that drew the eyes of everyone around us.

"Do join us tonight for cards, Lady St. James," he pressed. Then said to his wife, "That was bloody brilliant, my dear. Sell tickets next time, won't you?"

She gave him a prim smile and said innocently, "I have no idea what you are talking about, darling." Then she turned to me and said, "Forgive me for being so presumptuous, but I could not stand to let her win. Still, I hope you will join our table."

How could I say no after that? "I would, but I do not have a partner."

She waved that away. "One always shows up."

I smiled at her, the first honest smile to touch my face since walking out the door. "Then it would be my pleasure."

I could do no better than having this thorny rose at my side to protect me from ungentle hands, even if she had motives of her own. And Lord Ashcroft was active in the House of Lords, which meant he knew things I wanted to know, such as the state of the impending legislation and, if I was very lucky, whether the name Mr. Capstone was familiar.

Tea was optional, and they would not hold dinner until nearly eight o'clock. That gave me several hours to formulate a strategy for digging information out of the man. I also had to discover what my herbs were meant to do and see if they might give me any clue as to what happened to the housekeeper. Time was running short, and I could already feel the book slipping through my fingers.

I had to do all that... and make certain Percy was creating the most stunning evening gown I'd ever worn so I could shove it up that woman's pointed nose.

10

A Good Poker Face

GWEN

"It smells terrible," Sally said as she sat on the edge of our bed with her nose wrinkled, holding the leather satchel as far away as her arms allowed.

"You aren't meant to smell it, dear. I think," I said, setting down the tray I'd called for after arriving back in our room, "you're meant to drink it."

"Like a tea?"

"Exactly."

She looked doubtfully from the teacup I was preparing to the crushed herbs. "But you don't even know what's in there."

"I know of a few of the herbs, but you are correct. I do not know what this will do."

"Then don't drink it," she pleaded when I took the bag from her and began measuring out enough for a teacup. "What if it is poison?"

"There are many uncertain things in this life, Sally. But I know that woman would not have given me anything that will harm me."

"How do you know?"

"I'm not entirely certain. And never try to use that excuse on me because I will not stand for it."

She snorted.

I poured hot water into the cup and stirred the leaves. While the tea steeped, I took off my shoes and plumped the pillows so I could relax and allow the herbal properties to take place safely.

"My lady—" Sally began, but I raised a hand and said, "There are many kinds of magic, Sally. The woman who gave me this has a soul as clear as a pane of glass. She couldn't have given me anything harmful if she tried."

She crossed her arms. "That sounds like a bunch of excuses that just mean, *I don't know.*"

"Maybe you'll believe this, then. I lost my twin sister when I was sixteen. She was... let us just say that I have not been whole since she disappeared. The best chance I have to bring her back is to find the housekeeper in exchange for the grimoire that will explain how to open a portal to the Sunset Lands."

"That's where the faeries live. Do you mean to say your sister went to the Sunset Lands?"

"Went," I said, "or was taken?"

Her face paled.

"We have always believed that the barrier separating mortal lands from the Sunset Lands was absolute. Impenetrable. But last year, we discovered it was not."

"During the ritual," she said, clasping her hands together as her mouth twisted in disgust.

"Yes. The old woman knew what I was looking for. She gave me this, so I plan to use it. Perhaps it will do nothing, but it may let me see what happened to Ms. Honeycutt. That is a chance I must take."

Sally looked down at her hands. She was turning into such a lovely, thoughtful woman, and likely asking herself to what lengths she would go if something were to happen to Sam.

She did not respond, but there was no need.

"Will you make certain Percy's next dress arrives if I am indisposed?"

Sally took a deep breath and nodded. "Of course."

"Good girl."

I picked up the teacup and sat on the bed. A rich, earthy aroma rose in steamy tendrils, bathing my face in moist warmth. I raised the cup and drank. Bitter warmth filled my mouth, but I didn't die. Despite what I told Sally, there was absolutely a chance the woman bewitched me, somehow. Her hut, alone, was enchanting. But that was a chance I must take.

I took another swallow. Sally eyed me intently, her feet crossed at the ankles beneath her skirt.

Despite the potential danger, I felt no guilt. Not for this. But I felt guilty that finding Ms. Honeycutt was a secondary concern to getting the book. I did not want to find her for her own sake. Which was wrong. She was a real person who deserved what help I could give, and yet...

I finished the tea and held the cup out to Sally.

As I lay there, wondering what to expect and when to expect it, my body grew heavy, as if putting down roots. Deep roots that reached the secret places of the earth. My branches began growing, shivering in ecstasy at the feeling of sunlight and tiny squirrel feet.

Leaves sprouted in a tingling rush, shades of silver-green that quivered in the slightest breeze. Another tree grew next to me, reaching out and wrapping its limbs with mine until we were entwined. Its golden leaves were heart-shaped, and whispered as the wind blew, telling tales of beetles and birds and the feel of rain on dry bark.

An impact, sharp and deep, made the both of us shake. The golden tree cried out, clinging to my branches with desperate pain. Another impact. And another. The squirrels ran from its branches to mine, and the birds flew away with cries of fright.

Sap ran from its bark as our joined branches broke. The golden tree shuddered. Color leached from its leaves, draining them till they were frail as old parchment. The color bled into my leaves, turning them from green and silver to gold.

It fell, tearing away my branches as well before it crashed to the ground.

I let go of my seeds in grief, and they floated over the dead tree, carried away into the air on a warm breeze over a vast forest stretching from horizon to horizon, dark with secrets and hidden life.

The sky grew dark, the horizon red. Fire along the borders of the forest. Other seeds floated there, released in a desperate attempt to safeguard the future as fire bit and gnawed and broke. Creatures fought beneath the smoke, small quick creatures with few limbs and sharp metal.

Everywhere they fought, life died.

Some creatures fled the battle, shimmering out of existence as my seeds fell to the smoldering ground, only to be covered in a layer of ash. The bodies of dead trees protected them until the rains fell again, and new life took root in soil watered with blood.

When I woke, Sally was leaning over me, both hands on my cheeks, eyes filled with worried tears.

"I'm okay," I told her and covered her hands with mine.

She let our hands stay there for a moment, then sat down, took a shaky breath, and patted her tears with a napkin from the tea things. I sat up, and all the guilt I hadn't truly felt before slammed into my chest with the force of a storm front. Sally was braver and kinder than I had any right to expect, and it wasn't fair to ask her to endure my choices.

"I won't do that to you again," I said, forcing the words out through the lump in my throat. "I promise."

When she raised her face, her eyes were clear and serious. "Don't."

I nodded.

She handed me a cup of water, and I drained it in a single, very unladylike gulp.

"What did you see?"

I considered whether to answer that. The vision had made little sense, and yet it felt deeply personal. Perhaps the meaning was locked away in a place I was not ready to examine. But Sally deserved an answer, so I explained the vision as she listened, eyes narrowed and hands clasped.

"Do you know what it means?" she asked.

"No. At least, not yet. Perhaps the meaning will come with time. That is the nature of some magic."

"It was magic, then?"

"Of a sort. Think on it, will you? Perhaps you are a bit more objective and will see things I cannot."

Sally nodded and furrowed her brow, staring down at her hands.

The last rays of sunset peeked through the window curtains, which meant it was time to begin preparations for dinner. How I might manage that with the hazy leftovers of a hallucination clinging to my brain remained to be seen.

I flexed my hands and sighed. "I take it the dress has not arrived?"

"Not yet, my lady."

"Stop with the honorifics, brat. I've learned my lesson. Shall we go trouble Percy for a gown?"

Her eyes brightened.

We set off to accost the man, only to run into him in the hallway. A paper-wrapped garment was draped over one arm, and the expression on his lovely face was part satisfaction, part harried genius.

The hall was empty, so I took Percy's arm and dragged him into our room.

"I do believe I have outdone myself," he said as soon as the door closed. Then he stopped, looked around our disheveled room, and said, "Lady St. James, you are... are... how can you live like this? What is all this mess? Where is my dress?"

"Calm down, mother, it is hanging safely right there. And it's no business of yours if I want to live like a magpie."

He ran one hand down the flawless front of his shirt and waistcoat, clearly disturbed, but reigned in his disgust at my untidiness and laid the dress across the bed.

"Now," he said, "you must understand something before I show you this dress. You are already seen as... eccentric. So I must take that and twist it into something fashion-forward, or they'll never believe it; not with a gown like this. I intend my boutique to carry only the most avant-garde fashions, in any case, so I will use you to establish the trend. This is not like any dress you have worn. Am I understood?"

I laughed. "Are you here to dress me or lecture me? You are the genius, I merely a clothing rack. I trust your judgment."

He smiled at me as if I was a very good girl for saying so, then peeled the paper back to reveal the dress. My mouth popped open and Sally made an *ooh* noise.

"Percy, I cannot wear that."

"You most certainly can."

"But—"

I stared at the gown and tried to imagine myself walking into the dining room wearing it. The skirt was full, and the bodice fitted, which was expected of an evening gown. Even the color, red of deepest claret, wasn't uncommon. But that is where the similarities to modern fashions ended.

The dress was, in fact, two dresses. A thick, lustrous velvet on the outer gown with delicate gold embroidery along the bell-shaped hem and neckline. Beneath was a chiffon so sheer it had to be layered for modesty. When the wearer moved, the chiffon underskirt would part and flutter in sections as the velvet train trailed behind, inviting the viewer to catch a peek of a leg that would never show.

And the bodice itself would be scandalous if it wasn't perfectly modest. Percy created the velvet outer dress to cut across the bust at an angle and form a drooping, off-the-shoulder strap on one side. Below the velvet, the chiffon underdress had been ruched and pinned as if to promise a glimpse of the skin beneath, if you saw it from the right angle.

The visual effect was sensual trickery; the dress appeared to only fully cover one breast and hinted that it might display my bare legs even though everything was safely covered. And the contrast of rich velvet to sheer silk with gold embroidery... I could not imagine myself in it.

"They can stare," Percy said. "They can talk. They can gossip. And you know they would do that even if you were a modest wallflower. But they cannot impugn you for wearing it. And dresses that convince people to talk will eventually convince them to buy. Besides"—he pushed my jaw closed with two fingers—"you want to charm information out of people, don't you? No one will be able to resist you in this."

I looked to Sally for help, but she was enthralled by the thing. Was I truly about to attend my first high society dinner in years wearing a beacon of sexual desire?

I flexed my hands, cracking the knuckles in a series of pops, and said, "I am holding you accountable for the outcome, Percy."

He held up the dress and said, "I will take full responsibility."

The last social event I attended was Mama's ball, and that affair was carefully controlled to include only those guests she was certain would not cause a spectacle.

This event was composed of the most influential members of fashionable society with no expectations or boundaries. I was on my own for the first time since destroying my engagement at nineteen; a situation I promised myself I would never again endure.

But I would, now.

For Lia.

Supper began at eight, but until then we would mingle, and I searched the room for any remotely friendly faces but saw none... because they were all staring at me askance. Eyes widened, mouths gaped, chattering ceased, and my cheeks went up in flames.

Damn, you, Percy.

Lady Chatsworth sailed toward me through the crowd, her expression placid, as if women in sinfully red dresses regularly appeared to seduce her guests. "Lady St. James, I am so glad you joined us," she said in a warm voice pitched to carry. "With your busy schedule, I was worried you might be pulled away. Let me steal you for a moment, you must tell me your designer!"

She linked arms with me and turned us away, then leaned in close as if she were convincing me to divulge all my secrets. "You certainly know how to make an entrance, Lady Gwen."

"I assure you, it is entirely the fault of my designer, Percival Bywater. He assured me I could wear nothing less than avant-garde for one of your soirees."

She raised both brows and said, "I am convinced you could not wear less, not without truly scandalizing the entire party. That is a convincing illusion."

"Shall I go change?"

"Of course not. The only thing to do now is to behave as if it is the height of fashion. They will believe it, and I miss my guess if twenty women are not wearing something similar—if less daring—next month. Any news?"

I peeked over my shoulder to be sure no one could hear us, and said, "Did you know Ms. Honeycutt was visiting the cunning woman in your woods?"

She stared at me blankly. "Who?"

"The woman who lives in the hut in your woods, between Chatsworth Estate and the village."

"There is no such hut. I have been through those woods countless times."

"What a strange thing, considering I visited her there this afternoon, and she told me Ms. Honeycutt had been there on more than one occasion."

Lady Frances frowned, her gaze dropping to the carpet as she thought. "She said nothing to me, and I have sensed no other magic workers."

"It isn't magic, not precisely, not in the—" I stopped, recollected where I was and who might overhear. "Not in the common way. No channeling of energy or commanding of forces. She understands the inherent magic in living things and... asks for their help, I suppose, is the best way to describe it."

"Yet she did not know where Ms. Honeycutt has gone?"

"No, though I have a few theories, and I intend to gather more information tonight."

She glanced around the room, lowered her voice, and said, "I suggest you hurry. If I must invite you to stay once the party is over, my reputation will certainly suffer and my usefulness to the sisterhood will be severely decreased."

"I understand."

So, she wasn't merely a witch, if any witch could be said to be merely anything, but also a political tool. That was good to know. We parted by mutual agreement, our conversation having done the dual duty of exchanging information *and* clarifying that I was here under Lady Chatsworth's sponsorship.

Sponsorship or not, that didn't stop several unaccompanied gentlemen from introducing themselves and wantonly staring at my décolletage. A few of them seemed genuinely interested in conversation, but I knew exactly what they wanted, and it wasn't my body.

I was the next Duchess of Wainwright, whenever I took up the title, and whoever married me would become one of the wealthiest men in the realm; as my one-time fiancé made painfully clear. Knowing that would have made them easy to dismiss even if they weren't shallow and deceitful.

Besides, I told myself as I crossed the room to the window, *it hasn't been so long since I've had a man in my bed that I'd settle for an aristocrat. I would proposition Tony before I stooped to*—I stopped that thought in its tracks and pinched my arm under my gloves. Where on earth had my mind gone?

It must be the damned dress.

When Percy made something, he didn't just make it beautiful or functional; he made it joyful to wear. It felt good to move in, to feel the silk rustle against my skin, the velvet brush the insides of my arms. Who knew simply wearing a dress could be an act of sensuality?

When dinner was announced I nearly jumped out of my skin, then realized, with dawning horror, that they would expect me to take my place in the line, which would enter the dining room according to rank. These people, who already despised me, would have to watch as I took my place at the front.

I raised my chin, threw my shoulders back, and sailed across the room with all the aplomb I could fake. They eyed me as I passed, and I pretended not to notice. I was technically a duchess, though I never formally accepted the responsibility of the station. That made me the highest-ranking person in this room, and they could not touch me.

Except they could. I felt every heated stare like a dagger in my back when I took my place just behind our hostess. The rest of the meal progressed in much the same way, and I forced myself to look happy and amused while listening for any hint of information I could use.

There was none in the vapid conversation. That made dinner both painful *and* useless. Escaping to the drawing room was a blessing, and the sight of Lady Ashcroft hurrying toward me afterward was a comparative relief.

"I regret we were seated at opposite sides of the table for dinner," she said, taking my arm familiarly. "You would not believe how dull the conversation was at my end."

"I would believe it," I assured her.

"Nothing but society gossip and politics," she continued. Her tone said this was a common complaint.

"Politics is not your preferred topic of dinner conversation?"

She laughed. "I live with a politician, remember?"

"How could I forget? He must have a lot to say lately, with all the contention around the legislation to admit elves and dwarves to the peerage."

"You cannot guess how much. When the topic was first introduced, Lord Ashcroft was in favor and even spoke of helping draft the legislation, but he has since changed stances. I cannot account for the change other than all the time he is forced to spend with Lord Rutledge on their subcommittee. That is a gentleman whose company I prefer to avoid, when possible."

"I am acquainted with the man."

"Then I suppose I need not say another word. And to be honest..."

One of the safest ways to encourage a person to talk is to ask them questions related to whatever topic they most enjoy complaining about. Lady Ashcroft complained happily for a quarter of an hour, and while I gleaned several interesting bits of information, none of it helped me get any closer to Mr. Capstone or the mysterious disappearance of the housekeeper.

Worse than that, I found that I actually liked the woman's quick mind and calm but humorous temper, which was a stupid thing to do when she was probably as carefully fishing for information as I was.

The men appeared, breaking up the comfortable groups of chatting women, and all of us trooped off to the game room to waste copious amounts of money gambling and drinking and smoking expensive cigars. All the while, the bored or lusty would sneak off to engage in secret trysts the rest of us would pretend to know nothing about.

A few people set about dancing while the rest of us formed card parties or smoked on the balcony in cliques that let everyone else know which powerful friendships were being formed and maintained. Lady Ashcroft escorted me to a table where her husband was already seated.

"Ah," he said, looking up at me with a handsome smile, "Lady St. James. I am glad you're joining us, after all. Have you ever played poker?"

"It's an American game," an elvin man butted in before I could answer. "It can be crude and abrupt but it's great fun." He leaned forward and said, "It's all about the bluff," and winked.

"I think I can muddle through," I said as I sat.

A servant began placing drinks and napkins at every setting.

"Lady Gwen, may I present the Honorable Mr. Jestin Slimfeather, head of the Sussex Artisan's Guild, and his wife, Lucilla."

The elvin couple and I exchanged bowed heads, and Lord Ashcroft continued, "We've changed the rules a bit to accommodate partner play. Rather than basing your bets on your own hand, you'll bet based on the cards from both hands and how you think they can be combined. The trick is"—he held up one finger—"you cannot confer with your partner. At least, not openly."

"That is the fun of it," Lady Ashcroft said as she brushed out her skirt. "You can see your partner's hand and try to communicate in suggestions or vagaries, but if the other players pick up on your cues, you will never be able to bluff them."

"So it's a more social version of the game," I said.

"Exactly."

"Unfortunately, I do not have a partner."

I turned to peruse the room, hoping to see a willing card player. Dwarven lamps glowed through the haze of cigar smoke, making each table a point of light in the intimate semi-darkness. Despite the laughter and general camaraderie, there was no one in this room who would willingly ruin their reputation to be paired with me.

"Lady Gwen. Seeing you again makes my heart burst with joy."

The sound of *that* voice, deep and resonant without being loud, felt like being wrapped in a cashmere blanket. I knew who it was without looking, and wasn't surprised when I turned to see him.

The stranger—*my* stranger—strolled toward us, long-limbed and confident, wearing darkness like a cloak. His finely carved mouth curved in a sardonic smile; his hair, just a little too long to be fashionable, curled in blue-black waves over his ears and the back of his collar. And his eyes (*god's breath,* those eyes) dark and wicked, raked from the hem of my dress to my eyes with lazy insolence, as if he had the right to look at me wherever he pleased and for as long as he pleased.

"I thought we established you do not have a heart, sir," I said as he took the place next to me. No one objected.

"Only because you're holding it in these lovely hands," he retorted before kissing my knuckles and smiling at me impishly.

I jerked my hand back, turned away from him, and found amused—or bemused—expressions on the faces of the other players.

He leaned toward me. "You refuse to ask how I do, even when we have not seen one another since that charming soirée at your mother's home."

I shot back in a furious whisper, "You are, of course, referring to the night you danced with me against my will, whispered a cryptic remark in my ear, left me holding a clue to a murder, and then disappeared without telling me your name, correct? Or has my memory failed me?"

He leaned down, his voice low and meant only for me, and said, "I knew you wouldn't forget."

The dealer ignored our verbal jousting and dealt with quick flicks of his wrist while I tried not to scowl at my partner, who leaned comfortably back in his chair where he could easily see my cards. Or he would have been able to if I hadn't kept them so close to my chest.

"I cannot help you win if you won't share your cards, *my lady*," he said.

The other teams were busily looking over one another's cards, though they couldn't talk about their hands and couldn't trade. I scrutinized their expressions instead of replying to my infuriating partner. If I said what I wanted to say, that would be the end of trying to fit in while I searched out clues for the missing Ms. Honeycutt.

Mr. Slimfeather maintained a calm expression, but his wife's cheeks were flushed. Lady Ashcroft's brows knitted together in thought, and Lord Ashcroft tapped his index finger on the side of his hand. I still hadn't looked at my partner's cards.

"Lord Ashcroft," the dealer said, "the betting begins with you."

We lost the first round to the Slimfeathers.

"How much are you willing to sacrifice to keep your secrets?" My partner asked. That his voice made goosebumps run up my spine and down my arms made me even more determined to keep my cards to myself. I could stand to lose money, especially if it meant costing *him* money.

And I doubted Lord Ashcroft would be particularly talkative if I emptied his pockets.

We lost the next hand to the Ashcrofts, despite Lord Ashcroft holding his breath over a fantastic hand.

"Don't you tire of hiding? We could win, if you were willing to share," my partner said.

The Slimfeathers won another round. I managed to control my competitive impulses quite impressively, hanging onto ruining my partner's night as a consolation, until Mr. Slimfeather said in a patronizing tone, "Don't worry, Lady St. James, the game isn't as easy as it looks. It might take you a few tries to understand it.

We won with three of a kind, you see, which is higher than Lord Ashcroft's pair of eights."

It did not matter whether he thought he was being kind. His tone was a match to the tinder of my temper, which was already desiccated from being suppressed for so long. I *was* sick of losing; sick of keeping quiet, of letting people say what they would to avoid confrontation and keep the peace.

And I was sick of pretending their words didn't matter, didn't hurt.

Anonymity wasn't a disguise I could wear anymore, so I could no longer justify silence as a key to peace, and in that moment I would rather have burned the game room down than lose another hand.

Jaw locked, I picked up my next hand and leaned back, so my partner and I could see one another's cards. He smiled slowly, lips curling in pleasure, but I ignored him. I had a pair of twos—diamonds and clubs—a jack of spades, a queen of hearts, and a ten of spades. He had the eight of clubs, a three of diamonds, a two of hearts, and a queen of spades.

The twos were a sure thing, but Slimfeather's wife was pink, again, and Lord Ashcroft's index finger tapped loudly against his cards. They both had good hands, to begin with. My partner tilted his head and raised one black brow; a question or a challenge, or both. I pulled the queen and both twos from my hand and tossed them on the table. He laughed, delighted, and tossed everything but his queen.

It was all or nothing, despite the slim chance of pulling the cards we needed in the only suit that mattered.

The dealer gathered our discards, tossed the new cards back at us, and the betting began.

11

Yellow-Eyed Strangers

SAM, THE PREVIOUS MORNING

When Sam fell off the back of the carriage, he was so tired that he didn't quite realize what had happened. One moment he clung to the luggage rail as the first faint traces of sunlight began stealing into the sky, and the next he was on the ground rolling bonelessly beneath a hedge.

It took a moment for him to register the impact of the fall. A small wheeze of pain escaped as he curled into a ball, listening to the rattling of carriage wheels, loud in the silence. Carriage wheels. If he let the vehicle get away, he didn't know how he'd find Lord Ashcroft again. What would the Cutthroat King do if Sam came back empty-handed? If he ever made it back at all.

He rolled onto his belly and watched the carriage bump down the country lane. Even if he could force himself to his feet, he'd never catch it. But the carriage slowed and turned toward a road sign that said *Chatsworth Village*.

Chatsworth. He could remember that.

Sam scooted painfully, wedging himself as far beneath the hedge as possible, and fell unconscious.

It was late afternoon when a passing cart woke Sam from his exhausted slumber. He pried his eyes open and yawned, sending the curious squirrel, who had been sniffing at his satchel, running for the closest tree. The beast scampered halfway up, then turned around and chittered at him reproachfully.

Sam edged out from beneath the hedge, grunting while his muscles screamed at him. He pushed himself into a sitting position and opened his satchel. The two remaining sweets were squashed against the inside of the pocket, plastered to the leather in a goopy pancake. When he fell that morning, he must have landed on top of them.

It had been a while since Sam felt genuine hunger, the hollow pain that stabbed your guts like a knife. He shamelessly pried the sticky mess off with his fingers and shoved the sweet gobbets into his mouth, then licked his fingers clean and took a sip from his canteen.

This time last year he would have rejoiced over such a breakfast, but he had no time to dwell on the past. Lord Ashcroft could be anywhere by now, and Chapman probably already discovered his absence, so Sam hauled himself to his feet and started walking the soreness out of his muscles.

Chatsworth Village looked like something one might see on a postcard, and the people were prosperous enough, but they kept a suspicious distance and glared at him as he passed through. He felt their eyes on him even when no one was around.

He was dirty and disheveled, and that certainly wouldn't get him any answers, so he made up a quick backstory, cleaned up his leaf-ridden hair in a window reflection, and strode into the dry goods store as if he owned it.

"Hello," he said brightly.

The elf woman behind the counter looked at him down the length of her slender nose. "Can I help you?"

"Sorry to be a bother, ma'am, but can you tell me if Lord Ashcroft has come through? I'm delivering a letter"—he held up the satchel and puffed his chest up, importantly—"but I don't know if I'm behind him or in front of him, whether I should wait or go on."

She considered him, taking in the quality of his clothes, and decided that boys will get dirty no matter who they worked for. "What does his coat of arms look like?"

"A flowering tree on a green shield," he said. He'd been plastered to the thing for the last eight hours, he should know.

"Hennie?" she called.

A dwarven lass appeared from the back room, her arms filled with empty sacks. "Ma'am?"

"Did a coach come this way bearing a green shield with a flowering tree upon it?"

"Yes, ma'am, early this morning as the sun rose. Went yonder to the big house for the great to-do, there."

The shopkeeper nodded, and the girl went back to her chores.

"There you have it," the woman said, but kept her eyes on Sam as if she expected something of him.

He shifted uneasily, then dug a sticky ha'penny from the depths of the satchel and bought a couple of peppermints. She ignored him after that, so he doffed his cap and hurried out the door.

High Street connected to the manor lane, separating the village into a T shape, with the stream on one side and the common buildings on the other. The manor sat by itself at the top of a gradual slope of lawns and gardens, with a forest off to the right. Ladies in dresses dotted the lawn like small white flowers, and servants with silver trays that flashed in the sunlight scurried between them.

He would never be able to sneak into the manor with so many people about, and the public house across the street, with a sign engraved *The Crooked Nag*, wouldn't open till the early evening. So, Sam decided to—what was the word Lady Gwen always used? Reckon-oiter?

He strolled around the village, trying to ignore the feeling that he was being watched by the suspicious townsfolk while he peeked in shop windows. Eventually, Sam found what he was looking for: a series of three vertical lines with a horizontal line along the top scratched into the doorpost of a tinker's shop that sat on the edge of town. It was a bit of Theives' Cant, a sign only people born into the right world understood.

Sam checked to see that no one was watching and slipped inside. Behind the counter, a small mouse of a man fiddled with a watch, staring hard at the gears through thick spectacles that made his eyes look huge.

"Be with you in a moment, young sir," he said.

Sam dug into his bag, fished out the silver coin, and dropped it onto the counter with a snap that made the small man look up from his task. His already pale face lost all color, and his mustache twitched as he stared at the coin.

"Wha—what does *he* want, here? I pay my dues, same as everyone."

Sam understood the fear. The King's Coin was a regular silver piece that was recast with the figure of the smiling man on the face. They were only given to people in the direct employ of the King, and no one wanted to be presented with one unexpectedly.

Sam picked up the coin and said, "If I give you messages, can you see they get sent back to town?"

The proprietor gave a jerky nod, fished a bit of sealing wax out from behind the counter, and passed Sam a pen and a piece of paper. He scribbled a note, sealed it, and pressed the face of the coin into the warm wax. When he pried it up, the little face with its slit throat and empty eyes stared back up at him in a silent scream.

He left without looking back, trusting the man's fear to see the job done. Now that Sam was in his employ, willingly or not, he was a dagger in the hand of the King, and the King had long arms.

He eased the door closed behind himself, feeling sick when the lock *snicked* into place, and every hair on his body stood up straight. Someone was watching him, and not just suspicious villagers. Hands casually in his pockets, Sam strolled away from the tinker's shop without a care in the world. At least, that's what he hoped the watcher saw. One didn't show weakness to predators, and he was certain in his guts that whoever watched him wasn't friendly.

Should he turn back into the village where there were at least people and buildings to hide in? A branch snapped. Sam spun as a shadow flashed across the road and disappeared into the trees. He squeezed his fists so tightly that the edges of the silver coin bit into his palm.

What was that? Peering into the shadow beneath the canopy, he could swear he saw something or someone move. Were those... eyes? Yellow eyes?

Sam wasn't stupid. He didn't intend to walk into the woods after a moving shadow, but he also couldn't stop himself. Without his permission, his feet tromped through last year's dead leaves, legs moving mechanically, carrying his body farther into the trees until the village disappeared.

Then the eyes came closer, floating in a field of darkness. Dreadful cold settled over him, dampening every thought and feeling. Somewhere, in the very back of his mind, Sam screamed and clawed at the invisible walls that stopped him from directing his own limbs.

Yellow filled his vision, drowning the world in a foggy haze that told him to let go, to stop fighting. But the voice did not stop screaming. Following an instinct deeper than thought, he reached up to push himself away from the eyes, and his hands came in contact with something cold and hard.

Screaming. His voice, and another screaming together, a sound so piercing that it rode the ragged edge of human hearing. Sam fell.

He ran. With every step, he came back to himself, waking up from a nightmare or floating to the surface of murky water.

Trees flashed by while the screaming continued, and Sam fled with every bit of strength in his sturdy legs. Where was the village? He needed to get back to people, back to houses.

The screaming stopped.

"Help!" Sam yelled, but it came out in a breathy gasp. The shadow chased him, pushing air before it like a breaking wave that caught at his heels, slowed his strides, pulled him inexorably backward.

"Help!" he screamed. He didn't want to die out here alone where no one would find his body. And then the Cutthroat King would come for Sally. Sam lowered his head and *ran*.

"Here!" a voice floated toward him. "Here, boy!"

A little cottage sat in the clearing, an old woman hanging out the half-open door with her wild hair caught in the breeze that dragged Sam backward.

"Keep running, boy! Don't stop!"

Fear crawled up the backs of his legs and sunk its claws into the base of his spine. The shadow was close. It was going to catch him. It was going to kill him. He opened his mouth and screamed as he ran, and he didn't stop screaming till he tripped over the threshold and the cottage door slammed shut behind him.

Something hit the door with a mighty thud, and the one-room building shook so hard that pieces of straw fell from the roof in a shower. He couldn't get his breath.

A voice, cold and high, said, "Let me in."

The old woman put her back to the door. "There is no place for you here."

A blast of wind, and then a man's face appeared at the open window: a yellow-eyed, grey-skinned face wreathed in a black hood. Despite that, it would have been a terribly compelling face, except the emblem of the Cutthroat King stared back at Sam from an angry red brand on his cheek, just as it had from the melted sealing wax. He tightened his fist around the coin.

"Open the door, old woman, and let me in," the man said, and the voice was sweet and pure and stinging, like a winter wind. The words were not directed at him, yet Sam wanted to open the door the same way he wanted to scream an insult at someone who hurt him.

"Close your eyes, boy," the old woman commanded. Her voice was warm and worn, like the earth or an oak tree, and he wanted to obey her voice the way he wanted food or air. The competing forces kept him still and trembling, but Sam closed his eyes. He wished he could close his ears.

"Open the door and I will give you pleasure you have never conceived of," the yellow-eyed man promised. "You will drown in my kiss, and my fingers in your guts will feel like warm spring rain. Make me wait, and you will watch as I tear out every slippery inch and eat them like freshly caught eels."

Sam trembled, hands clenched so hard his nails dug into his palms, but a warm hand settled on his shoulder. "He cannot come in," the old woman said. The promise would have been more reassuring if her hand hadn't been shaking.

"Give me the boy, and you may live. Is this not a fair offer?"

"There is no place for you, here."

The following silence was terrible. Sam's stomach climbed up to hide in his throat. The shadow would tear through the walls, jump through the window, and kill them both.

"Why protect him? When he dies, no one will mourn him. When *you* die, where will they go for help, old woman? Who will show them the ways? Who will listen to the earth for them? Give him to me and live to serve these wretched people another year. The boy is not worth your life."

"He is."

After a moment of silence, the shadow said, "Very well. I am patient."

And he was. He began walking slowly around the hut, his footfalls nearly soundless. Hours passed. Night threatened, and still, he walked.

The old woman looked at Sam for a long time, but he couldn't return her gaze. He hid his face in his knees. Finally, she turned to her table and began gathering herbs. The scent of spring rain and freshly baked bread filled the air, and a shiver ran down Sam's arms. It was a clean smell, one that seemed to clear the air of the little hut.

The sound of walking ceased.

Sam dared to climb to his feet. Was the shadow gone? Had it given up?

The ground shook and a mighty cracking sound split the air. He spun toward the window and saw, to his horror, that the shadow had only changed tactics. Instead of waiting for them to grow desperate, he found an axe somewhere and was chopping down the closest tree with mighty blows. Leaves rained down as the blade bit deep into the wood. When he was done, the ancient elm would fall... and crush the cottage.

"Come here, boy."

He turned frightened eyes on the old woman. She seemed smaller than before, as if her stuffing had been pulled out and left nothing but an empty sack. In one hand, she held a clay bowl filled with a pungent paste.

"Take off your clothes and cover every inch of your body with this."

He stared at the bowl, uncomprehending, and gestured to the window. "But he—"

"The tree will hold on as long as it can, but if we are in this hut when it falls, we will both die. Every protective herb I have is in this paste. It is the only chance I can give you. Go on, now." She pushed the bowl at him.

Sam swallowed and undressed until he stood shivering in his skivvies, then took a handful of the paste and smeared it across his chest. The old woman helped, covering his back, neck, and arms as he rubbed his face, chest, and legs. She stuffed all of his belongings into his satchel as a great, ripping crack split the air.

"When I open the door," she said, "put your feet on the path and run. Do not look back. Run until you reach the big house. Your lady is there. You will be safe."

Fear squeezed Sam's heart in its talons. "What about you?"

Her smile was warm and resigned, but not sad. She touched his cheek, and said, "You are worth it, Samuel Dawes." Then she jerked the door open, the trunk of the tree split, and she said, "Run!"

Sam took off, pelting down the path with tears streaming down his cheeks. The shadow could be right behind him, those yellow eyes mad and hungry, hands outstretched.

A flash of blue light lit up the darkening forest, followed by a scream and a blast of wind that ripped leaves from the trees and nearly took him off his feet, but Sam never stopped running.

12

Nursery Rhymes

GWEN

"I've never seen anything like it," Lady Ashcroft said again, squeezing my arm in excitement. "Neither of you spoke a word the entire game, but you won every hand. It was like magic. Edgar—Lord Ashcroft, I mean—has never lost so much, but I daresay he did not mind, for it was like watching a magic show!"

I tried not to shiver, remembering the feeling that my partner knew exactly what I was thinking during every hand. A blink, a smirk, a raised brow, or the shrug of a shoulder was enough for one of us to know what the other was thinking. It was almost like falling into the ocean and realizing you had only been a drop of water all along.

It hadn't discomforted me until now, when the game was over and I had time to remember it... that and his dark eyes touching my face, my neck, or my hands as he waited for me to pull a card.

But the game ended, the party broke up to endure, or enjoy, the other distractions, and my partner disappeared into the crowd before I could demand answers: like his name, how he was involved with the kidnappings and murders a year and a half ago, and how he had known to give me the necklace that tied everything to Lady Monmouth. Those things seemed like very important questions now, but at the time, I was too furious to even think of them.

"Forgive me," I said, "but do you happen to know my partner's name? I was so distracted I forgot to ask."

"Oh! Of course, it was... ah—I'm quite certain he said it was..." Her voice trailed off, brows drawn together, but then she laughed. "I am certain he introduced himself, but I cannot for the life of me remember. I must have had too much sherry already."

"Lady Ashcroft—"

"Edith," she interrupted, squeezing my arm again. "Please, you must call me Edith. I feel as if we are fast friends already and I know you are too kind to hurt my delicate feelings." She looked up at me, pouting from beneath ridiculously long lashes, and I could not stop myself from snorting with laughter.

"Then you must call me Gwen."

"My, my, if it isn't the new arbiter of fashion for the season!"

Lady Covington descended upon us, sneering. She was deep enough in her cups that she hadn't even bothered to hide her disdain behind a mask of civility as she tripped over the carpet while approaching us.

"Lady Covington," Edith said with the vocal equivalent of an eye roll. "How lovely of you to join us."

"Well, you did promise me a chance to examine this most *striking* gown," she said, making a wide gesture with her drink. Liquid sloshed over the lip of her cup and onto the floor.

"Fashion forward, don't you think? Even Lady Chatsworth said so," Edith noted, relying on the opinion of our hostess to cool her fervour.

"Lady Chatsworth is such a *generous* hostess. But of course, Lady St. James must want to show off the work of her designer, and who could blame her? The lines are so daring, they draw the eye of every man in the room. You had better keep Lord Ashcroft on a close leash," she finished with a cruel laugh.

Between intimate friends, it might have been a passable jest, but Edith's cheeks darkened with angry color, and despite her skill with verbal fencing, she was still a lady, born and bred. She was mortified at the suggestion.

And I may have been my mother's daughter, but I did not play by her rules, and seeing Edith's embarrassment made a little flame ignite in my chest.

"Surely Lady Covington, a woman as popular as you are, would not mind if a few eyes stray my way? If you are afraid the competition will make you less likely to snag a wealthy husband to rescue your impoverished estate, I can assure you, you are safe. I have no intention of marrying."

All the color drained from her face and she said, "How—" before she mastered her surprised anger enough to control her tongue.

"How did I know?" I asked as if she had been in earnest. "Well, my dear, you are rather telegraphing it. If I am not mistaken, you are wearing every piece of jewelry you own, and a gown two years out of fashion that has been poorly altered to be suitable for today's event. The stitching there, on your bust where the gown was lowered to display your assets, is loose. Aside from that"—I waved my hand—"you have been chasing every single man in the room all night long. One does not have to be a detective to see your plight."

Her face broke out in angry red splotches, and her hand curled so tightly around the stem of her glass that the fabric of her gloves creaked across her knuckles.

She leaned forward and hissed in a furious whisper, "I will not be insulted by a ruined woman who jealously murdered her own more beautiful sister and hid her body in the woods. No one said anything because you were the daughter of a duke. Thank the goddess your fiancé learned what a monster you truly are before he could marry you. You should be in prison, not attending parties with normal people!"

I staggered backward as if struck in the chest with a mallet.

People had created all kinds of stories to explain what happened to Lia; most of them involved a secret lover or a kidnapping. But this cruel interpretation sliced through my self-righteous anger like a thousand flying daggers, leaving bleeding holes in my gut.

As if I could ever have hurt my sister.

A red haze fell over my vision, making everything look flat and unreal. Both women backed away from me, their mouths popping open in surprise, their eyes round and panicked like cattle about to stampede. My skin burned and every muscle in my body coiled and tightened like a guitar string held at the breaking point. I would hurt her for suggesting such a vile thing. Make her scream for forgiveness. The next time she heard my name, her heart would shrivel with the memory of what I—

I was standing on the balcony with cool evening air against my heated skin. I blinked and the world slipped neatly back into multi-colored, three-dimensional normality. My throat was dry, and I swallowed painfully. How did I get here?

My mysterious card partner appeared at my side as if out of nowhere, and his mere proximity was enough to send all other thoughts flying from my head like frightened pigeons. "You really should learn to control your temper, my lady. It is bound to get you in trouble, someday. If I had not escorted you out of doors, you may have struck one of those poor women."

"I don't have a temper," I said, blankly. That was true, I didn't have a temper... at least, not one I ever had trouble controlling.

"You are a liar," he said, smiling indulgently at me as he leaned back against the railing on his elbows. Had I truly scared Edith away? Why couldn't I remember? That question would have to be answered another time because the mysterious stranger was eyeing me with sardonic amusement and my ire rose to meet that self-satisfied expression.

I focused on him as he stood completely at ease, looking like carnal sin in a suit. "Excuse me?"

"You. Are. A. Liar. Lady Gwen. You have a temper that could burn mountains to piles of smoking ash, you simply suppress it.

Suppress it often enough, for long enough, and the explosion will tear your world apart."

The amusement faded from his voice, and he looked at me with serious dark eyes, eyes like a starless sky you could fall into and keep falling forever. It was disconcerting, just like everything else about the man. Why was it so hard to keep my train of thought when he was near and looking at me like that?

"*I* am a liar?" I said, at last, unwilling to let him distract me. "And what of you, sir? A man who appears at parties uninvited and gives women clues to stop murders, then disappears into nothingness? Who are you if not a liar?"

"I have never lied to you," he said, his voice carefully neutral.

"Lies by omission are still lies."

"Are they? Are they really, Gwen? Think on that answer."

"I would prefer to think about why you refuse to tell me your name."

He smiled again, then stood and raised his arms to the side. "I never refused. I distracted you, instead."

I put my hands on my hips and glared at him, wishing desperately that I had my umbrella. He could use a good blast to the chest. "I require your name, sir, or I have nothing left to say to you and must ask you to leave."

His smile faded into something dangerous, his eyes steady. "And if I refuse?"

"Then I will make you leave."

One corner of his mouth twitched. "You prefer to attack me instead of thanking me for saving you. What has become of your manners?"

I blinked. He'd changed the subject and said something ridiculous. That was *my* trick. "Saved me? Do you have delusions of heroism as well as terrible manners?"

"I saved you from attacking that peacock of a woman," he said, gesturing toward the game room behind me.

"I don't need saving, sir. Please take your misplaced chivalry elsewhere."

He stood up and prowled toward me, head cocked to the side. "You are so quick to dismiss me, my lady."

The urge to run or hide flared up from somewhere deep in my mind, but I stood against it, refusing to back down. He was tall, lithe, too confident, too graceful. Dangerous. He stood close enough to feel the heat of his body and leaned down to whisper in my ear, "So quick to push away everyone who wants to help you. Why are you eager to stand alone?"

He walked around me, his scent sharp and wild, like an icy breeze across the moors before the first snow falls.

"And you *are* alone, my lady," he whispered into my other ear, making goosebumps run down my neck. "I mean to help you, again. Why not accept it?"

I wanted to spin and grab him by the lapels to demand answers. I also had the ridiculous impulse to kiss him into silence, and that mental image made my already dry throat clench around a nervous swallow. Neither of those courses of action was a good idea.

Instead, I said in a low, hoarse voice, "Exactly why do you think I need your help?"

"Because you have strayed into deep water where the monsters live. And I do not want to see you hurt."

The last was said as if it were dragged from his lips. I turned and stared up at him, but the light of the party was behind him, throwing his face into shadow so I could not read his expression. "Why?"

Silence dragged between us. He slowly, almost reverently, placed both hands on my bare shoulders, letting them hover for a moment before touching my skin. An electric shock ran across my chest and I sucked in a surprised breath. His thumbs slid along my collarbones, delicate as the brush of moth wings, and an unwilling but not unpleasant shiver ran down my spine.

With slow, deliberate pressure, he turned me until I faced away from him, the grey moonlit lawn stretching out in an unbroken line to the dark forest. His chest pressed against my bare upper back, and the ridiculous urge to lean against him made my breath catch.

"Why would I help you? Because you deserve it," he said against my neck. The heat of his breath made my skin prickle deliciously. What was wrong with me? It was as if my body had severed all ties with my brain and decided that we were going to indulge in the things this stranger made us feel, even though I wanted to punch his infuriating face.

Then he hummed a tune, one that felt as familiar as any nursery rhyme, vibrating through his chest and against my back. Words appeared in my mind, but I could not tell if I was remembering them from some long-lost song, or if he whispered them into my ear. They swirled around me in beckoning curls and eddies, caught me in their spell, and dragged my mind away from my body.

You cannot see their faces
though under moon they ride
through glen and downy heather
'cross moor and mountainside.

My child, beware the Reavers
when moon is full and bright
if you see the shadows riding
venture not into the night

Their horses never tire
you cannot run or hide
they will catch and fetch you
Back to the other side

My child, beware the Reavers
when moon is full and bright
if you see the shadows riding
Venture not into the night

No glamor, rune, or magic
Will help you turn the tide
stay safe by fire and circle stone
when the Reavers ride

When the music stopped, I fell slowly back to myself, leaving behind visions of riders in the moonlight. Two men stood in intimate conversation on the lawn, standing at the edge of the window light. I might have thought they were lovers except the one facing the manor was Lord Ashcroft and the other wore familiar dark clothing that hung in folds, torn at the edges, with a hood covering his head.

I turned and ran for the stairs, barely registering that my card partner had gone.

The balcony was on the second story, with curving stairs on either side leading down to the lawn. Holding the skirt up, I took the stairs two at a time, my blood racing hot in my veins even as my skin was cold with dread.

Edith's husband was meeting with the dark figure who fired a gun at me not eight hours ago.

"Lord Ashcroft!" I yelled as my feet touched the grass.

He stood alone, unmoving, and my heart somersaulted. He was alive. Where had the figure in black gone? I was certain I saw him but... could that have been a figment of my imagination, a bit left behind from the nursery rhyme about Reavers?

Lord Ashcroft hadn't turned at my call, only stood staring at the house with a blank expression.

"Lord Ashcroft," I said, coming to a stop in front of him. "Are you well?"

He stared past me as if I weren't there.

"My lord," I said, patting his cheek.

No response. I had been wrong. His face wasn't blank; it was slack in a kind of post-ecstasy relief. After a moment, he wobbled, a tree in a strong breeze, swaying to a song I couldn't hear. Was it the moonlight, or were his cheeks pale?

"Edgar!" I yelled and slapped him.

His face snapped to the side, he stumbled, then righted himself and shook his head. "What?"

"Lord Ashcroft, are you well?"

The man blinked, adjusted his collar and cravat, and his eyes regained their former cleverness. "Lady St. James? What are you doing out here?"

"I saw you on the lawn. I thought you might need help."

"Help? From what?"

"From the man accosting you. Who was he?"

"Man?" he said, laughing. "What man? I simply came out to enjoy the weather and a respite from the madness inside. Have you had too much to drink, lady? Shall I call a servant to see you back to your room?"

I stared at him blankly. The dark figure *had* been there with him, standing incredibly close, as if whispering. I examined his face for the telltale signs of lying I learned from Tony, but his expression was clear and guileless. I wanted to shout at him, hit him on the head to jog his memory, but hysterics like that would only confirm what these people already believed about me... if my insulting Lady Covington hadn't already done the trick.

"Yes," I said as defeat settled heavily on my shoulders. "I would like to go back to my room."

"Allow me," he said and took my arm.

I let him lead me up the stairs as I tried to understand what I had seen and why Lord Ashcroft didn't remember it. The figure was now tied to both the rioting in New London and to a weekend party in the country. Who was he, and why was he here?

"Edgar?"

I looked up at Edith's voice to realize we stood on the balcony, Lord Ashcroft and I, and Lady Ashcroft stood in the doorway, her face balancing somewhere between surprise and pained disappointment.

I opened my mouth but Lord Ashcroft said, "Lady St. James is indisposed. Let us call someone to take her back to her room."

Edith's face was like a breaking dam doing its best to stop the cracks from allowing water to leak through. "Of course," she said, glancing between her husband and me.

I wanted to assure her that nothing happened between us, but after Lady Covington's cruel insinuation, it would only sound like guilt.

"Lady St. James," a breathless servant said from the balcony doors. "Your companion has sent for you. She said it was urgent but declined to explain. Forgive me for being so forward, but she was crying."

Dread skittered down my spine with sharp-clawed feet.

What happened to my girl?

13

The White Tree

GWEN

I picked up my skirt and sprinted down the hallways, trying not to create catastrophic scenarios in my mind. If Sally needed me desperately, she would find me on her own, propriety be damned. Wouldn't she?

I skidded to a stop and jerked open the door to our room, *what's wrong* on the tip of my tongue, only to see Sally sitting on the floor in front of the heater with a nearly naked young boy lying in her arms.

"Sam?" I breathed.

Then my wits returned, and I closed the door.

Sally wiped tears away with the heel of one hand and said, "I went for a walk after dinner; this room feels small, after a while. And I heard someone crying. Sam came stumbling out of the woods with this all over him."

She smeared one finger down his arm and showed me a green-ish paste. His small body was covered in the stuff, and half of it had rubbed off on Sally's dress where he lay across her lap. The rest was on a rag Sally must have used to clean his face, lying forgotten on the floor.

I knelt next to them, heart pounding. Sam was unconscious but breathing, and the paste, some kind of ointment or salve, filled the room with a fresh, clean scent.

"How did he get here?" I said.

"I snuck him in," Sally admitted. "I didn't know what else to do."

"No, darling, you did exactly as you should. I meant, how did he get here, so far in the country?"

She said, "I don't know. He could barely breathe and he was crying and then he just..." She shrugged, shaking her head, silent tears trailing down her cheeks. The hope in her eyes was the kind that cuts you just to see it, the kind that is hanging from the edge of panic by bloody fingernails. "Will he be okay?"

"Of course," I said, using my best soothing voice. But, in truth, I had no idea. And not knowing was terrifying.

We finished cleaning him up, transferred him to the bed, and wrapped him in warm blankets before I called for tea. One benefit of attending a weekend party is that the guests stay up very late and the staff are on call. So, while I would never dream of waking Charlotte or Mrs. Chapman for something so simple as tea and sandwiches, everyone in the manor was already awake and prepared.

When the tea arrived, I added a good deal of sugar and coaxed Sam to drink a bit. He swallowed the first mouthful, coughed on the second, and then sat up and out of my arms, his eyes wide with terror.

"Run!" he tried to scream, but it came out in a hoarse whisper.

"Sam," Sally and I said together, "Sammy, it's okay. You're safe. Shhhh."

His eyes, so wide the whites shone, flashed around the room as if terrors were hiding in every shadow. It took several moments to calm him, and once he was calm, he drank nearly all the tea and ate every sandwich.

Once he was recovered enough to speak, I mimicked Mama's tone of voice, and said, "Samuel, what happened?"

I wanted to know how he came to be here, but that question was much less important than finding out why he was mostly naked, smeared with a salve, and wandering in the Chatsworth woods.

His lip trembled, but he clenched his jaw and said, "There was a monster, Lady Gwen. I know that sounds crazy, but... it was like a man, with yellow eyes. It chased me, but I hid in this hut with an old lady. It chopped down a tree to fall on the house, so she rubbed this paste on me and made me run. She said—" His voice broke.

Sally made a distressed noise and wrapped her arms around him.

"She said to run to the house, and don't stop running, and don't look back."

It must have been the woman in the wood.

"What did the monster look like, Sam?"

"It... it was..." He started shaking, hands clenched into fists in the blanket as his eyes searched for words he didn't seem to have. "I can't remember. It was like a shadow, but I can't—it's like reaching down into a pond to pull up a frog only it slips through your fingers before you see it. I can *feel* the memory, but it's just not there."

"That's all right, Sam. It's not your fault. Can you remember anything else? Anything at all?"

He closed his eyes, and tears slipped down from beneath his pale lashes. "Just that he wanted me, and he wanted to come in, but she wouldn't let him. She saved my life."

He turned and curled into Sally, wrapping his arms around her waist and burying his face against her neck. She looked at me over the top of his head, worry and relief mingled on her face, and a question in her eyes.

Was I going to investigate what happened?

I stripped out of my evening gown, dressed in more suitable clothing, buttoned my jacket, tucked the pistol I recovered earlier that day into my pocket and grabbed my umbrella.

Tony appeared in the window after the seventh pebble struck the glass with a little *ping*. He stepped onto the road only minutes later, his blonde hair mussed and nearly white in the moonlight.

"What is it?" he asked, voice rough from sleep and, I had to admit, rather appealing.

"Sam was attacked in the woods, and I'm worried about the old woman who lives there."

"Sam? Wait. How—"

"No time," I said, grabbing his wrist and dragging him off into the dark.

I explained Sam's story, and my own, as quickly as I could while Tony scanned the ground with the beam of light from the torch I gave him. At least one of us was prepared.

Then again, I hadn't wanted to waste time fetching Tony in the first place and only jogged to his rooms because I promised Sally before leaving the house that I would warn him. So, I could be excused from forgetting that I did not, in fact, have night vision. What I did have was a friend with common sense who was probably also a better marksman than I.

The beam of light was steadier than any torch or lantern light would have been and picked out the path easily from amongst the undergrowth. It absolutely destroyed our night vision, but without it, we would have only seen shifting shadows under the canopy, full moon or not.

Now and then our passage disturbed the pixies, who floated out of their leafy bowers and flickered irritably. Their pale green glow added to the torchlight, and since my imagination was already primed to look for monsters, I was more than grateful for the extra illumination.

Before long, Sam's footprints appeared in the dirt. We followed them, noting where they stopped, turned, disappeared, and then reappeared a few steps later as if he'd either jumped or been picked up. An icy chunk of dread lodged itself in my throat when Sam's stride lengthened, his footprints digging into the path at the toes and leaving flicks of dirt behind.

"He was terrified," I whispered, touching a print and imagining him running headlong through the wood.

Tony spun the flashlight, but no yellow eyes reflected the light back at us, and the crickets and night birds continued to sing happily. That was a good sign. Animals know when dangerous creatures are about, and monsters affect them more significantly than mundane predators.

"You said the old woman's hut was on this path?" Tony asked as we continued.

"Yes, but I came at it from the other side this afternoon, so I'm uncertain if—"

The words died in my throat as Tony's light raked across the wreckage. A great elm tree had toppled directly onto the center of the hut, blowing the building apart. Stones, broken pieces of clay pottery, branches, and chunks of wall lay scattered as far as fifty feet from the original structure. Crumbling pieces of wattle and daub jutted up from either side of the tree trunk, the only proof a warm little home had once existed here.

"Look at the trees," Tony said. He turned and shone the light on the other, smaller trees that ringed the clearing. They were bare, naked to the stars, as if each leaf had been plucked.

We inched closer and followed the trunk back to the stump, where the blade of a long-handled axe was sunk into the wood. There were deep, finger-shaped indentions in the wood of the handle. I ran my finger across the marks and looked up at Tony, eyes wide. Axe handles were hardened, oiled, and primed for rough use. The strength required to damage the wood with one's hands was worrying.

Tony shone his light along the length of the tree, and white hair glowed like a beacon from where the old woman lay, propped against the trunk. I tried to tell myself that, even if I ran straight here without stopping, I would have been too late, but I couldn't quite force myself to believe it.

My stomach tried to climb out of my throat and empty itself on the ground.

I must have made a sound of distress because Tony stepped between me and the body and pulled me against his chest, one hand on the back of my neck and the other across my lower back.

"Don't look," he said roughly.

But it was too late. The image of the sweet old woman with her guts in her hands and her throat ripped out was burned onto the backs of my eyelids. I had seen death more often than most; the bodies of people killed by animals, and savaged by werewolves, but those were the results of hunger or wanton violence.

This had been purposeful pain and cruelty. Whoever killed her positioned her body in such a way that anyone who found her would know it.

I let Tony hold me for a moment and tried to pull his warmth into myself so I could use it as a shield.

"You don't have to do this," he said when I straightened.

I touched his cheek, then stepped around him to examine the scene and learn what I could. Wind destroyed most of the tracks but it was clear the old woman fought. Her footprints were firm, dug in, and in some places moved in surprising patterns, like the katas used by martial artists. The footprints of her attacker hardly touched the ground, with greater distance between them, as if he moved fast and light.

At some point, he picked her up, and around her final resting place, there were no prints at all. I suspected that if I examined her back, I would find it broken from where she struck the tree when he discarded her.

No blood on the ground despite her wounds, which were disturbingly precise. This hadn't been the work of a hungry, savage animal; it was purposeful. And it had hurt.

My eyes filled with tears, making the whole scene blur, and my stomach cramped with the need to scream. She had been kind and generous, and that was true magic in such a selfish world. I fell to my knees next to her, brushed the hair out of her face, and took her hand in mine. Her expression was surprisingly peaceful, a wrenching contrast to the way she died.

"If anyone has ever found peace," I whispered and kissed the back of her hand, "I pray it is you."

I placed her hand on her chest, but her fingers were curled around something: a long, white tooth that pressed against the center of her palm. She had grasped it so tightly the tooth punctured her skin, leaving it sitting in a little pool of blood. I looked up, around the clearing and the chaos, and remembered the peace I felt when I first stumbled upon this place.

I took the tooth, still wet with her blood, and began digging with my bare hands.

"Gwen?"

I didn't answer, just dug until I had a nice, deep hole in which to bury the tooth. Why? She had wanted me to. I couldn't say how, but I knew it in my bones.

"Gwen, I've got to report this," Tony said.

"And say what?" I said, tiredly, as I dropped the tooth into the hole and scraped the dirt back in to fill it. "That a vampire killed an old witch in the forest?"

"A—vampire?"

I pushed myself to my feet and brushed the dirt from my knees. "Do you have a better way to read these clues? Sam said it was a monster who looked like a man, who wanted to get into the house but could not, with the strength to dent an axe handle and the speed to... well, you see it with your own eyes."

"I—there hasn't even been a vampire sighting in the whole of England and Scotland for more than fifty years."

"I could be wrong," I allowed, "but I cannot think of another way to understand the evidence. Is Scotland Yard prepared to hunt a vampire?"

"We have procedures," he said the words slowly, as one does if someone asks whether one can ride a bike one has not touched since youth.

They might have procedures, but no one practiced them in so long that they may as well not have any. That wouldn't have stopped Tony. He had thrown himself at a powerful witch without a second thought. Perhaps I could convince him from another, more personal angle.

"If you report this," I said, "the manor will be crawling with police within days, and whatever chance I have to find Ms. Honeycutt will be trampled beneath their boots, and with it, any hope I have to find my sister."

"This is my job, Gwen. A woman has been murdered, and it is my duty to bring her killer to justice."

"Do you truly believe you can stop the creature that did this?" I demanded, flinging my arms wide.

"It doesn't matter whether I can or not. I swore an oath and I have to try. You know this. Don't ask me to forsake it."

He was right, and yet I felt my only chance of reaching Lia, after years of study and searching, slipping through my fingers like so much water. It made me want to scream, to beg, to offer anything.

"I have to find her, Tony. I have to. I *have* to. Please, at least give me a couple of days."

"Gwen, I..." His voice trailed off.

I waited, but his eyes were glassy. "What?"

"Gwen, look!" He pointed, and I turned.

While we were speaking, something began growing. A white tree sprung up, stretching its limbs under the moonlight, silvery leaves quivering ecstatically, like falling snowflakes. The roots crawled snakelike across the ground, twisting and curling, and then diving into the earth. One root curled about, as if searching, then wound itself around the body of the old woman. It began pulling her backward, toward the trunk.

Tony jerked as if to stop it, but I grabbed his wrist. It towed the woman until her back was pressed against the smooth bark of the trunk, now already several feet wide. The tree groaned and began to flow around her, pulling her into itself a bit at a time, until finally closing over her peaceful face.

When it was done growing, the tree looked centuries old. There was no sign that a woman had been murdered there.

"I suppose that decides the matter," I said, staring up at the branches in awe.

"What?"

"Well, you cannot very well report the murder, now. There is no woman left."

Tony's jaw clenched, and his hands balled into fists. I touched his arm, sympathetic even in my relief that hope remained for finding Lia.

The clearing was now peaceful, despite the wreckage. One of the wise women died here, and this place had become holy, consecrated by blood spilled in the defense of the innocent. She sacrificed her life to save Sam, died a valiant death in pain and torment, and no one but the tree would ever know it.

"We can still find justice for her," I said, my voice hard.

Most of the guests already found their beds, or the beds of a lover, by the time we reached the house. A few determined gamblers were still at cards, but they were not interested in us as we strode through the room.

I found the nearest server and tried not to intimidate her with my expression, but I was so angry it was difficult to control my features or my voice. "Bring me to Lady Chatsworth, please."

Her eyes darted around the room as if looking for an escape route, but there was no one to rescue her, so she eventually curtsied and led us out of the game room. We found Frances in conversation with the butler just outside the butler's pantry, giving instructions for the next day's events.

"Lady Gwen," she squeaked in surprise, then shot a dirty look at the serving girl.

"Don't blame the girl," I said, a warning in my voice I didn't bother to hide. "I would have found you without her, but the process would have been much louder."

She dismissed the servants, said, "Come with me," and led us to her husband's study, where she closed the door and turned on the lamps with a touch. The room filled with a warm, steady glow.

She positioned herself behind the oak desk and folded her hands neatly in front of her, the picture of feminine perfection, and said, "I assume you have found something."

"A dead old woman with her guts ripped out," I said, savagely.

She flinched, one hand on her chest and the other covering her mouth. "What?"

"Something killed the old woman who lived in your woods, Frances. The people in the village are terrified to speak to me, and, to be quite honest, the facts do not match the story you've told me about Ms. Honeycutt. So, if you truly want her found, I suggest you tell me the truth, and you do it now. Otherwise, the inspector will report her death to Scotland Yard and I will be gone in the morning."

"I will have a dozen men searching your grounds within a day, my lady," Tony said, his voice flat.

Several emotions crossed her face, chasing one another like clouds across the sun. She didn't want to explain any more than she already had, but the idea of murder and an investigation, during her husband's birthday celebrations, no less, was too much for her constitution.

She took a deep breath, let it out slowly, and sat behind the desk. "Very well. Please, sit. You may as well be comfortable because this will not be easy to believe."

Tony looked at me from the corner of his eyes, then sat on a chaise near the cold hearth with his jaw set and nostrils flared. But so much angry, frenetic energy bounced around inside me so violently that I could only pace back and forth as Frances worked up the courage to speak.

She sat with her back straight, hands folded on the desk, and said, "Ms. Honeycutt technically came to work for me over five years ago. I say technically because she has, in fact, been working for my husband's family for so long that she is obliged to change her name and appearance every generation or so."

Tony sat forward and asked, "How can that be?"

Frances folded her hands. "Because Ms. Honeycutt is not human. She is a faerie."

14

The Truth About Faeries

GWEN

I stopped pacing and spun toward the desk so fast it made me dizzy. "Say that again."

"You may believe, Lady Gwen, as we all did, that the wall has separated faeries and mortals since shortly after the Great War. That there is no traffic between the mortal lands and the Sunset Lands. We thought the wall an impenetrable barrier..."

She let the thought hang in the air, and though her voice was soft, the truth struck like a thunderclap. I said, "But it is not."

Frances shook her head. "No. In fact, from what I gather, it is less like a wall and more like a net. That is a deeply imperfect metaphor"—she waved the thought away impatiently—"but it is perhaps the only one that might make sense."

"Explain," Tony said. His voice was unnervingly calm.

"To catch something in a net, it must be bigger than the holes, or weaker than the fiber the net is made of. But small things, and very strong things, might pass through. Either by slipping through the holes or breaking the net. And, of course, one must find the holes in order to pass through them."

"If that were the case, we should be overrun," I said.

She held up her hands. "I said it was an imperfect metaphor. I don't believe Thistle—that is, Ms. Honeycutt, could explain it in simple enough terms for me to understand, fully. Wait a moment."

Frances sat in thought for a long time, fingers steepled. Just as my patience was beginning to wear thin, she snapped and said, "The thinning of the veil!"

"What is that?" Tony demanded, brows drawn together. He was a bit out of his depth and irritated about it.

"Have you ever heard it said that there are certain days of the year or times when this world and the spirit world pass close to one another?"

"Such as Samhain?"

"Yes," Frances said. "People often say the same of locations, holy places, and so on. It's not a fairy story or a myth. As far as we can discover, those places and times warp the magic that holds the wall together, making rifts large enough for some faeries to squeeze through."

Tony said slowly, "As if I took hold of the net string and pulled the hole open."

"Something like it," she confirmed.

"What happens to the ones who don't make it through?"

She shrugged and shook her head in mute ignorance.

So, fae that met some criteria we did not understand could, during some times and at some places, cross the wall that separated the Sunset Lands from the mortal world. That must have been how they stole my sister.

"And Ms. Honeycutt was one of them," I said.

"Yes."

"So, faeries must look like humans, after all, if they can hide among us," Tony said.

Frances laughed. "No. At least, we cannot say for certain. Glamor is part of their magic, and so we only see what they choose to show us, but Ms. Honeycutt said the fae are as varied as humans, elves, and dwarves in appearance. What that means in practical terms? Who knows?"

The implications were so monumental that I took a seat, at last, to give my mind a chance to work without also trying to keep me upright. I searched literally half the world to find a way to reach across the wall, and the fae had been doing it for what? Centuries? Why? By all accounts, the Sunset Lands were created especially for them, as a kind of haven. Magic ran through their veins as surely as blood ran through mine, magic that would warp humans without some kind of...

"Frances," I said slowly, pulling on the threads that tied what she told us to the current situation and coming to an uncomfortable conclusion. "Why should it matter to you whether Ms. Honeycutt is fae?"

Of course, it mattered very much, and for many reasons, but if she confirmed my suspicion... Well, it would change the entire landscape of what we understood about magic.

Frances raised her chin, her pretty face set in lines of indecision. I doubted she had clear guidance from the leader of her coven on how to deal with this matter, and so could not decide how to move forward.

"Madame Matilda hired me to help you find the woman. Clearly, she thought it important enough to risk my knowing."

"Yes," she said. "Yes, quite right. Very well. Thistle, Ms. Honeycutt, agreed to lend us her magic. In short, to become a kind of magical focus for our spells."

"In return for what?"

I tried to ask the question without passion, but my anger was bubbling happily along below the surface, and she noticed the quiet menace in my voice.

"I don't believe that is germane to your investigation."

"How do you know what is germane and what is not? You were not aware of the cunning woman in your woods, and now she is dead, torn open by some kind of monster. Your villagers are terrified and whisper of black riders. And your fae housekeeper is missing. People are dying, Frances, and Madame Matilda hired me to deal with it. I will be the judge of what is germane."

Somehow, between beginning my speech and ending it, I had crossed the room and stood with my hands on her desk, staring down at her with all the fury I felt for the murder of the old woman and the torment of *my* Sam burning in my eyes.

She leaned back and away from me, and Tony put a hand on my shoulder.

"In return," Frances said, her voice unsteady, "she lives here quietly and safely, under our protection."

I snorted and spun away from the desk and Tony's hand. "Protection, indeed." Then a thought occurred to me. "How long have the villagers complained of black riders?"

She blinked. "Somewhere near a month, I suppose."

The black riders, the figure in black, the monster who killed the old woman... they were likely all the same. And Ms. Honeycutt had stood near the window one night, completing her final task of the day. Did she look out and see the figure in black on the lawn? Perhaps it scared her so much that she fled. That would mean she knew what it was... knew enough to be afraid.

I allowed myself a moment to calm down, to think rationally, and said, "Lady Chatsworth. If you would like me to find Ms. Honeycutt, do not keep any other information from me. If another person dies because you have not shared knowledge with me, I will consider you responsible. Do you understand?"

Her face paled. She was a member of a coven precisely because doing magic on her own would slowly break and twist her body, causing strange, magical deformities that nature could not explain. It was difficult not to remember Cassandra Monmouth standing with her arms raised as the magic sucked the life from her body, leaving only a dried-out husk.

Frances was cautious, not power-hungry. She was not as ruthless as I was willing to be, and she knew it. I would not dare take the same tack with Madame Matilda. That woman was more spider than flower.

"I understand," she said.

"I will maintain our ruse to protect your coven, but I expect you to protect your people by every means necessary."

She nodded shakily.

I left without another word, and Tony followed. We were halfway down the hallway when he said, "Has anyone ever told you you're rather scary when you're angry, Lady St. James?"

"Why would anyone tell me such patently false drivel, Inspector?" I replied, trying to sound lighthearted. "*I* am supposed to be the source of nonsense in this relationship."

"Perhaps because it's true."

I glared at him.

"There," he said, pointing at me. "You see? Terrifying."

"Oh yes, I can see how much I scare you every time you fight with me or tell me not to do something."

"Someone has to be the voice of reason."

"Who appointed you?"

"I suppose I did."

"Was this before I made a habit of scaring you, or after?"

"Gwen," he said, "you have scared me every day from the moment I met you."

I stopped. "Really? Why?"

He watched me intently, his brown eyes warm, hair mussed from our late-night escapades, and lack of sleep, but his expression was deadly serious. "Because you seem to have no concern for your own welfare. Because you have a habit of saying what you shouldn't say to people to whom you should not say it. And because I'm afraid of what I might do if you get hurt."

For a moment, we stood, staring at one another. I was caught between the desire to explain myself or to throw myself into his arms for being one of the few people in the world who cared.

I settled on saying, "I've spent the entire day in a series of painful situations. For the last two hours, I haven't been able to blink away the vision of the old woman lying in the dirt or stop imagining what would have happened to Sam if she hadn't protected him. The guilt of feeling... grateful. Grateful that it was her and not him. It makes me angry. I can't help it."

"Any parent would feel the same."

Something warm blossomed inside me at those words, but I quickly squashed it. I never desired parenthood, and having the title applied to me felt wrong. "I am not a parent. And you do not understand what she was, how special she was. The world lost something dreadfully important when she died."

"You are a parent. In the only way that matters, you are."

"Stop trying to make me feel better!" I shouted.

And then I was kissing him. I threw myself at him, wrapped my arms round his neck, and plastered my mouth to his with desperate need, my heart wild as a caged animal in my chest. He stiffened, shocked by my onslaught. But then his hands slipped around my waist, and he kissed me back.

His lips were soft, his hands gentle, but I didn't want gentle. I wanted him to crush me against the wall, to bruise my mouth with his, to make me feel something, *anything* but the helpless anger I couldn't seem to quench.

"Gwen," he said against my mouth, but I ignored him and bit his lip, begging him with my body for anything but tenderness. I pushed him against the wall, tearing at the buttons on his jacket, but he was stronger than me.

He held my face between his hands, held me away from him until I stilled. I could only stare helplessly up at him, my body shaking with unspent energy. He wiped my cheeks with his thumbs, brushing away tears I hadn't realized were falling, and said, "I will not hurt you, Gwen. Even if you want me to. You don't deserve it, and I... I *can't*."

I stumbled backward out of his reach, chest heaving, glaring at him through my tears. His lips were swollen, his eyes hurt and sad. I turned and fled.

There were still bottles of champagne in the game room, though the tables were empty and the servants were busy cleaning. I swiped one and drank from the bottle as I stumbled blindly onto the balcony, letting the night air cool the heat beneath my skin.

Tony didn't understand. How could he call me a parent when the children I was responsible for cried themselves to sleep a hundred miles away from their own beds? When Sam was nearly killed? I didn't deserve that title any more than I deserved to be free of the guilt I felt for knowing there was a monster in the woods and doing nothing to either protect or warn the woman who lived there. My concern was maintaining my cover so I could get my hands on a book that had been outlawed for centuries.

I was selfish, and an innocent woman died for it.

I deserved that guilt, and even Tony with all his kindness and warm kisses could not absolve me of it. The wise woman had been something special, something rare. She spoke the language of the earth as though she had roots and leaves of her own. The earth trusted her, protected her, so she could protect others, and she did it without expectation or pay. Now she was gone. My fault.

I tipped back the bottle for another drink, but it was empty. Why was it empty? I shook it, hoping to dislodge the rest.

"That bottle seems to be empty," a man said rather unhelpfully as he sat down next to me on the stairs.

I narrowed my eyes, trying to make him stop moving, and said, "*You.*"

"Alas, it is I. Come to ruin the one-woman party you are throwing. Has it been fun?"

"Go to hell."

My one-time card partner threw his dark head back and laughed. "You are charming, my lady. Quite my favorite person."

"You aren't mine."

"No?" He raised one sardonic brow. "That's a pity. I suppose you have saved that distinction for the handsome inspector?"

"Tony?" I set the bottle down with a clink, and he caught it before it could tip off the edge, placing it on the step farthest from me. "Tony won't take me to bed."

"Then he is a fool."

I sighed, unable to be uncharitable, even while drunk, even while talking to a dark stranger I would rather slap than share secrets with. "No, he's right. It wouldn't be fair."

"Why on earth not?"

I plopped my chin into my hands. "Because I could never give him what he wants."

"And what's that?"

"A wife. A home. A neat little relationship that fits into a box and makes him the protector."

He snorted. "Has he told you this? How do you know that's what he wants?"

"Because I *know* him," I said as if he were stupid. "And he won't accept half-measures."

"Half measures meaning... a wife or nothing?"

"Yes," I growled. "And I will never marry."

He tilted his head at me, making the window light strike blue sparks off his black hair. "Why?"

"Because my fiancé was right. No one will ever marry me for anything other than my father's estate and title. That will always be the most worthwhile thing I have to offer," I admitted, and felt a burden lifted off my chest. I had eaten that truth as an eighteen-year-old girl, swallowed and choked on it, and let it grow into something grotesque inside of me. Vomiting it up felt, strangely, like freedom.

He was as still as stone next to me, black eyes fixed on my face. He said, in a quiet voice that held an edge, "Tell me what he said to you."

It was the night of our engagement party at his family home. Everyone was invited. They laughed and smiled and congratulated us as we stood arm in arm, the picture of young love.

I had been alone for so long, and I was finally going to be healed, be whole, have a partner again, someone I could tell my secrets to and laugh with in the dark. So when he towed me to an out-of-the-way sitting room during a lull in the party, my heart pounded with excitement.

He kissed me, and I thought I would swoon. This was what love was like, to be wanted, desired. When he tried to slip his hand up my skirt, I froze. We were supposed to wait for that part till after the marriage. But he was the love of my life, and he wanted me, and his mouth was hot on my neck and my breast and it was hard to think.

But I managed to disengage our mouths and say, "Wait. Shouldn't we wait?"

"What for?" he said, rolling his palm over my breast.

"To be married, silly."

He stopped moving, stopped kissing, and leaned away. "What for?"

"Well, this isn't exactly very romantic. Especially for our first time. In the sitting room?"

"First time? God, Gwenevere," he said, rolling his eyes and shoving his hand through his hair. "What do we need romance for? No one was ever going to marry you for romance, anyway."

I stumbled backward, feeling as if I'd just stepped off a cliff. "What do you mean?"

"You cannot be an heiress and be that naive," he said as if I were stupid. And maybe I was. "You're going to be a duchess, Gwen. Whoever marries you will be a very rich man. Your father's title and money will always be the greatest inducement to marry you. You must know this. Your body is the least important part of this equation, so who cares what you do with it? Why not find pleasure now, when you want it?"

My illusions, so carefully built and lovingly maintained, shattered into a million pieces that cut me until I bled. I did not have a knight in shining armor, or a prince, or a brave sister with flashing green eyes to rescue me from the emptiness.

"I don't," I choked out. "I don't want it."

He smirked at me. "You did a moment ago. I can make you want it again."

He reached out to pull me back against him and shoved his tongue into my mouth. I snapped. When I finally came to, my ex-fiancé was sitting on the ground, dazed. His face was bloody, and the room was in shambles; broken tables, holes in the wall, and destroyed furniture that had been hundreds of years old. A man held me off the ground by the waist while my mother screamed my name.

"Everyone heard the story by the next day, and I have been persona non grata since then. I will never be as valuable as my money or title. How could anyone, even a good man like Tony, not be tempted by so much wealth? Besides, he is whole, and I am broken. He is a good person and I am not. It would be terribly unfair, and I love him too much to do that to him. So, I will never marry. Not as long as I am worth less than my title."

I was tired and hollow but somehow freer than I had been. Wasn't the truth supposed to do that? At least someone now knew what really happened, even if that someone was a dark stranger with no name.

I was free, but I was so tired.

The world started to tip sideways, but I didn't fight it. I wanted to sleep—so, why was I floating? I opened my eyes to see his sculpted features and long, straight nose. Sometime later, a bed creaked beneath me, and I curled into it with a sigh.

A quiet, comforting voice said into my ear, "There is nothing in this world—from the snow-capped peaks to the bottom of the ocean—worth more than you, Gwenevere St. James."

15

Croquet and Vampires

GWEN

To pry me out of bed and wrestle me into clothing suitable for outdoor games, it took both Sally and Percy, an entire pot of coffee laced with brandy, a cheese Danish, four sausages, and several threats of death and mayhem.

Sally was quiet and stoic during the process, but Percy needled me endlessly.

"I cannot fathom what made you think getting drunk at four o'clock in the morning was anything like a good idea. I would like you to explain how I am supposed to tempt the wealthy elite to purchase my fashions when they have to look past your bloodshot eyes to see them. Just look at the lines round your mouth! My model is an absolute lush. It's shameful, Gwen, that's what it is."

Percy said all of this while providing gentle ministrations and fastening buttons. It was nearly like being looked after by Mama.

Sam sat on the bed, leftovers from his own Danish smeared across one cheek, trying not to giggle.

Once I was marginally fit to be seen, they bundled me out the door. Their muffled complaints followed me as I trudged down the interminable hall to join the other wealthy elites on the lawn. Another two hours of sleep would have been far more welcome.

Despite the enormous hat providing ample shade, I do not recommend, under any circumstances, playing croquet in the glaring sun while hung over. Sunlight bounces off the lawn with more than average strength, the white gowns are positively glaring, and the laughing feels like razor blades in one's ears.

The party had been separated by activity: most of the women and several men gathered into teams of two on the lawn for croquet, while the rest of the men took to the other side of the property to shoot clay pigeons—which would have been much more fun but infinitely worse for my headache.

So I joined my partner, an elderly gentleman with round spectacles and clever eyes. As we waited for our turn to bash the unoffending little balls with our mallets, he stood with one hand on his comfortable stomach and smiled good-naturedly at the competition unfolding before us.

"I do hope you are a vicious competitor, my dear, or we will certainly lose," he said with a light German accent. "For I have a trick knee, and am content merely to stand in the sunshine and make my wickets."

"Then I am afraid of our chances, sir, because I have a splitting headache."

"Did you join in the festivities with a little too much enthusiasm?"

I stopped just shy of snorting but said, "You could say that."

He laughed, a jolly sound, and held out his hand. "I am Dr. Martin Hesselius. It is a pleasure to meet you."

My hand froze mid-air, and I said, "Dr. Hesselius?" then blinked away my shock and shook his hand, perhaps a little too vigorously. "Forgive me, sir, but I have read all of your published case files. Your investigations into the occult are some of the most logical and thorough I have ever read."

Pleasure turned his cheeks pink above his white mustache. "Well, then. It is kind of you to say so, miss...?"

"Oh! Gwenevere. Lady St. James."

"It is kind of you to say so, Lady St. James. You have an interest in the occult?"

We advanced in the line, only two teams from beginning the chase, and I said, "I do, indeed. I have traveled through Europe and parts of Asia and Africa to study it."

"Have you? Then it seems I have been partnered with a kindred spirit. It is too bad we will certainly lose this game," he laughed.

"So long as you are willing to put up with my questions, sir, I do not mind losing at all."

As it turned out, however, Dr. Hesselius was no slouch at croquet. His strikes were almost always accurate, and he methodically knocked other players in the wrong direction to advance our ball, all while apologizing and laughing at himself.

We did not win, but it was close.

"We acquitted ourselves rather well," he told me as we left the field of battle for iced lemonade in the shade of pavilions and umbrellas.

"Thanks to you. If you do have a trick knee, you disguise it rather well. You were brilliant."

"Pish."

I had begun forming an idea from the moment Dr. Hesselius introduced himself, and as we collected our glasses and retreated to an umbrella on the outskirts of the party, I decided to put it into motion. After all, how often was I likely to stumble across one of the world's foremost experts on the occult?

"Doctor," I began as we sat on the blankets, "if you dislike speaking of your profession while on holiday, please tell me. Because if so, I will change the subject. But if not, I have something that might be of interest to you."

His eyes sparkled. "One never tires of one's obsession, dear lady. I am only surprised to find someone here to indulge me. These affairs are dreadfully lonely but, of course, I could not say no."

I told him as much as I could about the dark figure without giving away Frances and the coven, or the grimoire. "Did the boy say the monster could not come inside, or would not?"

"He said the monster wanted to come in, but the cunning woman would not let it."

He sipped his lemonade, white brows furrowed in thought. "You already have suspicions of your own, do you not?" he said, finally, setting his glass down and looking at me squarely.

"I do," I admitted. "But I don't want to contaminate your impressions of the evidence. And if your conclusions differ from mine, I'm inclined to agree with you rather than trust myself. After all, the weight of experience is on your side."

"The weight of knowledge, maybe. But remember, I have gained much of my knowledge second-hand. Experience is its own kind of wisdom."

"And what does your particular kind of wisdom lead you to believe?"

He plucked a blade of grass absently and began tearing it into neat little squares. "Given what you have told me, I suspect the monster in question may be a vampire. But, if it is, it is the boldest vampire I have ever heard of."

"Why do you say that?"

"Well, vampires are generally secretive. Their survival depends upon it. If this creature is causing spectacles and interacting with people it has not killed or enthralled, it does so at great risk to itself."

"Is it possible the vampire is strong enough not to fear retaliation?"

His lips pursed. "I suppose that is possible, but is it probable? I cannot say. Mortals are much more dangerous to monsters than in the old days. Were I the creature, I would need a good reason to risk myself, so."

"What reason could force a vampire to expose itself?"

He shook his head. "Who can know such a thing for certain? The only vampire I have known to spend a great deal of time with mortals did so for a twisted sense of love."

"I have read that case file, though I admit I did think it somewhat fantastical."

The look on the doctor's face could only be described as melancholic. "It is, in many ways. And desperately sad."

I leaned back and let my eyes roam, unseeing, over the gathered crowd as I tried to piece together bits of information into something coherent. Could I guarantee the figure in black was the same creature Sam encountered? No. I could not. And what about the black riders? Just a country superstition, or had the villagers seen the vampire moving about in the woods?

Whether Ms. Honeycutt was related to any of it, I could not tell, but the vampire seemed to be the only clue I might be able to follow if I could find him. And I *wanted* to find him.

"How might one go about tracking a vampire?" I asked.

He sat up straight and raised his brows, mouth popping open beneath his mustache. "Why on earth would you do such a thing?"

"To stop it from killing anyone else."

"A vampire who is not afraid of making a spectacle is a dangerous foe, young lady."

I leaned forward and looked Dr. Hesselius in the eyes, allowing the facade I generally wore, one of polite, well-bred amusement, to fall away. Anger rose to the surface in its place, and I said, "So am I."

He considered me, sighed, and said, "I believe you. Very well. A vampire who does not wish to be found is nearly invisible. They cast no shadow, no reflection, and they can move as lightly as the wind. You may be able to follow the trail of a young vampire who has not learned stealth, but an older vampire?" He made a cutting motion with his hand. "Impossible without trained dogs, or perhaps a seer. You must either know where the vampire keeps its nest, find a thrall to track, or divine who its next victim is."

"As easy as all that, is it?"

He laughed. "I did warn you."

"A thrall is someone the vampire has enslaved," I said slowly, thinking as I spoke, "but they may not show any noticeable signs, is that correct?"

"According to my studies, you are correct. Unless the vampire crushes their mind, a thrall may be anyone. You may know if you found the wound from which the creature feeds but, as I said, this is second-hand knowledge. However"—he snapped his fingers, eyes lighting up—"some friends are coming to visit me, and they may be of more help. They will not arrive for another day or two, unfortunately."

"I do not know if we have that long to wait. How often does a vampire feed?"

He thought about it. "It depends on how they feed. If they take little sips from a thrall, perhaps every day. If they eat much, all at once? Perhaps weeks."

The old woman was nearly as dry as a husk, but she was also very small. I wanted to pull out chunks of grass and hurl them while I spewed curses at fate, but instead, I said, "You said there may be a chance to track the vampire if we know who the next victim is?"

"Yes, but it is not always easy to tell such a thing."

Sam said the vampire wanted him. My skin crawled in revulsion. I could never put Sam in danger that way, not even to catch the monster. But I had seen Lord Ashcroft with the dark figure, and while there was no guarantee that was the vampire, it was the only lead I had. Putting him in danger by asking him or tricking him into becoming bait would be wrong... but simply keeping an eye on him? There was nothing wrong with that, was there?

"I think I might have an idea, Doctor, though I need to work through it a bit. Thank you for your help."

He patted my hand, but said, "You may not thank me if my advice brings you face to face with such a deadly foe, young lady."

I smiled. "If I live through it, I will thank you, I promise."

"Why does that not make me feel any better?"

Once the chaperoned activities finished for the day, the party broke up into small groups for other activities. Some ladies went shopping in the village, others took open carriages for sightseeing in the countryside. I promised the doctor I would tell him when I had a solid plan, and hurried to my room to change.

After checking on Sam and Sally, who were playing cards while munching Sally's caramels, I slunk through the house and back to the housekeeper's room. Some piece of this confused puzzle was missing, and her room was the only place it made sense to look.

Knowing Ms. Honeycutt was a faerie in hiding made my early conjectures, like a secret affair, less likely. Not because humans and faeries couldn't reproduce, but because someone willing to make a deal with a coven of powerful witches was probably desperate... I should know. And I doubted she would be willing to compromise her position of expensive safety for something as trite as an affair.

Lady Chatsworth would not have dismissed her, even if she had; she was too valuable for that.

So I needed more information to complete the picture and force this whole affair to make sense.

The room was as orderly as I remembered, everything carefully arranged and placed just so: a pair of boots, a comb, hairpins, a serviceable dress, and a second uniform, all clean and neat. It felt more like a museum display than a room someone lived in. Whatever inner life Ms—no, Thistle was her real name—whatever inner life Thistle led was not lived in this room.

I stood in front of the single window and stared at the horizon. What drove her to leave her home, a place of literal magic, to live a life of service? Perhaps if I could deduce that, I would have a better idea of... My thoughts died away as I noticed the white tree. From this window, the landscape around Chatsworth Manor opened up like a painting, and there, in the center of the wood between the manor and the village, were the leaves and branches of the white tree that grew from my werewolf tooth and the old woman's blood.

Thistle would have seen nearly everything from this window: the village and little river to the south, the wood to the west, and the miles of land divided by stone fences. A hill rose out of the wood a mile or so to the west, and on its top, catching the late afternoon sunlight, was a circle of standing stones.

Had Thistle come through the wall there, so many years ago, and stumbled down the hill into her new life? How strange must the world have looked to her, then? My eyes flicked back and forth between the standing stones and the white tree, and then... the tea!

The old woman said Ms. Honeycutt came to her because she needed the knowledge of passing things and things that were. I began my search anew, this time with no regard for order. I pulled open drawers, turned out pockets, pulled off the bedspread, grabbed the pillow, and—there it was: a small leather sack, a mirror to the one in my room.

I would go down and—no. I promised Sally I would not ask her to sit through that again. I needed Tony. My stomach soured at the thought. In fact, I had been trying hard not to think of him since I woke up dizzy this morning. I'd imposed upon him terribly, unfairly.

The idea of looking him in the face today was unpleasant, to say the least. But I would do it. I had to. No matter how much it hurt. So I asked Percy to watch over the children, screwed up my courage, and walked to the village.

The Crooked Nag was open, and the ground floor was full of rustic folk eating bread, drinking beer, and singing end-of-workday songs. I passed them and took the stairs to the second floor, where the only two guest rooms were located. Now or never.

When Tony opened the door, his mussed hair and tired eyes didn't look just-woke-up-from-bed attractive, as they had the night before; he looked like he hadn't slept at all, and there was a better-than-average chance that was my fault.

"I have to try something, and I need your help, if you're willing. I know I don't deserve anything from you but—"

"Oh, shut up, Gwen. Come on."

He stepped aside and held open the door, rubbing one hand over his unshaven jaw. I was used to seeing Tony in a suit and coat, or

even a tuxedo. He always looked very purposefully put together. Now he wore nothing but trousers, a shirt open at the
throat, and suspenders. The expanse of muscle visible through
the thin cotton was distracting.

I took a deep breath and stepped inside. Into his room. With
him. Alone. That might not have been such a good idea. But
the door closed behind me with a *click*.

He said nothing. The silence was painful. I was the only
person who could break it, but it was nearly impossible to force
my mouth to say, "I'm sorry, Tony. I shouldn't have..."

"Attacked me?"

"That's not the phrase I would have chosen."

He peeled back his bottom lip with two fingers where a series
of little red cuts ran along the inside, from where I had smashed
his lips against his teeth in my desperation.

"Gods." I dropped my face into my hands. I had made him
bleed. Yet another black mark on my character. "I truly am
sorry. I didn't—I was wrong and unfair."

"Don't apologize. You were hurting. I'm sorry I couldn't give
you what you needed, I just"—he ran his hand through his
hair—"don't apologize. We're square."

I bit back the need to keep apologizing until he said he
forgave me, and held up the little sack, instead. "I found this
in Thistle's—Ms. Honeycutt's room. It's a kind of herbal tea
mixed by the woman in the wood. If I'm lucky, it will show
me what it showed her, something she needed to see. I can't
guarantee it will help me find her, but it might."

He frowned down at the sack. "Why do you need my help to drink tea?"

"I don't need your help to drink it, but I don't know what it will do, or how I will react. This tea was not meant for me, so it could make me sick, or I might say things during my vision that I will not remember, afterward."

"I see," he said, his voice rich with distaste. "And you believe this is necessary?"

"I do."

Tony went downstairs to fetch a cup and hot water, and I paced back and forth, trying not to examine everything in his room, unsuccessfully, or read the signs that said Tony had been distressed all day long... also unsuccessfully.

It was actually a relief when he walked back in and handed me the cup. I measured out the tea, let it steep, and found a comfortable place to sit.

"What shall I do, during this"—he waved his hand—"whatever it is you're about to do?"

"Just watch, I suppose, and stop me from hurting myself, or call for help if something goes wrong. And try to remember the words if I say or—or scream anything."

His hands flexed, but he nodded and sat on his bed, near my chair. I didn't particularly enjoy that experience the first time, and I had no great expectations now, but one word was a glowing ember in the center of my chest that burned every other concern to ash... Lia.

"Here we go, then. Bottom's up."

The tea was hot enough to burn and tasted of black licorice and ginger. It made me feel buoyant but sloshy, like water. Water flowing in swift rivers, joining with the sea, rising in great clouds, and falling again to leave black puddles on paved streets, and make knee-deep mud in country lanes where hopeless men pushed carts filled with the bodies of the dead.

Rain trailing down window panes, where beautiful beings in velvet argued and pointed at maps and threatened each other with steel bright as silver.

Snow that crunched beneath ragged boots with too-thin soles, stained with the blood of the fallen warriors who fought there.

Water in battered wooden cups that pressed against the chapped and blistered lips of desperate men, and elves, and dwarves.

Waves that crashed and spilled over walls, over streets, into homes, swallowing up whole cities and all the lives within.

When the vision faded, I found myself wet-cheeked, looking into Tony's face. He had dragged me onto his bed, and I lay across his lap with my head in the crook of his arm.

"Hey," he said softly, brushing the hair back from my forehead. "There you are. Are you alright?"

I tried to nod and say I was fine, but a sob escaped instead. I slapped both hands over my mouth to stifle the sound, but it was like trying to plug a bursting dam with chewing gum.

Tony held me while I cried, making little comforting noises. After the impersonal observations of the water, I needed the warmth of human touch like one needs a fire after a day spent in the snow.

When the worst of it was over, and I only sniffled, he kissed me. Just once, softly, no demands or expectations, simply the gentle, warm pressure of his lips that felt like a balm for my ragged nerves.

"I'm okay," I said, as he brushed his fingers over my cheeks.

"You sure?"

I sat up and nodded, pinning back the strands of hair that had somehow escaped during my vision to give myself a moment to process what I saw and, more importantly, what I understood from it.

Thistle had seen the Great War, the war between mortals and the fae, and all the death and destruction it caused. But, more than that, she saw it as a precursor, a foreshadowing of what might come, like looking in a mirror to see who is sneaking up on you.

Thistle left the Sunset Lands because she believed a war was coming. She left and hid here.

Once I finished explaining, Tony said, "If that's true, then why did she run? Why leave the manor?"

Why did she leave what she believed to have been a safe place?

"I don't know," I admitted. In my mind, I saw Thistle standing near the battered table, counting and recording the plates and bowls as moonlight spilled through the window across the hall. She saw something that scared her enough to drop the bowl, to run from the safety of the manor she lived in for dozens of years. What could frighten her so?

"I have a bad feeling the only way we are going to find out is if we catch a vampire."

16

Love Notes

SAM

There were no chances to escape since he'd woken up that morning. Sally refused to let him out of her sight, barely even leaving to use the water closet. Then Percy showed up and whatever chance Sam might have had to ensure Lord Ashcroft was still in the manor evaporated like piss on a street corner.

At least there was good food.

After losing a dozen games of cards and staring out the window for hours, Sam's nerves were so tight that if someone sneezed, he might have snapped in half. The monster was out there, somewhere, and the Cutthroat King would be waiting for his next update by post, but he could do nothing so long as he was shut up in this room.

He didn't want to leave it, of course. Who would be stupid enough to jump right back into the fire after getting burned? But Sam had little choice if he wanted to free himself and keep Sally safe. Escape ideas ran one after another through his head, until Lady Gwen and Tony entered the room.

Tony?

They slipped in as if trying not to be seen. Was someone following them? Sam's instincts pricked up like a cat's ears, and just as quickly tried to slink away when Lady Gwen turned those dark eyes on him.

"First," she said as she pulled out her hatpin and placed her hat onto the chest of drawers, "thank you, Sally and Percy. I appreciate your willingness to help. But now I have to ask something more of all of you. We must have a council of war."

"War?" Sally squeaked.

A blade of irritation cut at Sam's nerves. Sally was one of the bravest people he knew. She fought kidnappers, stole, robbed, tricked, and conned. She fought for them to have enough to eat when she was younger than he was, now. Why did she keep acting so scared?

"It's just an idiom, darling girl," Lady Gwen said, pulling off her gloves.

"For what, exactly?" Percy asked.

"We must come up with a plan to do something dangerous," Tony said, likewise slipping out of his jacket.

Lady Gwen brushed her sleeves out, laced her fingers together, and said, "Before we can do that, however, I'm going to need a few answers, Samuel. You are recovered, I assume?"

Could he lie? That expression was on her face, the one that made it feel like her eyes could see right through him. He reluctantly nodded.

"Then I would like to know why on earth you are here instead of at home, and how you came to be here."

That was the one question he did *not* want to answer. He lowered his head, as if in shame, but used the opportunity to give himself a chance to think. What was true enough that she'd believe it, but wouldn't give him away and put Sally in danger?

At last, he raised his head and said, "You was worried about Mr. Capstone—"

"*Were* worried," She interrupted. "Continue."

"I knew you were worried about Mr. Capstone, so I thought I could ask some of my old mates. They hear a lot, you know? Well, Billy"—he picked the name at random—"he sometimes runs errands to Parliament, and he said he heard someone called Lord Ashcroft say the name Mr. Capstone."

He hoped that part wasn't so much of a fabrication that she would see it in his eyes. All of it was partially true, and the Cutthroat King hinted that Mr. Capstone was somehow linked to Lord Ashcroft, or at least he would find the information he wanted the same way, so he wasn't exactly lying.

Her lips pursed, so he blurted out, "And I thought you would need to know, so I hitched a ride on the back of a carriage headed this way and tied myself to the footman's handle."

Sally made an incredulous noise, but Lady Gwen rolled her eyes toward heaven and said, "God's breath, Samuel Dawes" in tones of profound weariness.

Percy covered a smile, and Tony only looked grave, which was a better outcome than he could have hoped for.

"Why didn't you tell Mrs. Chapman or Mr. Yates? They would have sent me a telegram and saved you from—" Lady Gwen stopped and rubbed her temples, then took a deep breath and said, "Please don't ever put yourself in danger like that for my sake."

Sam folded his arms and stuck out his jaw. "I've been in danger since I was born."

"But I wasn't responsible for you, then. And I do not want to be forced to lock you up."

"I can take care of myself!"

"You were nearly killed last night!"

"That," Tony said in a deep voice that shut them both up, "is quite enough from the two of you. Samuel?"

"Yes, sir?" Sam said through his teeth.

"What do you think would hurt Lady Gwen worse: not knowing about Mr. Capstone, or knowing you were hurt?"

That cooled the head of steam Sam had slowly and happily been building. Anger felt a lot better than worry, but Tony neatly ruined that. He nodded in understanding.

"Gwen, Sam is competent and intelligent. You cannot simply lock him up, or he will resent you for it and *still* find a way to break free."

Sam blinked. How had the man known that?

Lady Gwen sighed and nodded. "You are right. I'm sorry, Sam. It's not that I don't trust you, it's that I don't trust the other people in this world who would harm you without thinking twice. It would break my heart, and I know your sister would never forgive me."

Sally looked between the two of them with wide, round eyes, but didn't say anything.

"Now that we've settled that," Tony said, clapping his hands together, "let's get down to business, shall we? Gwen?"

"After a bit of digging, we believe Sam's monster is probably a vampire."

Sam felt like he'd just been wrapped in a cold, wet blanket.

"A vampire?" Percy said, his voice thin.

"Yes," Lady Gwen said. "And the townspeople began complaining about dark spectres at nearly the same time our housekeeper disappeared."

"If that vampire got her," Sam started to say, but his voice died in his throat. He didn't like to think about what the monster with yellow eyes could have done to her.

"We don't know whether he did or not," Lady Gwen said. "But their appearing at the same time is a coincidence we cannot ignore. That means our best chance of finding out is to catch the vampire."

"You cannot catch a vampire," Percy said. "They're faster than humans, stronger than dwarves, and see better than elves. And if he did kill the wise woman in the woods, then her blood will have made him even stronger."

"That's only speculation," Gwen began, but Percy glared at her and said, "It's true."

"Very well, it's true. But it doesn't matter, because we must still find and stop him, whether he's strong and fast or not."

"How?" Sally asked.

The adults in the room all traded glances.

"Well," Lady Gwen said, slowly, "there are only a few ways to track a vampire, but one of them is to watch the next victim so you can be ready to spring a trap."

"How do you know who the next victim will be?" Sam asked as prickles of dread ran along the back of his neck.

"Vampires tend to focus on one victim at a time, hunting them, until they've dispatched their prey. Last night I saw Lord Ashcroft speaking to a figure in black, the same figure I fought in the woods earlier that day. When I reached Lord Ashcroft, he was dazed and unresponsive."

"You think the vampire enthralled him?" Percy asked.

"If that was the vampire I saw with him, then it seems like a reasonable explanation."

Sally frowned. "But it was daylight when he attacked Sam. I thought sunlight killed vampires?"

"Did you read that in the recorded folklore, or popularized novels?" Lady Gwen asked.

Sally blushed, and Lady Gwen winked at her. "Sunlight does, in fact, kill younger vampires, so the novels are not entirely wrong. But for older and stronger vampires, it is merely painful. That is generally enough to keep them either indoors or hidden during the day. So this vampire must be chasing something he cares enough about to endure it."

Percy, who did not look very happy, said, "You obviously have some kind of plan you'd like us to sign onto, Gwen. What is it?"

"I think we must use Lord Ashcroft as a lure."

"Will that work?" Percy asked.

"More people will die if we don't do something. And Lord Ashcroft will probably be the first."

Panic fluttered in Sam's chest. That couldn't happen, not until Sam had the information the Cutthroat King needed so he could prove he'd done his job.

"Why is that our responsibility?" Percy asked. "Shouldn't the police be investigating, instead? You have special units for monsters, don't you, Inspector?"

"The old woman's body is gone," Lady Gwen said. "There is no evidence of the murder to justify bringing them here."

Sally said, "Why not warn Lord Ashcroft? Doesn't he have a right to know if something wants to kill him?"

"Would you believe it if I told you a vampire was hunting you?" Tony asked. "Besides, if we warn him, he may simply lock himself up to stay safe, and the vampire may target someone we don't know about, someone we cannot protect. We have a chance to save Lord Ashcroft and stop the vampire, but if the monster targets someone else—"

"He could agree and decide to help," Sally retorted, her cheeks pink with anger.

"But what if he doesn't? Then we've lost the only chance we're likely to get."

His chances of getting out of service to the King were dwindling with every new argument. Sam had to find a way to escape this room and become part of the plan, or he might be the next person on the floor with their throat cut. Or it might be Sally.

"I could watch him," he said.

They stopped arguing. Four pairs of eyes fastened on him, but Sam ignored the urge to fidget under their gazes.

"Absolutely not," Lady Gwen said.

Sally sighed and closed her eyes.

Tony gave Sam the same penetrating look he'd given him when the three of them had driven off to rescue Sally, as if he could see past the stubbornness to whatever lay beneath.

"It might be a good idea," he said, at last.

Lady Gwen turned on him, her eyes flashing. "He has already been a target. I'm not putting him in that kind of danger."

"It's a vampire, Gwen. He's already in danger. But he is exactly the kind of person the guests will overlook, especially if Lady Chatsworth is willing to fit him up in servants' togs."

"Tony," she said, and her voice reminded him of the sound a cat makes before it tears into another cat.

"The boy has proven himself capable," he replied in a reasonable tone that would have been hard for anyone but Lady Gwen to argue with. "And if he stays inside the house, he'll be just as safe as if he were in this room."

"It is probably better than forcing him to stay in this room, where he's more likely to want to escape," Percy added.

"I have you both against me now?"

"And me," Sally said, crossing her arms and glaring at all three of them.

The worst thing he could do now was try to argue his own case. They were slowly wearing Lady Gwen down, and she got mad when she knew she was being unreasonable.

"Dammit," she said. Then she turned and pounded her fist on the wall. "Dammit, dammit! *Dammit*, Tony."

"I don't like it, either, but this is the situation we're in and we will need every eye and ear we can get."

"Fine," she growled at last, then added, "but I will smother you all in so much garlic, you're going to wish you'd never wanted to help."

The garlic wasn't that bad. Sam was used to it within the first couple of hours, but he did have to stay far enough away from the guests and other servants that they couldn't smell him.

Lady Gwen had also given him a cross that hung heavy in the pocket of the black trousers Lady Chatsworth's servants wore. Why the symbol of a nearly dead religion should matter to a vampire, Sam couldn't understand, and Lady Gwen didn't bother explaining, but he supposed that as long as it worked, it didn't matter.

The real torture was watching the guests on the lawn drink lemonade and eat something sweet he could smell but not identify. It smelled like almonds and sugar and something else, maybe vanilla? And he couldn't get close enough to snag one. He had to stay just inside the doorway as if waiting to carry a message or run an errand at a moment's notice.

But the position did let him keep an eye on Lord Ashcroft, who was currently playing tennis on the lawn and winning spectacularly, much to the appreciation of his wife. Which meant he wasn't

inside. Which meant his room was empty. He should be searching the room for information, but he didn't know which room
it was, and he couldn't ask without... or could he?

Sam made a quick stop in Lady Gwen's room at her writing
desk, scribbled something on a piece of paper, sealed it in an
envelope, then went in search of one of the older servants. He
found a staid-looking older boy, held up the envelope, and said,
"Lord Ashcroft wants this taken to his room."

The older boy looked him up and down with the kind of
disdain only the servants of the wealthy seemed to be able to
manage. "You must be the new boy."

Sam nodded.

"Well, what are you standing around for? Take it to his room
and leave it on his writing desk."

Sam looked down and shuffled his feet, and the older boy gave
a deep, resigned sigh. "You don't know where it is, do you?"

At the negative shake of Sam's head, the boy turned and
stalked away, saying, "Come on" over his shoulder.

Sam followed him back to the guest wing of the house and
memorized the route, counted the doors and turns, and nearly
ran into the older boy when he stopped.

"It's this one," he said. "Hurry, and don't let anybody see
you."

Sam slipped into the room, which had already been tidied by
the upstairs maids, and dropped the letter onto the silver tray
on his desk. There were several correspondences on the desk,
a mess of papers and letters. That was exactly what he needed,
but he didn't have time to look. He exited and shut the door.

"Good, you're quick and quiet. Just be invisible and you'll do alright. Get back to your post or whatever else the butler has you doing."

Sam returned to the door and searched the chatting crowd to find Lord Ashcroft's dark head. He was looking over a horse with some other men, touching it here and there, arguing about Sam couldn't guess what. What was there to argue about? It was a horse. A pretty one, but still a horse.

No matter what they were fighting about, it looked like it would occupy them a good long time. So he slid the second fake letter from his pocket and searched the crowd for Lady Gwen.

She was easy to spot because she stood in a wide, empty circle as if people feared getting too close to her. Maybe she was slathered in garlic, too. But she was feeding handfuls of oats to one of the horses being paraded about, so Sam took his chance.

He followed the same path back to Lord Ashcroft's room, watching for returning guests or servants with interested eyes, but most of them had their minds on their own tasks and paid him little notice. The door opened silently, and Sam slipped inside.

Before touching the papers, Sam grabbed his fake delivery, stuffed it back into his pocket, then made a mental note of the way the papers were laid out. He slid them just far enough apart to be read: a letter to his solicitor about something containing too many big words, a record of a horse he wanted to purchase from Lord Chatsworth, an invitation for some lord to join him at a club... it was all useless nonsense.

The urge to swipe every paper off the desk was so strong that Sam had to stuff his hands into his pockets. Perhaps there was something else, something in the drawers? He reached for the knob only to freeze when he heard rapid footsteps in the hall outside and a distressed woman's voice, muffled through the door.

Sam spun and slid beneath the bed as the door swung open. A pair of shiny black shoes strode into the room, followed by white skirts and patent leather boots. As quietly as possible, Sam scooted backward, farther into the shadows beneath the bed, barely daring to breathe as his heart thudded painfully.

"I wish you would not see him," Lady Ashcroft said, her voice pleading.

"Edith, we have been through this. You know why I must. This will be the most important piece of legislation to hit the floor in our lifetimes, and if it passes, it will change everything. Absolute political upheaval. The entire landscape of power in the Empire will change."

"I thought you supported seeing titles distributed to humans, elves, and dwarves alike?"

"I do, but that isn't the point. If we don't exert some control over how these changes take place, we could see all of the power we have fought so hard to gain washed away in a matter of a few years."

"But this is all so clandestine, Edgar, and trading in secrets like this is dangerous."

"What other option do we have? Right now, our sons stand to gain not just our titles and wealth, but the power of our reputation. That will matter, especially to Charles, as a second son. Would you have me throw that away or gamble it on the whims of the Commons?"

She stomped away from him, closer to the bed. Sam flattened himself against the wall. The bed creaked as she sat on it, her little shoes dangling off the floor. "I just do not see how someone trading in secrets can be trusted."

"Capstone has not been wrong yet," he said. His voice sounded like Sally's had when they were younger, and she offered to let him slug her back after a fight.

"Here, Sammy, look," she'd say. *"Don't cry. You can punch my arm. Will that make you feel better?"*

It had. But he didn't think that made Lady Ashcroft feel better.

"Being right does not make him *good*," she said.

"Good and effective are two different things, my love. And right now, I'll take effective."

"Must I make up some excuse for you after dinner, then?" she asked, and there was acid in her voice.

"If you would be so good, though I shan't be long."

"I do not like this business, Edgar."

"I do not ask you to like it."

She dropped off the bed with a little thud, then stalked over to the door. "Clearly, what I say does not sway you, and you'll do just as you like. But I do not want to know about it. And I hope you will take my advice and join us tonight after dinner rather than meeting with that man."

She slammed the door behind herself.

The lord sighed, swore under his breath, then turned to the writing desk. The sound of his pen scratching was loud in the silence, but lasted only a moment before he had done, and followed his wife.

He'd been so close. Ashcroft was meeting with Mr. Capstone, and they were trading in secrets, but what secrets? That wasn't enough information for the King to blackmail the man. But it was a start, at least. And he knew what time they planned to meet.

Sam waited till the hallway was silent, then slid out from beneath the bed and into the hall. He closed the door and turned smack into the chest of the butler. The man grabbed Sam by both arms and shook him once, hard.

"What are you doing, boy? Don't you know guests' rooms are off-limits?"

Sam's teeth clacked together. "Yes sir but—"

"Turn out your pockets," the Butler ordered, pointing.

His palms began to sweat. "But sir—"

The butler slapped him once, sharply, across the cheek. "Don't make me repeat myself."

Shaking, Sam reached down and pulled the pocket linings of his jacket out.

"And the trousers," the man said, his voice dangerous.

Sam pulled the notes out of his pockets, his stomach sick, and held them up. The butler snatched them, turned them over, read the names, and said, "You had better be more careful, you little fool. If you're caught running messages like this, it will hurt our lady's reputation. If you can't be discreet, find someone who can. Now get out of here."

Wait—did the butler just assume he was carrying notes between Lord Ashcroft and Lady Gwen? Love notes?

"Sir, I don't think—" he began, but the butler raised his hand again, so Sam turned and ran.

He should have written other names on the envelopes, but he hadn't much time, and he really, really didn't want to have to explain to Lady Gwen what he'd done.

Worse than that, he should tell her about Lord Ashcroft's plan to meet with Mr. Capstone, but he was afraid she would force him to stay back. Because if she did and he lost the chance to get the right information for the King... what would happen to Sally?

17

The Reavers

GWEN

My only consolation for allowing both Samuel and Sally to participate in something I wanted them nowhere near was the disgruntled look on Sam's face when we buttoned him up in his evening uniform. The collar was high and snug, the black buttons shining, and Sam looked as if he was having second thoughts about the experience.

Frances found a maid's uniform for Sally, and while she wouldn't be expected to serve, she could help keep track of Lord Ashcroft. Tony patrolled the grounds near the manor, keeping just beyond the reach of the light.

Percy planned on using his charm during the secondary dinner for the parties of guests to poke about for information, and I was responsible as the first line of defense until the man was safely ensconced in his room for the night.

Our hostess would watch and listen but refused to get involved in the affair, even if the vampire pursued Lord Ashcroft.

"You must understand my position," she said when handing me the children's disguises. "If the authorities discover me, I would be banned from New London, which would weaken the coven. It would jeopardize all the good we do, and everything we have been working toward. I cannot risk that."

"Not even to save a man's life?" I had demanded.

"I am trying to save more than the life of just one man," she said in that insufferable tone that implied she knew far more than I.

Now we smiled at one another across the dinner table as if we weren't trying to catch a vampire while using an innocent man as bait. And Lord Ashcroft, who chatted amiably with his dinner companions, was blissfully unaware of it.

I told myself that was best, but guilt still gnawed at me. Sally had been right, of course. He should know and make an informed choice. But if he did, circumstances might change too much to account for, and the trail of the missing fae housekeeper may grow too cold to follow. That was a risk I could not take.

After dinner, the usual routine of brandy and cigars in the smoking room for the men, and idle chatter in the drawing room for the women, ensued. We obediently trooped away from one another to our separate enjoyments until the smoking was done and the men rejoined the party.

This was the part of the evening I most worried about because it was the only time no one could track Lord Ashcroft. I let my gaze wander over the milling women and spotted Lady Ashcroft, stand-

ing near the hearth with her hands folded, lips pursed in indecision. She met my eyes, and her mouth firmed into a determined
line.

Dammit.

She crossed the room, never taking her eyes off me, and said,
"Lady Gwen, I must apologize."

I started. That was not how I imagined this interaction playing
out. "For what?"

She looked down at her hands, a little line of concentration
between her brows. "Last night when I found you and Edgar
arm-in-arm on the patio, I was weak. I allowed the baseless alle-
gations of a cruel woman to have some influence over my mind. I
am certain you saw it in my expression, and I am ashamed of it."

When she raised her eyes, there was such honesty in her face
that I could no longer fool myself into thinking of her as merely a
determined actress. She said, simply, "I hope you will forgive me."

"Lady Ashcroft—Edith. There is nothing to forgive. Your conclusions were understandable given the circumstances. I only
hope you can forgive me for not contradicting them right away.
But"—if she could be honest and vulnerable, then so could I—"I
am used to people thinking the worst of me, and trying to defend
myself often does more harm than good."

She took my hands and said, "You are too good. I felt on first
meeting you that we could be great friends, and I do hope I was
right."

I smiled at her through the guilt of knowing I was currently using her husband as a pawn in a most dangerous game. Hopefully,
she would forgive me if I kept him alive.

"Lady Ashcroft, Lady St. James, I hope you enjoyed dinner?" asked a young woman who approached us. She had kind eyes and a gorgeous wealth of dark hair coiled in dozens of shining braids adorned with beads and jewels.

We replied with the meaningless niceties polite society expected from such an introduction, and she continued, "I hoped I might get the chance to speak with you, Lady St. James, and ask who your designer is. Your gowns are always so eye-catching."

She was the first in a string of ladies who, bolstered by Edith's support or the possibility of salacious gossip, made their way across the room toward us. I sang Percy's praises and fielded their questions, all the while keeping one eye on the door.

When the men finally entered, Edith turned expectantly. Which one of us waited for her husband more impatiently I could not say, but when he failed to enter with the other gentlemen, the disappointment in her eyes made a lump rise in my throat.

"Lady Gwen, if you'll excuse me, I find I have a headache. I think I will retire for the night."

"Of course."

I patted her hand. She gave me a tremulous smile and left the room. The crowd slowly dispersed into smaller groups for chat or gaming, and I spotted Sally and Sam near the door.

Sally looked angry, fist clenched in her brother's coat, but Sam's face was pale and he pulled me across the room purely from the force of his gaze. Something was wrong.

I made my way across the room with exaggerated calm and took a glass of champagne, then situated myself nearby without facing them and said, "What's wrong?"

"I caught Sam trying to sneak out of the house," Sally growled under her breath.

Being angry with the boy for breaking our carefully outlined rules wouldn't help now. I could save that for later.

"What were you doing, Sam?" I asked.

"I should have—Lord Ashcroft didn't come out of the smoking room, but I saw him wa-walk into the forest," he panted, "out the window. I thought I could sneak up and catch him."

"And what?" Sally demanded, too angry to keep her voice down. "Capture the vampire yourself?"

I placed myself between the children and the rest of the party, blocking them with my enormous skirts, and said, "Where, Sam?"

"Out the front door, to the left."

"Get him back to our room and don't let him out of your sight," I told Sally, then slipped out of the party and ran down the hallway. I stopped only long enough to throw my coat on and pull my umbrella from the stand.

The night air was comfortably warm and the music from the other side of the house floated lazily on the breeze. There were no prints to follow on the gravel path or in the grass. I studied the tree line, hoping to see Lord Ashcroft, but the only movement was shrubs and trees bending in the wind.

Wait, was that a light? Tony. I picked up my skirt and darted across the grass. Tony must have caught his trail. But when I reached the spot, there was nothing but darkness and shifting patches of moonlight beneath the trees.

"Gwen?"

I squeaked, spun, and leveled my umbrella at Tony.

"What are you doing?"

"Sam said he saw Lord Ashcroft leave after dinner," I said, turning back to the wood with my umbrella raised, the runes warm beneath my fingers.

"You didn't see where he went?"

"Sam only said he saw him walk into the forest."

"What are we waiting for, then?" Tony said, took my hand, and pulled me into the dark.

Once we were far enough away that we weren't easily visible from the house, Tony flicked on his dwarven torch. I had to stop forgetting to use mine. He turned the dimmer switch down so we wouldn't be completely night blind and trailed the beam of light over the forest floor. It wouldn't have mattered if the beam of light was a hundred times brighter, because there were no footprints, no broken branches, nothing to hint that anyone passed this way.

But the birds and crickets were silent, and only the trees whispered.

"Something is wrong," I breathed.

Tony's fingers curled round my wrist. "Look."

He pointed into the distance where yellow light flickered between the trunks—the same light I'd thought was Tony.

"Could that be a pixie?" he whispered.

"No, it's too big."

"Do vampires glow?"

"Not that I know of. Quietly," I said and turned the handle of my umbrella until it clicked, releasing the safety on the blade inside.

We stalked through the wood toward the light, knees bent, every step carefully placed. My heart beat hard enough to make my ribcage vibrate. If my first encounter with the vampire had been anything to judge by, he was faster than me by a significant margin, which meant I must be ready *before* he moved.

Tony held his pistol low in one hand, and in the other, a stake carved earlier that day. Of more use, I hoped, was the bola in his coat pocket. The South American weapon was made of three weighted balls connected by a rope that, once thrown, would tangle around the vampire's legs and remove—at least for a moment—his single greatest asset: speed.

If Tony landed the throw, that is... in the dark, in the woods, with trees and branches and undergrowth everywhere. Alright, perhaps we were a *bit* under-prepared. But there was no going back.

The light grew brighter as we approached, bright enough to see by. I readied the umbrella, listening with every fiber of my body, but hearing nothing. The light was just around the next tree. I held my breath. Tony caught my eye and raised both brows in an *are you ready* expression. I clenched my jaw and nodded.

We sprang around the tree from either side, weapons ready for battle.

Instead of a vampire, we found a glowing woman... if such a mundane term as *woman* could describe her. She was humanoid in that she had a head, arms, legs, and mostly human features, but this creature was longer of limb and more elegantly built than any human or elf, perfectly symmetrical, and nearly seven feet tall.

Her eyes had no iris or pupil but were black from edge to edge above a long, straight, wide nose and impossibly high cheekbones.

Half of her hair was braided in a crown on top of her head, and the other half fell in shining waves that would have reached her lower back if they hadn't been floating on some unseen breeze. It was impossible to tell what color her skin or hair was because she glowed with a golden radiance that was almost blinding.

She had not bothered with clothes, and it would have been a shame if she covered up such an exquisite form. While I was certain the glowing woman was a female, there were no visible sex organs, just smooth lean muscle beneath glowing skin. Tony and I stood spellbound before her.

With infinite grace, she raised one long arm and pointed toward the east. Then, because we were too slow to obey, she floated off in that direction. I do not mean that metaphorically; she floated across the forest floor without ever setting foot upon it, her hair trailing in the air behind her. Tony turned off his torch (what need does one have for a handheld light while following a magical glowing being?) and we followed.

What else could we do?

After a hundred yards or so, the trees thinned and opened onto a grassy plain that stretched up the flanks of a hill to the ring of standing stones at the top. She pointed again, then faded like mist when the sun rises; one moment she was as solid as the trees, and the next as thin as smoke, and then she was gone.

Tony looked at the hill, then at me, and shook his head as if to clear it. "What just happened?"

"I do not know," I breathed, running my hand through the air where she floated only moments before.

"Why did she bring us here?"

"Again," I said, "I have no—"

The bushes on the other side of the clearing shook and cracked as a piteous cry broke the silence. I crouched behind the trunk of the closest tree and watched, umbrella ready, as Tony took shelter behind a low shrub and raised his pistol.

A pair of black horses stomped into the moonlight, trampling the bushes beneath their hooves. Their riders looked almost like medieval knights, except that their armor was made of bark, and antlers sprang from their helmets. Capes of spiderweb and moss trailed behind them on a phantom breeze, and they held between them a struggling figure.

I squinted, peering across the distance in the moonlight. "That's the blacksmith!"

They held him by his upper arms without effort despite his brawny size, and his heels dragged the ground as he struggled. "Don't take me, for pity's sake. Have mercy!"

Tony stood up, stepped out from cover, and fired his pistol into the air. It cracked like thunder, but the riders didn't notice, continuing their steady advance toward the tor and the standing stones at its top.

The blacksmith did notice, and twisted to scream, "Help! Don't let them take me! Help me!"

"Release that man!" Tony yelled, leveling his pistol, but the riders pushed on.

He pulled the trigger, the heavy thwack of the bullet striking echoed through the meadow... and nothing happened. The rider did not even flinch.

"Come on!" I yelled, and sprinted toward them, now nearly halfway up the hill. I had to be close for the umbrella to work.

Tony tripped behind me, cursing, but I ran on, my eyes fixed on the struggling man. A blast of force would lose strength as it traveled through the air, so I waited till I was about twenty paces away, snapped open the umbrella, braced my feet, and fired.

Before leaving the manor, we spent nearly half an hour taking turns punching and hitting the umbrella canopy to store energy, enough that the runes were warm beneath my fingers. When I released the blast, the umbrella kicked backward and nearly tore itself from my fingers.

The wall of energy hurtled forward and knocked the blacksmith out of their grip with enough force that the riders were left holding only the torn bits of his shirtsleeves. He hit the turf with an *oof* and rolled several feet down the hill. But the force did not so much as stir the rider's capes.

I pulled out the blade and braced myself, prepared for them to turn and charge, but they only spun their horses and followed the blacksmith, who was already sprinting down the hill.

Tony reached me, lifted the bola from his pocket, and pushed the stake into my hands. He set himself, swung the weapon around in a circle, and flung it with a twist of his powerful shoulders. The balls spun through the air, wrapped the rope around the horse's back legs, and twisted around to lock. At least, that was what should have happened.

But the balls simply sailed through the air, dragging the rope behind them, passed through the horse's legs, and bounced harmlessly off the turf. The bullet hadn't harmed them, the force had not touched them, and the bola might as well have stayed in Tony's pocket.

I jerked the blade free, set myself between the horseman and the top of the hill, and held my ground as they ran the blacksmith down and caught him before he reached the tree line.

Tony aimed again, but I told him, "Don't waste your bullets. We can't hurt them with lead."

"But they're going to notice your rapier?"

"My rapier," I said, settling into my stance, "is made of silver."

When the riders dragged the man back to the bottom of the hill, they stopped. I could not tell if they regarded me or simply looked in my direction, but they did stop.

"Leave him," I commanded, and lowered the point of the sword.

They each drew a single blade, something like a hand-and-a-half sword, held low in their outside hands. Without word or signal, the horses resumed walking, with no sign they intended to stop or treat with me.

This was not going to be pleasant. As soon as they were within striking distance, I slid to the right side and thrust.

The rider parried in a circular motion, our blades met with a silvery chime, and I struck again, but the rider parried with ease, leaned back, and kicked me in the chest. The impact was like getting hit with a sledgehammer, but Percy's wondrous jacket absorbed and spread out the energy, so while the blow took me off my feet and sent me rolling down the hill, it didn't kill me.

My blade flew from my hand. When I pushed myself to my feet with Tony's hand under my arm, wheezing and trying to get my diaphragm to cooperate, the riders already reached the top of the hill.

They dragged the screaming blacksmith into the circle of stones and disappeared in a puff of silvery smoke.

"What in the bloody everlasting hell was that?" Tony demanded once he was certain I wouldn't fall over.

"I think," I wheezed, "those were the riders in black the villagers mentioned."

"You said the riders in black were the vampire."

I rubbed my chest, hoping I wouldn't bruise. "I was wrong."

"That means our vampire is still out there."

"Yes. And we need to get back to the manor."

We found my blade and Tony's bola, then limped along until my pain mostly subsided. I was going to have to pay Percy more. If that kick had struck me without the coat, it would have crushed my ribcage.

"You said those were black riders," Tony said as the lights of the manor winked to life through the trees. "What are they?"

I leaned on him to hurdle a tree root—the muscles of his arms were solid and strangely comforting, even beneath his coat—and said, "There are many legends that include some kind of spectral riders, though the horses vary in color and appearance, but I have a feeling these riders are not the ones I've read about. I heard a poem recently though..." I trolled through my memory, trying to remember where I heard it, but couldn't seem to dredge it up. "I can't remember where. Anyway, it went something like, *No glamor, rune, or magic will help you turn the tide, stay safe by fire and circle stone when the Reavers ride. My child, beware the Reavers when moon is full and bright. If you see the shadows riding, venture not into the night."*

"That sounds like a nursery rhyme."

"Many nursery rhymes passed down wisdom in palatable ways. Turn advice into a poem and it's easy to remember. Make it a song and every child will sing it."

"Nothing seemed to touch them," he said, awe seeping into his voice. "Not my bullets or the bola, or even your umbrella. Why did your sword work? Silver isn't a good metal for a blade."

"It is when Delilah is done with it," I said. "And silver has magical properties. It has been connected to the moon for a long time. Even the alchemical symbol for silver is a crescent moon. If I had to guess, it has something to do with that. The rhyme did mention the moon, after all."

"Does any of this give us an indication of who they are or what they want?"

We broke through the tree line and stumbled onto the lawn with the moon shining on our backs. This was the last night it would be full, and since the poem mentioned *when the moon is full and bright,* perhaps this was the last night they would be abroad.

"I don't know. The term Reaver has been around a good long while, but I've never heard it applied to phantom riders before. And I cannot guess why they would kidnap a mundane blacksmith."

"How am I supposed to file a report saying a man was kidnapped into the mist by phantoms?"

"Don't file one."

He stopped, fists clenched, and said through his teeth, "A man has been kidnapped and a woman killed. I cannot ignore what is happening here."

"I have no answers, only questions. Do you think I would truly sit by and keep information from you when lives are at stake?"

"If you thought it would help you get your sister back?" His voice was acidic, and it stung.

I swallowed my own rising anger. "If I knew who they were, I would know how to fight them. I would not have let them kidnap that man if I could have stopped it."

He shook his head and turned away from me, his shoulders tight with strain. A moment later, he said, "I know that. I know. But that is two people dead or gone on my watch and I have nothing to show for it, not even a clue we can chase."

I wrapped my arms around his waist and laid my cheek against his upper back. He relaxed and sighed, pressing my hands with his own. There was nothing romantic in the gesture, just the offer of comfort and understanding. We might have stayed that way for several more minutes if we hadn't heard a woman scream.

Both of us were running before the sound ended.

"Back of the house," Tony said.

We rounded the corner in time to see a woman collapse onto the grass and a dark figure disappear into the night. Tony peeled off to chase the shadow, but I didn't bother trying to stop him. He would never catch the vampire, not in a foot race, and my eyes were for the woman, alone. I fell to my knees beside her, knowing I would need to apologize profusely—and with my wallet—for all the damage done to Percy's gown, and checked for breathing.

She was alive.

But there was a significant amount of blood on the bodice of her gown. I pulled the neckline back to reveal a bite just above her left breast. Not two neat little holes, like in the popular novels. This was a true bite, with torn skin and ragged flesh.

"Dammit," I said, grabbing a handful of my skirt and pressing it hard against the wound.

Tony stumbled to a stop next to me, panting.

I said, "Go get Dr. Hesselius, quickly" without looking up.

There was no way to know how much blood she lost, but she needed a doctor, and I would *not* let Edith Ashcroft die.

18

Enthralled

GWEN

We carried Edith through the servants' entrance to avoid alarming the rest of the guests and laid her on the bed in the doctor's room. He cut her gown open, then cleaned and dressed her wound, asking us clearheaded questions as he worked.

"You saw a shadow fleeing, you say?"

"Yes," Tony confirmed. "I chased it into the wood, but I couldn't keep up."

"A good thing. You would have made an easy meal in the dark. Lady Gwen, will you clean your hands and pass me that needle and thread?"

I took the bottle of alcohol on the dresser and doused my hands, then threaded a curved needle with the silk thread, and passed it to the doctor.

"Will she not wake?" Tony asked.

"Not in a vampiric swoon," the doctor said as he began stitching. "She may not wake for several hours, more if she has lost a significant amount of blood. But her color is good and her pulse is strong."

"What is a vampiric swoon?"

"Vampires have a nasty bit of magic that allows them to entice and enthrall their victims. If they wish to kill a victim, they can overwhelm them with this power, which causes them to swoon."

My blood went cold. Had we not been close enough to hear the scream, we might have found kind, generous Edith on the grass in the morning, her skin covered in dew, white eyes staring blindly at the sky. I shook my head to clear that grotesque vision.

"And if they don't want to kill their victims?" Tony asked.

"There are generally two paths the vampire may take: one is to feed enough to satisfy and move on, and the other is to create a thrall. To maintain their power over the thrall, they must feed from them regularly. If the thrall is weak, their mind may eventually break. If not, the vampire has a willing—or unwilling, as the case may be—slave, for as long as he chooses."

"A slave?" Tony asked, perking up. "How?"

"The vampire's influence over the thrall's mind allows them to implant ideas, desires, and even instructions the thrall will follow. The vampire may erase themselves from the victim's mind if they choose. But many prefer the victim to remember because they enjoy the fear as much as the food."

Dr. Hesselius spoke absently as he worked, as if reciting a text from a boring, oft-read book, but the effect of his words on Tony and me was the opposite. My cheeks heated as a mixture of fear and anger took hold like an oven in my gut. Most of this I knew from my studies, but the doctor had many years more experience than I, and my knowledge was broad rather than focused since I had been searching for ways to get to Lia.

Part of my struggle to complete this puzzle was simply not having enough pieces, but I began to see the details fit together and hints of the broader picture became clearer.

"Doctor," I said, watching as he tied off the stitches and finished dressing the wound. "Is it possible to break the enthrallment?"

His white brows drew together above his spectacles, which he pulled off and cleaned on his shirt. "Sometimes. If a vampire enthralls a person against their will, it is possible to prove to them, through enough evidence, that they have been enslaved. But"—he sighed and rubbed his forehead—"if the thrall has been a willing victim? I have never seen it broken."

"Why would someone be willing?" Tony asked, his face screwed up in lines of disgust.

"People are complicated," the doctor said. "Perhaps hoping they, too, might become a vampire one day. Perhaps for the pleasure of being fed upon. Who knows?"

"Would it be easier for a loved one to break the enthrallment?" I said.

"I believe it would. They have a deeper connection to the thrall, after all."

A large piece of the puzzle became suddenly clear; we were right to follow Lord Ashcroft, but maybe we had been wrong to keep this truth from him, after all. Sally, good-hearted Sally, had seen far more clearly than I, even if she didn't know it. If I were more willing to trust people, Lady Ashcroft may not have been attacked. And if I'd been more concerned with their safety and less with my own desires... Edith lay on the bed, her lips pale, salty trails of dried tears on her cheeks, and a bandage wound around her chest.

She was kind to me at her own risk, honest and generous when no one else dared. And now she lay wounded because I wasn't willing to risk losing the one chance I had to find Lia. God's breath. Did my selfishness know no bounds?

I turned to Tony and said, "Keep these two safe. Doctor, I think I have a plan to capture the vampire. One that should actually work." I hadn't been able to keep the self-loathing out of my voice with that last thought. "Are you willing to help?"

"In any way I can," he said.

"Good. I'll be back."

Percy was not thrilled with being woken in the small hours after midnight, and when he saw the blood, ragged tears, and grass stains on his gown, his face nearly turned purple. But then he looked at my face, and the anger melted into worry.

He said, "What happened?"

"I'll tell you if you come with me."

He threw on a dressing gown and followed me to my room, where I gathered up a sleepy pair of siblings and dragged them back to the doctor's room, grateful it was too late even for the most determined card players to be wandering about the house.

Once everyone was gathered in one place, I started asking questions.

"I cannot lay out my plan until I have every bit of information we have gathered. I moved too quickly today, and this is the result of my miscalculation." I gestured toward Edith.

Sally looked at the woman with an empathetic frown. Percy simply stood, solemn, but Sam swallowed and fidgeted—gotcha.

"So I'd like to know what you've all learned today if you don't mind. And you don't. So speak up."

"I only scraped up some run-of-the-mill gossip," Percy said.

"Any clue might help."

He shrugged. "Very well, then. Lord and Lady Ashcroft were a love match. Their third son died of scarlet fever, and she has not been able to conceive again. Lord Ashcroft is concerned about their inheritance, and since their son's death has spent most of his time politicking, even when Parliament is not in session. Lady Ashcroft seems to be universally liked. I did, however, learn some rather salacious gossip about an affair the Marquis of Rutledge had a few years ago with a mysterious lady."

"Save that story for when we've got time, and some wine and cheese," I said, feeling that a smile was altogether misplaced given the atmosphere, but Percy only winked at me, as if to say *goal accomplished*. It took a bit of the chill from the air and the weight from my shoulders, and I was grateful.

Sally cleared her throat and straightened like she was about to give a lecture or recite a poem, but she would not look at me. "Most of what I heard was—was about you, my lady."

I swallowed my discomfort and said, "Sarah Elizabeth Dawes?"

Her eyes, blue as a robin's egg, widened as they locked onto my face.

"What have I told you about calling me, *my lady*?"

The tension in her shoulders eased, and while she didn't smile, she relaxed back against the wall. Sam, by contrast, was fidgeting as if he had a frog in his pocket.

"What did you learn, Sam?" I asked, softening my voice as much as possible.

He squeezed his folded hands until his knuckles turned white, his eyes darting to Sally, and I thought he was more afraid of her response than of mine. After a moment of silence, he came to a decision.

Sam raised his chin and said, "I snuck into Lord Ashcroft's room."

Tony let out an exasperated breath through his nose.

"I thought I could find something in his papers about Mr. Capstone, or the vampire, but then I heard them coming down the hall, and I hid under the bed. Lady Ashcroft said she didn't want him meeting with Mr. Capstone anymore. She wasn't happy about them trading secrets."

From the little I knew of Edith's character, I wasn't surprised.

"He said that everything was changing, and they needed to be prepared to protect their son, and Mr. Capstone had always been right, so he was going to meet with him tonight." He paused and thought that over, then amended, "Last night after dinner. I thought—I thought I could find out myself and tell you, after. But then he left and went into the woods, and Sally thought I was trying to be sneaky—"

"Because you were being sneaky!"

He turned on her, his cheeks flushed an angry red. "I wasn't trying to—"

"That's enough," Tony said. His voice cut through their argument like a sharp knife.

"Give me a moment," I said, and turned to pace on the limited floor space.

From the sound of it, Mr. Capstone met with Lord Ashcroft regularly and Edith wasn't happy about it. She mentioned to me that his political goals had changed, but she attributed it to the Marquis of Rutledge, who was a ridiculously puffed-up misogynist. More likely, it was the vampire who altered his goals, but why? And how was that tied to Thistle Honeycutt? She was missing longer than the vampire had presumably been in the country.

"Sally was right. We need to tell Lord Ashcroft everything," I said.

She breathed a sigh of relief, and even Tony didn't disagree this time, not now that someone else was hurt.

"We need to find him, explain what is happening, and see if he is willing to become bait for the monster. Doctor Hesselius, if he believes us and breaks the enthrallment, will he be able to remember anything related to the vampire?"

"The few times I have known of it," he said, "the thrall recalled what the vampire tried to hide, although it took many days of recovery before they were able to do so."

"We don't have many days," I said.

"What makes you say that?" Percy asked.

"The vampire just tried to kill his wife. He's getting either desperate or more dangerous."

"What do you propose?" the doctor asked.

I cracked my knuckles. "An ambush."

He smiled.

I would much rather have gone to bed. I might even have taken Tony with me if I thought he would accept a fling. Instead, I dragged a sleepy, flustered Lord Ashcroft through the dark halls of Chatsworth Manor so I could shove his nose in his injured wife's face.

"I don't understand the meaning of this, Lady Gwen," he protested. "Why isn't Edith in bed?"

The fact that we found Lord Ashcroft in his room, sleeping like a drunk with absolutely no odor of alcohol about him, suggested he had, in fact, met with the vampire. He'd likely gone to bed without a thought in his head.

"I'll explain it all when we get there," I said, casting a glance at Tony, who ushered the man along from the other side.

The room was dark when we entered, dark enough that the light from our single candle only reached a few feet beyond the three of us. Percy and the children were back in my room, and the doctor sat by the head of the bed, swathed in shadow.

"Edith is in here?" Lord Ashcroft said, peering into the darkness. His voice was sharper, with a bit of his customary intelligence having chased away the befuddlement of sleep.

"She is," I said, "but first there is something you must know, my lord. You have not been well."

He snorted. "What do you mean? What can you know about my health?"

"More than you think," I said. "I know you forget things other people claim to have told you. And that sometimes you struggle to remember parts of your day, minutes or entire hours of time."

"That happens to everyone," he scoffed, but fear pooled behind his eyes. "I would like my wife, please. Where is Edith?"

I was making guesses, hoping to uncover the mental blocks a bit at a time, so I did not shock him when we finally revealed his wife. We needed him functional.

"You don't remember because you've been in thrall to a vampire," I said.

His face went through several lightning-fast changes in the candlelight; surprise, disbelief, anger.

"This has gone too far, lady. Give me my wife."

With that, he tried to push past me, but Tony dropped a big hand onto the muscle where his neck and shoulder met and squeezed. Lord Ashcroft stopped, fear rounding his eyes. "What is the meaning of this!?"

We had decided beforehand to let him see his wife at that point, but I had a hunch, so I reached up to unbutton the high collar of his nightshirt. He batted my hands away, and I slapped him. One sharp, openhanded blow that wouldn't hurt as much as startle him.

Likely, Lord Ashcroft had likely never been struck in his life. He stood there, mouth popped open in shock until I unbuttoned his shirt halfway down his chest.

"What is this, Lord Ashcroft?" I said, trying to keep the horror from my voice.

He looked down at his chest where I held the shirt open but only said, "What do you mean?"

"Try this," Doctor Hesselius said and offered him a mirror with a silver handle.

Lord Ashcroft took it in shaking hands and held it at chest level. All the color drained from his face when he saw what I guessed would be there.

A clean cut marred the skin of his pectoral muscle beneath the dusting of black hairs. It was an inch or so long, deep, and surrounded by bruising and small broken blood vessels, similar to a love bite one might see on the neck of conspicuous lovers.

One trembling hand reached up and touched the skin gently. He flinched backward so hard that the mirror slipped from his fingers.

I caught it, Tony caught him, and Doctor Hesselius turned on the light.

"The vampire has been feeding on you and controlling your mind, Edgar," I said, as gently as I could allow myself. "You know him as Mr. Capstone."

The name made Edgar jerk in Tony's hands. "No," he said. "Capstone is an informant, nothing more. He cannot be a vampire. How could you possibly know this?"

"I am an occultist," I said. "I assume you have heard of the study."

"But I've seen him during the day. He cannot—he can't. This is..." His voice died away.

He spotted Edith.

With a cry, he lunged to her side, and Tony let him go.

"Edie?" he whispered, touching her face with the back of his hand. He jerked the covers away and found the bandage around her chest.

Turning on us, his face a mask of fear and outrage, he cried, "What have you done to my wife?"

"We have saved her life," the doctor said and peeled back the bandage to reveal the wound. The vampire had not bothered with making a clean, reusable cut; he'd simply savaged her with his teeth. Purple bruises marred her neck and shoulder where he had grabbed her, probably when we heard her cry.

Lord Ashcroft fell to his knees by the bed, shaking. He clutched her hand to his chest, ignoring his own wound.

"I will see to him if the inspector will stay with me," Doctor Hesselius said, then patted my hand. "You get some sleep. Come to us in the morning, and we will make our plan."

Tony searched my face, his eyes warm with concern. "I'll stay."

There was nothing else to do. If we pushed the man now, forced him to remember, it would likely break his mind. So I left, dragging myself back down the empty, dark hallways until I reached my own door.

It wouldn't open. Why was it locked?

Panic had me rearing back to kick the door in when it swung open, revealing Percy's tired, but still irritatingly beautiful, face. Of course, he would have locked the door. That was safe.

He pulled me inside and handed me a cup. The bittersweet bite of brandy floated up to sting my nostrils. I swallowed it in a single gulp and wheezed, "Thank you."

The children were curled up together on the bed, Sally with an arm thrown protectively around her brother. My heart squeezed at the sight, and I sank down to stretch out my legs and lean back against the door. Percy sat next to me, moonlight from the window picking out the sharp planes of his nose and cheeks in pale blue.

"I'm afraid, Percy," I whispered after a moment. "I made a bad call, and nearly got Lady Ashcroft killed."

"The vampire did that, Gwen, not you. Try not to take credit for everything, will you?"

I snorted, but it came out sounding more like a whimper.

"You are one of the smartest people I know, " he said, bumping his shoulder against mine. "But even you cannot know everything. Take me, for example. I am the best designer and milliner in New London. Maybe even all of Europe. I am also ridiculously handsome. But that doesn't mean I don't sew a false stitch, from time to time."

"You know," I said, "it's your humility that I appreciate most."

"Don't get used to it. You've earned me four more commissions for evening gowns, which should cover my income for an entire year, so my ego is guaranteed to grow."

"You did that," I said. "Your gowns speak for themselves."

"That's true, isn't it? Very well, I take it back."

A moment later, staring down at my hands in my lap, I said in a small voice, "Percy?"

"Hmm?"

"What if you don't make them the dresses they want? What if you make the dresses you want, and they hate them, and they hate you for making them?"

He turned to look at me, but I couldn't return his gaze, because if I raised my eyes he would see the fear in them.

"If I did that," he said, "then I would apologize and repair the mistake, or make them new dresses. And they would forgive me because they would understand that I am just as imperfect as they are, and because my intentions were good."

"Intention doesn't always equal impact. Besides... maybe my intentions aren't good. Maybe I'm too selfish to be a good person."

"It's never too late to change things and become who you want to be."

"You make it sound so simple."

"It is simple, Gwen. Maybe not easy, but simple."

"It's too complicated to be easy, especially with the Reavers involved."

There was a beat of surprised silence. "The what?"

"The dark riders I mentioned. I heard a poem somewhere that referred to them as Reavers. They kidnapped the village blacksmith tonight and disappeared in the circle of stones. I couldn't stop them. I barely even made them pause."

"Why the blacksmith? That seems strange."

"This whole affair is strange."

He was silent for so long I began to wonder if he'd fallen asleep. His voice was subdued when he said, at last, "Then we have more than vampires to deal with."

"So it would seem."

"What do these Reavers want?"

"I wish I knew."

Because I had a terrible suspicion the whole thing was tied together in some unexpected way, and I would only discover it too late to save anyone.

19

Silver Bullets

GWEN

L ady Ashcroft's illness was the topic du jour during luncheon, and wasn't Lord Ashcroft such a devoted husband for forgoing the pleasures of company to stay by her side? As if his involvement with a vampire hadn't been the cause of the whole debacle.

That was unfair because I didn't know how he had become entangled with the creature in the first place, but it felt better to blame him than to shoulder any of the responsibility myself. There was enough of that on my plate, already, thank you very much.

When the guests weren't talking about the Ashcrofts, they were giving me sidelong glances and whispering about how Lady Ashcroft and I seemed to grow close. Wasn't *that* a coincidence? Tragedy did seem to follow me, after all.

I escaped as soon as I was able, practically throwing myself through Doctor Hesselius's door before slamming it behind me.

Tony jumped out of his chair, one hand sliding beneath his coat. When he recognized me, he eased back down.

"Don't make me go back there," I said, leaning against the door and closing my eyes.

"You'd rather face the vampire?" he asked.

"At this point? Absolutely. Speaking of," I stood and turned toward the bed. Edith was sound asleep, though her color looked better, but Edgar's haggard face told me he hadn't slept at all. He looked twenty years older, with dark smudges beneath his eyes and deep lines bracketing his mouth, which was thinned in distress.

"Have you slept, my lord?" I asked.

He shook his head, and locks of dark hair fell across his face. He rubbed his hand over his eyes and said, "Nightmares."

Tony and I exchanged a glance.

The doctor crossed the room to stand close to me. "He remembers, and it is torturing him. Lady Ashcroft woke long enough to drink some soup and swallow a little water, but otherwise, she has slept."

"Have you spoken to him?"

"Not of our intentions, no. I thought it best to leave that to you. But I must warn you, lady. If he becomes distressed to the point of harm, I will ask you to leave. I would like to help you, but I am a doctor first, and these are my patients."

I swallowed back whatever argument was trying to escape my lips and said, "Very well."

The chair next to the bed was empty, so I sat and took a deep breath. "Lord Ashcroft, I need your help."

He didn't answer, so I continued, hoping he was, at least, listening. "I want to capture the vampire who hurt Edith. And I am afraid that if we do not do it soon, he might escape and hurt other people."

Nothing.

I chewed my lip. If revenge didn't stir him, perhaps... "Doctor, how often does a vampire abandon a victim it has not killed?"

He saw the path I was trying to lead Lord Ashcroft down, frowned at me, but said, "Unless they are killed, a vampire always finishes its victims."

That was nothing less than the truth, as far as I knew, but I needed Edgar to hear it. "If we don't stop him, he will come back for Edith. Maybe not tonight, but it will happen."

He raised his head and turned bloodshot eyes on me.

I asked, "When he appeared to you, what did you see?"

His eyes flicked back and forth, searching inside his mind for answers. "He appeared to be a rather tall dwarven man with a black beard."

That fit with what the headmistress of the orphanage told us. She believed Mr. Capstone to be a dwarf who was paying her to provide children for false kidnappings, hoping for political gain through fear. She also had worn those high-collared blouses. Perhaps to hide the vampire's bite? We would never know, now.

He also appeared to Edgar Ashcroft as a dwarf. Why? To make humans suspicious?

"But I can see him now, in my memory," he continued. "As if there are two men standing in front of me but one wavers like steam. And those eyes. Yellow, like a harvest moon."

Sam had also seen yellow eyes. "What did he want you to do?"

"He never told me to do anything, only—only gave me information and asked questions. He..." His eyes filled with tears and he pressed one hand over the bandage that covered his wound. "I can't talk about it."

The doctor raised one white brow at me in warning.

"I want to make him regret what he did to you and Edith. And I want to stop him before he hurts her again. Will you help me?"

He looked down at his open hands, examining the palms as if there should have been something in them. "He is still in my mind," he said, voice filled with horror. "What can I do against him? What can I do?"

I stood and reached out to take both his hands—they were icy—and waited for him to look at me. Those eyes, once so confident and intelligent, were haunted.

I squeezed his hands and said, "You can fight; for Edith, and for yourself."

"What if—what if I can't? He'll kill us, all of us, I know it."

"Then we will have died trying to remove an evil from the world. But Edgar"—I pushed every bit of confidence I would muster into my voice—"we will *not* lose."

He searched my eyes, hungry and desperate, but afraid to hope. Whatever he saw in them must have been enough, because he swallowed, tightened his hands around mine, and said, "Very well."

We left Lord Ashcroft to the doctor's care for what few hours were left before we would all take our lives into our hands and attack a vampire.

"He looked better," Tony said.

"Perhaps having something to do helped."

"I suppose it would, but sleep might help more."

"Let us hope the doctor can coax him into bed, then."

"He'll be safe without a guard?"

"As far as I know, the vampire has only attacked people outside the manor, which suggests they have not invited him inside. They are as safe as we can make them. For now, at least."

Tony stared at his shoes as we walked, and I doubted it was to admire the thick carpets. "What's wrong, Inspector?"

He looked up. "Back to that, are we?"

"Only until you stop irritating me."

A half-hearted smile curled one corner of his mouth, but his voice was serious when he said, "After what that man has been through, I don't feel right asking him to do this."

I nodded as we turned into the hall where my rooms were located, keeping my voice low when we stopped just outside my door. "I know. But we must have the vampire so engaged, so distracted, that he does not notice us. If we give ourselves away, he'll flee before we have even a chance to stop him. And the doctor was not lying; it will come back for Edith until it kills her. Besides"—I rolled my shoulders to loosen some of the tension—"It's nothing he hasn't done before."

Tony didn't like my answer, but I didn't have a better one to give.

When I opened the door, Sally and Sam looked up from their respective books.

"No sign of Percy yet," Sally said as she closed her book.

Tony poured himself a glass of water from the pitcher on the bureau. "I thought he was only walking down to the village for some ribbon or something?"

"I'm not sure why," I said. "I have no intention of going to dinner tonight."

"Maybe they have particularly nice ribbons?" Sally offered.

"You may be right, my dear. Sam, would you care to charge up the umbrella?"

The boy dropped his open book and jumped to his feet, leaving Sally to pick it up and put it neatly on the windowsill before the pages could wrinkle.

"Sure," he said, smiling.

I popped open the umbrella, propped it on the back of a chair, and let him go to work. He had a serviceable right hook for a thirteen-year-old. He punched the canopy while I unloaded the pistol I had taken after my encounter with the vampire.

"Are those silver?" Tony asked, looking over my shoulder.

"Good question." I dug through my luggage until I found a small-ish leather case with alchemical symbols stamped into the clasp. "That," I said, holding the case up, "is what we are about to find out."

Tony and Sally both watched as I lay the bullet on a clean cloth, pulled a vial and a small dropper from the case, and worked the stopper out.

"Do you carry a chemistry set with you everywhere you go?" Tony asked.

"It is an alchemy set, not chemistry, though it naturally does chemistry as well, and of course I do," I said, pulling up a tiny amount of the clear fluid into the dropper. "At least when I do not have access to my kit at home."

"What is it?" Sally asked.

"This," I said, wiggling the vial, "is sodium hypochlorite. It is extremely caustic, so do not let the liquid touch your skin."

"What does caustic mean?"

"It will burn you," Tony said.

"It doesn't look hot."

"It is called a chemical burn," I said, letting a drop fall onto the head of the bullet. "And the same reaction should tarnish the metal if it is silver."

After a moment, the surface of the bullet became milky beneath the solution. "Yes," I said, carefully replacing my tools. "It is silver. Why would a vampire carry silver bullets?"

"You can ask him tonight," Tony said, as he began checking his own pistol.

"Tonight?" Sam asked, panting. His cheeks were pink with exertion and the runes on the handle of the umbrella glowed faintly.

He shook his fists out as I closed the umbrella. The handle was warm, just shy of being hot enough to burn. I would need to wear gloves.

"Yes, tonight. And no," I said before he could finish opening his mouth, "you cannot go."

"But—"

"You will go nowhere near the vampire," I said as he continued, "I can help!"

"Have you already forgotten what that thing nearly did to you?"

"No. And I'll never forget. That's why I can help."

I took his slender shoulders in my hands and said, "You will not leave this house without Tony or me. Do you understand?"

His jaw clenched and unclenched and his lips worked as if he were swallowing something he desperately wanted to say. The only thing that came out was a deeply reluctant, perhaps angry, "Yes, ma'am."

A knock made the four of us jump. "That will be Percy," I said, and pulled open the door.

A person who was distinctly not Percy stood in the hall with an envelope on a silver tray. I thanked the servant, who looked bewildered and closed the door.

"Tony? Why are you receiving mail in my room?"

He took the envelope and slid his finger beneath the seal. "I told the innkeeper to forward my mail here if I wasn't at the inn."

As he read, his voice slowed and his face took on an air of gravity. He folded the letter, stuck it in his jacket pocket, and took a deep breath. Oh, no. I knew those signs. When he looked up, his eyes confirmed it.

"What have you done?" I asked.

"Gwen—" he began, but I balled my hands into fists and warned, "Tony..."

"I've called in a few men from the local constabulary and they've just arrived."

"I see. So you'd prefer to get a few more people killed than trust me?"

"I would prefer," he said through clenched teeth, "to keep everyone as safe as possible, and the more guns, the better."

"How did your gun work last night? This is not a mundane criminal, Tony."

"Which is exactly why we need all the help we can muster."

"No. These men will only make it harder and more dangerous. More people, more noise, more body odor, and more heat, means a greater chance it will discover us before we spring the ambush. And they are not equipped, mentally or physically, to fight with a vampire."

"And you are?" he demanded.

I was tempted to show him exactly how equipped I was. In fact, the temptation was so strong that I clenched my fists until my knuckles popped to keep myself from showing him. Somehow we were inches from one another, and the coffee scent of his breath only made me angrier because it was a reminder he'd stayed up all night protecting the people I allowed to be hurt.

"I have trained, and I am experienced. I know what to expect," I said, with what I considered admirable self-control. "They do not. They will make mistakes, and they will die."

Tony, attempting to exert the same self-control, said in a similar tone of voice, "Their job is to put their life on the line to uphold the law. They agreed to the danger when they swore their oaths. You cannot ask them to sit idly by while the people they swore to protect are in danger."

There was no give in his expression. I could not convince him to call them off. Every hope I had of getting Lia back was tied to finding Thistle Honeycutt, and right now my best chance to find her lay in the vampire. And it looked as if I would not be able to do that without a gaggle of constables at my back.

"Fine," I said as I wrestled my temper back under control. "Fine. But they will not like what I force them to do."

We spent the rest of the afternoon in preparation. Percy did not return from the village, so I asked Frances to have one of her huntsmen guard each of the doors. She agreed, and asked, "Are you close to finding her? The celebrations end soon and after that, we will risk much more to keep you here."

I spun on her, my anger barely contained, and spat, "People have already died under your secrecy, and more are in danger. I warned you I will see to this matter as I see fit, and if you dislike the consequences, you should not have bribed me to intervene."

Her mouth popped open, like a landed fish, but I did not stay to see if she would recover her composure. There was too much to do. We charged the dwarven torches, letting them collect the last rays of light before the sun dropped below the horizon. Tony's constables were already in place and, as I had warned him, unhappy with their lot in life.

Sam and Sally were relocated to the housekeeper's room, where they could watch the forest and warn Lady Chatsworth if anything dangerous left the trees.

"Lady Gwen," Sally said, catching my arm before I left. "Please be careful."

"Of course, I will. And don't worry. If anything happens to me, your estate is in a trust that will ensure you and Sam are well taken care of until you reach your majority."

A flash of anger darkened her eyes. "I don't care about the money."

Sam glanced at his sister, shuffled his feet, and said, "The money is kind of nice, though."

Laughing, I pulled both of them into a hug. "I will come back, Sally. I promise."

I buttoned up my coat, reminded the children to keep themselves safe, and collected Tony, Lord Ashcroft, and the doctor.

"I had a telegraph from my friends," Doctor Hesselius said as he shrugged into a thick wool coat. "They landed in Ipswich and are hurrying to meet us, though I cannot say how long it will take them to arrive."

"We must proceed without them. Thank you for agreeing to stay with the children."

"Of course. I must also point my friends in the right direction if they arrive. I pray they will, for you will need the help."

We parted with the doctor at the stairs, ignored the surprised glances of the guests heading to dinner, and stopped at the servant's entrance. Lord Ashcroft was quiet, his skin pale and clammy, his lips nearly bloodless.

I touched his arm and said, "You remember where to go."

He nodded.

"And you are prepared?"

He glanced down at his chest, then pushed on the wound. Doctor Hesselius had reopened it just enough to let the capillaries near the surface soak through the cloth.

"I'm ready," he said.

"The vampire must be completely engaged," I said to the two of them. "We cannot move until he is so distracted that he will not notice us. Remember the signal?"

They nodded.

"Follow us in twenty minutes," I told Lord Ashcroft, and Tony and I set off for the forest, lanterns in one hand and pockets filled with weapons.

"Can we trust him to follow us?" I wondered aloud. If he didn't, our efforts would be meaningless.

Tony double-checked his revolver and slid it into a holster beneath his jacket as we entered the wood. "Did you see the way he looked at his wife? He'll come."

I tightened my grip on my umbrella. He'd better, because if the vampire appeared and we didn't have a distraction that would allow us to spring our trap, we might not make it out of the woods.

But it was too late to worry about that now.

It was time to catch a vampire.

20

The Kiss

SAM AND GWEN

"Stop pacing, Sam, you're making me nervous."

He glared at his sister and stomped on the floor as he passed her. Lady Gwen and Tony were about to go fight the thing that killed the old woman. The monster with yellow eyes. And he was here, safe in the house, with no way to help, while Sally watched him like a hawk.

Then there was the doctor in the corner, sitting on a chair and leafing through a book as if he didn't have a care in the world. Didn't they understand what was about to happen?

"Do you see anything yet?" he asked.

"No," she said. "Just darkness."

He stopped next to her and peered out the window. Light from the house spilled across the grass in bright green rectangular swaths, swallowed up by shadows before they reached halfway to the tree line. Beyond that was nothing but acres of canopy and the occasional bare spot where a clearing or bald hill poked its head above the treetops.

The leaves of the white tree stood out like a beacon in the moonlight. Sally noticed the same thing, because she said, "The moon is waning. I wonder what the tree will look like when there isn't so much light?"

She was right. The edge of the moon looked like it had been clipped off. There was still plenty of light, though. Enough, he hoped, for them to see by.

"Don't worry, children," the doctor said in his strange accent as he absently rubbed his bad knee. "They are as prepared as they can be, and have a better chance than most. Lord Ashcroft has an established relationship with the creature, which will make distracting it much easier. Most vampire hunters are not so lucky."

"You never saw that thing," Sam said, pacing once again. He had too much energy running through him to stand still. He felt like Lady Gwen's umbrella after it was all filled up and humming with power.

"Their chances will improve when my friends arrive," the doctor said. He sounded like an old farmer talking about the likelihood of rain, not someone who knew what it was like to be hunted by a vampire.

"Who are your friends?" Sally asked.

Her hands were clasped in her lap, fingers wrapped around the whistle Lady Gwen gave her to sound as an alarm. She held it as if it were the only thing keeping her together. Maybe she was as worried as him, after all.

"Famous monster hunters," he said, looking up from his book with a smile. "Though they rarely come to England. Your small island has been cleared of most of the more dangerous monsters, so there isn't much work for them. But in the wilder areas of the continent, there are still horrors to slay."

"Monster hunters?" Sam asked, a little spark of interest flaring to life in his chest. It wasn't enough to smother the worry, but it was enough to distract him, so he held onto it with both hands, like Sally gripping her whistle.

"Indeed. A rare profession, to be sure. One seldom sees monsters in cities with electric lights and dwarven lanterns, so people forget that the ground is not yet paved everywhere."

"I thought vampires would hunt where people are? Doesn't that make the city a good place for them?" Sally asked.

"For a few, it might. Perhaps for those younger vampires who still look a bit more human. But the old ones, the ones who have changed too much to look anything like a living human, would be easier to spot in a city, where they can no longer hide in the dark thanks to lamps. And we have better weapons now than we did when monsters ruled the shadows."

Sally turned back to the window. Tony and Lady Gwen had not just walked into the well-lighted streets of New London, but into a dark forest.

"Can't you do anything?" Sam asked. "Since you know so much, and all?"

"I would only be a hindrance. I cannot move as quickly as I once did. They will need every bit of their concentration, and if they had to protect me as well as themselves, everyone would be in greater danger. No." He pulled off his spectacles and wiped them on his shirt. "Better that I stay here so they don't have to worry about you, too."

Sam's right hand tightened into a fist around the knife in his pocket. That was easy for the doctor to say. He hadn't been there last year when Sam had found Tony and Lady Gwen tied up in the witch's house. If he hadn't freed them, Sally would now be dead. He couldn't get rid of the feeling that, if he couldn't get to them, something bad would happen.

Gwen

Tony and I positioned ourselves downwind from the site of the ambush, a small-ish break in the canopy that made as much use of the moonlight as possible so we wouldn't give ourselves away with artificial light.

Vampires couldn't smell fear the same way werewolves could, but they had far better senses than humans, and it was safer not to take any chances.

I put my back to the trunk of an ash tree, heart pounding, and waited. Tony hid behind a thicket of dense hedges and braced the rifle he'd borrowed from the Chatsworth Estate in the crotch of a low branch. He positioned himself to catch the vampire in a crossfire without hitting any of the constables, but only if Lord Ashcroft lured the creature to the proper spot.

With a long, silent sigh, I closed my eyes and tried to see the ambush in my mind. I let my hands relax, let my breathing slow, and with it my heartbeat. My senses grew more acute. Leaves rustled and crickets sang monotonous stridulation, the earthy scent of turf and decaying plants rose in a woodsy bouquet from the forest floor, and a spider skittered across the toe of my boot.

And then silence.

Crunching footfalls and snapping twigs echoed back to our hidden position, so loud they disturbed the entire forest. I fought to keep my muscles from tensing, my breath from picking up. We had to do everything perfectly. My fingers tightened around the butt of the pistol as the coppery scent of lord Ashcroft's blood filled the air.

The footsteps stopped, then signaled us by clearing his throat. He was ready.

"Mr. Capstone?" he asked of the night in a voice watery with fear. "I know you didn't call for a meeting but I've learned something you should know."

The vampire was close. I felt it, like rot in the air.

"You were right to seek me out," a voice—smooth, warm, honeyed—floated out of the darkness. I stopped breathing, and so did Ashcroft. Hopefully, the vampire was so distracted by the blood, he wouldn't notice the change in his thrall.

"What have you learned that caused you to put both of us in danger, my lord of Ashcroft?"

The voice was closer, intimately close, but seemed to come from everywhere at once, bouncing off the trees. If a spider could speak to a fly, it would sound like that.

"I—I overheard Mr. Coalfire during last night's card game," he said, his voice slowing with every word. "He said the guilds may... may strike if... if—"

His voice died away into a long sigh of ecstasy, and then a grunt. I risked peeking around the trunk of the tree. If Ashcroft had been compromised, we had to act now.

My stomach twisted in a mixture of morbid curiosity and revulsion. The vampire was already feeding. Perhaps the fresh blood was too much temptation to bear, or Ashcroft's news was not important enough to wait. He wrapped both arms around Ashcroft's chest, lifted the man, and plastered his mouth to the wound.

Edgar's head fell back as if in the throes of lovemaking, his fingers threaded through the vampire's dark hair almost reverently. It was uncomfortably, unbearably erotic.

It was also exactly what we needed.

I screwed my courage into place, stepped around the tree, sighted down the barrel, and squeezed the trigger. A silver bullet snapped the vampire's head back and away from his victim. Ashcroft crumpled like a boned fish and the vampire stumbled sideways with a scream that tore the air and cut at my eardrums.

A second crack of gunfire and a flash of light from Tony. That was the signal. Constables leaped from their hiding spots, flinging dirt and dead leaves in every direction as what looked like bushes and mounds of earth or fallen logs turned into men with guns, clubs, and Tony's bola.

Half a dozen shots rang out, and the vampire's body jerked like it was getting struck with heavy rocks. The constable with the bola unfurled the weapon, spun it once, and slung it, sidearm, at the vampire's legs. The balls zipped through the air, wrapped around his ankles, then twisted together on the opposite side, locking his legs in place. He lost his balance and toppled to the side.

"Stakes!" I cried as I sprinted toward the fallen monster.

Sam

A flash of light sparked beneath the canopy, lighting up the forest about halfway between the white tree and the bald hill.

"There!" Sally said, tapping on the window glass with a shaking finger.

Sam's heart jumped into a gallop. More flashes of light, followed by the sharp report of gunfire. If they were still firing, it meant the creature didn't go down in the initial attack. Tony and Lady Gwen were in danger. He turned to run, but Doctor Hesselius calmly stood between Sam and the door.

He skidded to a stop and said, "Let me go!"

"I cannot betray your guardian's trust by allowing you to put yourself in danger."

"Sam," Sally warned, grabbing his arm to lock him in place. He jerked against her grip, but she held tight. Someone knocked on the door and the three of them jumped in surprise.

"Come," the doctor said.

Sally turned back to the window, eyes fixed, one hand clutching the whistle she was to blow if the fight spilled out toward the house, the other fisted in his sleeve. A servant stood in the doorway.

"Doctor Hesselius? Your guests have arrived."

"Very good," the doctor said and followed the servant from the room.

The opportunity he needed was right in front of him and he couldn't move. In desperation, he twisted toward the window and said, "What was that?"

Sally rushed to the pane and pushed open the glass. "Where?"

Sam bolted for the hallway, taking the first few stairs before he skidded to a stop on the second-floor landing, face-to-face with the doctor. The old man considered Sam, then said to the servant, "On the other hand, please send them up to me right away."

The servant nodded and hurried away. Sam could have screamed with frustration. Doctor Hesselius turned to usher Sam back up the stairs when his knee gave out and he wobbled, losing his balance as he flailed, reaching for the rail but finding only empty air.

Time seemed to slow as the old man tipped backward, eyes wide with fright behind his glasses as his foot slipped. Sam lunged, fingers locking on the lapels of the doctor's jacket before he could tumble backward down the stairs. They sank to the carpet, panting. Dr. Hesselius braced himself on the railing and scooted back so he could clutch his knee with his free hand.

Sam couldn't see anything wrong with the knee but the doctor's forehead had broken out in sweat. "Are you alright?"

"My knee," he said between teeth clenched in pain. Sam considered the man on the floor, and Sally, where she stood on the third floor, halfway between the door and the window, unable to focus on both. More gunshots rang out, clear and sharp through the open window.

"Watch the forest!" Sam yelled, then turned and sprinted down the stairs past the doctor, who cried, "Samuel, no!" Just as Sally screamed, "Sammy!"

He ignored them both and took the stairs two at a time, running headlong down both flights to reach the ground floor, and nearly plowed into a golden bear of a man.

Sally had yellow hair, but hers was dark, like honey. This man's hair was as bright as wheat in the sun. He caught Sam by the shoulders, and said, "Woah, woah, where's the fire, boy?"

His voice was deep, like it came out of the bottom of a barrel, and his hands could have probably crushed Sam's skull. Next to him stood a woman, taller than Lady Gwen. Long dark hair fell down her back in a braid. She tilted her head and regarded him with the yellow eyes of a hawk.

A thrill of fear shot up his spine.

Both of them wore leather packs on their backs and woolen cloaks instead of jackets. The woman's was such a bright red that it reminded him of blood. Both of them wore the kind of calm, competent expressions he associated with dangerous people. If he had seen them on the street, he would have crossed to the other side.

But dangerous people were exactly the kind he needed to save Lady Gwen and Tony.

"Are you the doctor's friends?" he asked, breathless.

"We are," the woman said in a light French accent. She had a voice that made Sam feel like a cat who had just been petted. "Where is the doctor?"

"He sent me to get you," Sam lied, "there's a vampire in the forest and we need your help!"

They exchanged a glance, then the big man let go of Sam and said, "Where?"

Gwen

The constables reached the struggling vampire before I could close the intervening space, stakes raised to strike. Despite how fast I ran, the world crawled at a snail's pace, showing me every movement in painful detail. The vampire rolled to a sitting position and looked at me. His hood had fallen back when he'd fed from Lord Ashcroft, and the moon fell fully on dark eyes and stark features that were beautiful the way a gnarled, dead tree is beautiful: bones, and eyes, and skin recognizable as human, but only an echo of something that had once been alive, barren and twisted.

My shot had taken him in the back of the head, and a section of his skull was missing behind his right ear; he didn't seem to notice.

Instead of scrambling away from his attackers or trying to protect himself, he smiled at me. It was a slow, cruel grin. His lips and teeth were smeared with Edgar's blood.

"Wait!" I screamed at the constables, but it was no use. Before my heel hit the ground, the vampire jerked his legs apart, snapping the rope of the bola. He continued the motion, planting one hand on the ground and turning into a low kick that snapped the shin bones of the constable closest to him. The man screamed and tumbled to the earth, clutching his legs.

Tony fired another shot that buzzed past my left ear, but the vampire had already moved. He spun to his feet, caught a constable by the throat, and flung him against the trunk of the closest tree. The man hit with a cry and a wet crunch that didn't bode well for his spine.

The other two constables were too close for a clean shot at the vampire, so I yanked my umbrella up and pulled the trigger. The energy Sam stored by punching the canopy earlier that day exploded from the tip, stopping me dead and burning my palms as my heels dug into the dirt. The wall of force took the vampire off his feet. He spun sideways through the air but twisted his body like a cat and landed with nimble grace.

It had only been a matter of seconds, but three of the seven of us were already out of the fight, and the vampire was still smiling.

"Where is she?" I demanded, but gunfire from both constables devoured my question.

The vampire leaped in a ten-foot arc that brought him down between them. I raised the umbrella, but I wasn't fast enough to stop him from punching his fist through the chest of one of the constables. The wet sound of tearing flesh and breaking bone froze me.

I was aware of making a retching noise, but I could not move or tear my eyes away as the vampire reached backward with his free hand, grabbed the constable behind him by the front of his shirt, and threw him casually over his shoulder to sail through the air screaming. He landed with a crunch and didn't get up.

Tony charged through the brush behind me and fired two more shots that hit the vampire in the chest. He didn't even flinch. Slowly, almost thoughtfully, he pushed the dead man off his arm with a wet sucking sound, and stuck one finger in his mouth like a child with a lollipop.

His eyelids fluttered, and he said, around his finger, "She, who?"

"The fae woman, the housekeeper," I said, surprised at how calm my voice sounded despite the way my hands shook, and how badly I wanted to turn and run.

"A fae woman? I'm certain I would have known if I had a fae woman for supper. Their blood is fizzy and light, like champagne. Quite my favorite drink."

He wiped his hand lazily on the front of his black shirt. I raised my chin without lowering the umbrella and said, "Didn't those shirts drop out of fashion with pirates and poets?"

He chuckled. It was a horrible, tearing sound. "I don't pay much attention to fashion. Only to food."

Tony skidded to a stop next to me, rifle at his shoulder, his breath sawing in angry gasps. He didn't pull the trigger again, because it wouldn't do any good, but he didn't lower the weapon, either.

Only my first, unexpected shot had done enough damage to shock the monster, and that was because the bullet had been silver.

We sidestepped away from one another, keeping enough space between us that we couldn't be killed by a single blow. A stake was strapped to my back, but I could only use it if I managed to get close. And the umbrella still had one blast left.

"I presume I have the honor of meeting the distinguished Mr. Capstone?" I asked.

He sketched a graceful bow. "At your service. Or, rather, you will be at mine in a moment. You smell"—he pulled in a deep breath through his nose—"intriguing. I thought so when I first saw you in New London, and then again in the forest."

"So that *was* you at the zoo," I said, edging sideways, hoping to let Tony get close enough that a duel attack would immobilize him long enough to drive the stake home.

"You knew it was," he chided me. "Just like you knew I would be here, waiting for you. I smelled you on him, you know."

We reached the right angle, and I pulled the trigger. The vampire tumbled backward, putting him safely in Tony's line of sight again, and I sprinted forward, discarding my umbrella for the stake.

The gun barked. The bullet struck. The vampire did not even react.

He rolled to his feet and grabbed Tony by the lapels of his jacket between one breath and the next, staring into his eyes like a lover. Tony froze, his angry expression softening like melting wax until his eyes were dull and uncomprehending. His entire body relaxed, and the rifle slipped from his fingers.

"There's a good lad," the vampire cooed.

He didn't even bother to move when I attacked, simply bent like a tree in the wind, dropping Tony–who stood in a daze–and rolling his weight away from me.

I launched a series of strikes to close the distance between us. Left cross, right jab with the stake clutched in my fist, front kick. He dodged each one with no effort, smiling at me all the while.

"You are surprising, aren't you? Faster than you should be," he said as if we were having a chat over tea. Then he caught a punch that stopped my arm as if I had just hit a brick wall. "And stronger, too."

Then he punched me in the chest. If he had put his full power behind it, I doubted even the coat could have stopped it, but he was playing with me. The strike pushed me backward and heat from the transferred energy wrapped around my torso as the filament absorbed the blow and spread it out.

I darted back in but, in a blinding display of speed, he flung me away and launched himself at Tony. I landed hard, the coat heating once more. I lost my grip on my stake and rolled to a stop against a tree next to the body of one of the dead constables.

The vampire hefted Tony in the air, leaned in, and smelled his neck as if my friend were a glass of wine with a strong bouquet. A sound of purring pleasure rumbled from the creature's chest and bile burn at the back of my throat. God's breath, he was going to kill Tony and I was too far away to stop him.

"Leave him!" I heard myself scream. "He is under my aegis!"

It was a shot in the dark. By declaring him under my protection, I was putting myself in a position of power and relying on old rites and customs, such as guest rights, to form the rules of engagement.

For some magical creatures, such things were not simply customs but rules as inviolable as gravity.

Slowly, very slowly, he turned his eyes on me. "Aegis? What right do you have to enforce an aegis?"

He released Tony, who stood in a blind stupor, and stalked toward me. I pushed myself backward, using the tree to stand, and watched him come. The wound on the back of his head hadn't yet healed, but every other gunshot wound was nothing more than a hole in his ratty clothes. There was one mark, something like an angry scar on his cheek, a perfect circle with a deformed symbol in the center.

"He is under my aegis," I said again, breathlessly. "You cannot touch him."

A long sigh hissed between his teeth. One second he was ten feet away, the next he was right in front of me. He was close enough. I told myself to strike, told my hands to move, but they wouldn't. Between one blink and the next, he had both arms wrapped around my waist, pinning my arms against my sides, leaving the stake I'd taken from the body of the constable trapped uselessly at my thigh.

"And who protects you," he said in a low purr, his nose running along the column of my neck.

I wanted to pull away in disgust, but a vampire's magic extends beyond its ability to enthrall, and I had overestimated my strength. He laid his ear against my chest, letting me see in stomach-wrenching detail the dangling bits of bone and flesh hanging from the wound in the back of his head.

"Your heart is strong," he said, raising his lips back to the level of my throat and dipping his tongue into the hollow between my collarbones. "And poor Edgar is useless to me, now that you have broken him. Was it you who ruined him for me, changeling child? Perhaps you will make a suitable replacement, once you taste my kiss. Let us find out."

He bit me.

I heard a scream but didn't feel the sound leave my throat. Dark ecstasy rolled over me in a wave so close to physical release that my entire body shook with it. The pleasure began at the spot where my neck and shoulder met and uncoiled in shimmering black waves that loosened every muscle. He pulled his head back, arching against me, and made a humming sound low in his throat.

"Yes," he whispered, my blood on his lips. "You will help me, won't you? For a taste of my kiss, for the pleasure it brings? You will help me usher in a new era where the strong do not hide in fear of the weak."

He leaned in close and whispered in my ear, "You may not have any magic, but your blood is full of power. Is that what keeps you from my thrall, delicious changeling child?"

Something struck the vampire in the face so hard that he jerked away from me, screaming in fury, his arms thrashing. I hit the ground. My knees wobbled as I tried to regain my balance and bring my body back under my control.

Something black clung to the vampire's face as he windmilled, then launched itself into the air with a triumphant caw, leaving the monster spinning and thrashing. Instead of burning eyes, the vampire was left with a mass of torn, bloody flesh.

"Save the girl," the bird croaked from high above.

Aristotle.

I still clutched the stake in numb fingers. My damned wonderful bird had given me a chance. The only thing that made sense now was to attack. So, I launched myself at the vampire and screamed as I went.

21

Red Riding Hood Joins the Fight

GWEN

Even without sight, he was stronger and faster than I, and he still moved like water, sliding aside my strikes or turning, so they landed uselessly on his shoulder. He could both hear and feel me moving. I growled my frustration into the night air.

He hadn't taken Ms. Honeycutt. Several people died who might still have been alive if I had not involved myself in something unrelated to my mission. The anger burned hot in my stomach, spread up to kindle in my chest and out to my limbs, like heat lighting, making me faster.

I twisted in a high kick, then followed up with a low strike aimed at his legs. He sidestepped, growling in irritation, and said, "You cannot keep this up forever, and my eyes will heal. When they do, I will make a slave of you and use your body in ways that tear your soul apart a bit at a time, till your heart is nothing but a useless bit of meat that beats only for the pain I can give you."

The anger that kindled in my chest roared to an incandescent blaze as a series of faces flashed across my mind: Mr. Yates and Mrs. Chapman, Tony, Delilah and Percy, Sally and Saumel, Mama... and Lia.

"My heart," I snarled as I spun in the opposite direction, clutching the stake in both hands, "has never been mine."

I caught him on the dodge. The tip of the stake punctured his chest just beneath his breastbone at an angle and drove up sideways with a meaty pop, bathing my hands in cold, wet gore.

He made a sound, something like the air being let out of a balloon, and stumbled backward. Aristotle gave a triumphant cry. With a grunt, he pulled the stake out and wobbled, unable to catch his balance. Perhaps I had not buried it deep enough to touch his heart. I pulled in a breath, preparing to launch another attack, but something huge and tawny barreled past me like a speeding auto and crashed into the vampire with a terrific *whack*.

I tripped backward over my own feet, but strong hands caught me by the backs of my arms. I spun, swinging an elbow, but it was carefully diverted and locked into place.

"Not so fast, Gwen. I suppose it was our turn to save you," said a faintly accented voice.

I blinked and forced my tired eyes to focus on a beautiful, olive-skinned face and a pair of amber eyes. Eyes I recognized. "Alix?"

My knees gave out. She caught me and lowered me to the ground. "Who else?"

"I did not realize Doctor Hesselius and I were part of the same social circles," I said in a poor attempt at humor. My voice shook.

"Fate is a funny thing," she agreed. "You can imagine our surprise at hearing an old friend was working with you. We ran all the way from the coast after we landed."

Vicious snarling and breaking bones punctuated her speech.

"Is that Cyrus?" I asked as I tried to keep my head from swinging limply on my neck.

"It is," she said and pressed something into my hands. "Here, drink this. Courtesy of the Sisters of St. Christophe."

I raised whatever it was to my lips and swallowed. Cool, bright, with a touch of alcohol and something spicy. It burned down my throat and hit me in the chest like a train.

"God's breath," I coughed, as the world snapped back into focus.

"They should have named it that. I will tell them so," Alix laughed. She replaced the flask, then handed me a wadded-up cloth. "Here, you are bleeding. I will be back."

It took me a moment to realize what she meant. I pressed the cloth to the bite mark on my neck and surveyed the damage. Cyrus had taken his wolf form and, quite literally, ripped what remained of the vampire to soggy shreds. His dusky muzzle was dark with blood and something worse that he tried to clean by licking his forearms and rubbing his nose against them.

Alix reappeared, guiding Tony by both arms and sat him next to me. She pressed the flask against his lips with one hand and pinched his mouth open with the other. When he had a mouthful, she tilted his head back and covered his mouth with her other hand. He swallowed dutifully, then his eyes widened, and he jerked forward. She moved as he coughed and surged to his feet.

"What—" He coughed again, bending over and bracing himself on his knees. "What was that? Gwen?"

He spun, eyes wild, and saw me just as I said, "I'm here."

Alix examined the rest of the bodies, and Tony sank to the ground in front of me. "You're hurt. Here." He took the cloth from my hands and peeled it back. When he saw the wound, his face twisted with anger and disgust. I wanted to flinch away from his eyes, but I could not. The expression was more painful than the bite.

He folded the cloth neatly and pressed it to my neck. "I'm sorry," he said.

"It wasn't your fault."

"I pushed this. I brought them here. *Dammit*."

"Lady Gwen?"

Tony jerked to the side at the high-pitched voice to reveal Sam standing between two trees at the edge of the small clearing. His chest heaved as if he'd run all the way from the manor.

"What are you—" I began, then realized what had happened. "You led Alix and Cyrus here, didn't you?"

He nodded.

"Where is Doctor Hesselius?"

"He hurt his knee on the stairs."

"And you thought you'd just step up and help, is that it?" Tony asked.

Sam's eyes darted around, but he nodded. "Are you okay? Is he—is he..."

"Dead," Alix said as she plopped Edgar Ashcroft down next to us. His head rolled around on his neck and he made small whimpering sounds, but he was alive. When Sam saw him, his face went slack with shock and something else I was too tired to unpack.

"Lord Ashcroft?" Tony said, taking the man by the shoulders. "Edgar?"

"Here," Alix said and handed Tony the flask.

Cyrus padded up, muzzle mostly clean, and poked me in the ribs with his nose. He was closer to the size of a bear than a wolf, and other than the reigning stink of vampire viscera, he smelled a bit like cinnamon.

I dropped my free hand onto his neck and said, "Thank you, friend."

He bumped my hand with his nose and opened his mouth in a doggy grin, letting his tongue loll out the side.

Sam gulped audibly. "Is that—is he?"

"A werewolf?" I asked, tired. "Yes. How do you think I got the tooth?"

"You didn't fight a werewolf for it?"

"She did," Alix said, patting Edgar's back as he coughed. "But she pulled that one out of Cyrus's arm."

Both Tony and Sam raised their brows at me, and I threw my hands up. "Witches, you'll believe. Vampires, you'll believe. But a werewolf is too much, eh?"

"Well," Sam said, digging his toe into the dirt, "It's just that he's so big and you're, well—"

"A girl?" I asked, holding back what might have been hysterical laughter.

"Small."

I did laugh, then; let the stress and pain roll out of me in a peal of laughter that made tears run down my cheeks. I knew I would cry this out later, probably even throw it all up, but for now, the laughter felt good.

When the hilarity ran its course, I wiped my eyes and said, "Do you remember what I told you about the unicorn, Sam?"

He nodded solemnly, then his eyes widened. "Oh."

"Oh, indeed."

Lord Ashcroft started crying. He curled into a ball and made soft keening sounds that nearly broke my heart because I knew now why he cried. It wasn't just for his wife, or for the danger he inadvertently put them both in. And it wasn't for the secrets he may have shared, or the damage he might have done in Parliament.

He cried because he had been used, *invaded*... and he liked it. His body had luxuriated in the surrender and the forbidden pleasure of the vampire's kiss even while his mind despised it. It did not matter that magic manipulated him; he knew his body could not be trusted, not when it surrendered so willingly to the pleasure. He craved the thing he hated. That was gone, now, and whatever kind of man he was before his mind had been invaded was also gone.

I would throw that up later, too.

"We need to get him back to the manor," I said.

"Sammy! Sam!"

Tony and I both sighed in defeat. So much for telling the children to stay safe inside. Sally appeared through the trees a moment later, her white dress a beacon in the dark forest. Terror and moonlight made her face as pale as the dress. She saw Sam through the trees and came running.

He braced himself and she grabbed him by the shoulders, shaking him while yelling, "What do you think you're doing!?" Then crushed him to her, tears streaming down her face before she shook him again. "Don't ever do anything so stupid!"

Alix made a little noise she probably didn't realize I could hear. Her amber eyes were locked on the pair, her mouth softened into a sad line of longing. I wondered what the children would say if I told them Little Red Riding Hood envied them.

"Sally," I said.

She stopped yelling and shaking and hugging her brother long enough to look at me. Her eyes locked on the bloody cloth. "Oh, Lady Gwen," she breathed through her tears.

"I'm fine, dear heart. Can you and Samuel take Lord Ashcroft back to the manor and get him to Doctor Hesselius? The danger is gone now, and he needs to be with his wife."

She wiped her tears away but nodded, and came forward to take Lord Ashcroft's arm. "If you run away again, Sam, I swear I will tie you to the wall for the rest of your life and read you the sappiest, most romantic poetry I can find until your ears bleed," she told the boy.

Holding back more hysterical laughter, I said, "We'll be right behind you."

Alix waited until the children were out of earshot before she said, "Do they know how lucky they are?"

"They know," I told her.

Then the softness disappeared from her voice and she said, in her usual frank manner, "What should we do with the bodies?"

"Did none of them live?" Tony asked. His voice was rough.

"One did, for a while. He's gone now."

He nodded, cleared his throat, dragged a hand through his hair, and said, "We must leave the scene as it is until the sheriff can be brought in to examine it. These men died heroes, and that shouldn't be covered up."

He didn't direct his words to anyone in particular, but I knew he was talking to me. I didn't disagree with him, though Lady Chatsworth might. I failed, anyway. All the clues ended here, with the vampire. I hadn't been able to save these men, and I wouldn't be able to save Thistle Honeycutt or bring Lia home.

"Come on, then," Alix said, getting her hands under my arms to lever me up. "Let's get you back to the manor, too. You smell horrible, by the way."

I snorted. Aristotle sailed down from whatever branch he'd been perched on and landed on Tony's shoulder, flexing his claws.

"Aristotle, how did you—never mind. I'm tired of trying to figure it out." Tony winced and tried to shoo the bird off, but he only squeezed harder and cawed in Tony's ear.

I reached up to grab the tip of his beak and give it a playful shake. "How did you find me, you willful, disobedient, wonderful bird? You're making quite a habit of saving the day, aren't you?"

"Save the girl," he agreed.

A hopeless wail rose over the tops of the trees; a long, agonized cry that stopped the four of us before we could move. The hair on my arms and the back of my neck stood on end.

"The Reavers," I said.

"The what?"

"The Reavers," I told Alix. "Spectral riders. We saw them kidnapping the blacksmith yesterday, but couldn't stop them. They didn't respond to anything but my silver blade. Even bullets didn't—"

Tony and I locked gazes. Hope—blazing and painful—sprang up to scorch my insides as I realized I had gotten everything wrong about this case.

"Alix? Cyrus? Are you up for another impossible battle?"

The woman exchanged a charged look with the wolf, perhaps remembering the first time we fought an impossible battle together and won. Cyrus barked once, decidedly.

"Can I have another drink of St. Christophe's magical drink, then?" I asked. "I'll explain on the way."

Tony and I swallowed another mouthful of the potent drink, gathered our discarded weapons, and the four of us took off at a run toward the hill with the stone circle.

Aristotle flew off ahead of us, high above the trees, and I recited the poem to Alix and Cyrus as we ran.

> *You cannot see their faces*
> *though under moon they ride*
> *through glen and downy heather*
> *'cross moor and mountainside.*
>
> *My child, beware the Reavers*
> *when moon is full and bright*

if you see the shadows riding
venture not into the night

Their horses never tire
you cannot run or hide
they will catch and fetch you
Back to the other side

My child, beware the Reavers
when moon is full and bright
if you see the shadows riding
Venture not into the night

No glamor, rune, or magic
Will help you turn the tide
stay safe by fire and circle stone
when the Reavers ride.

"That sounds like a... what do you call them? Nursery song?" she said.

"Something like that. But I think there was more truth to it than anyone knew. We know silver affects them," I said, gesturing to the pistol I'd given to Tony that still had two bullets left in it. "And the poem mentions shadows and moonlight. If we can keep them busy till the sun rises, hopefully, it will dispel them and we can save whoever they're taking."

I didn't add *maybe I can follow them back to wherever they're going* because I didn't want to worry anyone. But, if I was right, and these Reavers kidnapped Thistle Honeycutt, then I might still have a way to Lia.

"Keep them busy, eh?" Alix asked.

"You still have your knives?"

She snorted and pulled two long-bladed daggers from somewhere in her clothing, not even breaking stride. Of course she still had them. I carried my umbrella, whacking it on every tree trunk we passed until the runes on the shaft were hot enough to burn my hands. Inside, the silver blade glowed.

Cyrus loped alongside us, his tawny coat silver in the moonlight. I wasn't certain what he could do, but he was the most powerful werewolf I'd ever seen, and his family line was reeking with magic. It would have been stupid to count him out.

But Tony, with the last of the silver bullets, was our best hope of stopping the spectres.

We broke into the clearing at the base of the hill to find the Reavers already there, but—not there. Under the full moon, they seemed as solid as the trees and rocks. But in the light of the waning moon, only a day past full, they did look like shadows: bits and pieces of people, transparent in most places, casting flickering moonlit shadows on the grass.

And despite their mostly incorporeal appearance, they dragged another captive between them.

"God's breath. Percy!"

The figure writhed and screamed, "Gwen!"

Without making a plan or waiting for the others, I dashed forward, grateful for the split skirt that gave me more freedom of movement. Alix caught and passed me a moment later—a benefit of being a half-vampire, I supposed—and then Cyrus passed the both of us.

Tony squeezed off a shot, and the air shattered with the crack of it. The horse on the right reared as its rider threw back his hands and fell off the horse to land soundlessly on the earth.

Percy tried to twist free, but the other rider held firm and continued to drag him up the hill.

"Cut him off!" I shouted, pulling the blade free of the shaft.

Alix and Cyrus circled around to harry the mounted Reaver as I advanced on the second one with Tony at my back, blade drawn.

"If I can't take him, shoot him in the head," I called over my shoulder.

"Give me a line of sight," he called back.

The other rider, or his horse, screamed a sound at the very edge of hearing, like the cry of a hawk, but I didn't turn to look. I attacked the fallen Reaver. My body was sore, bruised, and tired, but I ignored that. Fear, anger, and the drink still sang in my veins with enough motivation to push me forward.

The Reaver noted my silver and drew his own sword with a transparent hand. It was the most solid aspect of him, like a shadow made corporeal. He wasn't on a horse this time. And I was ready.

I lunged, he parried, and the battle was on. We danced around one another, but I never let him close enough to strike me with anything other than a blade. He was better than me, his footwork impeccable, but I was angry. More than angry, I was desperate.

He parried and riposted, but I was waiting for that. I slid to the outside, letting my blade trace sparks up his so I could get in close, and twisted my shoulders to bring the blade up high. He raised his arm and the edge of my blade sliced along the place his shoulder should have been.

Smoke sizzled into the air, leaking upward from the wound, and his shoulder became more solid. I was so surprised by the effect that I didn't defend myself fast enough when he twisted to kick me. Heat spread out in a rush from my left hip as the jacket did its work, but it was already hot, and the sudden jump in temperature made me sweat. If I took too many more blows, the jacket would explode, with me inside it.

"Shoot!" I yelled. The gun barked. The Reaver's head snapped back, becoming corporeal, and it toppled backward.

I lay on the grass, panting, then shoved to my feet.

Alix and Cyrus attacked the other Reaver as if they could speak telepathically, one harrying, the other darting in to attack. The horse spun as quickly as any cow pony, while the Reaver defended with one arm and dragged Percy behind him with the other.

My friend hung at the end of his arm, screaming. His shoulder had been dislocated during the fight, and his beautiful face was twisted into a grimace of pain.

"No more silver bullets left," Tony said as he joined me.

"You don't happen to have any iron on you, by chance?"

"No. You?"

"No," I said, shoving my hand into my pocket as if I could prove it, and touched something hard. The stone I found outside the old woman's hut. She had patted it and called it a gift. A line from the poem followed that thought: *Stay safe by fire and circle stone.*

I pulled the stone out and held it up. It was a plain gray stone, worn smooth, with a hole just off center, like Dr. Hesselius's spectacles. I raised it and gasped. Through the circle of stone, the world looked entirely different. I saw the Reavers, but not as I saw them with my eyes. They weren't people or even humans, but constructs made of something else, something dense and blacker than the night sky.

My intuition said it wasn't magic, and it certainly wasn't flesh, because when Cyrus leaped between me and the Reaver, one light glowed red in his chest, and another shimmered out along his limbs like veins, wrapping around and through him. Was that his magic?

What were the Reavers made of, then, some sort of anti-magic? Their horses weren't separate from them, either, they were extensions of the construct. And Percy... Percy wasn't an elf.

"He's fae," I heard myself say. "Percy is a faerie. That's what they are!"

"What?" Tony asked.

I turned to explain and watched as the Reaver, the one we just killed, rose up behind Tony and raised its sword in a killing blow.

22

The Wall

GWEN

The blade began to fall, and there wasn't even time to raise my sword or cry out. Tony must have seen my expression change because he collapsed like his feet were cut from under him... but the blade followed him down.

I lunged forward anyway, knowing I was too late. The tip of the sword sliced Tony's shoulder and cut down to the center of his back. He dropped his gun and screamed as he fell.

My sword caught the Reaver's blade on the upswing while Tony rolled out of reach several feet downhill, gasping in pain. My mind spun away as I blocked, lunged, and parried, taking refuge somewhere deep inside of me, a place disconnected from the real world.

I watched my blade arc through the air, catching moonlight and shedding it like water, as the Reaver advanced to press his advantage as a better swordsman. But I thought about Edith Ashcroft and her generous spirit, and of the old woman and her calloused hands, and of the stares and whispers that followed me since I was sixteen. Since I'd lost my twin sister.

Lia had been everything to me; beautiful, with honeyed hair, dark green eyes, and an elegant figure. She was clever, funny, and brave. She was as charming as Mama and as regal as Papa. And she was kind.

Somehow she saw in me—the careful one, the quiet and shy one—a person worth loving, worth admiring.

You are the bravest person I know, Gigi, she told me, once. Geoff and Tilden, farmer's boys from Wainwright village, had challenged us to a tree climbing contest. Geoff and Lia started, and she beat him to the top, but when she came back down and touched my hand, I froze. I couldn't climb that fast, it wasn't safe. Visions of plummeting from the top and cracking my head on branches had made sweat pop out on my upper lip.

I did climb the tree and touched the knot on the top branch, but only several minutes after Tilden reached the ground. I stood with my bare feet on the springy limb, hugging the tree with sweat dripping off my chin, and reached out to touch the knot with shaking fingers.

When I reached the bottom, the boys had pulled my braids and called me a scaredy-cat. I sat in the dirt and cried.

Don't listen to them. Lia had said, spots of angry color burning in her cheeks. *They think that because they're not afraid to climb a tree, they're braver than you, but they're wrong. You climbed the tree even when you were so scared you couldn't see straight. Don't you know how special that is?*

When she was gone, there was no one left to see past my carefully built defenses to the burning heart inside. So, I took as much of Lia as I could, trying to make the parts of her I missed live inside of me until they became my armor. If Lia wouldn't have been afraid, I couldn't be afraid, either.

But Edith also saw something worth admiring beneath my armor, and the old woman, too, or else why should she have helped me with no expectation of pay?

She had said, *Drought causes deep roots. And the dandelion does not ask the rose where it may grow. You will see the truth through the eyes of stone.*

Eyes of stone. Fire and circle stone. Shadows and moonlight. Silver, iron, and blood. That was it. I knew how to beat them.

My arm muscles burned and my legs cramped from fighting at an angle on the hillside, but the Reaver did not tire. It couldn't; it wasn't alive. Its sword came down again and again, and the reverberations echoed up my arms and made my bones rattle.

Cyrus sailed through the air on his back and landed hard on the turf with a sharp canine cry. When the black sword came down again, my blade tumbled out of my hands and stuck in the ground. He stepped forward into a reverse cut on the upswing and I turned, raising my arms to protect myself. The blade hit the back of my shoulder and took me off my feet. I landed with a huff of expelled air, dizzy, my jacket now nearly hot enough to scald my skin with stored energy. Sweat poured down my face, making loose curls stick to my forehead and temples.

I shoved the hair out of my eyes and didn't feel the burn of a blade, so the cut was either deep enough to kill me or the jacket had once again done its job.

Satisfied that I was out of the fight, my adversary climbed back onto his horse and joined his partner. Alix couldn't fight them both, alone, despite the way her silver daggers flashed. The second Reaver gripped Percy by the wrist and they began dragging him again toward the standing stones.

I emptied my pockets onto the ground and tore the buttons from my jacket as I wrenched it off, never taking my eyes from the Reavers as their horses climbed. Tony's pistol peeked out of the grass, and I grabbed the butt as I ran, screaming at Alix, "Stay back!"

I bundled the coat into a ball and hurled it as far up the hill as I could, which ended up being closer to the top than I'd imagined. Raising the pistol, I aligned the sights, breathed out, and squeezed the trigger. The jacket jumped as the bullet struck. Nothing happened.

The riders rode on.

Before they reached the top of the hill, the jacket caught fire in spectacular fashion. First, a wisp of blue smoke, then a single spark, and the entire hillside in front of the horses bloomed with flames at least four feet high.

The Reavers jerked to a stop, pulling Percy to a cross position between them as their mounts stamped angrily. But the fire died as quickly as it caught. They waited a moment to be certain my dead coat had no other tricks to play, then urged their mounts forward again.

But my trusty coat did have one last trick up its metaphorical sleeve: it exploded. A crack like cannon fire shook the air as the blast ripped Percy out of the Reaver's arms and flung him into mine. Dust and clods of dirt pelted us as we fell.

We landed and rolled several feet, neither of us able to breathe from the impact. I wrapped my arms round his chest as I wheezed and kicked at the ground to put more space between us and the Reavers. To our right, Alix hovered over Cyrus, who had shifted back into his human form. He sat up and shook his head. I would have sighed in relief if I could have gotten my breath.

Percy struggled weakly, but he was in so much pain he was nearly incoherent. I couldn't pull him down the hill fast enough to get away from the Reavers. They turned their horses and were upon us before I could come up with even a sliver of a plan to stop them.

Pulling up on either side of us, they reached down to grab Percy's arms and began dragging him back up the hill. I didn't let go. My wrists were locked around his chest, and I dug my heels into the grass as I pulled in my first deep breath, straining against the power of the horses, and failing.

Apparently, I was no threat now that my silver sword was stuck in the earth somewhere on the hillside. I was enough of an irritation that the Reaver who had cut Tony leaned a bit to the outside and kicked me in the ribs.

White hot pain lanced across my torso and made my arms go numb. Without my jacket to protect me, my ribs broke happily, and I crumpled to the grass, landing on top of everything I had pulled out of my pockets earlier. The circle stone lay forgotten inside a footprint, and the dwarven torch dug into my hip. I rolled to the side to ease the pressure, holding back a cry of pain, and watching the shadows drag my friend away.

Alix and Cyrus rejoined the fight, but there was nothing they could do. Even the two of them, deadly as they were, could not stop the Reavers from advancing until the sun rose. I hadn't been able to hold them, and neither could they. After all, how does one kill a shadow?

With a cry, I grabbed for the dwarven torch, but my hands still tingled from the blow and refused to grip it.

"Come on, you blasted useless appendages!" I snarled, trying to force my fingers to cooperate through sheer bloody-mindedness. My thumbs slipped over the rune-engraved switch as the horses cleared the top of the hill.

"Move!" I screamed at my fingers. And they did.

The switch clicked into place, and a beam of trapped sunlight burst from the tip of the torch. I swung my arms around, crying from the pain, and pointed the beam at the crest of the hill. It hit the first Reaver with a burst of gold smoke, dissolving the horse beneath him and sending him crashing to the ground.

A second beam appeared from farther down the hillside and grazed the top of the second Reaver, where the helmet should have been. A tearing, high-pitched scream rent the air and it fell to the side, flinging both arms wide. Percy hit the turf like a sack of potatoes and didn't move.

Locking my jaw against the pain, I wobbled to my feet and aimed the torch. What was left of the Reaver shredded into little pieces of shadow that floated upward, like sparks from a fire, and dissolved in smoke.

Alix dove toward the last Reaver, silver daggers scything through the air too fast to track, and separated its shadowy head from its body. The second beam of light finished it, and for a moment, dissolving pieces of Reaver filled the air, floating like ash blown away by the wind.

"Tony?" I yelled.

"I'm here. I'm okay."

Where was Aristotle? Probably flown away now that the excitement was over.

My legs gave out, and I plopped onto the grass with a grunt atop the other things I'd emptied my pockets of. The circle stone was cold beneath my hand, and I curled my fingers around it and squeezed.

Unshed tears filled my eyes. Tony and Percy were still alive, still here. But whatever hope I cherished of finding Lia died with the Reavers. There were no more clues to follow toward Thistle Honeycutt, and from her to the grimoire.

"Gwen?" Alix said as she knelt next to me.

"I'm okay," I muttered. "Will you see to Tony? He was cut."

She held my face in her hands for a moment, examined my eyes, then nodded and jogged away as if she hadn't just fought two nearly invincible shadow monsters.

Soft crying floated into the air from the top of the hill. Percy. He was alive, too, and probably in terrible pain. Cyrus padded up next to me. The tip of one ear was cut cleanly away. He crouched, whined, and pushed his shoulder against me.

I took a handful of his fur in my good hand, and he pulled me to my feet to lead me to the top of the hill. It was easier to walk with his bulk to lean on, but it wasn't easy to see Percy curled in a fetal position, one hand protecting his dislocated shoulder, his face twisted in pain.

I sank next to him and made little shushing noises while I rubbed his back. No matter how much I wanted to, I couldn't replace his shoulder; that required a significant amount of strength and technique, and I barely stayed upright.

Alix appeared a moment later carrying Tony like a small child, despite the fact that he was twice as wide as she and at least a head taller. She lowered him to the ground next to me and began ripping strips off the bottom of my pant legs to wrap around his torso.

"The cut was shallow," she said. "Mostly, anyway. He's lost blood, but the bleeding is slow. He will live."

Tony winced as she tied the last knot. "Don't be so sure."

Cyrus padded away, then returned a moment later in human skin... in nothing but his human skin. He looked like the god of strength and majesty carved of granite and moonlight.

He lifted Percy upright, and Alix braced his other side. They positioned Percy's arm in an L shape, turned his wrist, and slowly twisted his wrist and shoulder toward his spine. There was a soft *pop*, and Percy slumped forward with a sigh of relief.

Cyrus patted him on the back, and Alix said to me, "Do you greet all your friends with monster hunts?"

The hilarity that bubbled up was completely involuntary, probably a reaction to the adrenaline, but I giggled until my stomach muscles hurt, my ribs burned, and tears ran down my cheeks. "Welcome to England."

Eventually, my laughter faded into silence. I would mourn my failure soon, but not now. Maybe after I slept for three days, and I could deal with losing Lia again. Or, perhaps, after a bottle of wine and a bit of laudanum. Or maybe I would box it all up and drop it into the hole in my chest, and try to learn to be content with the ache.

"What is that?" Cyrus said.

I blinked and raised my head. The sun stole the darkness from the sky while I'd been thinking, and blue and magenta stained the clouds above the tree line behind Chatsworth Manor, which was visible from the top of the hill.

At the edge of the forest, a golden glow floated between the trees, advancing toward the foot of the hill.

Tony said, "It's *her*."

The shining woman flowed up the hill like smoke, hair floating behind her, dark eyes calm and serene as the first rays of the sun struck the treetops. She stopped before us, silent, unmoving. The last piece of the puzzle fell into place.

A growl rumbled in Cyrus' chest, but I said, "Don't worry, she doesn't intend us any harm. Do you, Ms. Honeycutt?"

The sun rose over the back of the hill and crowned the creature in fire for a blazing instant before illuminating the rest of her. As the sun touched her, a mortal glamour materialized from the glow beneath her skin.

It was something like watching a light bulb go out.

Instead of a startling, glowing humanoid, a plain elvish woman stood on the grass with her dark hair pinned up and her hands folded in front of her white apron. When I say plain, you mustn't take that to mean the same thing it means when applied to humans. All elves are beautiful. She was merely beautiful instead of extraordinary, which, in elvin terms, made her plain.

"That's quite a disguise," I said.

She inclined her head and said, in a perfect west-country accent. "Of course, I mean you no harm. In fact, I wanted to thank you. I know you could not save Borchinus—you would have known him as the village smith—but you did try."

It took me a moment to respond because one of the fae just thanked me, and thanked me when she knew I understood what she was. She had acknowledged a debt, willingly, and in front of witnesses.

I nodded in understanding and said, "I was glad to do it."

"We should all be grateful to whoever gifted you the Hagstone."

"Hagstone?"

"The circle stone that lets you see magic."

I looked down at the smooth rock cradled in my palm. "No one gave it to me. Well," I amended, "the wise woman said the earth gave it to me."

Her brows raised. "Then it is a mighty gift."

My fingers closed around the stone, which was cool and heavy. It would certainly come in handy in this new world where faeries walked with mortals. Thinking of new worlds, I cleared my throat and asked, "Would you be willing to explain what has happened here?"

"I believe you have understood most of it."

Wrong question, then. "Who are the Reavers?" I asked, instead.

"I suspect you know that, too, or have puzzled it out."

"Will you tell us what the Reavers are?"

She smiled. "The Reavers are a construct of darkness created by a coalition of human witches and fae sorcerers after the Great War. They protect the integrity of the wall, looking for holes, and patrol the mortal lands to retrieve any faeries who have broken through."

"How does one create a construct of darkness?"

"It is not darkness in the way you understand it, but a reverse, an opposite. Magic flows with life, and life with light. Darkness is the opposite. This is why magic cannot touch them."

"Silver can."

"Silver is moonlight, and moonlight and darkness are mates, not enemies."

"Like the sun."

"Indeed. The sun, light, and life. Those are enemies of darkness."

That was why the dwarven torches had worked when nothing else touched them. Dwarven artifice was not magic, as Delilah was so fond of reminding everyone, but funnels and channels for natural forces. The torches harnessed light like a water wheel harnessed the power of water. I tried to work out what to ask next, but I was so tired, and my question came out barely understandable. "Why now?"

"A small crack might go unnoticed, but a large one is easy to spot, even from afar."

"So, too many faeries came through the hole you found?" Tony asked. His voice, too, was tired and shaky.

"The hole I *made*," she corrected, her head high. "Long ago, after the wall was built, when I refused to serve the traitor. But that is fae business, and none of yours."

"Will you return to the manor?" I asked.

"Once the hole in the wall is closed and the Reavers cannot return."

My heart sank. "They're not dead?"

"They cannot die. They are not alive. You have merely dispelled them."

"And if you close the rift, they cannot come back?"

She nodded.

"How do you close the hole?"

"By donating a little of my life, a little of my substance, as a patch. But I cannot do it on my own, and Borchinus was not strong enough to help me. That is why I hid when the Reavers appeared. But *he* might be strong enough," she said, pointing at Percy.

Percy raised his head. He'd done his best not to look at the woman, I thought, but once he did, he didn't seem able to look away.

She held out her hand. "Will you close the wall with me?"

My friend climbed to his feet, ignoring Alix's offer of help, and stood with his head bowed. "I will, my lady."

He took her hand reverently. They walked in unison to the top of the hill and stood in the center of the stone circle. Percy glanced up at me with apologetic eyes, then turned to focus on his task. Nothing seemed to happen, at least, nothing I could see.

I raised the circle stone and peered through it with my right eye. Their glamour fell away. Thistle was precisely as she had shown herself to us, but Percy was another creature, entirely. I still recognized him as Percy, oddly enough, but he was softer, rounder, without Percy's sharp corners and hard edges.

Rather than the up-tilted, widely spaced eyes of the elves, his were round and dark and long-lashed, the kind of eyes one might drown in. His skin was still dark but speckled with nearly invisible spots down his torso and flanks. And rather than pointed ears, his were smaller and closer to his skull.

Selkie.

Seeing them next to each other was like seeing sleek grey velvet next to a burning lamp. They faced one another, placed their hands together, and began to sing.

"By the moon," Cyrus said, sinking to his knees.

Their voices were high and clear and as sharp as a mountain spring, as beautiful as a single star in a black sky. The sound stopped the blood in my veins. Though the words were strange, they were familiar. If I just listened a little harder, a little longer, I thought I might catch their meaning.

When they stopped singing, the air shimmered and fell in a shower of golden sparks.

They collapsed onto the grass.

23

First Line of Defense

GWEN

How we got back to the manor and into our rooms, I cannot remember, but I woke sometime later with golden beams of light streaming through a crack in the curtains. A tray of food sat cold on the bureau, next to a glass of tea and a note that said "An extraction of willow bark and laudanum," in what I assumed was Doctor Hesselius's neat hand.

I drank the cup in a single go, waited for the pain to fade away, ate every crumb, and nearly licked the plate.

Sally helped me dress, though I paid little attention. Then she led me to an upstairs sitting room where Frances waited with Ms. Honeycutt, both of them smiling and talking animatedly.

"Lady Gwen," Frances said when I entered. "I cannot believe you brought Ms. Honeycutt back to us. Of course, I hoped you could, but after searching for so long, it seemed hopeless."

"Ms. Honeycutt brought herself back," I said, nodding to the housekeeper. "I only helped clear the way. I assume you know by now that the blacksmith was also fae and taken by the Reavers?"

Her smile disappeared. "Yes, I've been told."

"He is likely not the only one. I would imagine if you inquire in the countryside, others will have gone missing, will they not?" I directed the last part of my question to Ms. Honeycutt.

"Several faeries must have come through in the past year for the hole to catch the attention of the Reavers," she confirmed.

"I will look into it," Frances promised.

"There is a white tree in the forest," I said to Ms. Honeycutt, carefully controlling my voice. "I would take it as a personal favor if you would care for it."

She gave me a solemn nod that told me she understood this was all I wanted in return for her thanks.

"What of Lord and Lady Ashcroft?" I asked.

"Dr. Hesselius has not left their side, the dear man. Lady Ashcroft seems entirely recovered, though I'm afraid the road might be long for Lord Ashcroft."

"A run-in with a vampire will do that to you. Shall I assume you will carry word back to Madame Matilda?"

"An anonymous telegraph has been sent."

"Very well. Might I have the use of this room for the rest of the afternoon? I would like to have a few words with my party if you don't mind."

She looked surprised but nodded.

"One more thing, Lady Frances. Will you have a bath drawn in my room, please?"

She blinked at me, then said, "Of course."

As a historic manor, Chatsworth did not have the indoor plumbing of newer homes, so the servants carried a copper tub to my room and filled it with pot after pot of boiling water. I allowed them to cool it just enough that I wouldn't cook myself, then sank into the steaming tub.

It was hot enough to sting my skin and make me sweat, but I didn't care. I lathered the soap until the tub was frothing, and scrubbed myself until my skin burned and the water was pink with the blood from the wound on my shoulder.

If I didn't stop, I would scratch myself raw. Dirt could be removed, but I could not wash away the memory of the vampire's kiss, or how much part of me—a larger part than I was comfortable with—wanted to feel it again.

My skin crawled and my last meal threatened to make an appearance, but I ruthlessly stamped my reaction down until it submitted and hid in the corner of my mind.

Dressing was painful, thanks to the broken ribs. I managed it after binding my chest tightly and covering my wound with clean linen. Sally's help would have made the process easier, but she'd already seen enough, and my raw skin would only distress her.

I sent a servant with requests to the people I wanted to see, then trudged back to the room Frances gave me permission to use. Tony was already there, sitting on a chaise, back straight. He started to stand when he saw me come in, winced, and sank carefully back down.

"Don't stand up, you idiot," I chided him. "You should be in bed."

"I could say the same of you."

"I didn't get my back split open by ghost riders."

He waved a dismissive hand. "It's nothing."

"Have you had your stitches?"

He winced. Stitches weren't so easy to dismiss, and it was going to be hard for him to move for a while. I lowered myself onto the chaise next to him and put one hand on his knee. "Are you alright?"

He snorted. It was not a sound of amusement. "No. I am not."

"Will you be speaking to their families soon, then?"

"Tomorrow."

There seemed nothing to say, and my instinct for levity in stressful situations would not have been welcome, so I reached up with one hand, turned his face toward me, and kissed his cheek.

He turned into the kiss, frowning, holding his breath.

"I'm sorry. Truly."

"Me, too."

He took my hand, held it between his, and examined it. My knuckles were scraped, a fingernail had been torn during the fighting, and several scratches of unknown provenance decorated my palm. It was not the hand of a lady. Not the hand of someone soft, who would welcome his protection.

He kissed the back of my hand, and said, "This isn't going to work, is it?"

I curled my fingers around his, but I didn't cry. "I can't give you what you deserve, Tony."

"And what do you think that is?"

"Commitment. Promises of forever. Safety, or stability, or whatever you'd like to call it."

"What if all I want is you?"

I turned to look him full in the face, waiting for him to see me, to truly see me. "I would take you to my bed," I said. "I would happily make love to you until we were both too tired to stand. But I cannot promise you more than that because I don't think I have it to give. And I will never marry."

His breathing sped up and his cheeks were flushed, but he said, "Never is a long time, Gwen."

"I am—" I had been about to say empty, but that wasn't right. The hole inside me had been shored up by Sally and Sam, and by Tony and Aristotle, and there were even a few bricks in there from Edith. But I wasn't the kind of person Tony deserved, someone honest and good who would make and keep promises.

So I said, "I would hurt you. I don't think I could live with myself."

He took my chin between his fingers, and his gaze flicked from my lips to my eyes and back, making a rush of warmth flush from my chest to my cheeks.

Cyrus's voice echoed up the hallway.

"They're coming," I said.

He kissed me quickly: one swift, hard, heartbreaking kiss. Then he stood, sucked a pained breath through his teeth, and crossed the room to stand by the hearth, hands clenched into fists.

Cyrus and Alix entered a moment later wearing utilitarian clothes and looking like lions at a tea party. They held hands almost unconsciously and mirrored one another as they moved. The two of them were so deeply entwined they were like the sun and its shadow: he golden, she dark.

Percy followed them, walking gingerly and refusing to make eye contact. Sam and Sally strode in a few moments later, followed by Dr. Hesselius, who limped across the room to take Alix and Cyrus by the hands.

"It is a small world, Doctor," I said, "when monster hunters are involved."

He grinned. "I should be surprised to find you know one another, but it seems the most natural thing in the world now that I come to think of it."

"How long do you plan to stay in England?" I asked.

"We are gathering here for an expedition to Iceland. A village there is having trouble with a monster, so"—he shrugged—"perhaps a week, more."

"I hope I can convince you to visit me in town if you pass through?"

They exchanged glances, and Alix said, "I am still not fond of town. But for you? Maybe."

"I'll consider that a compliment," I said. Then I patted the chaise, and the children came to sit by me.

"Very well," I said. "I've asked you here to get a clear picture of what is happening because I have a feeling the events of the past two years are related and, likely, bigger than they appear."

Alix and Cyrus exchanged a meaningful glance. I cleared my throat and laid out what I suspected might be happening. "From what I have been able to gather, and Percy may correct me if I am wrong, faeries have been crossing the wall for nearly as long as the wall has existed."

Percy nodded without looking up.

"But those crossings have only been successful for individuals, those either strong enough or small enough to fit through the cracks?"

He swallowed. "Something like that."

"How long has it been since the Reavers have patrolled the country?"

"A long time. A hundred years, maybe."

"This suggests more faeries than before are crossing the wall, and they are either fleeing something, or they are the advance party. A group of faeries tried to cross the wall en masse the year before last"—Percy's gaze snapped up—"by giving a modified fae spell to a desperate witch. If we had not destroyed the spell, an entire party would have used it to enter the mortal world.

Vampires are back in England, and not only hunting here but trying to influence mortal politics. If I do not miss my guess," I turned to Alix, "monster sightings are on the rise?"

"Yes, ever since that affair in Haute Savoie."

Sam perked up and turned to me with raised brows.

"Yes," I said. "That is where I got the werewolf tooth and met Alix and Cyrus, but now is not the time for that story."

His shoulders slumped, and he sighed, but he didn't argue.

"I was traveling back to England when I met you there," I said, "and six months later, the kidnappings began. I think we may be looking at a concerted effort to prepare for something, but without inside information, it is hard to guess at what.

"The vampire said that he was using Lord Ashcroft, but that we had broken him and he was useless. He wanted to usher in some era where monsters would no longer need to hide. How he planned to accomplish that by engaging in political machinations, I cannot tell."

"He was Mr. Capstone?" Tony asked.

"It makes sense. He bribed or enthralled the matron of the orphanage, enthralled a member of the House of Lords, but to what end?"

"You might learn more from Lord Ashcroft once he has recovered," Dr. Hesselius said, "but that may take months."

Cyrus said, "So the vampire's presence was unrelated to the Reavers. He was here only because his thrall was here, and he needed to maintain control of the man."

"Where were you when I was trying to puzzle all of this out?" I asked.

"He was keeping me distracted on the ship," Alix said, giving her husband a naughty wink.

"So we have vampires involving themselves in politics, werewolves trying to overcome their natural aversion to silver, and Reavers roaming the countryside where they have not been seen in hundreds of years," I said.

"The vampires and the werewolves make sense," Tony said. "They want strength and resources. But what would drive the fae to cross the wall knowing the Reavers would be here to drag you back?"

Every eye turned to Percy, and his shoulders raised as if they could protect him from the attention. We had been trying not to stare for the last quarter of an hour, but now the ice was broken. We were all in deep water, and Percy was the only one who could give us directions.

He took a breath, dropped his shoulders, and straightened. "Crossing the wall is... it was the most frightening thing I have ever done. First, you must find a hole or someone who knows where one is. That, alone, is an act of treason. Next, you must force your way through, and no one knows how the wall will respond until they try, but it—it kills at least seventy-five percent of those who attempt it. And that only represents the bodies that are found. Most of us who live here are refugees. Trying the crossing is preferable to what we leave behind."

"Refugees from what?" Alix asked.

"It is hard to explain because we do not see morality the same way you do. That is"—he frowned as he thought— "the morality we adopt living among mortals is not natural to our kind. Some of us learn it well enough to make it part of our glamour, part of the mask that helps us hide, and some of us take it and make it our own. So trying to explain what happens in the Sunset Lands would not make much sense to you. Call it persecution and tyranny, if that helps, but even that is more complicated than it sounds."

"If our moralities do not align," Sally said slowly, "then how can you justify running from yours? What I mean is, if we don't mean the same thing when we say right and wrong, what makes the mortal lands better for you than the Sunset Lands?"

It was the wrong time for a smile of pride, but I felt the glow of it light up my face, anyway. Clever, insightful girl. Percy didn't hesitate to smile, but his smile was sad.

"May I ask you a personal question in return, Sarah?"

Sally blinked. We almost never used her first name. "Yes."

"When you lived on the east side and stole in order to survive, did you believe it was wrong?"

"Yes."

"But you did it, anyway?"

She looked down at her lap. "Yes."

"Did the other children believe it was wrong?"

"No," Sam said. "It was just getting our fair share from people who took more than theirs."

Alix hid a smile behind her hand.

"Then how did you come to believe it was wrong?" Percy asked.

She raised her chin. "My mother told me stealing was wrong. Even if I thought it was necessary, I still knew it was wrong."

"My mother knew, too. And faeries do not die of old age like mortals, so there are many who remember what it was like to live in the same world with mortal creatures. Just because our moral standard is different, that doesn't mean we all agree on it all the time."

I suspected that was a wildly simplified version of the truth, but everything I read aligned with the general principle that fae morality did not always align with that of mortals.

I said, "Following that line of thought to its logical conclusion: if more faeries are crossing the wall now, despite the dangers, something must have changed for the worse."

Percy nodded.

"Then I think it is safe to say that whatever changes are taking place in the Sunset Lands will also have consequences for mortals. Does anyone disagree?"

Everyone exchanged glances, but no one spoke.

"It appears," I said, locking eyes with each one of them in turn, "that we have just become the first line of defense to protect mortal lands from whatever is causing chaos on the other side of the wall. That includes you and the Triumphant Sisterhood, Lady Frances."

There was a shocked silence from the hallway, then Lady Frances Chatsworth stepped into the room looking as prim and proper as if she hadn't just been caught eavesdropping.

"I cannot make any promises or agreements on behalf of the Sisterhood," she said. "But I will relay everything faithfully to my coven."

"I'm certain you will."

It wasn't precisely a threat, but it wasn't *not* a threat, either.

After that, we established lines of communication and I promised to find out if Delilah might improve upon the current designs for telegraphs or manufacture us a way to reach one another more quickly and accurately.

Telegraphs were fast, but they required a station and a machine, and in the wild places Alix and Cyrus traveled, those amenities weren't to be found.

"You are one of the most capable people I have ever known," Alix said before she left, "but you are still human. You are not invincible. I know you think this"—she raised her hands to encompass the group—"means you are accepting help, but I know better. Don't do everything on your own. Some day you will fail and then where will the world be?"

She kissed me on both cheeks, Cyrus lifted me off the ground for the gentlest bear hug imaginable, and Doctor Hesselius promised to write and send me accounts of their encounters, with illustrations when possible.

Tony stood silently through the rest of the affair, then gave me a meaningful look that said, *we'll talk later* and left me alone with the children and Percy.

"The two of you had better get packed," I told them. "Rather, *you* should pack," I told Sally, then turned to Sam and said, "And you ought to think up an excuse as to why I shouldn't let your sister chain you to the wall when we get home. We'll leave in the morning, and yes, before you give me that look, we will take the train."

Sam was somewhere between frustration and elation, but Sally was perfectly content to drag him out of the room, giving me one backward, knowing glance before she left me alone with Percy.

He stood near the window, wreathed in filtered light, looking every inch an elegant elvin gentleman. But now I knew that beneath that glamour was a selkie with eyes as dark and fathomless as the ocean at night.

I rearranged my skirt, pretending that my ribs were not sending arrows of pain shooting across my chest, and said, "We can have the coach follow us with your luggage on the inside, if you'd prefer. I will hire a second footman and a guard to ensure your designs make it back safely."

"I would appreciate that very much. Thank you, Lady Gwen."

"I would also like to secure your services as my exclusive designer. Hire other artisans to create for your clients if you'd like, but I would like exclusive rights to the best designer in Europe."

He looked up, his expression somewhere between surprised and confused. "That would be very expensive," he said.

"You know spending my father's ridiculous inheritance is one of the great pleasures of my life. Besides, I cannot have that twat, Lady Covington, wearing gowns to rival my own, can I? Not now that Lady Chatsworth has deemed me the reigning fashion plate."

A grin fought its way across his face. "That is rather petty, Lady St. James."

"She did commission you, did she not?"

He nodded but said, "I cannot divulge my client list. That would be absolutely unprofessional and outre. How dare you ask it of me?"

"Name your price and I shall have my solicitor draw up the agreement, then."

The amusement left his face and his spine stiffened as if he were about to try and lift something heavy. "Gwen," he began, ignored me when I tried to interrupt, and blurted, "You saved my life and I have been lying to you for years. I can't accept this, not when—"

"Oh, Percy, shut up. You have saved me more times than I can count. Every kindness from you was a lifeline when I dangled by my fingertips. There are very few threads that keep me from falling, and you are one of them. Are we not better together?"

He crossed the room in a few strides and hugged me. I hugged him back, and said against his neck, "Besides, your jacket saved my life three times at least. I owe you more than I could ever pay. And I plan to use you mercilessly."

"Good. I plan to take all of your money. That makes us even."

I laughed. "Agreed."

24

A Job Well Done

GWEN

During the train ride home, I sat by the window, searching the skies for Aristotle. Every crow, raven, and magpie caught my eye, but none of them were him. I told Sam, once, that Aristotle was my friend, not my pet, and he was free to leave whenever he chose.

But I always believed he would stay. Perhaps saving my life had been his way of saying goodbye. If it was, I wasn't ready. Then again, I would never be ready, but he probably knew that.

Mrs. Chapman and Mr. Yates waited at the station and listened intently as the children described the wonder of travel by train. Sam extolled the virtues of being able to eat something hot while kicking up his feet and watching the scenery roll by. And all of this *without* being bumped around or stopping to change horses.

Sally appreciated the ability to read on the train, which was nearly impossible to do in a coach without getting a headache. The chat sounded carefree, but they all watched me from the corner of their eyes as if I were a teakettle about to boil and scald everyone.

I kissed Percy goodbye, and we entered separate carriages for the ride home. The children went directly to their rooms to clean up, but I stopped in the study. Aristotle's perch was empty, as was the head of his favorite statue. There were no disturbed papers, no shredded notes on the floor, and none of my fetishes had been stolen and hoarded in some dark corner, only to be found weeks later.

"He has not come back, my lady," Mrs. Chapman said from the doorway. "But perhaps he will. You know how much that devil loves to torture me. He will not let me off the hook so easy."

"I'm sure you are right," I said and turned to leave. "Watch the children, please, Mrs. Chapman. I shall be back before supper."

"But my lady, you've only just arrived! What can be so important that it cannot wait for tomorrow?"

I took her hands and squeezed. "I will return by supper."

Her mouth worked as if she wanted to say more, but she knew me well enough to know it wouldn't matter. I walked round to the stable and pulled out the auto.

I blasted down the street, weaving through traffic, wondering when Tony would return from the task of giving the constables' families the bad news. He turned me down when I offered to go with him, though I made him promise to bring me the information of the bereaved so I could set up trusts for them. If there was one blessing to having a neglectful father with literal tons of money, it was spending it in ways that would have made him cringe.

Those families would want for nothing, yet I knew it would not relieve an ounce of my guilt, or his. Thousands of pounds, millions of pounds, would never replace the life of a loved one or their place in one's life. This I knew all too well.

Patricia was at her post at the top of the stairs of the building on Tromwell Lane, as usual. When she saw me, she said, "Madame Matilda is not here, my lady."

"Very well," I said, passing her and striding toward the room where we first met. "Send for her. I will wait."

She stood there a moment, staring after me, then turned and hurried down another hall. Even in the summer, the room was chilly. Several feet of stone would do that, I supposed. But I didn't mind the cold. I sat by the dead hearth and stared at the ashes.

Sometime later, never mind how long, Madame Matilda entered. It might as well have been a presentation before the queen. She was the very picture of a fashionable woman with none of the exaggerations that made so many of my peers ridiculous. Most of her dark curls were pinned high on her head, leaving a tail of ringlets to fall over her shoulder, a contrast to the pale grey dress. She walked with consummate grace, unhurried, and stopped by the table to set down her reticule and pull off her gloves.

"I should have expected to see you, Lady St. James, but I told myself you would, at least, rest and refresh yourself before you came to close our bargain. I apologize for leaving you to wait."

"No need," I said. "I'll take the book and be of no further worry to you."

She snapped her fingers and the dead coals roared to life, sending a gout of flame spurting into the air before it died down and began chewing happily on what was left of the logs there. "Frances tells me you were successful in returning her housekeeper, but there were... casualties."

"Four men. A fae blacksmith. And an old wise woman who lived in the forest."

"We will send compensation to their families, then."

I paused. The Sisterhood claimed to be doing charitable work in New London, but I had never seen proof of it. "I intend to set up trusts in their names. You are welcome to contribute if you like."

She inclined her head. "Very well. I will have my solicitor call upon yours." After a moment of silence, she crossed to the hearth, rubbed her hands together near the flames, and said casually, "You know what Ms. Honeycutt is, then."

"Yes."

"Then you know, at least in part, why the Sisterhood exists."

I rolled my eyes. "You claim to be protecting New London against the fae?"

"Among other things."

"Why haven't you told anyone?"

"Why haven't you?"

We stared at one another for a long, tense moment, before I sighed and lowered my eyes, handing her that victory. I was too tired to care. "I would like my payment for services rendered."

"And I would like your word that you will use nothing you find in the book to target the Sisterhood or any of its members."

"I am not a witch, Matilda," I said, tiredly. "I do not have the power to use the book that way."

"I will have your word."

I stood up and raised my chin. "You have already given your word. Now keep it."

She took a deep breath and closed her eyes for a moment, raising her face to the sky. When she faced me again, there was no artifice or pride in her eyes. "I ask it for the safety of the women who trust me to guide and protect them. I did not offer you the grimoire lightly. It contains power. The book itself *is* power."

"Why offer it if you did not trust me to use it well?"

"I do. But power has a tendency to corrupt even the purest hearts, and I would have your promise as a shield for the women I love, if it should ever come to that."

I wanted to... well, there was much I wanted to do, and to say, but she used the one justification I could not ignore. I might have done the same in her place.

"Very well," I said. "I swear I will not use the book or what I find inside it to harm the Triumphant Sisterhood or its members."

She gave a solemn nod. "Promises have power, too, Lady St. James. Do not forget it."

"Madame Matilda, I would like to go home."

She regarded me for a heartbeat, then snapped her fingers again. The book popped into existence, or perhaps whatever veiled it from my sight popped *out* of existence, on the table. I did not wait for permission, but scooped the book up and held it against my chest, taking the first easy breath I had taken in days.

"I do not know what you hope to gain by offering this book to me," I said. "Or how you believe you are positioning us for the future. But do not, ever, attempt to use my love for my family against me again."

I turned and left without waiting to see how she would take my warning. I didn't care. I rushed down the staircase with the heavy book clasped to my chest and pushed open the door with tears streaming down my cheeks.

I had the book, the key to finding out how to get through the wall from this side. The key to Lia. It took several blinks to bring the streets of New London back into focus.

Tony stood by my auto, leaning one hip against the door, arms folded over his chest. I stumbled to a halt, sniffing but not daring to release the book to wipe my nose.

"It appears as if you need a ride, Lady St. James," he said.

"I thought you would still be in the country."

His mouth twisted into a bitter smile. "Turns out it doesn't take very long to tell someone their father has died. Or their son. Can I drive you home?"

"Alright."

Carriages, horses, and pedestrians passed in a grey blur, accompanied by the scent of horse dung, the never-ending cacophony of wheels, harnesses, voices, and occasionally, construction.

"I've only been gone a few days, and the city feels like a stranger," I said, watching the scenery pass and seeing stone instead of grass and trees.

"Funny how quickly perspectives can change, isn't it?"

"Tony—"

"No."

I bit my lip and tightened my grip on the book as he drove us carefully and responsibly back to the townhouse, and pulled around to the stable. The engine stuttered to a stop, and we sat for a while in silence. Tony pulled the silver franc from his pocket and turned it over and over, rubbing the surface between his fingers in unconscious agitation.

"You are..." he said, then gripped the coin so hard his knuckles strained against his skin, "The most frustrating person I have ever known. You're completely improper, you get yourself involved in affairs you have no right to be involved in, you don't give a damn about your own safety or honor, you as much as promise to break my heart if I give it to you and—" He let go the steering wheel, dragged both hands through his hair and dropped his head back against the seat with a mighty sigh. "And yet I don't think it's mine to give, anymore. I know this isn't the right time for either of us. But I couldn't let you go without you knowing that I don't intend to give up. I'm not as breakable as you seem to think I am."

I could kiss him. That disheveled hair, those earnest, determined eyes that were locked on my face with knee-weakening intensity... but I knew I wouldn't. And he didn't cross the distance, either. If I kissed him now, I would drag him onto the first horizontal surface I could find, though a vertical surface would work just as well, and we would use one another for comfort.

And it would be lovely.

But it wouldn't change the fact that we were not right for one another. At least, we weren't right, right now. When my jagged pieces were worn down by time and less likely to cut, perhaps we could be. If he was willing to wait for that day, I was too selfish to stop him.

The idea of losing Tony felt nearly as terrifying as the idea of loving him. So where did that leave us? Lonely, and in separate beds.

He walked me to the front door, kissed my hand, and walked away. I watched him go, holding the book instead of him.

"You made me a promise, Sam."

The boy sat across from me with his eyes downcast, jaw clenched, knees bouncing, and didn't answer.

"You promised you would never put yourself in danger like that on my behalf," I reminded him.

"It wasn't just for you," he said, looking up, his hands balled into fists. "It was for Tony, too, and for me. And I know we are only your wards, and I don't know what it's like to have a family that's not broken, but isn't that what you're *supposed* to do for each other? Why is it okay for you to do something dangerous for me, and not the other way round?"

I wasn't certain I could take much more today. After the events at Chatsworth, the book, and Tony, my heart walked a knife edge between overwhelm and a thousand-foot drop into darkness. And here was the boy, this intelligent, brave, stubborn, rotten boy jumping all over it with both feet.

"You're right, Sam. We are supposed to care for one another. And you and Sally are so much more to me than you can ever understand. I know I am not your mother, and I would never try to be, but fate or the gods have put you both into my care. It is my job to protect you, and if anything ever happened to you because of me? I don't know that I could live with that."

His knees stopped shaking, and the stubborn line of his jaw softened. He looked at me with eyes too wide and vulnerable for the tough, independent boy I knew.

He swallowed, then said in a voice tremulous with both hope and fear, "Is it because... is that because you—you love us?"

"Haven't I just said so?"

He stared at me, then flew across the space between us and wrapped his arms round me with enough strength to crack my ribs, if they hadn't already been broken. I didn't dare make a sound. The pain was worth it.

"Wasn't I supposed to be scolding you?" I said.

His laugh sounded suspiciously like a sob, but I didn't point that out, either. "You can keep going if you want to."

"No," I said, squeezing tighter. "This will work."

Sam and Sally were safely in their beds and Mrs. Chapman had fussed over everyone and scolded us long enough to suit her tender heart. Mr. Yates locked every door and promised to stay up and keep the lights on, just for tonight.

A note waited for me on the table near the study.

"Who delivered this?" I asked Mr. Yates.

"They did not wait to be identified, ma'am."

I stared at the paper, remembering the last time I received a nameless envelope. This one did not feel warm, and there was no hint of magic about it. Still...

"Will you wait with me while I open this, Mr. Yates? I'm feeling a bit jumpy."

He sidestepped, bringing his shoulder nearly into contact with mine. "Of course, Lady Gwen."

I gave him a wan smile and ran my finger beneath the seal.

Lady Gwen,

Forgive me for writing so soon and without your permission, but I could not in all good conscience wait. The service you have rendered Lord Ashcroft, and myself, is beyond any expectation or hope. Without you, I may have died, and Edgar would have remained—well, you know better than I.

Words cannot properly express my gratitude or sense of obligation to yourself and Inspector Hardwicke. Should you need anything, call on me.

I grew fond of you in a rather short time, but this kindness is far more than anyone might fairly expect of another. I pray you will consider me a loyal friend.

A thousand times, thank you,

Edith, Lady Ashcroft

"I would not presume, ma'am, but–" Mr. Yates said, then pulled a handkerchief from his pocket and pressed the corner to my cheek.

"Have I been crying, Mr. Yates?" I meant the words to sound lighthearted, but they were broken.

"Not in the least, ma'am. A bit of dust, I believe."

"Yes, of course. Thank you, Mr. Yates."

"I am at your service."

Had I hugged the man, it would have embarrassed him terribly. So, I gave him every bit of the most honest smile I could muster.

"Can I do anything for you, my lady?"

"You have done more than enough, Mr. Yates."

I hauled myself up the stairs, wincing with every step. The tea Doctor Hesselius prescribed for the pain wasn't quite as effective as the miracles Mrs. Chapman mixed up with her herbs, but I would not wake her now that the house was silent. There was still a bottle of brandy somewhere in my room.

The latch clicked and the door swung silently open. Someone had built a fire for me, knowing I preferred the homey sound and scent to the dwarven heaters that were more effective but lacked comfort. It had burned down, so I held the grimoire in one hand and placed another log onto the coals with the other.

It caught and filled the room with light as well as warmth. Summer nights didn't require fires for heat, but I needed it on a level deeper than anything purely physical and said a silent thank you to whoever knew it.

I didn't bother taking off my worn and, let's be honest, stinky clothing; merely sat in the armchair and held the book in my lap. There was no way to know for certain what I would learn from the years of accumulated magical knowledge inside. They banned the book for a reason. But the mere fact that non-magical people knew enough about the Mordegant Grimoire to ban it meant the knowledge was dangerous.

In a way, I would be trying to plot a safe path through a treacherous swamp, with no guarantee of a haven on the other side. And I would do it. I had to. If there was knowledge in this book that would help me bring back the other half of my heart, I would find it, no matter the cost.

I searched for something like this for a dozen years through books, across continents, and through perils that still gave me nightmares. Now I had it, a key that may open the door to bringing Lia home. Of course, I never expected the cost to affect Sam and Sally. How could I? And I hadn't expected how much it might hurt to love people again, or how much it would hurt to lose them.

"Save the girl?"

I jerked upright and white-hot pain shot across my chest, making me gasp. The grimoire nearly tumbled off my lap into the fire. I fumbled the book, clutched it to my chest, and spun. A raven stood there, oily black and nearly invisible in the shadows. Heart pounding so hard it hurt, I put the book safely on my desk and strode across the room, cursing.

"You deviant, rotten, flea-ridden, bloody, arsehole of a bird! Where in the hell have you been?"

Aristotle didn't care that tears filled my eyes, or that I was screaming profanities at him. He simply jumped onto my arm and chucked me under the chin with his beak, then rubbed the top of his soft head against my neck while making a purring sound.

I sat on the bed, kicked off my boots, and swung my legs up without undressing. Aristotle hopped off my arm, walked in a circle, then stood on my pillow and began picking at my hair, as if the tousled mess needed to be arranged just so before I could be allowed to sleep.

"Where did you get off to, eh?" I asked him, waggling my fingers at his feet.

He sidestepped my fingers and hopped onto the headboard where he could have mastery over the entire room. He said, as if it should have been obvious even to *me*, "Had to save the girl."

"You're making quite a habit of that," I said with a yawn. "Better be careful or you'll turn yourself into a hero."

He made a sound in the back of his throat somewhere between a purr and a laugh.

I closed my eyes and tried not to imagine the work it was going to take to find the right spell and modify it to be powered by runes. Of course, it didn't really matter how much work it would take or how much it cost. No price was too high. Now that Lia was within reach, nothing would stop me from bringing her home.

Aristotle made a contented little gurgling noise that was absurdly comforting and watched over me from his perch as I fell asleep.

25

The Cutthroat King

SAM

Sam didn't scream when they came for him. He wasn't even surprised. In fact, waiting made every sound, every knock, and every clop of horses' hooves a daily torture. Anticipation strung his nerves tighter than Mrs. Chapman's corset. So when the two men finally appeared after weeks of waiting, it was a relief, of sorts.

It had taken Sam several days to find a member of the underground who could deliver his sealed envelope. Everyone in the house must have agreed to take turns watching him because his only moments of privacy had been in the water closet and behind his closed bedroom door.

Now he was, once again, being escorted through the bowels of the catacombs beneath the old church by two of the King's enforcers. Only this time, he wasn't blindfolded. After all, he carried the King's coin in his pocket.

The bones of the old church weighed heavily on the stones beneath, bending the support arches and causing the tunnels to warp. Sam shivered as he imagined hundreds of tons of stone falling to crush him. He might have been happier blindfolded.

They didn't take him to the thieves' court this time but through a series of halls and rooms cleaner and better kept than the passages near the entrance. These had clean tile floors, carpets, and tapestries to act as a barrier between vulnerable skin and cold stone. But the place still smelled vaguely of mildew.

An unremarkable door at the end of a long hallway lined with oil lamps led to the chambers of the Cutthroat King himself. They hauled Sam to a stop, and the brute on his left knocked three times.

"Enter," came the muffled voice from inside.

They opened the door and pulled Sam through. This room was warm and smelled like tobacco smoke and something else, something wilder that Sam couldn't name. Several layers of rugs carpeted the floor, and a huge four-poster bed of dark wood sat in one corner, bedecked in draped fabric of all kinds and colors.

A woman climbed off the bed and strode toward them, and Sam's stomach curled up into a little ball. Her skin glowed in the firelight, and her dark hair hung in shining curls down to her hips. Thin silk clung to her curving body, and she moved with a liquid grace that reminded Sam of a cat.

She pulled a dressing gown off the back of a chair as she passed and slid into it, giving him a sideways smirk as she left the room. A dwarven woman slid out of the forest of blankets a moment later, and followed the first woman, giving the guard a lazy grin from red-painted lips. She was shorter and broader than the first woman, but muscled and strong, with dimples in her knees.

"Bring him," said the voice Sam had been hearing in his dreams for weeks.

He lounged in a chair by the hearth, one leg kicked up over the armrest, a pipe dangling from his fingers. Like the first time Sam saw the Cutthroat King, he wore snug black breeches and a poofy-sleeved shirt, but this one was unbuttoned down to his waist to expose his chest.

He was utterly at ease, the master of his environment, yet no one in the room made the mistake of taking that for granted.

"Sir," said the man holding Sam's right arm.

The King flicked his fingers, and the guards withdrew, closing the door behind them.

"It sounds like you've had quite an adventure, squirrel," he said after the door clicked shut.

Sam spent many nervous days imagining this moment, thinking of what he would say and how he would stand up for himself. All of those visions of bravery died when the King turned to look at him. Those dark, dead eyes belonged on crocodiles at the zoo, not in a person's face.

The King smiled. "Are you scared, boy?"

"Yes."

"Would you like to know why?"

He wasn't sure how to answer, so he said nothing.

The King turned back to watching the fire, his voice calm, cold, and without inflection. "The dangers you have encountered in your short time on this earth have been dangers to your body;

dangers to your life. Those are rather boring, mundane things. They can injure or kill you, but that is all they can do. I represent an entirely different kind of danger: the corruption of the soul. The twisting and darkening of the deepest parts of you that even death cannot touch. I am what you might be. What you will be, if I have any say in the matter. That scares you, because you are smart, and I have no place in my service for stupid people."

Sam bit his lips together. He understood that speech only in part, but even that was enough to make him squirm.

"I did what you told me, sir," he blurted. "Lord Ashcroft was a vampire's thrall. You can blackmail him with that."

"Ah, but that is no good to me now, little squirrel. Not now that he will no longer participate in the House of Lords. You have learned about Mr. Capstone, and I have lost my point of leverage."

"But I did what you said."

"Then it should be no trouble for you to continue doing what I say. Should it?"

Fear, disappointment, and anger swirled around in the cauldron of his belly until it exploded. "No! I did what you said, and now I'm done!" He dug the silver coin from his pocket and threw it into the fire. "You leave me alone and leave Sally alone!"

The King sat up and turned to face Sam, his expression amused and maybe pleased. "You charming little squirrel," he said, standing. One second he stood several feet away, and the next he clamped a hand firmly on the back of Sam's neck, forcing his head down. With a squeeze, Sam's vision constricted to a tunnel. He eased the pressure, and Sam's sight came swimming back.

"I admire your spirit, Samuel," the King said while hauling Sam toward the fire. The heat of the hearth stung his cheeks, and he tried to pull back, but the King's hand was like an iron chain.

"Few full-grown men would have the courage to defy me to my back, fewer still the temerity to say it to my face. That is a quality I can work with, a metal I can mold, if you will."

He leaned down and, with the bare fingers of his free hand, plucked the glowing coin from the coals.

It was only a few hours from dawn when Sam snuck back into the house the same way he'd snuck out of it. Mrs. Chapman wouldn't be up for another hour, at least, and Mr. Yates usually only woke twice in the night to check all the locks.

The house was quiet when he crept inside. He snuck down the hall to the study, pushed a chair against one shelf, and climbed up, wincing from the pain. Had Mrs. Chapman left any medicine mixed up for Lady Gwen's ribs? The shelf was empty.

He eased down and tried the secret drawer, just in case, but it was locked. He replaced the chair and wobbled up the stairs, leaning hard on the handrail. Light showed beneath Sally's door. It took several long seconds to open it quietly enough not to wake her.

She lay curled on the coverlet in the glow of a nearly spent candle, a book forgotten on the pillow next to her, blond hair spilling over the edge of the bed. When did her hair get so long? He watched her sleep for a moment, noting the peaceful look on her face. That was

an expression he never saw when they lived in the little apart-
ment in the Narrows.

He blew out the candle and closed the door behind himself,
carrying the picture of Sally in his mind back to his room. Sam
should have known that the Cutthroat King would want to
keep a useful tool, and that once he knew how much Sam loved
his sister, she would become a tool, as well... but he'd allowed
himself to believe, or to hope, that when it was all over, he
would be free.

But that was never the way of it. If there was one thing life on
the streets taught Sam, it was that the only way to be safe was
to be the most dangerous person around, more dangerous than
the people who would try to hurt or control you. If he wanted
to be free, truly free, he would have to learn to be dangerous,
not just fast and clever.

When he turned on the light in his room, a man stood by
his bed. Sam didn't scream, just stood and stared, wide-eyed.
He was tall, with pale skin, dark hair, and black eyes, more
handsome than the Cutthroat King, but strange and dangerous
in an entirely different way. He was familiar somehow, but Sam
was certain he'd never met the man before. It didn't occur to
him to wonder how the man got into his room.

"Show me," the man said.

The King had a deep voice, too. Hollow and cold. This man's
voice was commanding but warm and Sam found himself unbut-
toning his shirt without argument and holding the collar open.
The stranger approached and peered at the circular burn on Sam's
chest. It looked like his face wanted to twist into angry lines, but

he wouldn't let it. Fury filled the air around him like a living thing, and Sam felt it like heat from a fire.

"Alright," the man said, straightening. He reached into one pocket and pulled out a little tin with a smelly salve inside. "Put this on the burn two times a day. Once in the morning, and once at night. It will help with the pain and stop the wound from getting infected. Wear your shirt loose so it doesn't stick while the skin heals. Understand?"

Sam nodded.

"Good. Take care of yourself and your sister. I'll see what I can do. Now get some sleep."

It hurt to pull the shirt off over his head, but once it was off, the cool air felt nice. He opened the tin and smeared the salve on the wounded skin. The burning stopped, like a dying coal, and he sighed in relief. It smelled like lavender.

He stored the tin in the top drawer of his side table, slid beneath the covers, and arranged the blankets so they didn't rub the burn. His mind started to slip away into that land between dreaming and awake, where everything and nothing lived.

The yellow eyes of the vampire floated past, and the burning eyes of the Cutthroat King became the eyes of someone else he knew but didn't remember. He was running through the dark alleys of the Narrows, but the buildings turned into trees, and there, between them, was the hut.

The old woman opened her door and motioned him inside. She gave him tea for his pain, but it made his stomach hurt like the night after their father left when there was nothing to eat for two days. He cried because his stomach was so empty it felt like it was trying to eat itself.

Sally rubbed his head and sang to him until he fell asleep. In the morning she was gone to earn money or steal it, same as every morning, but there was a warm cinnamon bun on their rickety table. She hadn't even taken a bite of it.

How she had gotten her hands on it he didn't know and never asked. He never thanked her, either.

Sally was warm and safe in her room, with a full belly and a head stuffed with stories from books. A bit of pain was worth that.

When he woke in the morning, Sam put salve on the burn without remembering where it came from and made plans for how he could get out of the house regularly enough to spy on Lord Rutledge.

The End

Turn the page to read Chapter One of Spellbound, Book 3 of the Gwen St. James Affair

26

Spellbound

TONY

Anthony Hardwicke was one of the toughest inspectors to walk the streets of New London; he had arrested murderers, stopped kidnappers, fought vampires, and battled supernatural spirits...and none of it scared him as much as Thursday dinner with his parents.

His mother's face lit with pleasure when she opened the door, but as she hugged him, she whispered, "Today is not a good day."

He was grateful for her warning. It gave him a chance to prepare himself.

"Anthony is here, dear!" His mother called a moment later as she led him into the small sitting room.

A couple of mildly tatty chairs, a chaise with a badly repaired leg, a desk covered in little oil paintings featuring Tony and his brothers, and a table were the only pieces of furniture in the room. But it was warm, and his mother had added homey little touches, like a vase full of flowers dried before the weather turned cold, and bits of embroidery in wooden frames. The little brightly colored fabric birds stared back into the room with curious expressions in their button eyes.

His father sat by the hearth with a blanket draped over his legs, an unlit pipe in one bony hand, his white hair glowing in the firelight. Tony felt the familiar surge of pain like a knife in his chest, but he ignored it. It would pass.

"Good evening, Father," he said, kneeling by the chair and pressing the old man's hand.

"Tony," his father said, smiling. "Did you know I ate three eggs today? Three. Your mother was very impressed."

"As she should be. That is a prodigious number of eggs."

"Quite so. I'm going to need my strength for when I reopen the business and there is nothing so good for regaining one's vitality."

"When is the business to open?" Tony asked, beginning the first steps of the dance they repeated every Thursday night.

"As soon as I find a couple of investors, we'll be well on our way. And then your mother can stop selling those little bits of flimflam"—he waved his hand at the unfinished embroidery in the wicker basket next to her chair—"and I can fit her up in fine silks, again. No one looks as handsome in silk as your mother."

He gave her an adoring smile, took a puff from his pipe, realized it wasn't lit, and frowned at the bowl.

"Here, Father," Tony said, "I'll pack this for you."

"You always were a good boy."

He carried the pipe to the desk, opened a drawer, and pulled out a nearly empty packet of tobacco. His mother joined him, her expression defiant.

He tried to keep his tone casual as he packed the bowl. "You did not tell me you were selling crafts. And you didn't tell me father was out of tobacco, either. Why the secrets?"

"Parents are meant to care for their children, not the other way round. If I want to earn a few pounds a year to pay for your father's pleasures and small odds and ends, I have that right."

Tony clenched his jaw, took a deep breath, and let it out slowly. "I didn't mean to say you don't."

"Anthony," she touched his arm, forcing him to look at her. "You already do more than enough, more than any parent should expect from their child. This is the only dignity I have. Please do not make me feel guilty for it."

He fished a bit of tobacco from the packet, which lay almost empty and yellowing on the tablecloth, and swallowed hard. She had carefully repaired the cloth so many times there wasn't much left of the original design. It was a lovingly maintained illusion of gentility that would fall apart with the slightest stress, but his mother's neat stitches held the fraying edges together with relentless hope.

"Of course I won't," he returned, meeting her gaze.

She had such beautiful eyes, light blue and clear as the sky. As a child, he was convinced his mother's extraordinary eyes were a sign she was a secret fairy princess. Now they were surrounded by a mess of lines, propped up by purple pillows that were proof of the weight of her daily struggle to make their life joyful despite his father's injury. And for the most part, she succeeded.

But no amount of effort could return his father to the bluff, hardy man he had been before bandits waylaid him and left him on the street to die with empty pockets and a cracked skull. Neither his mother's clever stitchery nor his hopeful promises had been enough to keep his parents from walking the tightrope of poverty.

Bile burned the back of his throat as guilt flexed slimy fingers in his stomach. If his brothers would have seen fit to contribute more to their parents' maintenance, perhaps things would have been different, but...

His mother's grip tightened on his arm and her voice hardened as she said, "Don't do that to yourself. Don't you dare."

He schooled his expression, kissed her cheek—which always mollified her—and brought the pipe back to his father.

"Ah, Tony!" He said, looking up at his son with a smile. "Did I tell you I ate three eggs today?"

There was the pain, again, opening like a deep hole in his chest. "You did, Father. That was well done."

"It certainly was. Oh, my pipe! I wondered where it had gone. Thank you, boy."

They ate a simple stew with brown bread and butter, opting to stay by the fire instead of adjourning to the small dining room. The place had no hearth, and in winter it was far too cold for Mr. Hardwicke to bear.

Tony told them of his impending promotion to Detective, and his father regaled them with stories from his days as a merchant,

fending off pirates and bribing foreign customs officers. The experience was exactly as painful as every Thursday dinner.

When it was finally time to say goodnight, Tony made sure his
father had a freshly packed pipe, kissed his mother on the cheek,
bundled up in his wool coat, scarf, and hat, and hurried out into
the biting wind.

When he was promoted, their lives would be different. He would
buy dwarven heaters to keep his father warm, even in their chilly
dining room at night. And his mother wouldn't have to sell the
work of her hands just to have a bit of spending money.

Until then, every visit would feel like an arrow to the heart, and
the freezing winter air would be preferable to hours of having his
failures as a son thrown repeatedly, though unconsciously, in his
face.

He reminded himself to pick up a bag of salt for their stairs,
which sported a fine coating of ice, pulled up his collar, and tucked
his fists into his pockets. Despite the heavy layer of clouds, it did
not snow, though his cheeks and nose burned almost immediately.

The one benefit of the cold was that the air smelled clean instead
of reeking of horse manure, auto exhaust, or garbage warming in
the sun while waiting for trash collectors. His parents lived too far
from the Thames to suffer from the miasma that rolled off the river
during the hot summer months, which was why he paid so much
for their rent. His walk home was longer, but worth it.

The few people brave, or foolish enough, to be abroad so late
kept their distance, only glancing at him from the corner of their
eyes above scarves pulled up to protect their noses. He was tall
and broad across the shoulders, which made his current scowl even

more intimidating. They clearly thought he was not the kind of person to risk a chance encounter with at night. Good. He wasn't in the mood for even a passing conversation.

A cab rumbled past, the horses' hooves echoing off the cobblestones as the driver gave him a pointed look, but Tony waved the man on. He'd rather walk and work out his emotions on the unforgiving pavement. Still, his eyes followed the retreating vehicle as it passed beneath the electric streetlamps that buzzed and flickered.

A head of familiar tousled dark blonde hair caught the light of a street lamp half a block away, and Tony froze for a surprised heartbeat. Samuel? The teenager was the ward of his—what should he call her? Friend? Paramore?—Lady Gwenevere St. James.

The boy would soon be fourteen and had finally begun growing. Now that he ate well and regularly, he was filling out. In a few years, he'd been a strapping man, but the former pickpocket currently had the too-long limbs and awkward, coltish grace of someone unaccustomed to their changing body.

He should have been at the townhouse on Grosvenor Square, warm in his bed, not on the border of the east side at eleven o'clock at night. Tony altered his course, taking to the shadows of the row houses. He increased his speed but kept his gait casual.

Sam turned left on a cross street, passing through a pool of light and then disappearing into the shadows between lamps. Tony took the long way round, avoiding the light, and followed the boy onto Church Street. The homes and businesses in this part of town were a few short steps above neglect. They bordered the east side, where Sam had grown up, and while the neighborhood wasn't impoverished, it wasn't far off.

Abandoned buildings punctuated every block. Stucco had been added to the brick in the days when the inhabitants were affluent enough to hope for a better future. But progress crouched in the shadows like a hungry wolf, waiting to eat up whoever got left, or pushed, behind, and stucco had crumbled to expose neglected brick. Now the once-fine houses looked like aging actors trying to hide the passage of time beneath too many layers of makeup.

He gained on the boy a little at a time, but never fast enough to be noticed. Part of him was tempted to grab Sam by the back of the neck and drag him to Gwen and his sister, but the other part knew that if he asked Sam why he was creeping through Town in the dark, the boy would come up with a plausible lie and Tony would never catch him at this again.

He may have spent his entire career catching criminals, but Sam had spent his avoiding being caught. Helping the boy would be impossible if he did not know what was happening, so Tony kept his distance. They entered the south end of the neighborhood less than thirty seconds apart.

A crumbling gothic church dominated the landscape, looming over the houses like a vulture waiting for residents to crawl through its doors with their petitions in one hand and their coin in the other. Neither their coin nor their prayers had been enough to save the church from the erosion of time and progress, and only its bones remained to protect the graves of the parishioners buried there.

Sam stopped outside the boundary of the wrought-iron fence and turned his head to the side as if listening. Tony slipped farther into the shadows, not moving. The boy had good instincts. After a

moment, he hopped the fence in a single bound and wove
through the tombstones toward the doors. Before he crossed the
threshold, two men stepped out of the shadows and barred the
way.

Sam stopped, hands up, then reached one hand toward his chest
and pulled his jacket open. The guards stepped aside to allow the
boy through. He disappeared into the dark maw of the church.
Tony edged farther down the street, waited for the guards to
retreat, then crept up alongside the building to listen. The stone
beneath the broken stained-glass windows was cold against his
back, sucking up warmth through his jacket like a starving babe.

He waited, hearing nothing but the distant rattle of wagons
and the occasional echo of conversation or scuffing shoes. People
thought whispering was very sneaky, but anyone accustomed to
real sneaking knew whispered S sounds carried a long way in the
silence, and most conversations couldn't get by without at least
a few. But the only noises Tony heard were the breathing and
occasional shifting feet of the two guards inside.

Wherever Sam had gone, he either wasn't in the church, or his
business there required little conversation.

Tony circled the building once, then returned to the front of
the church and waited. If no one caught Sam sneaking out, and
he was certain Gwen would have mentioned something, the boy
must have a way home that kept him out of sight. He needed to
see what it was, so he waited.

It would break Gwen's heart to know her youngest ward was
creeping about the city at night, engaging in criminal activity. They
had no need of money since inheriting Claire Monmouth's estate,

so what on earth could force Samuel to return to a life of crime, knowing it would cause pain to both his benefactor and his sister?

Sally Dawes, Sam's older sister, was a pretty, good-hearted girl of nearly seventeen, who loved her brother with the ferocity of a mother bear. He had seen her work herself to exhaustion to learn anything and everything that might give her a leg up in the world: history, geography, chemistry, and alchemy right alongside etiquette and comportment. The girl was determined to make a good life for herself and her brother, and it would devastate her to know he was putting himself in unnecessary danger.

And Tony had to be the one to tell them. Or to tell Gwen, at least.

Didn't they already have enough hurdles to deal with in their relationship without adding this to the list? Apparently not, because he couldn't see a way out of telling her. He'd rather kiss her into insensibility, or bury himself—well, there was no use thinking about impossibilities.

Gwen was convinced she'd break his heart, and he hadn't been able to un-convince her, so instead of kissing the ironic smile off her face, he'd be explaining that the boy she loved was sneaking out of the house for potentially nefarious purposes.

He would find out how Sam had been sneaking in and out of the house, then catch him and give him the chance to come clean. If he refused, Tony would have to do it himself.

He had always believed the boy honorable, even if he was a bit of a scamp. Perhaps there was a good reason for him to be here at night, alone. Perhaps his excuse would make sense.

Tony hoped to hell that was the case, because he couldn't stomach the other option. If Sam was breaking the law, he didn't think he could hurt Gwen by doing his job and hauling the boy to Scotland Yard.

He was so distracted by his own thoughts he didn't realize he was being stalked until a rasping voice said from behind, "You shouldn't be out so late, guv."

Tony turned, half disgusted with himself for missing the tail, half relieved that he might be able to vent his anger on someone who actually deserved it. Sam disappeared around the next corner.

"It's dangerous in these parts, after dark. You'll want to get home safely, eh? We can make that happen, for ya. For a price, a'course."

The man speaking was about a head shorter than Tony but just as wide, with the forearms of a blacksmith and a jaw like an anvil. He showed off scarred knuckles by flicking a thumb across the bottom of his nose. A bowler hat was pulled down low enough that Tony couldn't see the color of his eyes. Clever.

What wasn't clever was trying to extort money from an officer with Tony's experience, an officer who was already aching for a fight. He said, with a hint of a warning in his voice, "I can find my way home just fine, thanks."

"'Fraid we can't allow that," the man said, raising his hands at his sides. "Wouldn't be neighborly to let you get hurt. Hard for a man to work with broken fingers. But don't fret guv, it'll only cost you a few pounds. Pull out your wallet and you can be on your way."

"This isn't the fight you want to pick, friend, unless you enjoy breathing through a broken nose. But I'm feeling charitable. I'll overlook your attempted extortion if you turn around, call off whoever is waiting to ambush me, and walk away."

The man snorted, pushed up his sleeves, and flexed his fingers, making his knuckles pop ominously. "So much for being polite and businesslike. Let me make this clear, eh? You aint the one making the rules, ol boy. Be a good lad and pay up, or you'll suffer worse than a broken nose for our trouble."

A chuckle came from behind him, a little farther up the street; the accomplice who would make sure he either paid, or regretted not paying.

"There you are," Tony said, turning far enough to keep both men in sight but staying close enough to finish the first man off before the other reached them. "Now it's a fair fight. Maybe. Come on, then. I have places to be."

The men exchanged disbelieving glances, and he waited. He couldn't strike first, not if he wanted to arrest the man for attempted extortion and assault. Not if he wanted to use force. And he did.

The first man shrugged, reached into his pocket, and slipped on a pair of brass knuckles. "Your funeral, mate."

He lunged.

The fellow was a brawler, strong and stubborn, but unskilled. Tony had spent more than half of his life training as a pugilist—it was one of the few legal ways he could take out his frustration with the world—so when the fellow threw a looping hook, he stepped to the outside, ducked, twisted his hips and struck the man in the diaphragm with a tight blow.

He crumpled with a gasp and flopped on the ground, trying to get his wind back. But Tony had hit him hard. It would be another ten seconds before he breathed again, and most fights didn't last that long.

"Disappointing," Tony said, turning to face the man's partner. "Can you do any better?"

Men who made their living on the streets weren't dumb. Harassing a random stranger for money involved little danger, especially working with a partner. Fighting one on one against a skilled opponent was another matter. Tony casually unbuttoned his jacket and flashed his badge from his waistcoat. The second man glimpsed the metal, then turned and ran.

Tony sighed, replaced his badge, and stripped the brass knuckles from the man who was just starting to breathe again. He removed the nippers out of his coat pocket and slung the rope around the man's wrists with practiced ease. Once he pulled the t-shaped handle into place, the man was securely bound.

"Come on, my lad," Tony said, hauling the man to his feet. "Time to go for a walk. You ruined my night, so I wouldn't be averse to another sparring match if you're still feeling tough. Here's your hat, let's go."

He dragged Bowler Hat toward the closest lockup, still fuming that he had lost the boy and been denied the release of a good fight. Tomorrow, he'd have to tell Gwen what he had seen and bear the look on her face when worry, disappointment, and fear replaced her usual humor and confidence.

That happened to his mother every time his brothers failed to write or call when they were home on leave. Every time they promised visits or money and disappointed the woman who raised them. The idea of Gwen suffering such pain made him clench his jaw against a growl of frustration.

He hoped his boxing club was open late because he desperately needed to hit something.

Also By

OTHER TITLES BY THIS AUTHOR INCLUDE

SERIES: The Gwen St. James Affair

Vanished

E ccentric social outcast Lady Gwenevere St. James knows many secret things: magic, alchemy, artifice, and even the truth about the long-forgotten faeries. But she does not know why common criminals are using rare and dangerous magic to kidnap orphans from the streets of New London.

After rescuing one young girl, Gwen vows to save the rest, no matter the cost. But the handsome Inspector of Scotland Yard is also investigating the case, and he thinks Gwen knows far too much about the kidnappings to be innocent.

To save the children, Gwen must dodge the Inspector, bully a coven of witches, and outsmart her marriage-minded Mama, all while managing a wily young pickpocket and a headstrong raven. But an unexpected secret hides at the center of the mystery, one that will force her to confront the most painful event from her past, and possibly sacrifice her future.

Moonstruck

Gwenevere St. James may be a lady, but she's never been interested in playing by the rules. Instead of ingratiating herself into high society, she spent a decade searching the world and studying the occult for a way to find her lost twin sister.

So when a coven of witches offers her a missing person's case in return for a book of spells guaranteed to locate her twin at last, Gwen cannot refuse, even if it means doing something she swore she would never do: attend a country party for the wealthy elite.

But the case is far more complicated and dangerous than she expected. Villagers whisper of ghostly riders in the night, and an unknown monster hunts the nearby forest, putting everyone in danger.

As people go missing and innocent bystanders die, Gwen must make a choice: how many lives will she risk for the thing she wants most?

Spellbound

Book 3 in The Gwen St. James affair will be released in 2023

SERIES: The Eververse Chronicles

The Founding Trilogy

The Laws of Founding

Legends and fairytales aren't all they're cracked up to be; especially when they're trying to kill you.

Since losing her father, Allie Chapter has stumbled through life, using friends, books, and alcohol to numb the pain. When she wakes up in the wrong world and gets kidnapped by supernatural forces, everything changes. Allie learns she is a Walker, blessed–or cursed–with the power to travel between different versions of Earth.

Allie must rely on Ronan, her devastatingly handsome mentor, to guide her through magical worlds she's only dreamed of, and teach her the Laws that govern all Walkers–Laws she must not break at any cost.

But a failed assassination attempt turns her dream into a nightmare. The Eververse is full of danger, and whoever wants her dead may also be behind her father's accident. As she searches for answers, Allie must decide what makes breaking the Laws worthwhile: love, or revenge?

But when she learns she is a Walker, one of the rare few with the ability to travel between different versions of Earth, an entirely new problem arises: can she master her powers fast enough to figure out why someone wants her dead?

The Founding Lie

The monsters we face aren't always the ones we expect.

As the newest member of the interdimensional police force, it's Allie Chapter's responsibility to find out who is stealing magical weapons and bring them to justice before war breaks out.

She's certain the thief is Goll MacMorna, the man who still haunts her nightmares, and she intends to prove it...no matter the cost.

She will either free herself from her nightmares or discover the real monster is the one in the mirror.

The Founding War

"Necessity knows no cruelty. She only makes demands, and we answer as seems best to us."

Allie Chapter went from aimless college student to interdimensional cop in less than a year. Now she's an outlaw, hunted by both sides of an oncoming war that threatens to destroy the Eververse. As her newly discovered magic grows in strength, Allie realizes she might be the only one who can stop the war and save countless innocent lives from obliteration. But her allies have betrayed her, and powers too large to comprehend are manipulating the battlefield, hoping to use her gifts for their own purposes. With no one left to trust, Allie must rely on her wits and her conscience to make the ultimate decision: sacrifice her future—and maybe her life—for the greater good, or save the people she loves and let the Eververse fall.

Acknowledgments

Books are not written in a vacuum, as much as it might feel that way to closeted writers crouching in front of their screens like dirty goblins.

No, books are a group effort that would not work without cover designers, developmental editors, alpha readers, beta readers, line editors, formatters, and the other skilled craftspeople of the book industry. I thanked most of these people in the aknowledgements section of Vanished, but there are a few people I want to thank for helping Moonstruck become the book it is now.

No writer should ever forget the unsung heroes of book writing: the folks who cheer us on and support our work just because they love the story and want to see it succeed.

Beta Readers Melissa, Angela, Amy, and Teri. You all helped me make this book better than it was, before. You have my unending gratitude.

The incredible subscribers of the Reader's Lounge, my personal community: Frank, Katherine, and Krista. Thank you more than words can say for your support!